CONTENTS


Prologue: A Crown by Candle-Glow . . . . . . . . . . . . 5

1. The Outcast . . . . . . . . . . . . . . . . . . . . . . . . . . 7
2. Between Bell and Beauchamp . . . . . . . . . . . . . . 19
3. "Young Folks Meaning Well . . ." . . . . . . . . . . . 25
4. A Son of the New Laws . . . . . . . . . . . . . . . . . . 35
5. Springtime Madonna . . . . . . . . . . . . . . . . . . . 39
6. Uneasy Inheritance . . . . . . . . . . . . . . . . . . . . 55
7. Tudor Curse . . . . . . . . . . . . . . . . . . . . . . . . . 77
8. The Designs of Spain . . . . . . . . . . . . . . . . . . . 91
9. Elizabethan Dalliance . . . . . . . . . . . . . . . . . . 105
10. Murder or Misadventure? . . . . . . . . . . . . . . . 125
11. Knot of Secret Might . . . . . . . . . . . . . . . . . . 143
12. Comings and Goings . . . . . . . . . . . . . . . . . . . 165
13. Summer Progress . . . . . . . . . . . . . . . . . . . . . 183
14. A Declaration to the World . . . . . . . . . . . . . . 207
15. Only Hours Away . . . . . . . . . . . . . . . . . . . . . 225
16. A Journey Upstream . . . . . . . . . . . . . . . . . . . 241
17. Clubfoot Hales and Crouchback Mary . . . . . . . 253
18. "The Picture of Myself" . . . . . . . . . . . . . . . . 271
19. Light in the Dark Depths . . . . . . . . . . . . . . . . 285
20. "As Time and Sequels Well Shall Prove . . ." . . 291

Afterword . . . . . . . . . . . . . . . . . . . . . . . . . . . 302

*The Second Sister*

*Lady Catherine Grey*

## PROLOGUE

# *A Crown by Candle-Glow*

"Escaped! Both of them?"

In the candle-glow of his London home, Edward Seymour, Earl of Hertford, stared aghast at the letter he'd received unexpectedly, while he was preparing for bed.

"As if 'tis not enough to have this accursed cold . . ."

A violent sneeze caused him to fumble the letter. Too late did he see the word 'Tower' burn from the bottom.

His servant moved the wax-candle and letter deliberately beyond his reach. The Earl found himself assisted to his chair and had his night-cap re-adjusted, but he signalled impatiently to peer again at the scorched paper.

"Stop fussing, man! Nearer with that candle, Tom. Nearer! If *you* were my age, you might read too close to the flame."

The Earl's gnarled hands tried shakily to smooth the paper and then pushed into reverse the habitual slide of his spectacles down his aquiline nose. He screwed up his eyes to focus better on the unwelcome news that grandson William and the Lady Arabella Stuart, first cousin to King James no less, had broken from their prisons.

"Captivity . . ." he muttered, "always the price to pay for marrying without royal consent."

But their sheer recklessness! Not only was it forcing upon him a world which nowadays he found so irritatingly loud and young. It was also history almost repeating itself.

How many people alive now, he wondered, could turn their minds back over half a century to 1560? The year when he, too, had secretly wed his princess of royal blood - the Lady Catherine Grey.

Yet *he* could remember those times so vividly. He'd once even been intended for her older sister, Lady Jane, that poor little nine-days' Queen! But he had loved - and been loved - by Catherine, the beauty of the family.

He smiled as he pictured her. Tiny and graceful was his Catherine, with wavy, red-gold hair. Few realized how close she had come to attaining the Crown herself. Through her, his descendants still held strong claims to the English throne, which made William's 'offence' with his rival claimant Arabella a doubly serious matter.

Frowning, the Earl considered the reply he must send regarding his favourite grandchild's escape. The first words at least posed no problem. He picked up his quill pen, dipped it into the ink and wrote:

*Hertford House, Cannon Row, Westminster,*
*this Wednesday night, 5th June 1611.*

And then what? He sniffed and laid the pen down. No simple task to condemn the actions of youth, as duty demanded. Not here, in the very room where he and Catherine . . .

"Catherine," he whispered. "My love for you - 'tis unceasing!"

He did not always know when fresh memories of her would be touched off. With her, and only her, he had known the height of his life, and many long years afterwards had been a crusade to have their union declared valid. This stirred within him another deep emotion. Something more than bitterness welled up again, as he recalled their humiliating treatment by the 'Virgin Queen', Elizabeth.

He stifled another burgeoning sneeze and eased himself back up in his chair. The thought struck him that to come to terms with his feelings, he must live his and Catherine's love story all through again this night. Only then could he turn his attention to William. After all, he was too wide awake now to seek precious sleep.

He dismissed Tom, and thrust away the letter, pen and attempted reply. And only the candlelight stayed close to guide the Earl on his reflective journey back through the years . . .

## CHAPTER 1

# *The Outcast*

"Where is it? What shall I do?"

The shrieks of a small, blindfolded girl echoed around Tower Green, until a well-muscled arm guided her to the block. And there she knelt.

"Lord, into thy hands I commend my spirit."

The axe rose and fell, and Lady Jane Grey's life was ended. Her blood spurted in a rich torrent over the execution scaffold and spattered the front row of spectators.

On Tower Hill, three more harsh thuds of blade against block despatched also her father, husband and uncle from this world.

Upstream along the Thames at Baynard's Castle, Jane's younger sister heard the boom of Tower cannons announcing their family's undoing and stared with tragic eyes towards the grim royal fortress.

There but for the grace of God, came the thought to Catherine Grey. Jane was only sixteen!

Catherine shivered in the February cold, by the riverside window of her bedchamber. A swift, downward movement brushed against her, but this was of a light and affectionate touch, and near to the hem of her gown. It came again and was about to do so once more when she bent to hold an uplifted front left paw.

"Good girl, Comfit," she murmured to the little spaniel, who had become so attached to her, lightening the lonely months of her marriage with companionship. Her loveless sham of a marriage to Lord Henry Herbert.

She stroked the dog gently beneath the chin, before Comfit rolled over onto her back. A rush of tears overwhelmed Catherine. The dog took on a mournful look too and was swooped up into Catherine's arms and hugged very close.

"Oh, Comfit, what life is there for us now?" she sobbed.

After a while of holding Comfit, Catherine began to feel calmer. She was glad to feel so. Especially when the dog's ears moved alertly and forewarned her of some flapping sounds approaching, even before she heard these fully herself.

"Lady Catherine!"

"Come in, Nurse Cousins."

The chamber door duly opened to let her old nurse flap in, followed by her maid, Helen Leigh. "I've brought you a hot posset to soothe you. Oh, Lady Catherine, you've not eaten above a few morsels again and I'll bet you've given most of those to the dog!"

"Please, Nurse ... not now."

"Well then, give the dog to Helen while you drink the hot posset."

"Thank you, but I would rather keep the dog and give the posset to Helen!"

Behind the nurse, Helen's chubby face broke into a grimace like Catherine's.

"O-o-oh! What am I to do about you, Lady Catherine?" sighed Nurse Cousins. "You know no good'll come of this. She's not even your dog, now that you're divorced. And though my Lord Herbert says you can have her for the rest of today, what of tomorrow when you've taken leave of her? Your lady-mother will be none too keen on you having pet dogs under her roof."

Catherine looked out of the window. The prospect of returning to her mother in truth chilled her more than the view before her, of the steely winter sky reflected on the river. But she hardly wished to stay here either in the same place as her ex-husband.

"Tomorrow - 'tis another day," she murmured. "I must have Comfit with me while I can."

Later that morning, Catherine saw the Earl of Pembroke, her former father-in-law, arrive by river at the castle. He was back from witnessing Jane die.

She gave Comfit another hug. Soon, the dog's ears were astir and her body tensed as she listened. A growl built up from deep in her throat at some distant-sounding commotion.

Raised voices reverberated ever nearer. They were added to at length by the noises of heavy boots marching along and the flapping of the nurse's skirts.

"My lord, I beseech you again. You cannot go to my lady like that," cried Nurse Cousins.

"Out of my way, woman. Or 'twill be the worse for you if you try my patience any more."

Catherine's body stiffened too as she heard Lord Pembroke's threatening words.

"Oh, have pity, my lord," squealed the nurse. "Have pity!"

The boots suddenly halted and so did the flapping. A scream quickly disturbed any silence. Then the marching resumed.

Pembroke did not even knock as he burst into Catherine's chamber. He advanced towards her, looking old and gaunt. Catherine shrank from him in horror, still holding Comfit. There were bloodstains on his face, and more on his clothes ... her sister's blood!

"She died well," he said gruffly. He swaggered forward all the more as Catherine moved back. "She left this for you."

He brandished a small book and thrust it at her. Comfit bared her teeth and Catherine received the book from him shakily. She feared that he would hit the dog with it otherwise, there in her arms - even though this was a holy book, Jane's well-used Greek Testament.

"You'll be off from here by first light tomorrow, madam, if I have to throw you out myself," he sneered. "And be assured that when you've gone, *that* will be taught a sharp lesson."

As he pointed a bony finger at Comfit, Catherine answered him vehemently, "How cruel can you be, my lord? She was only trying to protect me."

Pembroke's face twitched and his jaw jutted out while he gaped at her, momentarily taken aback.

"First light, remember! Good God, 'twas lucky I forbade my son to consummate your marriage, madam. It's made divorcing you all the easier," he retorted, before he stormed from her chamber.

Catherine ventured towards the open doorway, anxious

to know what had happened to Nurse Cousins.

"Knocked to the ground, she was, Lady Catherine," said Helen, as she helped the nurse into the room.

Catherine placed Jane's Bible on her coffer chest and Comfit gently on the floor, so that she too could offer assistance.

"Poor Nurse Cousins! I heard the scream."

"I was trying to bring Lady Jane's Bible to you myself, Lady Catherine, considering the state my lord was in."

"I wish it had been you or Helen."

The old woman brightened when she saw the book lying on Catherine's coffer chest. "Well, now I can bring this to you in a way, Lady Catherine. I reckon you haven't seen yet what Lady Jane wrote to you on some of the blank pages."

"Wrote to me? I'm sorry, I've had no chance to look."

"Don't you fret now." The nurse insisted on hobbling towards the book. She picked it up and opened it inside the front cover. "Such beautiful handwriting was Lady Jane's."

Catherine admired the perfectly-formed letters too as Jane's gift was handed to her again. She settled on the window-seat to read her sister's final message. Some of the words became blurred as her tears quietly fell. Beside her, Comfit watched her with a look of concern.

*Lady Jane Grey*

"My Lady Catherine, it does no good to linger here."

"Coming, Helen," sighed Catherine. Compliantly, she allowed herself to be handed into the boat in which her maid was waiting all too impatiently, early the following morning.

"We're going home. 'Twill suffice, surely, for the moment?"

"I suppose so."

But Catherine still felt far from certain about this as she sat down. Fortunately, Helen became too preoccupied with readjusting her own position beside Catherine to voice any further comment.

The boatman pulled away strongly with rhythmic, even strokes. Catherine tried not to look back at the riverside facade of Baynard's Castle and tried to shut from her hearing the now-familiar chimes of St Paul's close by. She had been cast out of the castle, where she had lived during her sister's last months. Doors had slammed and gates clanged behind her.

Wistfully, she pulled her cloak more tightly around her, fixing her attention on the sweep of the oars as they broke the surface of the water. She started to count their movements, one for each of her fourteen years.

She only reached double figures, however, before she was seized by a heart-warming wish that instead of oars making these patterns on the water, they were being made by the swans amid the streams and broad pools of her childhood home. And that instead of looking up to see the panorama of buildings on either bank of the Thames, she was gazing across at the deer wandering in meadows, while behind them rose the bracken beyond the avenue of oaks.

"I wish it were Bradgate," she admitted.

"Lady Catherine?"

"Home ... now, I mean."

"Me too," said Helen. "'Twere pity for the Greys to lose Bradgate after only their menfolk turned out in Wyatt's Rebellion 'gainst Queen Mary. She bein' so fond of you and your lady mother and sisters."

Helen assumed her eager, "If you ask me ..." expression and Catherine braced herself for an onslaught of further babbling. She nodded vaguely and began to yawn as politely as she could. Then she realized that for once she could curb the maid's tittle-tattling easily. Another set of sounds was assailing her from behind.

They came at first from the river bank and they started off with a series of high-pitched whimpers, then thin whining as if someone cried there without hope. And suddenly, they gave way to an indignant bark of protest, followed by a loud splash.

*Now* Catherine was happy to stare back at the castle! She hardly dared to believe the determined dog-paddle which was coming towards them, a pair of wavy ears bobbing up and down as the swimmer progressed accordingly.

"Comfit! I-I thought they had tied her up to stop her from seeing me!" panted Catherine. "How *did* she get out?" In the same breath, she instructed the boatman. "Turn the boat round. Please hurry!"

"As you wish, madam." He stopped rowing, and resting one oar, after a moment began to pull the boat round with the other.

"D'you think that dog'll willingly return to Baynard's?" said Helen. "We could be here all day rescuing her, taking her back, rescuing her again ..."

"Comfit is coming with us," said Catherine. "Having broken loose once, as you say, she may well do so again."

"But Lady Catherine, she's Lord Herbert's dog, not yours."

"Oh yes? *That* we shall sort out later. The dog herself has decided whom she belongs to. Turn the boat - quickly!"

"But, madam, under the circumstances ..."

*"Turn it round!"*

Catherine was ready to assert herself further, if necessary, to achieve her now fullest wish.

The re-directed boat stopped once more, but briefly, before it was pulled nearer and nearer the distressed dog. Comfit's threshing of the surface lessened visibly as her agitation eased.

"Little pet," murmured Catherine. Her spirits rose in joyful anticipation of their reunion.

"Aye, no doubting you're all in all to her, my lady,"

conceded Helen. "You've every right to keep her."

"I shall appeal to the Queen for her if need be!"

Even as she removed a towel from a bag containing a few possessions, Catherine felt strangely assured regarding her Catholic cousin, Queen Mary. Very strangely assured, considering that Protestants had put Jane on the throne for nine days the previous July to deprive Mary of her rightful place there. And then Wyatt's Rebellion had threatened another attempt.

Like Helen, Catherine plucked off her gloves in readiness for the spaniel's rescue.

"Come on, my poppet," Helen cooed. Her sturdy arm reached out to grasp Comfit's collar.

To her dismay, the collar worked loose. She overstretched to take hold of a length of frayed rope which trailed away from it. And the reckless resolve of both mistress and dog, on either side of her, spurred her to lean out yet further and support the frenetic front paws underneath.

The boat listed, rocked and drifted away, leaving Helen as much out as she was in. Catherine clutched onto her maid's cloak and skirts. Following garbled instructions, she tried to balance Helen by leaning "t'other way".

Helen's right leg and foot extended beneath the towel ruched up between them. Catherine saw these slowly begin to bend. Slowly, but surely - and her relief was unutterable as Helen eased herself upright, gasping, "Steady, now. Steady!"

And what a sorry sight writhed safely in Helen's arms! Comfit was plonked on the welcoming towel and wrapped in it speedily, before she could shake herself dry.

The boat turned again, now truly homeward bound. But for three of its four occupants, togetherness soared to a great crescendo of barking, wiping, licking and hugging.

By the time the boat passed Whitehall Palace, Comfit slept contentedly within the folds of Catherine's cloak and gown.

"I wouldn't have done that for no-one else, mind," Helen teased. "And 'twill be my pleasure to look after her for you, Lady Catherine, when Queen Mary welcomes you to Court."

"The chances of *that,* I fear, Helen, are ... well ... remote!" came Catherine's softly-spoken reply.

Remote indeed, so every indication seemed to suggest to Catherine. If she was still the beloved sister of a Queen, like in those nine days of Jane's reign, a royal barge would have been hers for this journey, not a boat. But it was either travelling home by boat, or enduring the noisome, filthy streets.

Catherine could not help but follow Helen's awed gaze towards the palace, however, where Mary and the Court were now in residence.

She caressed the slumbering dog and benefited from Comfit's usual calming influence. She had earlier undone the water-laden collar and frayed rope from Comfit's neck and flung them contemptuously back in the river.

What'll my mother beat me with, she wondered, for my supposed wrongdoing of bringing Comfit? The stick or the strap?

Although she shuddered at the prospect of either of these thwacking against her, Catherine felt braver with Comfit beside her. Braver, and stronger, to face the fear which sometimes suddenly beset her over her parents' years of cruelty to her and Jane. A total void had ever existed when she needed encouragement and solace from them.

Her sense of aching hurt about such mistreatment began to overcome her. She asked Helen to pass Jane's Bible to her from the bag of belongings and she clasped the book with both hands, opening it at the farewell message again. She read those parts which were greater in their meaning to her:

*Sunday, 11th February 1554. I have sent you, good sister Catherine, a book, which though it be not outwardly trimmed with gold, yet inwardly it is more worth than precious stones. It is the book, dear sister, of the laws of the Lord ... and if you, with good mind and an earnest desire, follow it, it will bring you to immortal and everlasting life. It will teach you to live, it will teach you to die, it will win you more than you would have gained by possession of your woeful father's lands, for if God had prospered him, you would have inherited his lands ... Trust not that the tenderness of your age shall lengthen your life, for as soon as God will, goeth the young as the old ... As touching my death, rejoice as I do ... for I am assured that I shall, for losing a mortal life, gain an immortal felicity.*

*Farewell, dear sister. Put only your trust in God, who only must uphold you.*

*Your loving sister, Jane*

Rejoice? At her sister's death? Catherine knew that she never could. She wished that fate had not denied her the chance of replying to Jane. What life indeed was there for her in going back to their dragon of a mother as a failure, landless, divorced, and all for no reason but the Greys' disgrace? Catherine dreaded also to contemplate that she now carried her family's claim to the throne.

As her tears smudged more of Jane's message, a left paw brushed soothingly onto her arm. A pair of bright eyes blinked up at her with a warmth of expression which she had so often longed for from her mother - instead of an acutely critical eye!

"Good girl," said Catherine.

Comfit wagged her tail. And then love broke from Catherine's entire being. She handed the Bible back to Helen and amid chattered endearments, she hugged her pet.

"A-a-ah!" Helen approved.

Catherine delighted to come closest to God in rare moments of mutual happiness like this. She knew that it was natural for Jane to advise her to seek Divine guidance through studying that gift of the Bible. But then, Jane was always so lonely except for her books.

Helen's certainly studying it, Catherine smiled to herself. Pity she's reading it upside down!

Catherine pretended now to confide her solitary thoughts to Comfit. She mused that maybe some consolation could be had from the Queen allowing the Duchess of Suffolk, her Mother Dragon, to continue living at Sheen Palace despite the family executions. That was more than the proud Duchess of Somerset had enjoyed after her "Good Duke" was beheaded. The betrothal of her son, Lord Edward Seymour, to Jane had then been ended too.

The wind helped the boat on its way. Sunlight glistened on the water droplets falling from each lift of the oars, as Catherine came in sight of Sheen. Even in sunlight, though, the palace seemed forbidding to her.

Slower, but longer strokes rowed the boat steadily towards the landing-stage. She saw figures stir within a dark arched doorway that she must soon go through. Comfit barked out a warning as two handsome young men emerged and came down a flight of steps to the water's edge.

Catherine shared the taller man's embarrassment at greeting her. But that was all she did share with Adrian Stokes, her family's former Master of Horse. She didn't know whether this was caused by his impending rise in status as her stepfather, or by her equally rapid loss of prestige.

Amongst his few, bluff words while he helped remove her and her maid, dog and belongings out of the boat, she was thankful at least that his fixed grin spared her a little longer from the coldness of Mother Dragon awaiting her indoors.

She was thankful too for the contrast of seeing a much friendlier face. Stokes' slightly-built companion dithered now outside the palace where he'd once dwelt in happier times, but his deep-set grey eyes rested in wonderment upon her.

A proffered left front paw brought the Good Duke's son - Jane's one-time betrothed - into the proceedings with both hands outstretched.

"My Lord Edward," Catherine smiled shyly, remembering to lower her own eyes in the manner instilled into her from childhood. "What do you *here?*"

The more congenial notion was already crossing her mind that by coincidence, this day after the tragedy of Jane's execution was also the eve of St Valentine's.

*The Ruins, Bradgate Park, Leicestershire.*

CHAPTER 2

# *Between Bell and Beauchamp*

The Lieutenant of the Tower bowed formally as he received his new prisoner. Some of his servants and even Tower guards and officials knelt. Some wept and cried out, "God save Your Grace!"

Elizabeth Tudor surveyed them through the rain. "My shoes are wet," she replied. She sat down on the steps leading up to Traitor's Gate.

"Madam, more of you than your shoes will be wet, unless you come inside!" said the Lieutenant.

"'Tis better for me to be here," she retorted. "I know not where you will put me, once . . . inside there."

The blustery rain persisted. In fear for her own servants' suffering, she reluctantly stood up at length.

"This March weather persuades me inside more than your words," she observed to the Lieutenant.

And so she underwent the indignity of entering the Tower beneath Traitor's Gate. The spectre was raised all too relentlessly for her of her mother's demise on Tower Green, almost eighteen years before. Queen Anne Boleyn had come in this same way then and never came out alive again.

After weeks in a vermin-ridden cell in the Bell Tower, Elizabeth had further grumbles. "A prize rat-catcher would be useful animal company," she complained to her interrogators. "Whether it's feline or canine matters not, so long as it can earn its keep! How long must I be close prisoner in this damp and stinking place?"

Amongst the many disadvantages of her birth was a strong sense of smell. Like her sense of hearing, this seemed to sharpen while she was so cut off from the outside world. All her pleas to see her sister, Queen Mary, continued to be refused.

"Your Grace must first clear yourself of all suspected involvement in Wyatt's Rebellion," she was told.

She learnt to discern the individual footfalls of her various captors. One late April day, she recognized the stately strides of the Lieutenant approach, preceded by the shambling of old Gage "the Cage", as she had nicknamed her immediate jailer. And behind them came three, possibly four guards, including that one whose heel scraped on every sixth or seventh stride . . .

A noise she had not heard was the hammering, which announced the building of a new scaffold. And yet its very absence she found intensely disturbing. Had Jane Grey's scaffold perhaps been left in place on Tower Green for the execution of the Lady Elizabeth?

"A swordsman from France, such as my mother had," was the request she had already determined upon if matters had indeed come to that. Not for her the butchery of the axe, but a quick, clean end!

Meanwhile her pallid face suppressed a smile at the familiar routine of old Gage struggling to unlock the door. Inadvertently, it heartened her in her resolve to play for time.

"Hurry, man," bellowed the Lieutenant. *"Tempus fugit."*

"A-argh! Curse this poxy bolt."

"Here, hold these. Let me try . . ."

The door groaned its usual echoing protest open to reveal that the gaoler carried boxes containing books and writing materials. At the welcome sight of them, Elizabeth queried teasingly, "More rat fodder for me, Mr Gage?"

"Good day to Your Grace," said the Lieutenant.

"*Good* day, Master Lieutenant? Good for those, no doubt, who come to gloat on me in this cess-pit once more!"

"Not at all, madam. We come to escort you out of here."

"Out! Out where?"

"To exercise, madam. The Queen's Majesty has granted you the liberty of the leads."

"Some liberty, Master Lieutenant, to be so accompanied by armed guards! Mr Gage, don't set those down in front of the window-seats . . . yes, away from the fire too, such as it is."

Elizabeth blinked hard as she emerged onto the wall-walk known as the leads between the Bell and Beauchamp Towers. The overcast morning seemed so bright compared with her slit-windowed cell. But as her vision cleared . . . Typical! The two guards before her obscured her view of the narrow leads' length. And being hemmed in also by the Lieutenant and the two behind her, she stared unimpeded towards the right. Oh, she could look this way without hindrance, fair enough. Down onto a sight which was even less inspiring - Tower Green!

"Aye, Your Grace, it has been taken down," said the Lieutenant, watching her, but then reddening suddenly under her close scrutiny.

"So . . . books? Exercise? No scaffold . . . Has the Queen, my sister, decided upon clemency?"

"I have not heard."

She turned from him abruptly then, scuttling the front guards forward into line in a swift, though soon rhythmic pacing. One, two, three, four, five, *scrape.* Another six strides, *scrape.* Six more, and at the next heel-scrape they were more than half-way across to the Beauchamp Tower, but the Lieutenant swept up to them, composure recovered.

"Wounded pride will not avail your cause, madam. There *are* signs that the Queen's anger is abating. What's left of the Lady Jane's family has been recalled to Court and I'm told that Her Majesty makes much of the Lady Catherine especially. But there again, she has never been in league with rebels . . ."

His captive could no longer keep her back to him once the pacing had to be retraced towards the Bell Tower. "The Lady Catherine?" she countered, even more testily. "That little nincompoop!"

"Lady Elizabeth, you would do well to remember that by the laws of this land, if the Queen bears no issue, Lady Catherine ranks next in the succession to yourself."

"And you would do well to remember that she is the daughter of an attainted traitor. Speak to me thus while you dare, sir, for God willing, I shall look back on this cheerless morning as from a bright and glorious evening. Offspring born to my sister at her age will be a miracle, and ere long, you may find that England is mine by right!"

Any minute now, she thought he would order her return to her cell. Or he might bow himself rigidly from her presence with scarcely a word. What a pity. She was enjoying this! And her, nought but a King's bastard, so many still believed, the daughter of an alleged adulteress and witch whose broken body lay buried in some old arrow chest in the chapel of St Peter ad Vincula's, facing Tower Green.

Elizabeth deplored the idea of softening her tactics, though all her escort appeared obviously disconcerted. But she needed more information. News, which she hoped would be good of other prisoners.

"It is not what's left of the Lady Jane's own family I would ask about," she stated with a quieter authority, as the pacing resumed towards the Beauchamp Tower. "It is, what's left of her husband's family - his brothers who, so far as I know, were imprisoned yonder." She pointed straight ahead.

"And still are, Your Grace," managed the Lieutenant warily.

"Still all condemned?"

"All," he confirmed. "No doubt they'll die bravely, like their recently-departed brother."

"Poor Guildford Dudley," she said, apparently subdued. "He was the youngest of them. And what of . . . Lord Robert Dudley? Is he well? I'll warrant no prison pallor makes *him* appear wraith-like, as I do!"

"He's well enough," the Lieutenant frowned. "His - er, *wife* comes to see him regularly."

"Indeed so," Elizabeth smiled wryly. She calmly resisted the impulse to shout at him, *Dolt!* Because Robin Dudley was already married, he could make no threatening claims on her affections. Because he was already married, he had been conveniently unavailable to marry Jane Grey and so was not lying now, in place of young Guildford, mouldering in his grave in St Peter ad Vincula's . . .

The sight of that chapel, she knew, should twist her heart for the mournful memory of some of its dead, including her mother. But when she focused on it her overriding feeling remained one of self-preservation. She had been less than three years old when her father had ordered her mother's execution and not yet ten when he had also sent her beloved young stepmother, Catherine Howard, to the block. She had not needed any further devastation to remind her how vulnerable women could be at the mercy of male domination. When she was fourteen, however, along had come that philanderer, Thomas Seymour, whose infatuation had endangered her honour as well as her own life.

Three strokes of the axe had been required to behead him. As for her, hardened to self-reliance beyond her years, survival was as much then, as now, a game of skill rather than chance. A game of deflecting rather than entirely avoiding danger, a game of dissembling and above all, of trusting no-one apart from a few, rare exceptions! Robert Dudley was such, a dear friend and companion from childhood, and she cared about him. Oh, how she cared - especially when she could do so from a safe distance!

"If Lord Robert is to die, I wish to see him too," she asserted, stopping near the walkway's Beauchamp entrance.

"I do not know if that is poss . . ."

"Oh, come now! Not even to say farewell?"

"The Lady Jane did not say farewell to Lord Guildford -

and he was her husband!" tried the Lieutenant, with an air of finality.

"Then more fool her! Clearly, she preferred instead to see his carcass carted in two pieces from Tower Hill!"

Clearly too, the Lieutenant should have known better! He bowed, muttering gruffly about seeing what could be arranged, and he disappeared into the Beauchamp Tower. She acknowledged his exit regally, whirled about and assumed the established pattern of pacing, awaiting his return with Lord Robert.

The Lady Elizabeth wished to grant audience not only to say farewell for friendship's sake but to assure herself that, in the event of her life and his being spared, Robert Dudley would give his support to her right to the throne totally and not to his silly little sister-in-law, Lady Catherine.

## CHAPTER 3

# *"Young Folks Meaning Well . . ."*

At Hampton Court, Lord Edward Seymour awaited Queen Mary Tudor's arrival with a happier anticipation than most of the other Protestant nobles assembled there. He played no part in their amused complaints, that *they* had not been plied with free ale and wine to greet her, and her new husband, like the citizens of London! He wondered how many had sent gifts of flowers to her sister, Elizabeth, now removed from the Tower to imprisonment at Woodstock.

It was not difficult for him to be seen to be loyal to Mary. The good Catholic Queen had been kindness itself to him, to the rest of the disgraced Seymour family and to Lady Catherine Grey's.

"Sweet Catherine," he smiled to himself, and his heart skipped a beat. He heard jokes around him about some apartments called 'Paradise' being designated for the royal honeymoon. Paradise for him, however, was anywhere he could even dream of seeing Catherine.

When a fanfare of trumpets announced the entry of Mary and her bridegroom into the Great Hall, Edward stood on tiptoe and craned forward to look above the shoulders of his peers. He just made out the girl's fragile form following Mary. Until now, he had felt closed in amid the brute strength of jostling and taller courtiers, but suddenly sensed some whispers of disappointment at their first glimpse of Philip of Spain. Could this thin, pale-faced prince be the horned monster of their imaginings, who burnt Protestants in his own lands and had caused Wyatt's Rebellion against his marriage to their Sovereign?

Edward also spotted his older sister Jennie amongst the rest of the Queen's ladies. He grinned and stood flat-footed. Freedom from bossiness a little longer, he reasoned - though knowing Jennie, she'd be keeping a sharp eye out for him!

She located him all too soon, when the bigger men behind whom he could hide, bowed low. A brief glance of affection was then exchanged, before he bowed.

He subsequently repeated the movement within the confines of female company. Catherine responded with a curtsey of billowing royal blue satin. Her natural grace of movement charmed him all the more for the delightful picture she made with two little dogs at her feet.

The Queen embraced him first. Her oddly mannish voice muttered joyously from behind small, narrow lips so like those on all the portraits of her father, Henry VIII, around the various royal palaces.

And next, old King Henry might almost have stepped down in person from one of those portraits, albeit in womanly attire. The same small-shaped mouth, the same piggy eyes and the same physical bulk loomed large and imperious over him.

"Ned, my son!" clucked the mouth benignly, before puckering into a tight-lipped smack against his cheek. The Duchess of Suffolk had called him "son" ever since the short time of his betrothal to her eldest daughter. But as another girl baptized as Jane extricated him from her, he noticed the Duchess send a look of venom towards Catherine.

*"Salve, Edouardus - frater meus!"* his sister demanded all his immediate attention.

*"Salve,* Jennie," he sighed. He hoped that she wouldn't add Spanish to the languages she was already so proficient in. Instead, he wanted Jennie Seymour's deepening friendship with Catherine to give him more chances of meeting the prettiest of the Queen's ladies without either her "Mother Dragon" - or his own - hovering near!

The Duchess's expression switched to one of over-benevolence when the Queen smiled as Jennie linked arms with Catherine. Ned beamed too, pleased that Catherine had made friends so easily with his clever and scholarly sister. Comfit seemed to sense his glad surrender to these more congenial feelings which her mistress evoked in him and began to flail out insistently at him with her front left paw.

"Comfit, how *do* you do!" he teased, travelling what was for him only a short distance down to spaniel level. He held the welcoming paw and also patted Amber, the puppy given to Catherine by Queen Mary.

"So full of enthusiasm, my lord!" a girlish voice bubbled forth.

He raised his face as if impelled to see the smile parting Catherine's rosebud lips and share the amusement in her lowered eyes. From this angle he could gaze into them direct.

Looking up at her was, for him, like seeing another living portrait. But she was a portrait in exquisite miniature of her Tudor grandmother, Henry VIII's beautiful younger sister, Mary, after whom the Queen was named.

What a fool was Pembroke's son, he thought, to repudiate the marriage vow, *With my body I thee worship.*

"*I* thee worship!" Ned himself so much wanted to tell Catherine. And yet part of his attraction to this tiny girl was in feeling tall and strong beside her when he drew himself again to his full height.

Ned was sleepless with excitement that night at the thought of the coming days at Court. Catherine's mother was setting off for Sheen in the morning. Seymour lands forfeited at his father's execution and recently restored by the Queen, were keeping his own mother, his guardian, busy for the time being. Mary herself had already disappeared with Philip into 'Paradise', not to emerge for several days. So this was the first time in all his sixteen years that he would be free of adult authority. And Catherine was near! A new, dream-like world seemed to beckon to him, but would its magic close round her in reality?

He was overjoyed to realize that Catherine had caught the same light-hearted mood. The July weather was pleasantly warm and he was with her at play in the inner courtyard straight after Mother Dragon had gone. Her jewelled headdress was swiftly discarded amongst a hotch-potch of other paraphernalia strewn across the lawn - a ball, a towel, an old woollen stocking, a silver comfit box ... And then he saw the glory of her Tudor red-gold hair, fanning out in beauteous abundance over her shoulders and down her back. Catherine laughingly scooped up the ball and tossed it for Amber to fetch. The puppy trotted back triumphantly with the woollen stocking in her mouth.

"We're into a 'Pull' phase at the moment, my lord," Catherine giggled, taking hold of the longer end. "And she usually wins!"

"Makes a change from howling when she hears singing at Mass!"

"Of that, my Amber is fully cured," the girl blushed.

He saw Helen move out of earshot, to try and entice Comfit away from under the fountain. He began to sing in a low, confiding voice, *"Sanctu-us, sanctu-us."*

The stocking was thrown hastily at him. "Oh, shame on you, my lord."

"Seize her, Amber. Seize her!" he countered, in mock revenge. "No, not me - Lady Catherine!"

Amber placed her head on one side, on hearing her mistress's name. She retrieved the stocking and returned to Catherine joyously for another game.

Catherine would have pulled again and again happily, but a bout of laughter hurled her to the ground. She lay, hugging puppy and stocking tightly, hair outspread around her face as if she smiled up from a pillow.

He went to help her sit upright. He believed that otherwise, either Helen or Jennie, who was now approaching them with a book, would harp on yet again about him staring at the girl "like she was an angel dropped from the sky".

Long after, when the chestnut hue of his short, dark hair had tinged to white and silver, Ned's memories of these days with Catherine were to dwell ever stronger within him. Days so fleeting, so idyllic. But the memories - their lasting gift! Her red-gold crowning glory span around her when they danced together while Jennie played the music. It floated behind Catherine when she skipped along by flower borders with her two pets frisking at her side. And her hair fell in gleaming waves to her waist when she stopped suddenly to delight perhaps in a butterfly, or a flower, the dancing light on water, or the lace patterns of leaves against the sky.

There was one day amid the acres of gardens at

Hampton Court when she walked up to him, followed slowly by Nurse Cousins. She showed him the four-leaf clover she was cradling in her hands.

"And I'll thank my lord not to make me go all giggly, while I'm carrying this," she announced. "Jennie promised to press it for me in her book if ever I found one. 'Tis no small joy to me, for once in my life, to have such a symbol of good luck."

"And to me - that my lady has found this."

Her face bent in appreciative study of the clover. Ned knew the soft lilt of her voice well enough by now, however, to detect its wistfulness. They had both suffered similar setbacks in their young lives and in his compassion for her, he went on, "Does it seem too great sometimes, Catherine - all the hurt you've been through as well?"

She nodded, but checked first from the corners of her downcast eyes that they were in the nurse's sight, though not her hearing.

"Good my lord," Catherine began.

"Call me Ned."

"Ned ... my sweet lord. Even now, 'tis not easy for me, to see my ex-husband and his father prancing about in attendance on Her Majesty. I was still under Pembroke's roof when he brought other Lords of the Privy Council there to dethrone my sister. If it hadn't been for Comfit, I'd have thought myself in hell."

"Comfit - she's all for you, eh? Loyalty undivided!"

"Yes, bless her heart. Like me, she was no use to Pembroke and son."

"So Jennie told me. Too maternal by half to be used as a sporting spaniel!"

Catherine smiled at him, but gently. Nurse Cousins was much closer to them now. Surely she could not object to him strolling with Catherine through the rich summer garden, though. Ned decided that he was also on his way to join his sister!

He noted that airing a few of her grievances seemed to bring Catherine a sense of relief. He had glimpsed only from the view of an embarrassed outsider the excessive subjection her family life had entailed and he sympathized with her dependence for love on her pets. She would not preach at him, like his mother and Jennie did, if he talked out some sadness of his own.

"Since Seymour property was returned to me, I've learnt just how *much* use it was to Pembroke!" he said ruefully.

"So Jennie told *me!* She said how great is your love for your Forest of Savernake, and I am sorry that he has still kept part of it."

"Aye, of all our Wiltshire estates granted to him at my lord father's death, trust Pembroke to keep a valuable part of Savernake." Words tumbled from him with increasing speed as each step took them nearer to Jennie. "It's the part where my father had begun a great new house. And the building materials were taken by Pembroke for *his* country home. How well I could have used them myself, Catherine, to repair our old home at Wolf Hall! After all, King Henry rushed there to wed my Aunt Jane after Queen Anne Boleyn's execution. 'Tis tragic it's so ramshackle now."

Catherine's eyes met his with tenderness, despite her nurse being near.

His breathing quickened. "Catherine, are you thinking perhaps of Bradgate?"

"A little. I was thinking more of my sister. She was whipped, Ned, most cruelly, when your betrothal to her was broken off and she still wished to marry you, and not Guildford Dudley."

She looked pensively down at the clover. A youthful voice spoke invitingly inside Ned, *We have only one life. Let it be lived!*

How glad he was that his betrothal to Jane Grey had not worked out as first planned. He realized only now what small consolation even lordship over all parts of his much-loved Forest would have been. Small consolation if, in his falling for Catherine, both of them had been wedded to others!

But they were free, and they had each other's company. He said softly, "Somehow, the future seems less bleak. At least Her Majesty doesn't blame us personally for our misfortunes."

Catherine's eyes were brimming with tears, but she braved a smile, unafraid with him to laugh and cry both at once.

As the summer cooled into the early autumn, Ned hoped for further moments together with Catherine. He resigned himself mainly to moping around his mother's home at Hanworth, bemoaning the meagre finances which made impossible the three days' hard ride to see his Forest at this beautiful turn of the seasons.

Jennie welcomed his frequent visits to her at Court. "More than I ever expected!" she reminded him, each time.

She certainly did not expect him to turn up one afternoon in the palace gardens, carrying a pet monkey. His finances had stretched enough also to dress it in tiny courtiers' clothes. He presented the little creature with a great flourish to Catherine. Her face shone with delight.

"Any ideas for a name for him?" Ned asked, affecting a studious, deep-thinking stance.

"Clover," Catherine immediately replied.

"Clover? But, dearest Catherine, it's male!" said Jennie.

Catherine paused briefly, then insisted on the name as before.

In her elation at introducing the newcomer to her other pets, she caught one of the hanging sleeves of her gown on the thorns of a rose-bush.

Ned moved swiftly to release her, and Jennie looked jokingly this way and that. "Such stirring to action, brother! I assumed that somewhere a drawn dagger pointed at you," she shrugged.

Soon a situation arose which took all of them unawares. When Jennie fell suddenly ill, the Queen was amongst those who kept anxious vigils at her bedside. Then to Ned's initial disgruntlement, Mary decided to allow Jennie home to Hanworth to convalesce. To his later amazement and joy, Her Majesty also determined that his sister's best friend would accompany the invalid!

Amid the general despair, while Jennie was still very weak, the Seymours' mother could no longer maintain the usual strictness over Ned. Comfit's nurturing instincts found fulfilment in attempting to herd him and Catherine together. The girl was reticent in her demeanour, but in a quiet corner of the corridor near Jennie's chamber, she could not hide her distress at the possibility of losing her friend. Jennie had become like her own older sister to Catherine.

"Don't worry, Catherine," he said. "Jennie'll be all right."

"Oh, my good Ned ... D'you really think so?"

"Yes. You'll see. She's always recovered from illness the minute she puts her mind to it. Mark my words, she'll soon be back ordering both me and thee around!"

Catherine's eyes twinkled at him in shy amusement.

"I'm glad that ours is a gentler sort of fighting spirit than is usual in our two families," he added, unashamedly. "Catherine ... can you love me?"

"I am honoured to, my lord -" She trailed off into drawing a heart-shape on his shoulder, with their initials intertwined.

"Beloved," he whispered, and kissed her hand.

She slipped away from the house with Comfit shortly afterwards to marvel at the changing shades of autumn colours in its grounds. He let several minutes drag by, and then he also went out. Comfit dashed up to him and rustled through fallen leaves in front of him, looking for him to follow her. They came upon Catherine trying to catch the leaves as they fell. Ned took her hands to capture jointly a russet leaf, just detached from a branch above them. But it rested on another, in solitary defiance.

From holding her hands to holding her closer and their lips meeting, all happened so instantly, that neither of them faltered towards a longer embrace.

They thought that only Comfit saw any expression of ardour between them. But the question of how much they meant to each other began to receive wider notice within the Seymour household.

"Helen's gossiping has probably set other tongues a-wagging," Catherine confided to Ned.

"'Tis more likely Jennie, beloved," he sighed. "Whenever she's ill, she guesses at so much more!"

Ned tried to divert Jennie onto Greek philosophy when

she confronted him with the first sign of interrogation over Catherine. Her wan face stared up at him and overruled him with the tell-me-truly-or-you'll-be-sorry tactic, which she so invariably adopted. He suddenly felt far from chivalrous.

"All right," he asserted himself. "Yes, there is goodwill between myself and Lady Catherine, and I wish to seek her hand in marriage."

Jennie shook her head. "The Queen will never allow it. Don't you know, brother, that she inclines towards Catherine for her successor? The true-born Lady Catherine, who does her bidding, unlike her bastard sister Lady Elizabeth, whom she heartily distrusts!"

She signalled to him to prop up the mound of pillows which supported her. Ned thumped them vigorously into place. "That's enough!" she chided him. "To be sure, Catherine's such a winsome little thing. 'Tis a mortal shame that she might also wear a crown one day ... Otherwise, Ned, she'd have made an ideal wife for you."

"You'll wed neither her nor anyone else, my lad, before you come of age," another voice rounded on him. A voice which sounded characteristically crusty, as their mother burst in upon their conversation from behind the heavy bed-curtains at the opposite end to them. "Do you think I saved you by sundering your betrothal to one sister, only for you to go and lose your head because of another of them?"

So you alone saved me? he thought. That's rich!

In his annoyance at her chuntering against both him *and* Catherine, Ned did his best at least to appear manly. "Mother," he said, "young folks meaning well may well accompany! And I trust I may have Lady Catherine's company, here and at Court. We've not been forbidden by the Queen." He looked intently then from his mother to his sister and reminded them, "Lady Catherine has been sent here as our guest by royal commandment, though the Queen knew that I too would be at Hanworth. Therefore, Her Majesty's feelings in this matter cannot be doubted."

"Just think on another matter, you hot-tempered young fool," snorted his mother.

"What other matter?"

"Lady Catherine's mother has recently miscarried of her second son. Strange, how such a large woman has borne only frail girls and a boy who died as a baby! But these Tudors have produced so few healthy sons. Are you sure your little lovebird can provide you with one?"

"I'm sure that I wish to rebuild my inheritance, with Lady Catherine as my wife."

His bold words caused the Duchess of Somerset to renew her vigilance over her impoverished son and continue to barrack him each day, but nothing could gainsay him in his love for Catherine. Her presence soothed his mind, his heart, his very soul for a further six weeks. During these, she was at greater peace with herself because of Jennie's recovery and Ned was thankful that his sister took so long about it!

Before Catherine and Jennie returned to their duties at Court, some news came which stunned and silenced Ned's mother. The Lady Catherine's romance with Lord Edward Seymour seemed to be of less concern to the kindly Queen and the Tudor succession than Jennie would have him believe ...

At the advanced age of thirty-eight, and after only a few months of marriage, Mary Tudor's 'miracle' to secure her throne had happened: her heir would be born in the spring!

CHAPTER 4

# *A Son of the New Laws*

In every church throughout the realm, the Queen's subjects prayed for her safe delivery of a sturdy prince. From northern hills and dales to islands in the English Channel, many genuinely wished her well at first, believing it was high time that one member of their gifted ruling house should assure the succession with a bevy of sons who could survive to manhood. Or would she add to the Tudor tally of embarrassment over this, the foremost of duties?

In Guernsey, Perotine Massey typified expectant mothers of every rank in opting to give her child the King's name, Philip, if she bore a son. Like others too, she prayed much during all the discomfort of pregnancy that when the ordeal of childbirth came, the baby would live, if not herself. They were so engrossed through those months in fact, she and her own mother and her sister, Willemine, with preparing for her first-born that they did not understand all the changes which the King's and Queen's new laws were bringing to their little church. Nor all the questions that the dean and curate plagued them with, about the Catholic faith and the Latin Mass, so different from the Church's teachings followed by everyone in the previous reign of Queen Mary's Protestant young brother, Edward.

The sensations of another being moving within her body, and the visible, tangible changes outside it as her pregnancy advanced, were naturally compounded by the strangeness of a world suddenly inconstant over religious doctrines. Doctrines that were the only ones young folk like her had ever been instructed in, the only ones those of her mother's age could latterly remember.

Her mother and sister were sharing her agony when she went into labour. Alongside her as the contractions began to tear at her, increasing, increasing . . . jerking her into a frenzy as she choked, gasped, tried to bear down to expel the child despite the restraints against her. Her every sinew seemed to be bursting and in this heat, the effort roasting her hair with her skin . . . In this heat. Oh, the heat! Could her torment really be as bad as this? She writhed, and pushed - amid her screams, called out, prayed aloud for the child to be saved.

But no-one heard her. No-one, because in her pain, the cord which had been tied too slackly around her neck, worked firmly into her mouth, forcing her to clench her teeth and so to mute her cries.

And by the time Perotine's child was born, a son, alive, the air was heavy with grey-black smoke and the stench of charred human flesh from the inferno leaping around three women bound to stakes with iron chains.

The crowd looked on in a silent paralysis of horror. The grim spectacle before them was worse than any of the tales of burnings they had heard of from elsewhere in the kingdom. A half-scorched infant was plucked squirming from the flames, with hastily dampened faggots. An infant for whom his mother seemed to cry out some name before her lips burnt away.

He did acquire a name, of a sort, when the Queen's official bailiff on the island lurched forward with boot-stomping vigour.

"Cast it back, that heretic's brat!" he barked at the executioners.

The men appeared to hesitate and some onlookers began to hiss at him.

"Fail you not," he warned, bellowing above the jeers by now erupting from sporadic pockets of the crowd. "At your uttermost peril, fail you not. Aye . . . and if any of *you* - or *you*," he leered round, "should presume like these to sin against Holy Mother Church, be assured that flames will consume your earthly bodies too, just as fire everlasting will burn your souls in hell."

At his command, guards then stood in readiness facing spectators, in case so much as a voice or half-clenched fist should be raised in protest while the day's slaughter spewed into memory in a baptism of fire. The throng was shifting, however, even as flames crackled over the tiny victim's cry. Shifting away, backs turned abruptly in silent revulsion, and some retching their green bile of nausea before they were far enough from the scene.

Enforced silence could not stop the recounting of the incident in all its detail, from the very moments people reached distances which seemed safe from the guards. Then the words *murder,* and *martyr,* gushed forth unchecked.

"They were my neighbours," sobbed one woman. "They were good and honest."

"What are things coming to? Executing a young, pregnant woman!" whispered another frantically.

"Execution? 'Tis martyrdom!" yet another corrected her.

Perotine's neighbour dabbed the tears from her cheeks while she nodded and joined in again. "'Tis unbelievable how harsh things have become since that Good Seymour Duke of Somerset ceased to be our Governor."

"Aye, he did his best for the island," agreed her companions.

"And for the whole realm when he was Lord Protector for that boy, King Edward. He'd never have let Perotine or her baby burn."

The second woman shuddered amd also broke down. "A babe. An innocent baby, murdered! Nothing will ever justify it!"

The story of Guernsey's "Baby Martyr" continued to stand out amongst the tales of other victims mercilessly burnt at the stake elsewhere. Numerous victims, who included the blind, the old, the crippled, the young and the very poor. And many subjects throughout the realm began to curse their Roman Catholic monarch and looked to the day when "Bloody Mary" no longer reigned.

Yet, if there appeared to be one rule for the poor, and another entirely for the rich, such a difference depended on possessing enough money to escape abroad. Money could not protect from the flames any high-ranking Protestants of insufficient means left behind. And accusing fingers were pointing, making many walk in fear for their lives. Family trauma closed in further around the Queen's sonless kinswoman, the Duchess of Suffolk, after Suffolk's own Dowager Duchess joined the exodus to safety in exile.

Spanish Philip's dwindling blacklist of suspected heretics was widely known. And now nearer the top of the list of those who could not afford to flee, were the remaining Greys and Seymours.

## CHAPTER 5

# *Springtime Madonna*

*"Remember, Catherine, I love you."* Ned's much-missed voice flowed dreamily into Catherine's innermost thoughts, while outwardly she mouthed the usual, nightly litany in the Queen's bedchamber. She had not seen him for all of April, since Mary retired from the Court to await the royal birth.

Catherine remained on her knees in an attitude of apparent prayer, even after uttering the final "Amen". The pressure of a hand on her shoulder then alerted her drifting mind back to reality, as Jennie levered herself stiffly onto her feet. Catherine's semblance of piety nevertheless earned her a nod of approval from the Queen.

If only Jane had been content to dream during all these Catholic rituals, Catherine wished. If only Jane had been less of a martyr-type!

She stood up and smoothed out the folds of her gown, now that another day's repetitive round of devotions was over. They seemed a small price to pay for being able to delight still in all that was beautiful, and gather people and pets around her to love.

Her two spaniels restored her spirit to match that of the springtime, when they welcomed her return to her own chamber with Jennie. She eased herself down onto her floor-cushions and they imitated her wholeheartedly. Catherine's need for diversion through relaxation and play with them seemed all the greater because so much depended on one unborn child. A new Tudor cousin might mean she could marry Ned soon, if Queen Mary permitted.

Amber was fully-grown now, but at the slightest sign of

encouragement from Catherine, she still turned on the playful antics of a pup. And so her favourite toy landed in Catherine's lap. The old stocking was tossed, fetched back and then the shared enjoyment of a game of 'Pull' began. How much better this was to Catherine than being haunted by Helen's voice, making her flesh creep some nights with the words of a chant the know-all said was rife all o'er the country:

> *'When folks with vi'lence are burnt to death,*
> *We wish for our Elizabeth.'*

I hope that Elizabeth knows nought of this in her prison, thought Catherine. Or else she'll be even more stuck-up!

Catherine relished the prospect of Mary's child demoting Elizabeth as well as herself in the line of succession. She became immersed in her game with Amber and her heart, in contrast, opened to offering up prayers to her Maker. But these were meaningful prayers. Pleas from the very depths of her being that Ned was abiding by the law and showing his face at Mass, as he had promised her he would. She prayed too that her step-grandmother, the Dowager Duchess of Suffolk, was now safe in some Protestant haven free from all threat of persecution.

"It's like a little Maypole dance," Jennie's voice trilled from a nearby chair.

"Mm?"

"Amber, toing and froing at her end of the stocking."

"Ah . . ."

"Ah . . . mm!" laughed Jennie. "No need to tell me - you wish you could be with you-know-who. Well, 'tis understandable."

"I . . . er, he -"

Jennie made the sign of the cross, with a look of earnest enquiry at her friend. Catherine nodded in reply, ruffling the fur along Comfit's front paw at the same time with her free hand.

"He'd better be!" said Jennie. "You know, last night I dreamed of a large, tall gentleman stalking into Mass with little *frater meus* tucked under his arm."

"Charming! It's lucky I know how much you care about my lord."

"Yes, but when he's not around for me to organize him, I sometimes cannot rise above fatigue!"

"Go easy, Jennie. I'd hate for you to be ill again."

"I wouldn't be overly pleased myself! Dear Catherine," Jennie nudged at her affectionately, "how can I ever know what you see in him when love, so people say, is blind? But I do wish you happier dreams than mine."

Catherine smiled and murmured, "What's so blind about loving him through different eyes than yours?"

She pictured Ned again, reiterating his love for her at their last, brief meeting and holding her in his arms as though perhaps there would never be any other meetings between them. He gave her confidence to express herself without always needing words.

And she longed to be with him, that was for certain! But what was not certain yet was *when* she could be with him. Custom demanded isolation of the Queen and her ladies from male company till after the birth, even that of male pets. Poor Clover had chattered with fury when he was separated from Catherine.

Meanwhile, only Mary's chaplain and King Philip could spend time with the royal mother-to-be and her attendants. Philip entered the Queen's apartments on the following day and greeted each of her ladies with his habitual kiss, full on the mouth.

Catherine always succumbed to her sense of icy panic at the sight of his yellowed, jagged teeth closing in towards her and the cold slaver of his lips across hers. But it was another ritual to be endured, uncomplaining, however much she may wish to wipe away his kiss on the nearest kerchief or yearned for Ned's embrace.

He had come to visit his wife because false tidings had

spread that she was delivered of a prince. Bonfires had blazed and church bells pealed throughout London, until stopped by his command. And beneath his precise and patient manner, he seemed distinctly grumpy.

He went into Mary's bedchamber and was alone with her. Several stormy words were overheard between them, however. Then without warning, he summoned "Lady Cattrin" into their deep-voiced presence.

A narrow shaft of light slanted into the Queen's chamber from the only window which was not hung with tapestry. Through its transparent, silvery rays, Catherine did not feel surprised to notice that Philip frowned down at the swollen belly which yet showed no sign of releasing the eagerly-awaited heir. Catherine's wary demeanour goaded her outward appearance to its most becoming subservience.

"Mary, the meeror of mercifulness," Philip droned, rather scornfully. "Is that not what a poet once wrote of Your Majesty?"

Mary stirred angrily, uncomfortably, amid the scarlet coverings of her bed, despite her usual cordial glances on seeing the girl. "I tell you again," she barked. "Elizabeth is no daughter of Henry VIII, but the result of an ill-starred affair between Anne Boleyn and Smeaton, a low-born musician. And since she's been brought here from Woodstock without either my foreknowledge or consent, and now lies 'prisoned above the gatehouse, there, by my express wish she shall stay."

"No daughter of Henry VIII, uh? Is your eyesight now so bad that you cannot see the family likeness between her and your cousin Cattrin?"

Catherine's carefully averted eyes suddenly dilated, in her indignation at being compared with such a trouble-maker to the Queen.

That Elizabeth! she fumed inside. *Why must she dominate everything!*

"Lady Catherine far excels her in looks!" retorted Mary.

"Catherine is much smaller, like myself, and her complexion is perfect - whereas Elizabeth's is sallow!"

"Smaller, preetier - *si!* But before you feed her ears any further, look!" He jerked Catherine's face up towards the light and her view of the gold and blue and russet silken fringe edging Mary's bed coverlet was suddenly substituted by another close-up of his teeth.

She was constrained by the pressure of his sword hand beneath her chin. So Catherine plumped for gazing unobtrusively heavenwards, as she wished to do rather more vehemently. Philip went on, "The shape of the face . . . ees the same, the forehead very high, the nose . . . long and straight, the chin a little pointed . . . the redness of the hair . . . the hands, very slender, very prettily displayed . . ."

"Beware of Elizabeth's witchery," cut in Mary. "She shows off her whole self to the best advantage. Would that instead of all her preening, she could look as Madonna-like as Catherine!"

The Queen's words nurtured yet further Catherine's youthful and poor impression of her haughty cousin.

"The ways of weemin," snapped Philip.

He let go of Catherine's chin, but his tone of irritation tended to accentuate her Madonna-like looks. Always, when she felt especially afeared and intimidated, her every move had seemed compelled to try and achieve perfection. Appearances of innocence, reverence, subservience and rapt attention had saved her from sharing a number of the thrashings, nips and other parental torments inflicted on her more outspoken sister, Jane.

Catherine also felt drained of energy now. That was a tendency she definitely had shared with Jane after family storms and strife. What price that Jennie would leave her in peace, though, after this royal battle of wills? At the earliest opportune second, she'd likely be pounced upon to tell what all the "weeping and gnashing of teeth" was about in here!

The scene before her was the closest enactment of those words of woe from the Bible she had ever come across. But her sympathy for the weeper was also tinged with a watchful admiration for the way Mary still remained so resolute that she would not abide Elizabeth near her.

"As heiress to your Crown, she has more right than any other English lady to be present at the birth!" insisted Philip tersely.

"A position she would presume upon to the utmost."

"No less perhaps than you presume, madam, to forget your sacred duty of obedience to me."

"I vowed to love you perfectly," protested Mary, "and that I would never forget. Nay, surely this is not a question of obedience, but of placing the interests of our child above all else. You had Elizabeth brought here to safeguard yourself, by courting favour with her in case the child and I are called to God. You do not know how she will hover round you like a honey bee around a fragrant flower - before she stings! Have you forgotten how only a year ago you were urging me to send her on poor Jane's path to the block? And do you think that even for a moment *she* has forgotten?"

Intimations of regret over Jane would ever be a kind of musical salve to Catherine. Philip, however, made a stilted half-turn which revealed his face near the shaft of light. With narrowed eyes glaring fixedly at Mary, he assumed an air of disdain.

"I am *far* too busy," he declared, "to concern myself with such trivia, as what Madam Elizabeth has or has not forgotten. Or to stand here beeckering all day with a quarrelsome wife." He turned on his heels to leave.

"I beg of you, Philip, do not go to her," called Mary plaintively, but still unrepentant in her distress.

"Go to her!" he said, looking back at Mary very correctly. "And face a woman who is not so unlike you as you think?"

Then he uttered his parting shot, "For her known

wilfulness and obstinacy, I believe Elizabeth ees also very much a Tudor! Would that you were both as withdrawn as Cattrin."

After that, Catherine went instinctively to help re-unite Mary's fumbling hands with her great consolation of her prayer-book.

"Withdrawn, hm, little cousin Catherine?" she croaked in gentler tones. "Back-handed compliments for us both from His Majesty."

Catherine steadied the book for her, and the Queen peered intently with her near-sighted eyes at the prayer for a woman with child.

"Not one babe, Your Majesty, but a fine set of triplets to comfort and cheer you," said one of the midwives.

"Born without danger, Your Majesty!" added a nurse. "Here is the mother, see. Of similar height and age to Your Majesty."

Mary clasped her hands in pleasure, as the mother came to her bedside and knelt.

While the Queen blessed each child and sought reassurance about their birth from this woman, Jennie whispered to Catherine, "We all heard those snatches of Tudor bluntness while Her Majesty was with you and the King! Let's hope this will help her."

"'Tis well done," smiled Catherine. "Her Majesty needs much loyal support."

Jennie beamed at her. "*Organizing* to be done now!" she enthused.

Soon Jennie was in full and forthright flow amongst Mary's attendant army of ladies, midwives, nurses, maids and cradle-rockers for them all to rally round the Queen with words of further encouragement. And Catherine's long-practised tendency to murmur at appropriate times, when she listened to others, became much used amid the animated talk in the Queen's chamber.

"Each day I awaken, thinking, 'Will it be today?'" said Mary to the midwives.

Their voices rose in reply above those of other sympathizers.

"Not long now, Your Majesty."

"Thursday week, 9th May. The birth will be over at the very latest by then."

"And the King will be too jubilant to recall any rash words of his."

"Rash words, aye, a sign of the jitters that anxious fathers-to-be get, Your Majesty! P'raps they even brought on His Majesty's bowel complaint again . . ."

Mary smiled broadly at them and began to warm to the idea of packing Elizabeth off back to the Bell Tower after the birth.

Later, Catherine told Jennie about the disdain she had seen on Philip's face.

"He does not return her love," she confided disconsolately.

"I think that the wars of his own country are preying on the King's mind at this time," considered Jennie. "He must needs be away perhaps, but like the rest of us has to wait upon events here."

Catherine compressed her lips, not entirely convinced. But in her weariness, she simply could not say for sure how clearly the Queen had observed her husband's expression.

"Remember that he was some distance from her in a dimly-lit room," said Jennie, "and her shortness of vision was misted by tears."

Catherine tried to stay hopeful, therefore, about marrying Ned long before he came of age, but the 9th day of May passed by with the royal cradle still empty.

She and Jennie overheard the midwives remark about

Her Majesty's deflating stomach. This was more than a trifle unnerving for the girl who wished she was safely third instead of second in line to the throne. But *watching* the Queen actually start to squeeze at that stomach was positively alarming!

Catherine's display of concern was easily interpreted as being purely for the Queen.

"Lord love you, Lady Catherine," said Mary huskily, "but I'm told there's nought amiss! 'Tis because this shrivelling bulge is said to be a sign of impending delivery that I have ordered a confession of guilt to be wrung from Lady Elizabeth, if she's ever to find mercy from me. I'll have no more of her cunning."

"May it comfort Your Majesty that the date for the birth was only slightly in error."

"Why, thank you, sweet cousin. And now, God willing, we look towards another Thursday week."

*Another Thursday week!* True to her upbringing, Catherine did not gulp, but swallowed with politely hesitant poise. Another Thursday week seemed so far ahead to her that she began to think Ned must have had some gift of prophecy, when he held her close last time as if they would never meet again . . .

"23rd May," added Mary after a pause. She knew no reason why the girl's hesitancy should be due to anything else but carefully working out the new date.

"Yes, Your Majesty."

"Or failing that, around the time of the new moon early in June."

"Or . . . around the new moon in June."

"*Early* in June, Lady Catherine."

"Yes, Your Majesty."

Catherine crossed her fingers very firmly beneath the delicate frills of lace, edging the wrists of her sleeves. She hastened back to the solace of Comfit, Amber and her floor-cushions as soon as she could.

Mary also started to sit on a pile of floor-cushions, and

for longer sessions than Catherine.

"Is this another Tudor family trait?" asked Jennie. "One which develops when its members are troubled?"

"Is it?" smiled Catherine. "We've been here on our cushions at *play* for weeks."

"And weeks!" echoed Jennie. "Whenever I see you set your chin firm like that at times of threat to your hopes, there's no doubting your resemblance to your kinsfolk! But whereas you, Catherine, look quite entrancing down there with your pets nestling beside you, Her Majesty on her cushions looks . . . as though she's in a *trance.* Prayer-book in one hand, oft squeezing at her stomach with the other!"

"Perhaps when the babe is born," said Catherine pensively.

"Aye, perhaps then her present mood will pass."

When 23rd May, and the next five days also went by uneventfully, Mary was at last roused from her floor-cushions.

"She said *what!*" her voice growled through from her bedchamber.

The humming drawl of Philip's response was, in contrast, scarcely audible to Catherine and the other females assembled in the outer chamber.

"That rather than confess her treason, Elizabeth would stay in prison all the days of her life if she has ever offended me in thought, word or deed. Pah! Was ever an anointed monarch insulted with such brazen defiance? She must tell another tale, husband, ere she is to be set free!"

Late at night on the 30th, Catherine was suddenly sent for to attend upon the Queen. She obeyed with all due urgency. Memories of early tribulations were still very strong inside her, that an immediate summons to see elders in authority over her meant she was about to be roundly castigated. She told herself purposefully, however, that in truth the Divine dilly-dallying over the birth was now almost over. Queen Mary's fervent prayers would be answered in the coming hours. And some fitting words, which had to be prayed fifty times in every rosary, coursed through Catherine, as of recent habit: 'Hail Mary, full of grace. The Lord is with thee. Blessed art thou amongst women. Blessed is the fruit of thy womb . . .'

When Catherine arrived in the royal bedchamber, she knelt before the Queen with extra deferential dignity. For Mary often praised this quality in her, and to Catherine's disappointment, Mary was alone in the room. Lank strands of greying hair straggled across her grim and ashen face, as she sat enthroned on the dais, a fur-trimmed cloak around her.

"Rise up, cousin," she muttered, "and come and stand at my side. This is your right, being the nearest *English* royal relation in good and loyal service to her Queen. Would that others could be so obedient."

Strangely, her voice became more gravel-throated and she seemed to talk across to the wall tapestry.

No sooner had Catherine gone to her appointed place than she suffered an involuntary tremble in her legs. She felt relieved that her gown hid this. Usually, it only happened at the sight of Mother Dragon. But now it was at the sight of the particularly disobedient 'other' being ushered in!

Elizabeth seemed so menacing, with her piercing stare as she peeled off her scented gloves and twitched her nose at the ill-smelling air. She even put them on again before deigning to kneel before Mary.

Catherine quaked and swallowed as discreetly as she could. Elizabeth was in a quagmire of trouble, maybe deserving death. Yet she had swept in with about as much penitence as if . . . as if she were Mother Dragon about to mete out harsh punishment!

Mother Dragon must have passed on some of herself to Madam when she became her godmother, thought Catherine.

"I am Your Majesty's true and humble subject," declared Elizabeth.

"But you will not own up to your crimes," said Mary. "You remain adamant about your innocence and no doubt you'll say only that you have been wrongly imprisoned."

"Never must I speak thus to Your Majesty."

"But you might, nevertheless, to others."

"No, I implore Your Majesty to think well of me as your loving subject and sister for all our earthly days."

"God knows," quavered Mary's voice across to the same wall tapestry again.

Catherine then thought she heard some breathing from there. It checked at once any temptation for her to steal surreptitious glances at the tapestry. Mother Dragon might be lurking behind it, watching and listening also to the Tudor sisters. In case that was so, Catherine appeared to stand immovably straight as a statue on her feeble legs and to listen far more intently than she truly was.

Mary started to choke. She seemed impatient, yet reluctant to disgorge her next words, "Ince . . . in*cent* . . ." She placed a hand briefly across her mouth and the other clenched round a fold of her cloak. "Innocent . . . or guilty, I . . . forgive you."

Forgive you, repeated Catherine to herself. Forgive Elizabeth, the stinging bee!

But before she could guess how such a change might affect herself, someone *did* augment their threesome from the direction where she had not risked a look. Someone who caused Elizabeth's thin, high-arched brows to arch even higher, in imperious surprise.

"Welcome, seester," said the newcomer.

"Your Majesty."

Philip grandly helped to raise Elizabeth up from her knees and inflicted upon her a greeting kiss. So Catherine half-gleefully saw her suffer some punishment after all, this woman heartily detested by the Queen.

How could it suddenly be right, though, for him next to hold one of the rebellious creature's gloved hands and link her in a human chain with her good sister by entwining his other hand with one of Mary's?

Catherine felt bemused and tired at the end of a long day. But she was obliged to continue listening, as the conversation moved on to greater matters: the war between Spain and France . . . The need to uphold the will of King Henry VIII with regard to ensuring an English-born successor to the throne, should Queen Mary and her baby not survive . . .

"His Majesty would not tolerate my young namesake, Mary Queen of Scots, claiming my throne," said Mary, "with or without her future husband, the French prince!"

Philip stepped forward from his stance between the Tudor sisters and curled the end of his neat beard upwards, as he placed himself nearer Catherine.

"Mark my words well, Lady Elizabeth and Lady Cattrin," he warned. "I am bestowing on both of you my friendship and support. And in return, if either of you marry during this war, you must take husbands acceptable to Spain, as well as your Sovereign Lady."

Catherine was jolted by this latter demand. What shall I do? cried her inner voice.

"I shall never incline towards marriage," said Elizabeth.

Her assertion stoked up a hubbub of lecturing about "Duty" and "Unthinkable" and "Marry, you *must!*" from both Philip and Mary.

"Eet ees *eemperative* you must!" added Philip.

"Imperative," Catherine blurted out. Then she realized that she could try to gainsay Elizabeth in the safety of Queen Mary's company. "You should say sorry for all the hurt you cause Her Majesty."

"I shall say sorry when there is need!"

"Lady Catherine is right," said Mary, "but Lady Elizabeth is forgiven."

Catherine feared she might suffer from Elizabeth outside Mary's presence for daring to speak against her. But her more immediate thoughts were of marrying Ned.

I must plead with the Queen for us as soon as the King

goes off to fight for Spain, she reflected.

Perhaps sanctioning her love-match might be fine retaliation, she hoped, for Mary against Philip for his championship of Elizabeth. And further retaliation too, if Mary's sunken, watery eyes had indeed noted the falseness of his love for her.

Catherine was determined that *her* romance would somehow triumph!

The weeks of June slipped beyond the new moon into full summer. Mary sobbed to her ladies one day, "It is God's punishment. God's punishment for not burning enough heretics."

She lifted her hands in a gesture of utter despair. The diagnosis that she was pregnant had been wrong all along, and the rigid arrangements for her lying-in were unnecessary.

"I'll write to Ned to visit me," said Jennie afterwards. "The Queen has shuttered her mind to any other reason why there was no child. If rumour be true, the King's seed was too weak."

Jennie tried to comfort Catherine when Mary, instead of sending letters to other rulers, happily announcing a royal birth, circulated orders to the bishops of each diocese to burn more heretics at the stake.

"Oh, Jennie," whispered Catherine, trying to hold back her tears. "Rather than marry Ned, I shall be lucky if he even stays alive!"

Ned resumed visiting Jennie at Court in July. "Postponed," he said to Catherine about their marriage aspirations. "Abandoned, beloved . . . never!"

Jennie pushed her friend gently closer to him, melting away the slight shyness which Catherine had first displayed on seeing Ned again after almost four months.

"Hark that I have noticed - you don't greet *me,* moving as if in time to the unheard melody of a lute!" Jennie attempted to banter. But she did so with a decided air of resignation to the inevitable, as sheer delight added to the romantic ardour in her brother's face when a tiny arm drew itself softly through his arm.

"Poor deprived thing!" quipped Ned.

"Oh, indeed, brother. But until a more auspicious time, it *is* under the guise of dutiful visits to me that you can continue to see Catherine privately, without causing comment."

"And a good guise it is, too."

"Yes, Ned. And if for no other reason than your love of Catherine, you keep yourself safe by bowing your head to Catholic rites, that is most welcome to me."

"Jennie, I'll be such a model of discretion that the most assiduous of tittle-tattlers will be leading a quiet life!"

"Poor Helen," chimed in Catherine, sharing a rueful smile with his sister.

"Aye!" he agreed.

"That's good to hear, Ned," Jennie beamed. "It's such a challenge to us to keep Helen quiet, that sometimes when she's within earshot, we resort to improving Catherine's Latin by telling each other our secrets in that language. And when Catherine's Latin falters . . ."

"As it frequently does," admitted Catherine beguilingly. "I use so many 'ums', it must still sound like Latin to her."

Ned laughed. "Well, from now on, *all* of us'll have to outwit her. Are we in perfect accord over this, my ladies?"

"Perfect," said Catherine.

"Perfect," said Jennie, and set her chin determinedly, in imitation of Catherine.

## CHAPTER 6

# *Uneasy Inheritance*

The autumn of 1555 marked the first full year since Catherine and Ned declared their love. To Catherine's relief, Mary parted company from Elizabeth gravely and politely one October day. The Queen had given her sister permission to leave Court and live in the royal residence at Hatfield.

"It's odd that Lady Elizabeth's new Governor is called Pope!" Helen was heard to joke . . . repeatedly.

Mary clearly did enjoy being rid of Elizabeth. She lavished affection and favour on Catherine, though, and also the girl's increasing family of pets. Forlorn sights of her rocking in her arms the puppies born to Comfit, and later to Amber, were a far cry for the royal household from her nickname.

"'Bloody Mary' - that's how my subjects revile me," she often sighed. "Much more so, since the King departed overseas. But it could be any time now when he returns to me."

Philip, however, did not come back until March . . . March, of 1557! The war was blamed for keeping him so long from her, for keeping their marriage childless. Catherine saw Mary sitting up in auguish, far into many nights. The Queen wrote to him of matters in England, and reproached herself with each passing month for not consigning enough Protestants yet to faggots' flames. She despaired further that the candles reflected fewer and fewer flecks of the Tudor red-gold that her hair had once been.

Catherine's accustomed place was closest to Queen

Mary, amongst the ladies who stood ranged about the throne whenever ambassadors or messengers were received. She watched with compassion as Mary went to the very water's edge at Dover when Philip left again in the July. Afterwards, Catherine was also dismayed to see her sink back onto floor-cushions, in abject desolation. Mary's belly swelled and deflated, as before. And though a gift of baby linen arrived for her from Elizabeth, the Queen's attendants no longer regaled her with platitudes about a precious heir to entice Philip back to her. Whispered rumours about tumours in her woman's parts began to prevail.

But by the winter, even Mary admitted, "His Majesty will not dare to reappear in my realm in person. Isn't that what my subjects will say now? I only let him have English soldiers for the war against France to please him."

"Alas, Your Majesty, the garrison he left at Calais was too small," said the messenger sent by the Governor of Calais. "The French were coming in such force to capture the town."

"And now it is lost," sobbed Mary, "after England owned Calais for so long. The damage to our trade will be enormous and my people will deride me even more."

Catherine later whispered into Comfit's attentive ears, "Bad, *bad* King Philip." How different were his clammy-cold salutations from the kiss which then alighted like the caress of a gossamer-winged butterfly on this, the most dear of all beloved pets!

She and Mary and Elizabeth were still tied to Spanish interests, however. Much as she took comfort from Mary's apparent apathy over coercing Elizabeth into a Spanish marriage, Catherine baulked at causing potentially further upset to the bitterly lonely, heretic-burning Queen by seeking permission to match herself with her English Protestant sweetheart.

But . . . come Ned's coming-of-age, the lofty objections of his mother could be overruled and he would be the head of his family, with full dominion over their lands and finances. *Then* would be a wondrous easier time for petitioning Mary than at present! Catherine trusted that the war would perhaps be over and Mary, in better health, might yet be avenged on Philip by giving her blessing to "Lady Cattrin's" love-knot.

In the meantime, the girl's heart urged her for pity's sake and for past kindnesses well remembered, at least to commiserate with Mary in all her sorrows. Quiet sympathy soon sounded towards the dejected Queen so hesitantly, however, that Mary leant forward on her floor-cushions and thrust a lock of hair behind her ear, in order to listen.

"I dare, from love of Your Majesty . . . to express profound condolences not only for the King's neglect of you, but also . . . his *desertion,*" murmured Catherine.

"Not only that," lamented Mary, in harsher tones of shared perception. "Not only that, but when I am dead and opened, you will find Calais lying upon my heart."

As the months of 1558 approached the summer, Ned decided at last to make a preparatory visit to his Wiltshire lands. Each month was bringing him nearer to his coming-of-age and the change in status this would assure him. Meanwhile, he gained a valuable ally in his father's former steward, Sir John Thynne, whose knowledge of the Seymour estates in that county was unsurpassed.

Ned often pictured Wolf Hall standing elevated, amid its undulating surrounds in Savernake. His old home seemed to watch and wait for him to come back and live in it again, and looked sorry at its neglect. With impish grins, he liked to contemplate its renovation, funded partially by the hefty fines he would impose on any poachers caught in and about his Forest!

But before he could ride off from Hanworth towards Savernake, he had to obtain a loan from Sir John Thynne for the expenses of his journey. He visited Hampton Court also, to bid fond farewell for a while to Catherine and Jennie.

"And give my heartiest commendations to the Great-Bellied Oak!" Catherine teased him over his love for his Forest.

"I'll render you great-bellied!" he retorted, easily encircling her tiny waist.

"Peace, children," intervened Jennie. "As for me, I shall wish to discuss the size of my allowance upon your return."

"Upon my return," he said merrily, "and not before!"

Catherine's hand pressed gently on his shoulder. "D'you wish that you were also coming to Savernake?" he murmured, and she nodded. "No more than I, Catherine. No more than I! And yet, wouldn't you rather see the oak trees at Bradgate again, instead of mine in Savernake?"

"No longer," she said dispiritedly. "Not since the oaks there were pollarded in mourning for Jane's death."

As always, he felt so attuned with her in their long-lasting "perfect accord" that words of warmth flowed from him, to make her smile again.

"I shall travel up the down into Wiltshire," he grinned.

"Travel up the down?" she laughed. "What do you mean?"

"I'll ride partly on the ancient Ridgeway, Catherine. It goes along the crest of the downland. Quite a climb up to it!"

"God keep you safe, my lord," she hugged him. "For sure, you have some curious names for hills there - and hoary old oaks!"

"What mischief are you planning now, brother?" said Jennie. "The best way there is the old road towards Bath."

"Mischief? I am merely minded to *savour* my homecoming to the area, Jennie!"

Long, eager anticipation of this unfolded into captivating reality when his journey eventually brought him onto the Ridgeway. He had left his accompanying servants to continue along the old Bath road as far as his castle at Marlborough. Now his chestnut steed, Esturmy, carried him across a land of hill-forts built in remote times of mystery. And views spread both before and beneath his euphoric gaze. Villages and churches, and higher landmarks, like the fir tufts atop Martinsell rising above Pewsey Vale . . . and woodlands, the greatest expanse of all stretching darkly away from Marlborough . . . and this was *his* - Savernake!

A lump rose in his throat. He patted Esturmy and then breathed with smiling, half-unbelieving relief at the extent of summer foliage clothing his trees in the miles towards Wolf Hall, farther on in the distance. Could the reports he had heard be all that true about the amounts of timber being filched from his Forest?

As he rode on, he tried to distinguish the various Forest divisions known as bailliwicks, which dealt with sundry abuses of his vert and venison. There indeed were more quaint names to make Catherine's eyes twinkle, he chuckled to himself. He recited them in a manner which to him, at least, was as lyrical as poetry - Panterwick and Westbayle, Iwood and Vernbayle, Hippenscombe, Southgrove and the Broyle.

He was glad that he could now recompense a little the friendly travails taken by Sir John Thynne on his behalf, by sending some venison to him at his Wiltshire home, Longleat. But Ned felt far less neighbourly when he discerned on Savernake's eastern edge the *purlieu,* the small wood of Wilton Brail, still held by Catherine's former father-in-law. He reaffirmed to himself that *that* old schemer, Pembroke, would gain nought else from the Seymours!

When he looked beyond the western edge, ill-will and sullen resentment were thankfully dispelled by marvelling at its vastness in olden times. The 'forest' part of its name had then meant a royal hunting reserve rather than venerable woodland, and treeless tracts of open land almost as far as his eyes could see had resounded to the baying of kings' hounds.

He did not begrudge his ancestors their hereditary wardenship over so large an area generations ago. For none of his predecessors had the distinction of owning the Forest, until it was given to his father when he was Lord Protector of the realm for King Edward. Its size was much shrunken by then.

And none of its previous Wardens knew the sheer pleasure of owning Savernake! Ned prided himself. He much regretted that his well-loved father had been too weighed down by matters of government and wars with Scotland, however, to have time for more than irregular interest in its concerns. The Duke's Vaunt, a favourite old oak named after the Good Duke, had seldom been seen by him in the last years of his life.

Ned consoled himself a little, nevertheless, with the realization that if power had never so preoccupied his father, Savernake would not have belonged to its present, appreciative young lord. And though rough and gnarled as aged oak bark his own features may one day become, however long he lived, the care he intended to take of the Forest would be part of revering his father's memory.

On the descent into Marlborough, he espied a group of horsemen across the way ahead of him, slowing as they approached.

Esturmy also slowed, as of necessity, hooves negotiating the slope with caution and stopping slightly every now and then to maintain their balance. Ned concentrated on his horse's progress, encouraging him with expressions of their confidence in each other. Being small and lightweight worked to his advantage, for a change, whenever he was riding, in the lack of burden he imposed on any equine companion that would otherwise hamper its agility.

An unmistakably local rendering of "Zur-r", for "Sir", from one of the horsemen caused Esturmy's ears to prick up to full alert.

Ned braced himself to see which of the riders merited

this appellation and was astonished to recognize the foremost of them here . . . a receding hairline revealed by a doffed velvet cap, a close-cut beard covering a heavy, square-shaped jaw . . . He had no need to *send* any venison to his father's longtime steward, after all, for the very same seemed to have come to some pains to collect it! Why the face of the second rider in the group appeared to be patterned with congealed blood, however, was a soul-plummeting matter at which he could only begin to guess.

"How now, Sir John," Ned called amiably. "I did not expect -"

"Nor I, my lord," replied Sir John Thynne briskly, as they reined in their horses. "I came personally to see how you fared on this your return to Seymour country, not expecting your arrival there to be without escort! 'Twould not be wise, my lord, not wise for you to enter Marlborough on your own now that there has been some trouble."

"Trouble? In the town, d'you mean? Or the Forest?"

"Both, m'lud," said the bloodied rider, "though 'twas catching thievin' varmints in Westbayle that I came to be beautified like this."

"Your efforts are most praiseworthy, my friend. Master Weeks, is it not, my forester of Westbayle?"

"At your service, m'lud."

"And so as that service remains good value, let's enlighten his lordship more on our way back whence we came," said Sir John. "Time passes. Your seeking of solitude wouldn't seem half so enticing, my lord, if - like for me at the time of His Grace your father's arrest - it meant solitary confinement in a dank cell in the Tower!"

Beset by a nagging suspicion that he himself was deemed to be providing poor value for the money loaned him by Sir John for his journey, Ned tried to emulate Catherine's diligent manner of attentiveness, at once still carefully considerate of his animal friend and listening intently to the revelations of his fellow-riders. He even adapted to his forester's blow-by-blow account of events with well-received gruntings in the local vernacular.

"So, the thievin' varmints were caught lopping off branches with a hatchet," he summarized earnestly. "And for turning on you while you strove to confiscate the hatchet, they've both been put in stocks hard by the castle. But those wounds of yours, Master Weeks . . . I trust will heal soon?"

"Nobbut scratches my missus sez, m'lud, thank 'ee. Compared with they, d'ye zee, as varmints'll look betime townsfolk's finished peltin' refuse at 'm in the stocks."

Sir John heaved impatiently. "Not the homecoming you had bargained for, eh, my lord, if any of the rabble had taken it upon themselves to pelt refuse at *you* on your lone and unsuspecting arrival?"

"Indeed not!"

"But remember, you are as a stranger hereabouts, having been away for these past few years. And a lone, lordly stranger presumed to be carrying money may be no safer from the unruly elements of a crowd than two beggarly wood thieves confined to stocks."

Ned's brow furrowed at Sir John's apparently unerring propensity for words such as value, bargain and money. The Good Duke's son preferred to think that Thynne's sense of duty to the Seymour family should prevail over monetary matters which caused its future head himself to feel beggarly. Had not the Duke been an exemplary master to John Thynne, enabling him to acquire much property and advancing him to a knighthood?

With a dignity far less diffident than that of his beloved, Ned responded to the onus he now felt upon him to impress.

"Blessed be heaven that I'll be entering the town in the company of local men known hereabouts," he began, to voices of agreement. "But despite my long absence, Savernake's spell is on me even more strongly than in my childhood and I have no fear of crowds. My father is still extolled by the people of this realm for all his attempts to improve their lot. *And* my horse is named after the loyal line of ancestors who ran this Forest for almost four hundred years before us Seymours. Sir John, if any of you had thought to bring that time-honoured symbol of the Warden's office, the Esturmy horn, for me to carry at my homecoming, I would swiftly be no stranger here!"

"I had sundry building matters at Longleat on my mind, my lord," excused Sir John. "I am become much more a local man myself, I have to admit, since my release first from the Tower and afterwards from the job of Comptroller to the Lady Elizabeth's household until she went captive to that dreaded place! And if such is your wish to wear the Esturmy horn slung from your shoulder -"

"It is my wish."

"Then I shall be happy to ride with you thus arrayed, through the Forest to Wolf Hall."

"And I should be glad of your excellent counsel on a myriad of building matters there!"

"Ah, *that* I can promise to the minutest detail, my lord. Well do I remember riding ceremonially with your lord father from there one day, and his blowing of the Esturmy horn to welcome King Hal to Savernake. You were scarce out of your swaddling bands then and your father new-made Earl of Hertford. But as for now . . ." Sir John shook his head and tutted. "You'll find ample opportunity for the task of rebuilding it if, as I do nowadays, you avoid all connections close to the throne."

"Thank you for the forewarning about Wolf Hall," said Ned. His silence over his incurable attachment with a connection still close to the throne had been well-practised for nigh on three years now. He believed in all sincerity, however, that Queen Mary would approve his life being joined with Catherine's once he attained his majority next year. Her Majesty might even raise him to his father's pre-Dukedom title - Edward, Earl of Hertford.

And Catherine, Countess of Hertford! his mind romanticized . . . Countess of Hertford? Or Queen?

For there remained an intriguing possibility that he might one day blow the Esturmy horn to welcome her, as England's rightfully reigning monarch, to Savernake.

"To the Lady Elizabeth, I must give credit where it's due, though," Sir John went on in his fiscal vein. "She runs her household very frugally. It's to be hoped she rules her realm as absolutely when she succeeds her sister! Aye, *and* that she'll come to her senses over marriage."

"How could she still say no?" scoffed Ned dismissively, to snide guffaws about coy virginity from the other riders.

Like them, he could never imagine Elizabeth not marrying or producing heirs, if only to keep rival claimants such as Catherine from the throne. In his opinion, the clever creature might even give birth annually, in order to spite his lady. She would not realize that in pushing Catherine further down the line of succession she would in fact be doing *both* the would-be Earl and Countess of Hertford a great favour, enabling them the better to live the contented life of their dreams in the country.

Such reverie about their future together was blissfully absorbing for him. But on reaching Marlborough, the cracks of a whip and piercing screams above the clamorous din of a crowd caused Ned to concentrate on the bleaker present here at the very edge of his Forest. He avowed his aim that neither Catherine nor any heir of theirs would ever come home to be confronted with a scene like this . . .

Some of the men, women and children who were straining and swaying on the fringes of the uproar turned to gawp instead at the horses and riders coming towards them. Hailing Weeks and Thynne, they gradually started to press back, and formed an opening into which the Westbayle forester rode promptly.

"Aye, that be one of 'em, m'lud," he yelled as Ned followed him closely and watchfully towards the centre of the crowd. "A ver'table spit-cat, more than t'other varmint 'e were! Scratted and scratted at me."

The veritable spit-cat lay sprawled in filthy, ragged hose

and breeches, stripped naked to the waist and bleeding, but was hustled to an upright stance by a man who respectfully doffed his feathered hat to Ned - the chief forester, John Berwick.

"'Ere, 'e be an *'er!*" exclaimed Weeks.

"An 'er more troublesome than 'e rogues twice 'er size," said Berwick. "Wriggled one foot out of the stocks somehow, she did, tryin' to escape. Stop snivelling in front of his lordship, 'ussy!"

"Nay, I mind not her snivelling, Master Berwick," said Ned gravely.

The unkempt girl looked up at him, briefly with less mutiny in the eyes peering through the dirt and dung on her face. Then her head drooped again with surprising grace. She was tiny, like Catherine, and almost as finely proportioned, but so emaciated and her breasts as well as her back showed marks wrought by the lacerating thong of the whip.

He was moved with pity, and at once motioned to Berwick to let her gather up her jerkin so as to cover her modesty. "What's your name, girl?" he asked.

"Frank, sir . . . Frances." She seemed aghast at being spoken to with courtesy.

Sir John appeared to be also somewhat out of countenance. "My lord, pray tell me if I err in perceiving in you a further legacy from his Grace, your father."

"A further legacy, Sir John?"

"A legacy, my lord, of that leniency towards the poor - that too much gentleness which won the Good Duke such renown." And with this observation both foresters readily concurred. "But beware! Surely we, of all people, need no reminding how a lack of ruthlessness ended his rule as Lord Protector?"

Before Ned mustered an apposite response to Sir John, however, Frank returned his courtesy with a warm and clear-voiced enquiry which greatly kindled the plaudits rippling through the crowd about his father's gentleness.

"The Good Duke - your *father,* my lord?"

Ned forebore to look at Thynne as if to say, "I told you so". Instead, he answered her amid the popular, even thankful expressions of affection for the Good Duke. "Yes, I am my father's son . . . and proud of that fact!"

The encrusted corners of her mouth managed an upward curve, into a taut but lop-sided smile. "In our village, how we prayed for him and rang our church bells when we heard false tidings of his acquittal."

"Where is your village?"

"Alas, it is no more. Only the church left there now, my lord. 'Twas many miles from here, where the soil was heavy -"

"Why *was?"*

"Well, the church was turned into a sheephouse and the fields into sheep pastures, and hedges put all round them. We'd nowhere to grow our food."

"Enclosures," frowned Ned, in total understanding. "What evil has been done to the poor by taking common-used lands from them! An evil my father sought to remedy."

"Oh, my lord, if you can - please help us . . ." she implored.

"Help you! You and whose army, brazen 'ussy?" suddenly exploded Weeks. "Wouldn't surprise I if you ain't gained practice for damaging m'lud's trees by breaking down some 'edges!"

Unknowingly, the outraged forester provided timely diversion for Ned, from the feelings of perplexity which momentarily overcame him.

"How many of you are there to help?" he asked, stalling a direct reply so as to recoup his composure fully in front of the crowd.

"Only me and my brother Kit, my lord. We're all that's left of our family."

"And where are the rest of your villagers?"

"I know not. In Lunnon, maybe. All scattered in search

of employ."

"Hm . . . hard work'd make better use of you and your brother's energies than stealing, that's for sure. *And* a more fitting punishment for your offences than the stocks or the whip . . ."

But it seemed hardly appropriate that he should tell them to come back next summer, when he would no longer be under age and might set them to labour, repairing Wolf Hall with some of his Savernake timber!

Then, a potential solution lifted him - an inspiration bursting upon him with the bright intensity of sunlight penetrating in a brief, golden nimbus through verdant foliage.

He quickly ascertained whether Sir John's sundry building matters at Longleat included punishment for unsatisfactory work.

"Verily!" affirmed Sir John. "No meat for work I deem less than perfect, be they maidservant or mason."

"No meat. 'Tis as I thought."

"Discipline, my lord! Discipline and hard, hard work. The only means of obtaining high standards."

"And when did you and your brother last eat, let alone eat meat?" Ned addressed the girl, having noted an indrawn gasp from her at the earlier mentions of food. "Days ago? Longer than that?"

"Much longer, my lord, it does seem."

"But you hoped to eat meat this evening. What was it?"

"Coney, my lord . . ." her voice trailed off penitently.

"Cooked coney! Which well explains why you were gathering timber, and why you tried to escape." She whimpered agreement. He then observed wrily to Sir John and the two foresters, "And for this, my friends, these young folk are made miscreants. What say you, Sir John - is there scope for two proven, able-bodied additions to your workforce who'll be waged and well-fed, providing they work hard? Two able bodies, who've already tasted of the harsh existence which would await them again if they fail to do so!"

"There *is* scope, my lord. I wish for Longleat to be completed quickly. The longer is taken by bad workers, the more it costs me!"

"Of course. And you, girl, once your wounds have been tended, would you exert yourself as expected in Sir John's employ and cease all mischief?"

"I'd fain lose a limb than not be of good and honest service," she cried gratefully.

"That is well, Frank. For I fear that at your present rate of mischief, you mayhap would incur an ear or a hand being cut off one day! And now, assuming Kit still has his tongue, let's hear if he's prepared to work likewise."

"Christ's blessings on you, my lord. I'm willing to work very hard," called her brother.

"My lord, the Good Duke's son!" breathed Frank, with a smile of thanks as Kit was released from the stocks.

"I'll detail all arrangements concerning them," Sir John assured Ned. "My daily list of instructions to my steward at Longleat seems to grow and grow!"

"I hope to *shorten* my own busy travel agenda from now on," Ned replied, as they both dismounted and handed their horses to the care of grooms.

He was soon refreshed enough to look discerningly at the remains of the once-royal castle at Marlborough in its present state. He wished with a sigh that King Arthur's magician Merlin, reputedly at rest in the great mound beneath the keep, could reverse all the slow ravages of decay he noted, and make the place more habitable.

Sir John appraised the castle separately at first. "A sturdy mansion could be built here re-using this castle's solid stonework," he observed, when he came up to Ned again.

"Maybe," smiled Ned. "Four fine potential residences have I in this one small area of Wiltshire, eh, Sir John! A castle at Marlborough in much disrepair, a house at Easton Priory which is all but derelict, I know not what at

Amesbury and . . ."

"Er, I bought the lead from Amesbury for use at Longleat, my lord."

"Ah! A roofless priory at Amesbury, therefore," Ned continued, "and a half-timbered, half-tumbledown manor at Wolf Hall!"

He wasn't overly dismayed about the lead-stripping at Amesbury. Of greater import to his immediate interests was the same-time discovery that his association with John Thynne had served a useful purpose to them both. Ned turned to glance at the knight thoughtfully, and felt less beholden to him.

He was then regaled with a barrage about how unsuitable timber-framed structures were for the new, classical architecture, compared with stone. "The beautiful symmetry of the new style at my own house has provoked praise far and wide," explained Sir John, "but alas, some resentment closer to home amongst those whose old-fashioned mansions cannot boast such harmony of proportion."

Beyond the building jargon, Ned also deduced that Thynne was in need of friends from the long-established local families.

And so, 'ere be one such friend! Ned mused.

He recalled that his father's liking for the new-fangled architecture had never seemed irreconcilable with love for the Seymours' ancient heritage. He therefore eked out his own very basic knowledge of the subject into what he hoped would sound a passably intelligent reply.

"I fully accept that the new classical, *pilastered* windows which my lord father introduced in England for the construction of Somerset House would be, er - *unsuitable* on our old-fashioned Wolf Hall," he began. He was pleased how with mildly pointed jibes, he had bluffed his way so far. "But I feel sure a greater symmetry can be achieved there, in the heights and breadths of windows and doors!"

"Well said, my lord. Well said!"

"You think so?"

"Wouldn't have said so if I didn't think so! We can work out harmonized measurements in ratios of three-to-two," Sir John visibly enthused. "Three-to-two - remember that, my lord. Now, let's to re-unite you with the Esturmy horn!"

*The Esturmy Horn, depicted on a monument in St Katherine's Church, Savernake Forest*

Nothing could diminish Ned's sense of rapture at his reunion with such a familiar old heirloom from his boyhood. He received the Esturmy horn from his chief forester, as if it were a friend. Its adornments of silver and ivory were exactly as he remembered them. He contemplated the four bands of silver all around it, embossed with their little hunting scenes of hares and hounds, and lordly stags - and even a unicorn. And he joked that the unicorn would not be entirely inappropriate if Elizabeth became Queen, the mythical beast being a symbol of virginity.

Many more old friends were the Savernake trees that seemed to greet him on his resumed ride towards Wolf Hall. Oak and elm and beech reached out to form arcades of overhanging branches. Yet each to him was so individually expressive, of shape and height, expanse and trunk girth. He rejoiced that he could never admire any one of them merely to assess its door or stair-making use, as did the highest-ranking of his companions. Sir John was fastidious even to the thickness of a hypothetical door and the requisite size of nails!

But just as power had prevented the Good Duke from

enjoying Savernake, so the trappings of affluent country housebuilding appeared to have blinded Sir John to the beauties of the countryside itself. Each thus set an example for Ned *not* to follow, even if time brought fearful changes as yet impossible to foretell.

From the end of a leafy glade, the loud and melodious laughs of a woodpecker echoed over Sir John's deliberations about a wall he was not happy with at Longleat. Words such as "botched" and "idiots" were accordingly relegated to the background of Ned's listening. He heard the bird tapping at a tree and his keen eyes espied it all too briefly, in a colourful mingling of its green, red and gold against grey bark, before it disappeared beneath the fork of a bough and gnarled trunk.

Forest scenes fortunately contented him further as a group of his red deer darted by. Then the woodpecker's music sounded merrily again, amid the coos and chirps of the other birdsong in sylvan depths beyond its abode. And still Sir John could not decide whether, or how far to move his wall . . .

Numerous other deer roamed and browsed at will in the rolling area of parkland surrounding Wolf Hall. Ned was disappointed to notice amongst them, however, several of the lesser, leaner sort termed 'rascals' by forest folk.

Characteristically, Sir John reverted to monetary talk, in what Ned took by now to be a well-intentioned, if rather singular attempt to cheer him. "Let's hope that the wool from your hardy Wiltshire sheep, grazing yonder, sells for a fair price again this year. Their meat is no tastier than the rascals'."

"No tastier, no."

"But still too good to feed to idle workers!"

Ned brightened again at Thynne's guffaw over that. "For my other flock, though, what those sheep represent is inestimable," he said.

"Other flock, my lord? What other flock?"

"Why, the flock of my tenants now coming, look, to

welcome us!"

"Oh . . . hmm . . ."

"It's beyond me, you know, Sir John, why other landowners around the realm don't give nearby acres in exchange to their poor tenantry, as my father did when a part of this manor became sheep pasture. The fate of that Frank and other such unfortunates should never have happened."

In a short distance Ned was waving, acknowledging, smiling to right and left as Esturmy ambled up the small eminence on which Wolf Hall and its Great Barn stood.

To his tenants and their families, he was "Young Lord Edward", and if a few seemed unsure initially whether he was indeed their Good Duke's eldest boy, the ancient horn hanging at his side swiftly convinced them. That, and his "Beautiful 'Sturmy - ain't zeed 'e at Ulfall since 'e were a colt!", as one fresh-faced old man chortled.

Like the Seymours, these people all had local ancestry stretching back for generations. Many amongst them had festooned the Great Barn with garlands for the wedding festivities of King Henry and Queen Jane, in which they had taken part there over two decades ago. The familiar faces of these might seem more lined or weather-beaten to Ned since he had last seen them, some of their smiles now half-toothless, but he was much heartened by their warmth and that he himself appeared "all growed up" to them!

"Well, beautiful 'Sturmy, here's journey's end," he praised, once they were in the grass-grown courtyard of his home.

On dismounting and wiping travel dust from his face and hands, he had an impression of warped beams and crumbling plaster between the upright timber laths of the surrounding walls. He reached into his pocket and gave a sugar-work reward to his horse.

In the excitement of requests to come and look at the Great Barn well stored with hay, come and inspect the cleaned-out stables all strewn with fresh straw . . . Ned opted first for the stables. He commented breezily that at least he knew where Esturmy and the other horses in his party would be resting comfortably this night. "As for myself and Sir John here," he added, "if the Ulfall bedchambers slope downhill much more than they did on my last visit, I for one might be sleeping in the Great Barn with all the hay or sharing 'Sturmy's stable!"

"'Twouldn't be the first time yon Great Barn has been temp'ry lodgin' for nobles, o'course," laughed Berwick, accepting the Esturmy horn from Ned once more into his safekeeping.

"Oh ah! Even our Good Duke and his lady wife slept in there a time or two when owd King Hal cum 'ere with all the Court," piped up the old man again, as Ned and lively rustic company started trooping after Esturmy and his groom towards the stables.

"Not with all the hay, though?" quipped Ned, well imagining what her haughtiness, his mother, had thought about staying overnight in a barn!

"Oh no, not with all the 'ay! Heh, heh, not a stalk of it in sight for m'lady."

Along with the ebb and flow of continuing mirthful noise, and sounds of tired horses being rubbed down by grooms in the stable-yard, some talk drifted across to Ned on matters other than Wolf Hall.

"Pleasant young man, m'Lord Edward."

"Aye, thank God 'e be lot like our Good Duke."

"Afeard was I of another Lord Thomas . . ."

"Ooh, 'e were a lad, Lord Thomas Seymour! Messin' about wi' that Lady Elizabeth. Ne'er were two brothers more different than 'r Good Duke and 'e."

"Mebbes *'cos* of his messin' Lady Lisbet found out all wasn't right with 'er down below an' talks such twaddle about allus bein' virgin."

God's wounds! thought Ned. If that's so, Uncle Thomas has left a lethal legacy to this realm. But only mebbes 'tis so!

Whatever the truth of similar rumours at Court about abnormalities in her woman's parts, mentions of Elizabeth seemed fated to keep intruding upon Ned's present concerns with Wolf Hall. The stables and the Great Barn were, thankfully, pronounced still to be in a sturdy and watertight condition by Sir John. The magpie walls of the goodly-sized house leaned in all directions, though, and the bed and clothes chest in Ned's chamber sloped hilariously on different inclines. Ceilings were cracked, iron window-frames were rusting and panels and wainscots were mouldering. Yet amid Sir John's suggestions, the next day, for new floors as well were confidential warnings against very plain, disparaging speeches about Elizabeth.

"My lord, I've seen those quelling eyes of hers cause the strongest men to tremble at more distance from her than the length of your Long Gallery," he declared, in what to Ned sounded like his most unedifying tone so far.

"Uncle Thomas Seymour seems never to have quailed before her! In the picturesque words of my tenants . . ."

"Better if you were to discourage your tenants' words on that episode, and her - alleged impediment," Sir John cut in, "be they picturesque or words too foul to be repeated!"

The vehemence of the warnings had been reasoned away by Ned the first few times as caused by fretfulness over Longleat. He began taking heed therefore, not so much because of that vehemence, but because they corroborated with what Jennie had been able to tell him of Catherine's awe-filled encounters with the Tudor 'stinging bee'.

"I *will* bear what you say in mind, Sir John," he said - he hoped more tactfully. "But my sister Jennie knows as well as any of the Queen's ladies how Her Majesty despises Elizabeth."

"Aye, and something to Her Majesty's cost, eh?"

"Be that as it may, I am much obliged for your advice, whether it's about the august virgin or pointing out essential repairs and improvements here. Especially when you have decisions to make and orders to give for the building to progress at your own house."

"My lord, I thank you for that consideration. Repair work here can soon go ahead, you know, when the Savernake leaves have fallen and started to grow again," said Sir John, almost poetically for him. "Wolf Hall will not worsen unduly afore then. But you are right, I must needs return now to Longleat."

"I revert to my earlier plan, therefore. I'll despatch some bucks' venison to you, before I leave here myself."

"Very kind! But send it on ahead of you - or bring it with you."

"With me, Sir John?"

"Aye, my lord, and you'll be most welcome. By all means, visit others of your manors. Visit Amesbury, visit Easton - and be not too sad that the tombs of your forebears there have also become time-worn in your absence. And then, stay a while with my family and me at Longleat . . . We have a new table game in the completed parlour now to absorb us away from the noises of building!"

"A new table game, eh," smiled Ned. He assumed this to be the backgammoning game of 'tables', which he played with fair skill.

"Indeed, my lord . . . Shove ha'penny!" replied Sir John affably as they shook hands.

A few weeks later, Ned ended his sojourn in Wiltshire and reluctantly left Savernake to return to Hanworth. Yet at his departing on Esturmy, he felt compensated, by the prospect that his and Catherine's four-year long courtship was perceptibly closer to accomplishing the desired ecstasy of their union.

But as autumn leaves fell for the last time in Savernake during Ned's minority, Queen Mary was struck down by further, serious illness. She was dreaming of little children like angels, singing and playing music before her, when she died one frosty November morning.

The new Queen was the daunting, quarter-century old

Elizabeth. And until such indeterminate time as *she* wedded and brought forth her first-born, Catherine was now the heiress of England, in the eyes of many people.

*The Great Barn, Wolf Hall*

## CHAPTER 7

# *Tudor Curse*

Lord Robert Dudley bowed his tall and impressive form before Elizabeth.

"Your Majesty."

"Aye, 'tis true, Robin!" she rejoiced. After giving him one smooth, slender hand to kiss, she showed him a black and gold enamelled ring lying in the palm of the other. "Mary's betrothal ring, never to leave her, night or day, during her life. I sent Sir Nicholas Throckmorton to bring this here to me at Hatfield, as proof that she's dead."

"Cautious as always," he said admiringly, "even in these moments of glory."

"In these moments of glory, there's much to remain cautious about, Robin! After all, my sister pardoned and freed you to fight in Philip's war. But I thank you, my Eyes, for keeping me informed as well of Spain's continued support for my succession. Now I trust that you'll always live up to my nickname for you."

She surveyed with regal pleasure the obeisance in his bow to this, but then warmed coquettishly as she went on, "Officially, you will be my Master of Horse, with a prominent place near me in my coronation procession."

If there had been no members of her household in attendance on her, she would have affectionately pinched his smiling cheeks at that. And more so when he looked at her through the encircled thumb and forefinger of each hand, forming the symbolic 'OO' for eyes, which he used in signing his letters to her.

"May Your Majesty's Eyes ask who gave the late Queen's betrothal ring to Throckmorton?"

Her relaxed manner at once stiffened into that of Tudor Sovereign Queen again. "It *should* have been our affected little goose, the Lady Catherine," she told him sombrely, "but, in the event, another of your sisters-in-law, Lady Jennie Seymour, performed the same. Her featherheaded friend was too distraught at Mary's passing."

"The featherheaded little goose. Ha! I'll arrange to escort her myself back to her mother at Sheen, if Your Majesty so commands! Spain may press you to designate her as your successor. But I care only for your right to the throne and I'll fight to uphold that."

"Dear Rob, my lord of unflagging loyalty!" she said, her voice softening once more. She placed Mary Tudor's betrothal ring into a jewellery box held out by another stalwart friend, her elderly servant Blanche Parry. "I have thought upon a compromise regarding Catherine Grey. I will not have her close about me as Mary did. Nor will all the ways to Sheen be crowded as they were here with people who deserted my dying sister to switch their allegiance to me, once I was at long last named to my birthright. But I'll appoint her *and* the youngest of them, crouchbacked Mary Grey, as ladies only of my Presence Chamber rather than my bedchamber. That way I can watch both of them and keep quiet what's left of the Grey brood."

"I would urge vigilance also over the Seymours."

"The Seymours?" The softness which had belied the sharpness of her previous discourse was returned to harsher tones. "Do you dislike all the families into which your brothers married?"

"I saw Ned Seymour gloat when he watched my father beheaded."

"Well, your father sent his father to the block on false charges, my lord! Wouldn't you have gloated, if you'd been in Ned's situation?"

"Not as openly as he did, Your Majesty."

"I'll brook no ill-feeling towards the younger Seymours,

my lord - providing they give me no cause! The girl, Jennie, is bright, accomplished and I like her well enough. And as for Ned, who's soon to come of age, I find him a bit of a milksop, but I'll restore him to his father's old earldom of Hertford at some fitting moment."

"And that'll keep quiet what's left of the *Seymour* brood," Robert speculated.

"Even quieter if he becomes Earl of Hertford before I am crowned and so could join his peers in my coronation procession."

Elizabeth arched her brows, though benignly with Robert, at the quizzical expression his darkly handsome features assumed. "Little Lord Hertford would hardly be visible in Your Majesty's triumphal procession to your coronation," he noted.

"Sir Majesty's Eyes," she laughed, "I am full persuaded by you that the timing of this revived earldom should make the Seymours guess about my motives!"

"Yes, Your Majesty, and rightly so."

"Ideally, therefore, it must harness their allegiance, as was my plan - yet check any hint of their ambition ..." she further considered. "But enough of that for now. I have a plan which requires your aid, Robin, for the timing of my coronation."

"Let that be soon," he said with absolute certainty, "while Your Majesty's star is so much in the ascendant."

"Soon it must be," she agreed. "None of us needs the fortune-telling skills of Mistress Blanche here to know that my accession is in question in some quarters, until the crown is placed on my head! However, her influence *has* been brought to bear on the timing, my lord, and not unrelated to stars."

"How so? I am both intrigued and eager to assist!"

"There is a tall Welsh cousin of Blanche's also called my Eyes," Elizabeth explained. "Or rather - my Secret Eyes, who imparts coded knowledge to me from home and abroad under the plausible cover of his studies. Like both of us, he narrowly escaped execution in Mary's reign - for casting my horoscope along with hers and Philip's."

"My old friend, Dr John Dee - I thought as much!" Robert smiled, as both she and Blanche Parry nodded. "Well, well ..."

"And less of the old, thank you, my Lord Robert!" Elizabeth teased him. "I'll grant you Dr Dee has some half-dozen years of seniority over the two of us. But nothing more, though it may seem remarkable that such a great intellect is not yet full-bloomed."

Although she resumed slower, more serious tones in speaking the praises of this other staunch supporter, her voice sounded mellower than before. Mellower, because of the regard she logically accorded to a fellow-scholar, whose questing mind would ever offer hidden guidance in her service, as the trusty Blanche often stressed.

"With my star in the ascendant for I know not how long, Robin," she said, "the heavens must smile their assured good omen on my crowning and anointing. And so I bid my Eyes consult privately with my Secret Eyes, through Blanche's good offices, and ask him what date my stars foretell as the most propitious for me. You may say to Dr Dee, as if I were present myself, that I predict no hurt will come to him for drawing up my horoscope this time!"

A few days later, before Elizabeth braved the muddy November road from Hatfield to London, Blanche ushered Robert back into her presence. He carried with him a small scroll conveying the information she sought. She responded to both of them with due satisfaction as it was unrolled on a nearby carved oak table.

Her astrologer, her Secret Eyes, was advising the date Sunday 15th January for her coronation.

"Sunday 15th January 1559 it is, therefore," she decided, and was full of high spirits as she pointed out his avowal of constancy in her cause. For above his complicated chart of lines, figures and symbols, John Dee had penned the word 'EveR' as a heart-lifting pun on her new queenly initials.

"Elizabeth Regina," breathed Robert, with wonder. He then showed a lively interest in Dee's coded signing of the document at the bottom. It was distinguished from his own secret symbol to her by the addition of a lucky number. It read 'OO7'.

"Talking of numbers, lucky or unlucky," said Blanche in her musical Welsh accent, "Your Majesty will avoid taking formal possession of the Tower on the previous Friday?"

"God's death, Blanche, and here's a merry conundrum from Dr Dee!" Elizabeth chuckled. "Nay, I'll not tempt fate by arriving in that place on Friday the 13th."

"But it behoves Your Majesty to be there *by* that date, for the coronation procession to Westminster would be on the Saturday," Robert reminded her, sharing her appreciation of the irony.

"Oh, we'll be there on the Thursday, the 12th, Robin," she replied. "Dr Dee's conundrum has helped me solve another one of my own at the same time . . ."

A grim smile of Tudor Majesty settled across her face as she added astutely, "I'll make young Ned Seymour the Earl of Hertford on Friday the 13th . . ."

Catherine travelled in the coronation flotilla from Whitehall Palace to the Tower. As she passed by the place where Comfit was rescued from the Thames almost five years before, a flurry of snow fell. She was thankful that her pets were being well cared for by Helen during her absence at Elizabeth's coronation. Yet tears glistened her eyes, that Comfit was now showing signs of ageing. Catherine feared too that she may already have lost some of Jennie's companionship and all that could imply about meeting Ned.

Jennie had not suffered the dishonour of being demoted by the new regime at Court, and so Catherine caught occasional glimpses of her friend amongst the ladies of the Privy Chamber in close attendance on Elizabeth. Gilded, and alive with music, was the state barge conveying them downstream, ahead of Catherine and the other ladies of the royal Presence Chamber.

Catherine resented her exclusion from that splendid vessel. She held hazy, but entirely contrasting memories of once accompanying Jane in it on this very same journey. She recalled too the amazing sight of her older sister's train being borne by Mother Dragon after they embarked at Tower Wharf.

Catherine so wished she could relive those memories sometimes with their elfish little sister, Mary, who was beside her then, as now. But though there was courtesy between them, she had never found any rapport, compared to the affection of her bond with Jane.

"The weather seems to grow more chilly," she sighed.

"Yes," said Mary, blinking up at her with bulbous eyes.

"Are you warm enough, my dear?"

"Yes," came the subdued reply again.

There was no enquiry about whether Catherine herself was warm enough. She felt truly sorry for this strange, aloof girl, however. Even the yards of luxurious velvet and cloth of gold, given to each of Elizabeth's ladies for coronation gowns, couldn't enhance Mary Grey's hunchbacked appearance. "Crouchback Mary" was Elizabeth's nickname for the poor creature. Such cruelty to her small, fourteen year old sister made Catherine more disgruntled about this reign of a mere two months.

When the new Queen landed with her retinue at Tower Wharf, the noise was deafening from the gun salutes, wildly cheering crowds and fanfares for her.

Catherine discerned only one flicker of emotion from Elizabeth, in the shadow of this terrible fortress.

"Which key is for my old room in the Bell Tower, Master Lieutenant? The one with that poxy bolt!" laughed Elizabeth, when the jangling keys of the Tower were presented into her gloved hands.

Off came the glove of her right hand for the kneeling

Lieutenant to kiss. Catherine saw the jewelled rings on the slender, tapering fingers sparkle, as they did on most days, when that hand dealt one or other attendant lady a sharp slap worse than any of Mother Dragon's.

Catherine lit her expression into her most winning, listening smile at the Queen's remark. Although she did not drool with fawning adulation like others around her, she believed her smile was enough to chase away any suspicion of her stored-up grudges. Some favourite of Elizabeth might deign to watch her, as she stood tucked away in the background.

Her dignity hid her feelings the next day too, in the potentially more glaring atmosphere of Ned's investiture. It even cloaked her tenderness for him, as he knelt before Elizabeth in his rich, ceremonial robes of earl's estate.

"How oft have I dreamed of this signal honour to our family," Jennie had said of this occasion. "I have imagined royal hands girding a jewelled sword around my brother and placing a golden coronet on his head."

"But by the hands of Elizabeth, in the Tower, on Friday the 13th?" Ned had retorted, about the stark reality of the situation.

Catherine could hear Jennie straining to contain a heart-rending cough, however, while Elizabeth's secretary, Sir William Cecil, read out the patent for the new Earl of Hertford's title. The cough had afflicted Jennie often, of late.

As Ned eventually arose, wearing the jewelled sword and golden coronet of his exalted rank, Elizabeth suddenly sounded almost kindly in her command, "We give you leave, my Lord of Hertford, to take your poor, ailing sister for some air once you have changed from your fancy-dress!"

"Yes, Your - Your Majesty," he bowed.

A hurried whispering from Jennie's direction and a rustling of skirts by old Blanche Parry towards Elizabeth, then surprised Catherine more. "Oh, and let Lady

Catherine go with them, Your Majesty. Lady Jennie will be glad of her friend's good company."

Elizabeth snorted, but agreed.

Mistress Blanche further ensured that Jennie, especially, wrapped up warmly before the two girls ventured out from the White Tower with Ned. For good effect, they muffled up in their hooded cloaks, and Jennie's gloved hand held a large kerchief across her mouth. Catherine and Ned flanked her on either side, seeming ready to support her if she experienced any difficulty in walking.

"To outward view, the only thing between you two is me!" Jennie whispered from beneath the hood and kerchief. She chuckled, winking surreptitiously at Catherine.

To inward view, however, the threesome's bright-eyed looks conveyed to each other their collective happiness at this permitted interlude together.

"'Twill take more than a few changes, Catherine, to break our perfect accord," continued Jennie.

"And not all changes are for the worse," Ned announced, in a low voice too. "Amongst more property granted to me, I'm to have my own establishment - a 'Hertford House' in Cannon Row. So I'll be able to plague you with even more visits when the Court is either at Westminster or Whitehall!"

"Such ordeals for us!" Jennie teased, while he rubbed his hands partly in mock glee.

"Brrr! Where do you wish to walk to, my ladies?"

"Not here. Not with its dismal associations for all of us," Jennie shuddered.

And Catherine nodded, her teeth also chattering agreement to that. She found herself huddled even closer to the other two, and not only because of the cold and semblance of assisting Jennie. The sight of Tower Green and the sepulchral chapel of St Peter ad Vincula loomed in the fading light before them! They each averted their gaze from the square piece of ground, edged with white stones, which marked the execution site.

"Sometimes, Catherine . . ." confided Jennie, "I think of the old curse said to have been laid on Anne Boleyn and her daughter by your step-granddam's mother, Lady Willoughby. So far, it seems to have been fulfilled through us Seymours!"

"My step-grandmother is not back from exile yet," said Catherine evasively. "Her return will be another change for the better."

There was certainly no denying, though, that her companions' Aunt Jane had supplanted Anne Boleyn in Henry VIII's affections. Nor that their Uncle Thomas's rumoured adultery had once brought the beheaded Anne's daughter, Elizabeth, in danger of the block too.

"So where *shall* we walk within the Tower precincts?" Ned resumed.

"The way out," Jennie decided. "I would see by what route we shall leave this place in the procession tomorrow."

"Good idea. 'Tis the way I came in on Esturmy this morning, through the Middle Tower, past the Lion Tower."

"Onward, thence, my Lord of Hertford! There's daylight enough to escort your poor, ailing sister and her dearest friend past the guards at the Middle Tower - and beyond, for Catherine to visit the lions."

Ned grimaced at his sister's organizing. But Catherine was pleased at his swift recovery from his awestruck demeanour before Elizabeth.

At the gates of the Middle Tower, the guards saluted England's newest peer of the realm, with a respect which Catherine had not much seen towards Ned before. They then halted the progress of an incoming consignment of ale and mead in casks, for their own celebrations of the coronation, while "the right honorable, the Earl of Hertford" came by with their ladyships, his sister and her friend.

Catherine now saw Ned shrug, as Jennie's forceful insistence on going towards the Lion Tower took her a few paces in front of them. His eyes communicated to Catherine a look of sheer enthralment in his desire, his love for her.

Their arms brushed lightly in contact, as they followed Jennie to the keeper's lodging at the base of the Lion Tower, where a coin from Ned achieved their objective of visiting the royal menagerie.

Snowflakes began to dance amongst flickering shadows, while the keeper led them by torchlight through a small courtyard towards a low arched door. It was an atmosphere which, in gathering gloom, made Catherine instinctively want to shrink very near to the two Seymours. The urgings of her heart quite overcame her when Ned graciously and gallantly ensured that Jennie continued determinedly on, ahead of them.

*"Stop kissing!"* hissed Jennie. She planted herself firmly in front of them and issued a timely harsh cough, as the keeper turned round to guide her and Catherine safely through the doorway.

Demure innocence seemed to Catherine best suited to the circumstances and her face readily supplied the appropriate expression. She was aware, however, that either Jennie's or hers might crease up into amusement any moment at the boyish nonchalance on Ned's face, as he sauntered into the semicircular building after them.

They stood in a stone-flagged area, between parapets protecting the royal observation gallery and arched cages securing the animals behind latticed bars.

"What a fine fellow!" Catherine enthused at a large and prowling lion.

"A king of the beasts in name also, my lady," replied the keeper in like vein. "Styled Edward VI that one, having been born here in the young King's reign. But do not be enticed too near to any of the lions, for if a paw so much as grabs hold of a hand, it has been known to rip a whole arm from out its socket."

To a chorus of gasps which did not lessen Catherine's

admiration for that lion's majestic beauty and strength, they were conducted on to dens containing other creatures - tigers, leopards, lynxes, an aged wolf, a jackal, hyenas, bears and eagles.

When the keeper saw Catherine backtrack to study the wolf, he said affably, "Close prisoners these beasts are, my lady, as much as any of Her Majesty's in the Tower. But they're well-fed and probably live longer here than in the wild - as witness by this fellow, now fortunately quite scarce in England!"

"Having been snarled and growled at by such fearsome brutes, sir," said Jennie, "I think even Lady Catherine would never favour freeing them!"

"Nay, never!" murmured Catherine emphatically. "Wolves are perchance not so scarce as we think. They still roam in the wild hills of the north. And sometimes they stray further south. My sister was once attacked by a huge wolf near Bradgate, after which it was slain . . ."

"So she survived a wolf attack, only to be . . ." Jennie's horrified voice faltered without her even bringing herself to mention Jane's tragic end.

"Aye."

"Oh, Catherine!"

As the keeper glanced from Catherine to Jennie, and back to Catherine again, Ned intervened to break a potentially awkward silence in a manner which Jennie might have done.

"Whilst thanking you for showing us Her Majesty's close prisoners here, sir," he said, "we should start retracing our steps through the Middle Tower, ere the curfew bell is rung."

"In truth, my lord Earl, I believe my lady your sister hearkens to its sound already," smiled the keeper.

The curfew bell then tolled from the turret at the top of the Bell Tower. Catherine thought that in the eerie light, she may possibly see the spectre of her headless sister at any part of their return into the Tower for the night.

Her hand clasped briefly with Ned's, as they neared the doorway out of the Lion Tower.

"Fear not," he whispered, caressing her ring-finger, which she then used to draw a tiny heart-shape on his hand.

No-one else apart from Jennie knew how much Queen Mary's death had been a blow to their hopes. The old curse allegedly placed on Anne Boleyn and Elizabeth, however, seemed set to continue being linked with the Seymours!

Catherine observed with calmness the first street pageant performed for Elizabeth during the long, slow procession on the following afternoon of 14th January.

'Tis good to feel like this! she thought happily.

Ned and Jennie were riding in their assigned places elsewhere in the cavalcade. She found the live portrayal of Anne Boleyn garish in this pageant, and that of Henry VIII too much a reminder of Mother Dragon. But the perfect accord had been re-asserted yesterday and it was shielding her from matters untoward. She warmed to the idea of her secret love blossoming into open expression, no later than the coming spring.

Elizabeth too had a deep, mutual love, but hers was with the Londoners and abundantly expressed. Catherine heard her cousin's usually caustic tongue make many tender speeches at frequent stops in her golden litter. There was a mood of optimism, now that the burning of Protestants had ceased. Wagers had even been placed as to whether this Queen was a wise or a foolish virgin, if she risked losing such love by failing in her womanly duty to provide her realm with a Protestant heir.

Elizabeth had furnished Catherine with mostly unfavourable impressions, but never that of a fool. And so the girl contemplated how quickly pressure from peers and people alike would prevail over Her Majesty's stubbornness to wed. Catherine dwelt on this and her future with Ned, rather than the sight of two of the Dudleys immediately behind Elizabeth in the procession. She was glad that Ned was some distance ahead of them and this spared him from witnessing such favour to the family who caused his father, the Good Duke's death.

Both she and Ned had to contend with watching stony-faced Lord Pembroke the next day, however, as he walked beside Elizabeth into Westminster Abbey for her coronation. Once Elizabeth was invested with the full sovereign regalia of the crown, orb, sceptre and coronation ring, Catherine soon consoled herself with a more congenial view. She enjoyed seeing Ned himself, when his turn came amongst his peers to approach the enthroned monarch in homage, in time-honoured tradition. Catherine then drifted through the rest of the glittering pomp and ceremony in a fantasy of sharing kisses with him!

Near the end of January, a delegation of Lords of the Privy Council and several Members of Parliament blithely put before Elizabeth the matter that was now called "the prayer" of all England. They formally petitioned her to choose her consort, so that princely successors born to her within holy matrimony would one day glory in *her* name, as she and her subjects did in that of her father.

From the looks which subsequently glazed on all their faces, Catherine saw that she was far from alone in not reckoning on Elizabeth's extraordinary reaction. The coronation ring was paraded vehemently by her before each and every petitioner, to their utter consternation.

"This," their Queen reminded them with scornful hauteur, "this is the token of my holy matrimony, and I marvel it should have escaped your fragile memories so soon that less than two weeks ago I was wedded to my kingdom, to my England!"

She was more than equal to the task of overwhelming into silence those who could not contain their astonishment.

"Dare not to reprove me again for dearth of offspring to

glory in my name," she went on coldly, "when all my subjects, without exception, are my children!" Nor did her voice dispense with its strident tone as she further snapped, "*If* one day I decide upon wedlock with a king for you, I give my word that my choice would be as loving as myself towards my people. But if I do not, I nothing doubt that God will send you for my successor whoever has most right! I would rather have the tribute on my tombstone that I lived and died a virgin."

No less of a Tudor rage began to seethe inside Catherine, on hearing this virginal 'mother' thus berate some of her 'children'. The information that she, the successor who nowadays had most right, was not to be officially recognized either, stiffened her resolve more than ever for her love-match. She had not been spared more of her unhappy home life with Mother Dragon only to serve an odd and disagreeable kinswoman at Court!

Catherine was not yet sure how she would impress upon Ned the increased urgency for their marriage to rescue her from both. But having noted how Elizabeth had reduced such a prestigious deputation to half-jibbering wrecks, she knew that his approach for royal consent could not be by direct, personal interview, as it would have been with Queen Mary.

## CHAPTER 8

# *The Designs of Spain*

A group of the Queen's ladies gathered in lighthearted mood around Blanche Parry, one February evening.

"Tell each of us our fortune, Mistress Blanche," the cry went up.

While eager hands extended towards Blanche, Catherine temporarily abandoned her embroidery and Jennie put aside her lute.

"Well, now!" exclaimed Blanche. "I do trow this will not be too displeasing to Her Majesty. Better than taking all of you to see future husbands in Dr Dee's new magic mirror, when she so extols the merits of single blessedness for you."

Catherine shared a covert grimace with Jennie. Single blessedness, indeed - for all of us here too, their look implied!

Catherine was flushed with excitement in the hope of hearing what Blanche was presently explaining to one of Elizabeth's Boleyn cousins - that the heart-line on her left palm revealed a strong and true love in her life. She did not know whether her cheeks were the same high colour as Jennie's had recently acquired, which burnished her friend's face with an apparent glow of health despite the coughing. But voices agog with questions, and whispered asides, were growing tantalizingly nearer while she awaited her turn.

According to the more persistent entreaties, however, Blanche was proving too cautious! She predicted a long life, possibly happy, for a few of the ladies and an unspecified number of "many" children also for some. For

Jennie, there was the unsurprising observation that her head-line was most marked and she would attain her aim in life, whatever that might be.

As Jennie's main aim in life was to see her brother marry Catherine, the subtle rapport of the two friends suddenly registered between them a glance of entire satisfaction with Blanche's vagueness.

"Here's to - whatever!" said Jennie.

Blanche began to study Catherine's palm and spoke with hushed reverence towards her.

"The lines do say, madam . . ."

"Yes?"

"The lines do say that if ever your ladyship marries without Her Majesty's consent in writing, you and your husband will be undone, and your fate worse than that of my Lady Jane!"

"Now, Mistress Blanche, no cause for such alarm," Jennie was swift to interpose, as she placed a reassuring hand on Catherine's arm.

"My thoughts exactly!" Catherine murmured in agreement.

She wondered whether Elizabeth perhaps even suspected her secret love. Blanche's use of palmistry had seemed to arise spontaneously, but she might possibly have contrived this whole charade to issue a veiled warning from the Queen.

Catherine gave a little shrug. In any case, the episode had served to confirm her belief that the best and easiest approach to Elizabeth, requesting such permission to marry, should indeed be in writing!

Catherine delighted in Ned's increased number of visits to Court when he began to set up his own establishment at his house in Cannon Row.

"I travel to Savernake with you in my dreams," she told him. "I wish to forsake life in Elizabeth's service at the earliest possible chance!"

"I'm an imaginary visitor to Savernake too," he smiled, "and a very restless one at that!"

During March, new developments caused him to initiate tentative moves in the challenge of affirming their love to a wider world . . .

Peace negotiations to end the French war in which Philip of Spain had involved England did little to alleviate Elizabeth's ill-temper. The French King declared that his daughter-in-law, Mary Queen of Scots, should be the rightful Queen of England and instigated her to include the English royal arms on her personal standard. He then incensed Elizabeth further by refusing to restore Calais.

"These events have made her become more of an irritable *wasp* than a bee," said Catherine, in the privacy of Jennie's chamber during one of Ned's visits.

"And we all know that a waspish Elizabeth may victimize you, Catherine," added Jennie.

Catherine shuddered, and Ned put his arms tenderly around her.

"'Twill be better when you can enjoy life in Wiltshire as my Countess," he said.

Jennie smiled, "Well, our Sovereign cares not for the presence of wives at her Court, Ned. And so, let the difficult stream of your romance now be forded more visibly to bring Catherine to the safety of marriage and out of Elizabeth's immediate reach."

"Such eloquence!" Ned grinned. "This difficult stream of our romance has been so very nearly forded in seclusion, Catherine . . ."

She placed her hands fully on his shoulder and propped her chin on them pertly. "Yes, my lord?"

"So very nearly forded," he said again, and kissed her, "that in all truth there would be greater risk for us now in turning back than in venturing forward. I'll visit both our formidable matrons about us, afore I was minded to do so in the spring."

But the mid-March visit to Court by the ambassador of Spain was to accelerate Ned's journeys even more to see his mother at Hanworth and Catherine's at Sheen.

Don Gomez Suarez de Figueroa, Count de Feria, strutted into the Presence Chamber with his wife for his audience with Elizabeth.

"Your Majesty, I have come to tell you that you may no longer toy with King Philip's recent proposal of marriage to you. His Majesty will marry another Elizabeth - a French princess, when the peace treaty has been signed."

"Hm. He did not wait very long for me. Four months!" snapped Elizabeth.

"May I remind you, madam, that to His Most Catholic Majesty you owe your throne, and . . ."

"No, you may not! It is to my people that I owe my throne, sirrah. So tell *that* to your master."

"My master will be made cognisant of eet, madam. For you cannot deny that after supporting your-r . . . access-eeon, His Majesty then offered to protect you in marriage *and* relieve you of those matters of government which are too onerous for weemin to shoulder."

Catherine waited with bated breath to learn what pitch of rage Elizabeth would reach in reply.

The Queen retorted with the answer, which to Spanish ears was most wounding. "I could not have married him anyway, for I am a heretic!"

When de Feria's proud figure eventually straightened up from clearing his throat, he shook his head slowly, but grandly, as if to admonish her for her little joke. He professed the continued friendship of Spain and all its mighty Empire for her poverty-stricken realm. The devising of any fresh stratagem to counter her abrasiveness, however, appeared to have failed him as surely as Spanish influence here was waning.

Later, Catherine began to fear that Philip had perhaps instructed his ambassador to effect other means for maintaining his influence in Elizabeth's England.

She was walking with Comfit in one of the galleries at Whitehall, when there came a furtive tap, as soft as a kitten's, on her shoulder. She knew straightaway from Comfit's reaction that it was no-one hostile.

One of Queen Mary's former ladies bent to accept the dog's outstretched left forepaw. Jane Dormer, now the Countess de Feria, said very quietly, "I hope, Lady Catherine, that *you* will not shun me. The Queen has banned me from entering the royal apartments, after my lord husband's latest audience with her."

"Banned you? But why?"

"Annoyance, I suppose, at my husband's tidings about King Philip. She couldn't treat my husband thus, for fear of offending Spain. But I'm still one of her subjects, for as long as I remain in my native land."

With considerable ease, their conversation then fell upon the mutual theme of how much better life at Court had been for them in Mary's reign. Their sighs changed into pleasant reminiscences of their days as agreeable colleagues, and they settled side by side on the seat in a nearby window-recess, with Catherine nestling Comfit on her lap.

Jane Dormer seemed eager to prolong their meeting. "Ah, our late dear Queen was rarely discourteous to anybody whose behaviour did not warrant it," she recalled.

Catherine nodded solemnly in response, for here was someone else who had known incivility from Mary's successor without poor conduct to justify it!

"In Spain, 'tis said that our present Queen is wrongly advised," Jane went on cautiously.

"In what way?"

"In . . . her shabby treatment of you, for one! I do pray that 'twill not be to her injury if she so persists. You are her successor."

Catherine lowered her eyes, then whispered, "She does not wish me to succeed her."

She resisted the temptation to touch upon her own

heartfelt shrinking also from the prospect of the throne. The mentions of Spain now overshadowed this conversation, and she remembered too that the Dormers had once spurned a Seymour marriage into their family, saying that the Seymours were not good enough for them.

Catherine felt Comfit's body tense and was thankful that possible speech was further checked, as the little spaniel barked at an approaching footfall.

The Count de Feria arrived at the window-recess and bowed low to Catherine from the gallery. She inclined her head in acknowledgement, but kept her eyes lowered and calmed her dog. It was an excellent means of avoiding his pompous gaze.

When the ambassador addressed his wife, he sounded cheerful, even excited, compared with the candid tone he adopted towards Elizabeth. Catherine attributed this to his inevitably greater fluency in his native tongue. His English-born Countess seemed to pause once or twice, however, in answering him in Spanish - a language which Catherine could not understand.

Catherine politely made her excuses to leave them to their personal talk, but de Feria implored her to tarry yet some minutes with them.

"It ees a pity, dear Lady Cattrin," he added, hovering imposingly at her side of the window-recess, "that you fear the Queen is not desirous of you succeeding her. And this grieves you."

She glanced up at him most warily, but more disarmingly than she first realized.

"Nay, dear madam, there is no need for you to say," he went on. "For I see that it does. And silence becomes maidens."

Catherine had no difficulty in complying with such a hint. She found that silence so became her during the rest of his sermonizing that he mistakenly assumed too that she would neither change her Catholic faith nor marry without his approval!

"Look how your Queen glories in her father!" he said. "For my part, I do not think she would go against his will, which is so clear that if she dies without children, the Crown goes to the descendants of his younger sister and not those of his older - to the most noble Lady Cattrin and not the alien Queen of the Scots. Nor will Elizabeth lead Henry VIII's kingdom back to the iniquity of heresy."

At last he ceased in his intensity. But she could only surmise at the true purpose of this curious encounter and she still chose to say nothing. Not even to point out to him that no-one yet knew what Elizabeth would decide for her people in the matter of religion.

"I am obliged to you for leestening to me so graciously," he added. "The art of leestening is sadly lost in these our days, except to a few. And blessed are they with wisdom beyond many of great learning."

"I shall ponder upon such an excellent notion!" Catherine replied quietly. "And now, I pray you will excuse us." She gathered Comfit gently into her arms and stood up. "My lord ambassador, my lady Countess, I give you - good day."

De Feria bowed ceremoniously and his wife curtseyed, as Catherine stepped back into the gallery. She then made good progress away from them along this, until she thought she glimpsed Jennie in the courtyard outside. She went into another window-recess to check. Comfit was set down on the seat, while Catherine leaned happily across it and stretched an arm up to rat-tat-tat on the window and wave to her friend.

Her arm stalled in mid-air for an instant and she placed her hand on her chin. She had noticed that although Comfit's ears stirred in picking up sound, the dog was looking fixedly towards the direction they had come from, rather than at herself.

"Stay!" Catherine whispered in command. Puzzled, she peered out from the recess.

The gallery seemed deserted. But as she turned once

more to the window, a burst of laughter told her that the de Ferias were still there. The thought occurred to her that they probably believed she had gone by now, for with the laughter were also some words . . .

"Well, what did I tell you! Such a pleasant contrast from the heretic."

"Ah, si, si!" Then followed something else from de Feria which was too indistinct. He ended, however, with two Spanish words Catherine had often heard in connection with King Philip, "Don Carlos."

"Don Carlos?" repeated his wife.

So that was their purpose . . . Catherine reflected, trembling. She could guess why they were talking about Philip's son. They wanted her to marry him!

Spain's ambassador must remain oblivious that her art of listening had extended thus far. Catherine therefore peered out again more prudently. She made sure that the gallery itself was still clear, lifted Comfit up and carried both her dog and herself off as noiselessly as she could. And as speedily too, in case Jennie had chanced to see them at the window and came hareing in to meet them.

They soon neared the courtyard. As Catherine had anticipated, Jennie was approaching. She tiptoed circumspectly for a few paces alongside them and immediately caused Catherine to giggle.

"Oh, Jennie, you do exaggerate sometimes!"

"Not at all! But I wish I could emulate your gracefulness."

All joky imitation ceased, however, once Catherine had enlightened Jennie in private about the conduct of the de Ferias.

"Don Carlos - but, Catherine, he's an imbecile!" cried Jennie. "Yet I'll wager that you're right. The Spaniards seek to wed him to England's heiress. They've failed to get our Queen into Philip's clutches, and this would be the next best arrangement for them."

"I'll say *'No!'* to this idea," gasped Catherine, "like

Elizabeth herself has always refused Spain."

"Dearest Catherine, Elizabeth's commonsense won't allow her to marry off a strong claimant, such as you, into a foreign power. Spain might use you against her."

Catherine brightened, though only for a few moments, before she saw Jennie's lively expression suddenly grow pinched. "But for one element in this," her friend continued, "I would say that the risk of Spaniards kidnapping you to achieve their plan is too far-fetched."

"*Kidnapping* me? Jennie, where are you going?"

"To obtain leave to visit my brother and spur him straightaway into action, if he's to avoid the danger of losing you," said Jennie breathlessly.

"Of *losing* me?"

Jennie hugged her hurriedly. "Until now, I've given Jane Dormer the benefit of the doubt over her family's attitude towards mine in bygone times," she declared. "But believe me, Catherine. This Dormer, with her Spanish designs on you, won't have a chance to assert that my brother is not good enough!"

Ned arrived to see Catherine's mother at Sheen. This time, the situation was somewhat different from the occasional courtesy visits he had made there for several years. He had always habitually shied away from telling her how deeply he loved her second daughter, having once been cast aside as a husband for her eldest.

And his ears were still ringing from the dreaded session with his own mother at Hanworth. "All right! Marry her, if you must," she had eventually conceded. "But on Her Grace, her mother's broad shoulders rests full responsibility for consent to this match, as well as securing that of the Queen."

Ned encountered an immediate difficulty with this latest Hanworth edict, the very minute that the Duchess of Suffolk greeted him.

"Ned, my son! 'Tis good to see you. Would that I could rise from my sickbed."

"My lady. I-I'm sorry to learn that you have lost another babe."

"Another *boy,* Ned," she wailed. "When this one survived those first crucial hours, you know, I hoped . . ."

He nodded sympathetically, but for the moment was speechless, being too embarrassed to utter any polite platitudes about a speedy recovery. He could tell from her bloated face of despair that such words would be wasted.

"There will be no more boys for me now," she continued bitterly. "I have sent to Court for my daughters to come to me, as I fear to die before I can speak with them. They're all I have."

*All you have, woman!* thought Ned. Her lack of joy from her motherhood of a gem such as Catherine much lessened his sense of compassion. He swept away all hesitation in letting her know how for once she could greatly help her daughter.

"Your Grace," he said, fervently. "It is fitting that before your daughters come from Court, I ask your goodwill for the Lady Catherine to marry me."

Suddenly there was a hint of a gleam in her eyes. "So you would truly be my son?"

"I would. And I'd cherish your lovely daughter more than any foreign prince might do," he replied, before informing her about suspected Spanish interest in the girl.

"I will consult with Mr Stokes, before I give answer, Ned. Please would you call my husband to me."

She had sounded reasonable to him. But he was left in suspense, in an adjoining room, while she was alone with this former Master of Horse she had wedded so quickly after the executions of Catherine's father and sister. Ned stared at the closed oaken door, which concealed them from him, and he succumbed to brooding about another rejection by the Grey family. He would feel *that* more keenly than the previous one.

He bemoaned the potential influence of mere horse-masters in determining his adult life. Not only Adrian Stokes here, but that swaggering one at Court called Robert Dudley - a son of his father's enemy and staunch henchman of Elizabeth . . .

The door opened at last. "My lord, Her Grace asks to talk with you again now," said Adrian Stokes. His customary fixed grin inspired Ned with little reassurance.

When Ned was back at the bedside, the Duchess said briskly, "Well, my son, 'tis one of the things I like about you that you would have my plain answer."

"My lady?"

"I believe that you would be a most worthy husband for Lady Catherine. And after what befell my Lady Jane, I dare say that 'twere better she is matched with one who loves her, rather than a foreign prince who may use her as a pawn to further his own power."

While she spoke, Adrian Stokes watched over her carefully. He now added, "Her Grace is not yet sure, however, my lord, if she could countenance the Lady Catherine publicly renouncing all claim to the throne, should this be a condition of the Queen's consent. So, in the interim -"

"Yes?"

"We would advise you to make discreet suit to such lords of the Queen's council as you think are most your friends. At least - that is one means of placating Her Majesty about the marriage."

"I like this advice well and will try to follow it."

"Adrian will assist me with a personal plea for you to my goddaughter, Elizabeth," promised the Duchess. "A letter, which we shall devise to that purpose."

"That is good. In fact, I was about to venture the same idea to you, now that I have your answer!" said Ned.

"My lord, let us wait concerning the letter," said Stokes, "until my Lady Catherine comes here. Then we could set to work on a rough draft of it, once we are assured that she too wishes for the match."

"She will," clucked the Duchess. "My Catherine has been well brought up."

*Her* Catherine! At first, Ned wondered if his ears were playing tricks on him. Then he recalled how suddenly and conveniently Catherine had been awarded the same acknowledgement whenever Queen Mary had praised the girl in Mother Dragon's company.

Ned swallowed before speaking again. "My earnest prayer is that Your Grace will grow strong enough to follow up your letter to Queen Elizabeth, with a personal Court visit and plea."

"What a son I shall have of you, Ned!" she smiled.

When he returned to Sheen two days later, the Duchess summoned both him and Catherine immediately to her presence.

"Daughter Catherine, I have found a husband for you," she announced grandly, extending an arm solemnly towards Ned. "Would you be a faithful and obedient wife to my Lord of Hertford?"

He and Catherine glanced at each other with tenderness. She shared his amusement at her mother taking all the credit for *now* providing her with the lover who had wooed her so devotedly for the last four and a half years!

And yet, the sounds were truly magical to him, to hear Catherine say, "My lady, I am *very* willing to be so. For I love Lord Hertford dearly."

So the stream of their romance was forded further out from its seclusion. After Adrian Stokes ordered writing materials to be brought to the sick-room, the Duchess began to dictate to him: "A nobleman bears goodwill to my daughter, the Lady Catherine . . ."

*"My Lord Earl of Hertford bears goodwill?"* her husband queried from his scribbling.

"My Lord Earl of Hertford?" she actually consulted the young pair.

"My Lord Earl of Hertford," agreed Catherine.

"I'll start again," said Stokes, crossing out his preliminary line and checking every few words with the others as he re-wrote.

"And I do require the Queen to be a good and gracious lady to her," continued the Duchess.

"And I do very humbly require," suggested Catherine cautiously.

"Very humbly?" snorted her mother. "And I do *humbly* require."

"Hum-bly re-quire," repeated Stokes, as his quill pen scratched along. "Good and gracious lady to her. Yes?"

"And that it would please Her Highness to assent to . . ."

"That it would please Her *Majesty,*" said Ned.

"Her *Majesty,*" beamed the Duchess at him. "Yes, of course. My *son!* Now, where were we?"

"To assent to . . ."

"The marriage?" enquired Stokes.

"Hm. That it would please Her Majesty to assent to the marriage of Lady Catherine *to the said Earl,*" oozed the Duchess.

The discussion then moved on to draft out the letter's further possible shape and she momentarily sank back, producing a great dent in her pillows.

"The marriage . . . which is the only thing I desire before my death," she considered aloud, "and should enable me to die the more quietly."

Stokes sharpened and tested the nib of another quill in readiness for more jumbled scribbling.

# CHAPTER 9

# *Elizabethan Dalliance*

"What is it?" snapped Elizabeth. "You know I'm in no mind to receive petitions nowadays."

How often since her childhood had she seen the look of silent reproach on the face of her old governess, who now knelt before her in the Privy Chamber!

"Oh, get up, Kat, if you've no good account to give of yourself," she ordered.

Such a remark being virtually guaranteed to unloose Kat Ashley's tongue, Elizabeth accordingly waited.

"I beseech you, Your Majesty, for God's sake to marry," cried Kat, "and so make an end to all the gross slanders being bruited about you and Lord Robert."

"Marriage is a serious step to take, Kat. Dost think my people will cease to love their Queen who in six short months has brought them so much? I've brought them peace, rescued their Church from the fold of Rome and let Mary's exiles come streaming home, no longer in peril of burning."

Elizabeth had been looking forward to using such statements of fact in defence of any attack against her increasing attachment to Robin Dudley during her first springtime of power. She revelled in her authority, though Kat's tone was too acutely reminiscent of the troublous times when Thomas Seymour had come a-courting her.

"Would to God that these achievements in the glorious start to Your Majesty's reign do not end in disaster!" returned Kat, more shrilly. "'Tis said that my Lord Robert and you are already as man and wife. Worse, that this is adultery as he has been wedded these past several years.

Can't you see that the more such talk spreads among your people, the more their image of their loved Sovereign Lady will be sullied? If their love were then to fade ... Oh, Your Majesty, to hear of you so maligned after the dangers we have come through together . . ."

"Go on, Kat."

Elizabeth sensed that although Kat had *not* been looking forward to speaking out, her statements had also undergone some preparation - doubtless with the aid of Blanche Parry, to ensure that the words were adequately memorized!

"If the love of your people were to fade, what also of their allegiance? From the start - and long before - the reign of Queen Elizabeth was looked for to be a golden age! The consequences are unthinkable . . . and had I known I might live to see such calamity for Your Majesty, I . . . I should have strangled you in your swaddling bands."

With that, Kat sank back to her knees, drooping like a wilted flower.

"Do get up again! You're over-wrought," said Elizabeth, sounding herself more impatient than she intended. For she had at first stiffened, in the manner which would have betokened trouble for anyone other than Kat who had given *quite* such audacious account as that last outburst - rehearsed or not.

While Kat endeavoured to obey, limbs creaking as she struggled to stand, Elizabeth reassured her, "Kat! I know that these incisive words come forth from your true-hearted loyalty. But we are neither of us in mortal danger now, as in that . . . earlier time. So have no fears."

In her unnamed reference to Thomas Seymour, Elizabeth hoped to distance Kat's mind from the tribulations they had both endured then. "Robert's company makes me happy. Don't begrudge me that after years of suffering."

Her brow darkened again, however, but more gradually, irrevocably, as Kat proved to be none too easily fobbed off.

Back came the vexatious pleas for her to marry.

"Delay much longer in choosing one of Your Majesty's many suitors, and God may wreak a bitter vengeance," warned Kat, shaking her finger despairingly. "If you were to depart this life untimely, leaving no heir of your body or no *named* successor, what legacy will there be for your people?"

"The Almighty will provide for my realm, as it was His doing to preserve me and raise me to be your anointed Queen."

Elizabeth's ire had increased at the broaching of such a thorny matter. From Kat, of all folk! She had already noted Catherine Grey acknowledge various expressions of kindliness from both her faithful Blanche and Kat. So the moment was ripe, she decided. Over-ripe to curtail this confrontation, once and for all, by using another advantage of her sovereignty: the absolute royal declaration.

Kat began to speak again, but Elizabeth silenced her with a glare.

"We princes are set as it were upon stages, in the sight and view of all the world," she asserted. "And not one of *my* subjects has reason to slander Lord Robert and their Queen. If my royal wish is to be favourably disposed towards him, it is in reward for his steadfastness in my service. Not for aught improper between us . . . yet, had it been my pleasure for such, there is no higher authority in my realm who could have said me nay!"

"Tsk," muttered Kat.

"The days for saying, 'Tsk' to me are past. You may go now, Kat."

Elizabeth simmered for several minutes. She called for music to soothe her, but this soon failed in its purpose. Instead, she sent for Blanche Parry and told her, "I wish to see my Eyes again. Fetch him to me at once."

"One for Ulfall, one for me. One for Ulfall, one for thee . . ."

Ned beamed at the jovial faces of his Savernake officials, as the coins received from fines were counted after his first Forest Court.

"Though I be of age now, I do fear to have entered upon a second phase of childhood!" he joked. "Always gives me good heart to be back at Savernake."

"'Tis good to 'ave you with us, m'lud," enthused Richard Weeks, to choruses of assent in the local burr. "Make 'em think twice from now on, thievin' varmints round 'ere."

"Fair long lists of 'em in this 'ere Lat'n," observed John Berwick, proudly perusing his written records of offences and punishment fines.

Ned's smile broadened further. The chief forester's attempts at Latin were jumbled up with English words and made Catherine's laboured scribblings in the ancient language seem almost erudite!

"Fair old list o' Lat'n names too on these 'ere coins, 'bout Queen Lisbet."

"Oh ah, but not the kind o' names that we be callin' 'er!" said Weeks. "Cavortin' roun' with a married man, son of 'im as sent 'r Good Duke to the block. Scandalous what a *vur-r-gin* Queen we got!"

Some of the other foresters joined in with the banter.

"Scandalous."

"'Igh time she was wedded and big-bellied."

And high time too, Ned knew, that he tried to call a halt to such gossip - at least in his presence! He had already had a surfeit of his tenantry around Wolf Hall being agog with speculation about Elizabeth and her married horse-master, as well as that other affair with Lord Thomas Seymour when she was only fourteen . . .

"Let's just concentrate on counting coins now, men!" he said. "Remember how speedily Her Majesty restored my lord father's old earldom and more of his lands to me."

He beamed at them again, and nodded at their burring of apologies. He had spoken firmly, but not unkindly. At one time, he would have followed his strong impulse to elaborate on their remarks, maybe with anecdotes of Elizabeth passed on to him mainly by Jennie. Despite such participation seeming hardly right for a peer of the realm, Ned felt more inhibited by the truth of Sir John Thynne's warning to him at Wolf Hall last summer about Elizabeth.

Then, it had seemed partly a joke. An ominous one, but a joke. He had not reckoned upon her becoming Queen for some greater lapse of time. And he was still amazed that the lethal legacy, perhaps unleashed by what his tenants termed his Uncle Thomas's "messin'" with her, had already materialized enough to cause much ado amongst her subjects.

Just concentrate on the coins, he reiterated to himself.

Links with Elizabeth were haunting his present, deepest concerns, but this money imprinted with her likeness had brought him compensation well exceeding its actual worth. It was providing him with a start, a real start, to fulfilling his good intentions to renovate Wolf Hall!

He turned to considering appropriate divisions of the funds available so far for different building materials, and did not temper his high spirits. Not even when Berwick noted lightheartedly, "M'lud, you zound like Zur-r John!"

The challenge of tasks at Wolf Hall helped to absorb Ned away from his chagrin at how easily other people seemed to have forgotten *their* good intentions - namely, with regard to his betrothal. The letter of appeal to Elizabeth was still in draft form when he set off on this latest visit to Savernake. Catherine's mother had decided on copying it out rather than only signing it. But each attempt had been thwarted by some further recurrence of her illness. Ned hoped and prayed that a completed letter had been sent by now and the whole matter resolved during his absence from London.

Upon his return, however, he found that expectation

was in vain. His more frequent visits to Court from Hertford House at least offset this dispiriting fact and sometimes his visits to Sheen were timed to coincide with those of Catherine.

"Jennie says that your Savernake men are right. You do sound like Sir John Thynne," she teased him, during a rare moment out of earshot of other people at Sheen.

*"Not with you!"* he whispered, tickling her neck below her chin and then kissing her smiling mouth. "'Tis all this delay . . ."

They both glanced furtively around to make sure that no-one else shared their secrecy. Ned earned a playful dig from her elbow for bridging his palm above his eyes to look out in Jennie-like mimicry.

But without Jennie to act as their lookout, their next embrace was snatched, compared with their deep and ardent kisses in her chamber at Court. Catherine grew tense at noises coming from different directions.

"How much longer must we still depend on hidey-holes and corners?" she sighed.

Ned had time to kiss her hand, before her stepfather clomped by towards her mother's chamber. They quickly covered up their feelings by reverting their conversation to the repairs at Wolf Hall.

Once back at Court, Jennie's chamber was a comfortable refuge, where noises dwindled into insignificance for them. They were able to express their love more freely, exasperated that they must continue to be so secretive. And all the while, Elizabeth could flirt shamelessly in public with someone else's husband merely because she was their Sovereign.

Their arms stayed entwined as they spoke between embraces.

"Your mother seems to think all urgency for us is past," mused Ned, "simply because de Feria is gone from England, after Elizabeth snubbed his wife once too oft. Does she want me for her son or not?"

"Oh, she does, Ned! But sometimes in her infirmity, she's sure that she has written and sent the letter. And no-one can convince her otherwise."

"Whenever she has recovered a little since I came back from Savernake, the Queen has fallen ill!"

"Divine retribution," said Catherine.

"What ails her today?"

"The same old pain."

"The same?"

"Yes. You know . . . about two yards high and called Robert Dudley!"

Ned burst into laughter. "Well, I've heard much scorn of him, of late, but none so apt or sweetly said as yours!"

Then he whispered her name tenderly and kissed her, and added, "Yet 'tis mild what my beloved says of him, unlike the wishful thinking I have endured of Robert Dudley this spring."

"My lord?"

"Sometimes, when longing to hold you on lonely and wakeful nights, I have again close witnessed *his* father's beheading. I've seen the lame executioner shamble across the scaffold in his white butcher's apron - but oddly, the victim's blood bespattering it at the block spurting from Robert Dudley himself."

"Nay, let's not wish that on him, Ned."

"Not on anyone," he affirmed, "including other courtiers, whom I suspect he has incited to nickname me 'Little Hertford'! But I digress . . . Didn't Jennie say some kind of burning fever still afflicts the Queen?"

Catherine shrugged, her rosebud lips overcoming a pert flicker of a smile. "I heard that she was let blood this morning from her foot! But maybe 'twas to bring on her monthly course. Hers seem to be so infrequent."

"Oh?"

"If you like, *I'll* sound like Helen and repeat every little detail she learnt from a couple of royal laundresses about the Queen's few menstrual cloths and -"

"Ugh! No, thank you. I do implicitly accept what you first said, and I'll try strict moderation to sound less like Sir John!"

At the delightful sensation of Catherine reaching up to place her lips on his, Ned's arms strengthened, as ever, to support her. He could tell from a lithe half-turn of her body so close to his that another matter had surged to the fore with her.

"Well, I'm listening." he said.

"I wondered whether we might ask the *other* Duchess of Suffolk - when she's home from exile soon - to intercede for us with the Queen."

"Your step-granddam?" Ned queried gently. "Catherine, why, when she's associated with a curse on Elizabeth, which has apparently been fulfilled by Seymours?"

"My dearest love," murmured Catherine, "that so-called curse was never meant to implicate your family. My step-granddam was a friend of your lord father, remember."

"'Tis an irony," he conceded, "that this lady's Spanish Catholic mother, Lady Willoughby, pronounced the curse. Yet 'twas in the reign of a Catholic Queen that your step-granddam herself fled into exile for her Protestant faith."

"She has a ready wit, Ned, which I think will please Elizabeth!" Catherine smiled. "Perhaps she still has that dog she dressed up in Mass vestments and named after a bishop . . . Ah well, there *is* something else about her, which for us is of the greatest importance."

"And what's that, beloved?"

"She highly approves of marriages where there is love."

They kissed again, their youthful spirits raised by this knowledge. It meant that at the homecoming of Catherine's step-grandmother, the Dowager Duchess of Suffolk, they'd have someone else to turn to for help.

Catherine assumed that Spanish designs on her had departed with the ambassador, de Feria, and his wife overseas, and her fears accordingly receded that she might be pounced upon by kidnappers at any turn. During the summer of 1559, however, Elizabeth continued to flout all accusation and outrage over her liaison with Lord Robert.

The Queen required minimal excuse to clasp hands with him like two lovers. Even in the comparative seclusion of her Privy Chamber this provided excellent cover amid their caresses for her to receive through him messages from her Secret Eyes.

Elizabeth was glad that the seemingly interminable and trying month of July would soon pass into August. In the meantime, the warm physical contact of linking her arm through Robert's, to study in confidential manner the coded symbols of the latest message helped to relax her.

And so did the sight of 'EveR' at its start, no less than the familiar '007' at the end, signed by a friend who had never failed her.

In between, she saw a single circle, then a dash and brackets, which she knew from Robert's concerned face that he also had swiftly interpreted.

"Mars!" she whispered, and he nodded in agreement, neither of them needing to utter more. For this was Dr Dee's symbol warning of danger to her throne.

*Danger* . . . echoed through her thoughts. Danger from whom - when or where?

Undaunted, she recognized the remaining symbol, a figure nought with a short diagonal line passing through it.

What riddle is this for me, Dr Dee? Elizabeth mused, wryly. As always she found such a quirky means of communication much to her taste. She sought to indulge her personal inclinations more, by testing the handsome, pensive man beside her.

"France," she said, and waited with a lively interest to hear what he might make of that. An army of invasion from there, perhaps, now that the French King's death in early July had raised the Queen of Scots and her husband to ultimate power in that realm? For they still had the effrontery to covet the Tudor throne, having gone on boldly sporting the royal arms of Elizabeth's England along with their own of France and Scotland!

Robert's muscular arm tensed beneath his padded sleeve while she anticipated his response. But his movements in bending his head protectively towards her were achieved with a most manly grace.

"Not France, Your Majesty," he whispered in her ear, as if in intimate endearment. "Spain!"

"Ha!" she laughed, both her beautiful white hands squeezing gently at his arm. Her smile then radiated up to him that he had answered well.

"A goodly poser, Rob," she murmured, and added as he kissed her hand, "My Eyes, be watchful for clues to its meaning."

"Dear lady . . ."

August began with Elizabeth and her Eyes remaining mystified by the goodly poser from Dr Dee. In her quest for a solution, she was also receptive to whatever might emerge through her regular conferences with her secretary, William Cecil - her Spirit, as she increasingly liked to nickname him. So far this summer, he had been unusually reticent in giving his honest opinion of her more attractive and informal conferences with her Eyes. These qualities accorded Robert unannounced access to her.

But when Mr Secretary came to them one morning, especially alert and self-confident, she discerned at last in her Spirit an implied lack of oneness with her Eyes.

The document which he placed with cool efficiency before her did not require her flourishing signature, but as with all such items she gave it a thorough preliminary read.

"Hm! Here we have one of your 'troublesome, fond matters' with a vengeance, eh, Sir Spirit," she observed.

"Indeed, Your Majesty."

Elizabeth felt a grim sense of satisfaction that before her

was the hitherto elusive solution to Dr Dee's secret message. Her discovery controlled for now her infinitely greater sense of wrath. That was expressed for her instead by Robert, when she saw his hand tighten into a clenched fist while she let him also read the letter from her ambassador to Spain!

"What madness is this?" he cried. "King Philip would counter the Scottish Queen's usurping of Her Majesty's royal arms by kidnapping that little featherhead. And he'd marry her to his own son and heir, before proclaiming her the true heiress to our Sovereign Lady, Queen Elizabeth!"

"Kidnapping the Lady Catherine . . ." Cecil began calmly to correct him.

"*The* Lady Catherine!" scoffed Elizabeth. "Gentlemen, I take fullest heed of the warning underlined in this."

While Cecil nodded sagely at her words, Robert returned his attention angrily to the letter, "So the Spaniards think she has a discontented mind, do they, as she isn't regarded by her Queen!"

Though the truth of the latter part of this statement had just been amply displayed, the stark fact which Elizabeth's mind had at once begun to address was that Catherine *was* regarded by Spain.

"One way or another, she must be watched more closely," affirmed the Queen.

Still looking at the document with contempt, Robert agreed with her wholeheartedly. Her Spirit, too, bowed in acknowledgement. But the unhurried manner in which he carefully gathered up the letter hinted pointedly at his own views. If she would but marry and cease her dalliance with her horse-master, a 'troublesome, fond matter' such as this situation need never have arisen!

The thoughtful, heart-shaped face of the Dowager Duchess of Suffolk appraised Catherine after an absence of almost five years.

"Well, Catherine! The loveliness of your Tudor ancestress has come out even more in you during my wanderings in exile."

Catherine felt strange to be so complimented by one of her own family during a visit to Sheen. Yet despite her mother being so ill, the thought that the Dragon was nearby restrained Catherine's personal pleasure at meeting her step-grandmother again.

With strict adherence to her upbringing, she sank smoothly into a curtsey and prepared herself to utter a formal greeting as she rose.

But she was affectionately hugged instead, and her whole being softened. "My lady, welcome! Welcome back to us," she smiled.

"'Twas the Lord's doing, my dear, to bring me and mine safely back! How we shall glorify in His Name soon in our old home."

After they drew apart, the Dowager shepherded forward her infant son and daughter, born to her late in life by her second marriage. Their bow and curtsey seemed to Catherine so refreshingly free from the parental coercion she had suffered at their tender age.

"I'm delighted to see them," Catherine acknowledged.

"God willing, we'll never lose my son's inheritance again," avowed the lady, taking each child warmly by the hand.

Catherine responded with sympathetic murmurs as her step-granddam talked more of the family home in Lincolnshire, which had been confiscated by Queen Mary when the Dowager escaped abroad and was now newly returned by Elizabeth.

"When you pay your respects at Court before going home, Your Grace," said Catherine in a confidential tone, ". . . there is something I -"

Her voice, unfortunately, did not carry above that of the Dowager.

"Court? Ah, yes! But before duty is done to Her Majesty tomorrow, I must speak with my friend and neighbour, William Cecil. God's Church in England still has similarities with Catholic worship, and he has influence to speed up change. I pray that Her Majesty will honour the true faith as notably as the last Queen was attached to the Mass."

"And *I* pray that in Your Grace's friendship with William Cecil, there could also be another matter to talk of - before duty is done to the Queen."

The Dowager cast a discerning, if doting glance at Catherine. "Of this other matter, I now know full well, Catherine," she replied. "I see for myself that you indeed love Lord Hertford, as I heard from Mr Stokes. You have my approval, my dear. And since you cannot, *must* not marry without Elizabeth's, let's see what help God allows."

"My lady, thank you!" said Catherine.

She was sitting at her mother's bedside when Ned arrived at Sheen later the same day. Catherine had already enjoyed hearing her step-granddam mildly reprove the invalid over her failure to send the letter to Elizabeth. She brightened further when she glanced at Ned from the corners of her eyes. That endearing, boyish wonderment he expressed at sight of her - it lit his face even before he bowed!

Catherine's eyes stayed lowered, however, once the two Duchesses resumed their conversation. Those cold, prickling sensations which had beset her since childhood whenever her mother merely tutted, were threatening to make her feel queasy as usual.

"Re-draft of the letter, did you say?" her mother moaned to the Dowager.

"A few small changes, that is all."

*"All?"*

"Look, dear, why not let Mr Stokes and my Lord of Hertford go through the letter again while I'm away visiting Her Majesty? And if my own beloved husband joins them, he'll bring a fresh mind to it."

"Humph! I want the letter to bear my signature!"

"It will. Now calm yourself."

Ned addressed both Duchesses, "I shall be ready to get on with the re-draft at a moment's notice."

"Patience, my lord, for a little longer!" smiled the Dowager. "My audience with the Queen is timely enough. Meanwhile, I'd like to discuss with my husband some ideas for the re-draft and how best to sound out Mr Secretary Cecil about conveying it to her."

Such congenial plans as these enhanced Catherine's thoughts well into the next day, while her step-granddam was at Court. Like Catherine's mother, the lady had remarried beneath her rank to a gentleman of her household. His name was Richard Bertie and the marriage expressed the Dowager Duchess's dislike of loveless, arranged unions, for it was a love-match.

Bertie's careful re-drafting of the letter with Adrian Stokes and Ned earned for him the heartiest of embraces from his noble spouse on her return from Court. Catherine felt elated to observe them. And then, miracle of miracles, Mother Dragon was at last cajoled into scrawling out her copy and signing it!

How straightforward everything happily seemed for the Dowager to indicate when she could deliver this to Elizabeth, probably via William Cecil.

"Well, the Lord has rewarded your patience, Ned," she said, exchanging smiles with him, before she handed the letter to him. "And I shall pray for His continued goodness to guide you in taking this to Queen Elizabeth."

Catherine thought at first she may have misheard. But if she had misheard, why had Ned suddenly blanched and dropped the letter on the floor?

"M-me?" he gasped.

"Yes, my Lord Earl! The only young peer ennobled early in Her Majesty's reign, are you not? And also blessed with a sister at Court who is much esteemed by her?"

"B-but I thought that you . . ." By this time, Ned was struggling to unfasten his doublet at the throat and beads of sweat had broken out all over his brow.

"Alas, I have been overseas too long," replied the Dowager. "I couldn't even sound out William Cecil on Lady Catherine's and your behalf. He does not have such confidence with the Queen as I expected - mostly due to her dalliance with Lord Robert. However much I wish to negotiate through him, Ned, on this and the hastening of true religion back to England, 'tis impossible while she is thus preoccupied. But I *shall* ensure there is no semblance of Catholic ritual in the worship of God on my own domains."

"Aye," mumbled Ned, mopping his brow unsuccessfully with his hands, because they too were perspiring.

Catherine made a move towards him, but then she stood still as he spoke to her step-granddam and mother more fully.

"My honourable ladies, like Mr Secretary Cecil, I cannot worm my way into the Queen's good graces, cringing before her as *some* others do. I . . . I'll meddle no more in this matter."

Ned then bowed rather forlornly to the assembled company and made a stumbling departure from the chamber. After a few moments, he was heard calling to his servant.

"Tom, see that Esturmy is saddled."

"Yes, m'lord."

Catherine instinctively picked up her skirts. She gratefully acknowledged a supportive nod from her step-granddam and ventured after him.

Her mother tutted, and ordered, "Come back here at *once*."

But Catherine was not deterred from her purpose. She was aware, for the first time in her life, that if she had remained in the same room, her mother's conduct would have provoked her to a storm of anger.

Ned whirled about on hearing her. He caught her hands and covered them with kisses. Catherine pictured Esturmy carrying both of them across the ford of a stream, more swollen behind them than it was in the short distance ahead.

"Ned, you once said there'd be greater risk for us in turning back," she reminded him gently.

"So ask your step-granddam to pray that God will guide us to another means than this!" he said, gripping her hands very tightly and then letting them free. "In the meantime, beloved, I *am* going back - to Savernake - and hope that I'll stop shaking more than any of my Forest leaves afore I get there."

In Jennie's chamber at Whitehall, Catherine looked on anxiously. Jennie was complaining of dizziness after another severe bout of coughing and held her hands to her head.

Catherine collected herself to summon help immediately if the dizziness caused Jennie to faint this time. The growing chill of October, only weeks before the first anniversary of Elizabeth's accession, had made her friend ill again.

"I'll send word to Ned that you are sick," said Catherine softly, "and I'll ask him to come and see you."

"Nay, Catherine, he won't drag himself from Savernake for me," Jennie gasped.

Catherine sighed deeply to herself, *Or me?* Two months he has been gone without a word!

Jennie's eyes continued blinking rapidly, but she began to rally. "Where's Comfit?" she enquired. "'Twould be such a help to me to enjoy her company."

Fresh dismay swept over Catherine, as she briefly hesitated to answer. With Jennie in poor health, Ned faraway to the south-west and her step-granddam to the north, and her mother edging nearer death, she had dried her tears concerning Comfit after sharing them with Helen.

"Oh, Jennie, Comfit will never be able to see you or me, or anything again."

"Where is she? What's happened to her?"

"I fear that Comfit has gone blind."

"Blind? Oh no, Catherine! When?"

"Well, Helen first noticed last night that she was blundering into walls and furniture in my chamber. But we didn't know for certain till we had some daylight this morning."

"I trust that the poor little pet will still recognize me by my scent," said Jennie. "Or else, perchance by my coughing . . .

"She still wags her tail when people she loves come near!" replied Catherine. "Jennie, I so much want to look after you and Comfit."

"So let's carry her into that new little nook the Queen has granted me, and console each other! In fact, while I'm in such favour now with our Sovereign, I'd like to talk to you, Catherine, about the prospect of me taking your mother's letter to Her Majesty."

The 'new little nook', Jennie's recent mark of privilege from Elizabeth, was a private sitting-room separated off from the common room used by the Queen's ladies.

Shortly afterwards, Catherine observed Elizabeth and Robert Dudley walking further away down the corridor outside this larger sitting-room. They were fully engrossed in each other and the sight of them added more anguish to Catherine's present worries. Especially her perennial nightmare of a life of spinsterhood at this woman's Court. Or a former dread, which again unnerved her - that of being waylaid by Spaniards and married against her will.

For a moment, Catherine was beset by feelings of shakiness. But she entered the common room, encouraging Jennie across to the door of the little nook, "Not far now." She was astonished at the calm and dulcet tone of her voice.

"No . . . not far, thanks!" Despite sounding breathless,

Jennie attempted a smile and gestured reassurance that she could reach their desired destination unaided.

So Catherine turned her attention to Comfit, who nestled in Helen's solid arms. Her outstretched fingertips stroked the dog's chin lovingly and in return a warm, pink tongue licked at her hand.

She did not heed footsteps nearby, from someone who spoke her name. If this had been a call for assistance by Jennie, it would not have seemed to intrude upon her. But her name was repeated more loudly, "Catherine . . . Dear sister, our lady mother has sent for us. Her Majesty has given us leave to set off for Sheen as soon as we're ready."

Inwardly Catherine cried, That's *enough!*

She felt so vulnerable. And as usual, she was confronted with the old, hurtful reminder of the great lack of solace from her family.

Catherine paused before looking round to reply, but in her annoyance, verbal arrows were launched from their sheath all together at Mary Grey. "Set off for Sheen. Just like that. No matter what else I might be doing! Must I be at every old termagent's beck and call? Can't see beyond the end of your nose, can you - I have others to care for too! Must I neglect them for the old Dragon, like the horse-master neglects his poor, sick wife, with her malady in her breast? Horses are not all he mounts at Court!"

She stopped simply to catch her breath, before pronouncing more words on this last contentious theme. But she saw her sister withdraw a few paces backwards, while looking at the doorway to the common room. As Catherine frowned in reproof at Mary's movement from her, she heard Helen also step backwards, still holding Comfit. Suddenly, the sounds of voices and laughter around the room ceased.

Catherine gaped at Comfit, taken from her immediate reach, and she began to regret her recklessness. Even more so when a pair of female figures changed their stance in the light of the open doorway. She next saw Kat Ashley, head shaking with sorrow towards her, skirts rustling with a reverential movement to one side. And then Catherine cupped her hand to her mouth - finding herself face to face with Elizabeth in full and terrible Tudor majesty.

Though the royal lips did not flicker, the searching, quelling eyes stared unblinking at Catherine, and powerful hatred and ill-will shot out at her from their glinting depths.

## CHAPTER 10

# *Murder or Misadventure?*

"It has pleased Almighty God to call out of this life the most noble and excellent princess, the Lady Frances, late Duchess of Suffolk," proclaimed the royal herald in Westminster Abbey.

On hearing such eulogy, Ned tried hard to keep any derision from his face. Hardly noble and excellent to her daughters, he thought.

The few November days that Catherine's mother had survived into the second year of Elizabeth's reign were enough for this, her funeral Communion service, to be the very first read out in English rather than Latin. Like other Protestants in the congregation, he was happy with such a significant reform.

But he watched tensely while Catherine, as the Chief Mourner, knelt on a carpet laid for her before the high altar. There seemed to be no end to the girl's suffering. Now she was publicly being forced to feign a grief she could never feel.

Beloved, forgive me for my neglect, Ned cried out silently. He was sure that somehow she would hear him.

His first autumn at Savernake since childhood had been a source of beauty and wonder to him during his latest absence from London. Only Catherine had been missing from his happiness in Wiltshire, though never from his heart. He hadn't felt confident about sending messages to her, for fear of these being intercepted and heaping further adversity on her. Instead, his love for her had driven him to occupy himself with work on Wolf Hall.

'Tis safest for us to meet through my visits to Jennie for

the time being, Ned reflected.

He hoped for a glance his way from Catherine, however slight, when the funeral ceremony was over. Minutes seemed more like an hour of heart-racing before she turned slowly in the cumbersome mourning apparel to make a remark to her train-bearers. Her eyes widened and softened at beholding him for an instant. From beneath the handkerchief she clasped so prettily to dab at her cheeks, her mouth quivered into a kiss for him across the space dividing them.

Ned contented himself with that moment, during the next few weeks that Catherine was away from Court at Sheen. His final view was of her leaving for there in a carriage with her sister Mary. Part of his mind was still too much in turmoil for him to realize how far he should blame himself for panicking the previous August about approaching Elizabeth, and afterwards leaving Catherine so alone.

He had learnt from Jennie that Catherine's mother had eventually added a postscript to the letter, an extra plea which said that her request for this love-match had sadly become her dying wish. The intention was that the letter could be presented to Elizabeth even after the Duchess's death. But now, after Catherine's unfortunate outburst in Elizabeth's hearing, nobody - not even favoured Jennie - could risk venturing to the stinging bee with that missive. Adrian Stokes had consequently destroyed it.

A new month and year began before Catherine returned to Court - January 1560. Ned preferred not to think back to the time of the coronation twelve months ago. Nor did he attempt to guess what was in store for himself and Catherine in the next twelve, if God still preserved the rule of their unpredictable monarch.

Elizabeth gave special attention to Catherine within hours

of her resumption of duties in the Presence Chamber.

"Rise up, cousin! We would not have you kneel before us so timidly," she ordered.

"Yes, Your Majesty."

"It does become you, Lady Catherine. Yet we rejoice that there is also boldness and spirit in you, of which we have made note. And we would have you closer about us. From now on therefore, we wish you to attend us in our Privy Chamber."

Ned heard the usual public din of the Presence Chamber noticeably subside at Elizabeth's clear speech, but not enough to catch Catherine's evidently satisfactory reply.

"Since you've each hushed your noise for us, even your frantic whispers," Elizabeth declared mockingly to all in the room, "hear this! The Lady Catherine being our near kinswoman and back in our service now bereft of her mother, we would call her 'daughter' rather than 'cousin'. Indeed, we may adopt her."

What ruse is this? thought Ned. He had the same uncomfortable feeling of distrust he had known when Elizabeth made him an earl on a Friday the 13th in the Tower!

Whispered snatches of the Queen's words hissed around him, as she swept Catherine off into the Privy Chamber. While the former din rebuilt, he realized only too well what Catherine's thoughts would be about ridding herself of one brutal, domineering mother and in such a short time acquiring another much worse.

Later, when he visited Jennie's chamber, he saw that the modest, compliant aura of Catherine towards Elizabeth had dissolved into laughter with his sister.

"I'm so glad that Jennie was close by the Queen, when I came back to Court," she admitted.

Ned took her in his arms and she clung to him wholeheartedly. "Sweet Catherine, it's like I've lived a lifetime waiting for this reunion," he whispered.

A knock came at the door and they both sat down,

smiling, while Jennie went to answer. Helen entered, carrying Comfit.

Catherine looked at her maid quite serenely, as Comfit was lowered onto her lap. "Thank you, Helen."

"Anything else, dear Lady Catherine? Or that'll be all?"

"All for the moment, I think. And thank you again, Helen."

Ned accepted the left paw proffered to him. But he watched, a little puzzled, at the warmth in which Helen bobbed her ungainly curtsey and left the room.

"No doubt you still use Latin to cover your secrets from her," he said. "I hope she doesn't carp about your courtesy, sweetheart, 'midst the rest of her gossip about you."

"Helen has been *most* loyal," Jennie chided. "She understands as well as I do. There were extenuating circumstances behind Catherine's loss of temper near the Queen. Affection and pity for two of her loved ones here - and want of the company of one who was then absent!"

"Extenuating circumstances," he repeated. "To us three, yes. And to Helen, God be praised. But to Elizabeth - I think, *no*, my ladies."

"Even though I only echoed what the whole Court are tattling about the Queen's Eyes, Ned?"

"Even though you only echoed what the whole populace from here to Wiltshire are tattling about him, Catherine! That doesn't alter the fact we must not be deceived by this 'adopted daughter' tactic . . ." He broke off, as he surveyed both girls grinning at him. "Oh, stick to lute-playing and spaniel-cuddling, the pair of you, and let me save wasting my breath in future!"

"As you wish, my lord," teased Jennie.

"I'm much too accustomed to an unloving mother and daughter tie," added Catherine, "for Elizabeth's latest idea to change my opinion of her."

"We must hold to our accord of secrecy as before," said Ned, "and be extra mindful of tittle-tattlers, the stinging bee and her Eyes."

"And also her Spirit," suggested Jennie.

"Aye," Ned agreed, "especially as he too has a town house near mine in Cannon Row!"

"And all subjects of Spain," murmured Catherine. "Philip's new ambassador is much like Count de Feria in cultivating my art of 'leestening'."

"De Feria's English wife is probably prompting him," said Jennie, "though she is overseas."

"Maybe. I know Jane Dormer would be sad to hear about poor Comfit. But if she ever comes back to England, I'd be watchful of her with a friendly courtesy," smiled Catherine gently.

"Like you were so convincingly with Helen in here!" he chuckled.

A much cooler form of friendly courtesy was royally maintained by Elizabeth towards Catherine for the rest of the winter. And Catherine graced her accord with the two young Seymours by seeming suitably appeased, although their uneasiness and suspicion regarding Elizabeth lingered. After their various traumas since August, the lovers hardly dared to believe that a tranquil interlude which set in for them during January could possibly last into the coming spring. But continue it did, and on beyond, into the summer months of 1560. Outside attention, including Helen's, was diverted well away from Catherine by fresh tale-spreading about the Queen, Robert Dudley and the further impact on her realm of a new war.

An English army marched north in April to repel a French invasion, which was threatened from Scotland. Soon afterwards, Robert openly bragged that in a year's time, he would occupy a far superior position than Master of Horse.

Robert Dudley - King of England? A notion which made even lifelong servants like Kat Ashley recoil in dismay! Both Catherine and Jennie were bystanders to her vehement words to Elizabeth.

"Such impertinence to Your Majesty," Kat wailed.

"What is my Lord Robert about? Victory for your army in Scotland would have restored your reputation in the world! What prince will *want* to marry you if Your Majesty is further dishonoured?"

"God's death, Kat!" replied Elizabeth. "You prate to your Sovereign of Lord Robert aspiring higher. You're assuming for yourself a position above that I assigned you. Keep all your surveillance over my ladies in future. *That* remains your place."

As the slurs on Elizabeth and Robert grew fiercer, these overshadowed English success in the short, but costly Scottish war. The scandalmongering centred on a sinister new implication: how would Robert Dudley rid himself of his wife?

"I need only listen to Helen, to know what my tenants will also be talking about!" scoffed Ned. "Some rumours are that he'll poison his wife, others that he'll murder her more cruelly if the poor soul doesn't die of her illness."

"All the criticism now makes the Queen very agitated," said Jennie.

"'Tis little wonder!"

"Yes, Ned, but I fear that the show of courtesy towards her 'daughter' might not last much longer."

"They are very close, though, Elizabeth and her Eyes," said Catherine, "despite the hostility against them. Perhaps if she does marry him, their happiness could change her and she'd be more approachable about us."

"I believe your love will yet find a way," smiled Jennie.

Ned looked at both girls with shining eyes and kissed Catherine. He found his thoughts returning to the very beginning of their romance, to the halcyon times immediately after Queen Mary Tudor's marriage and their future was briefly filled with promise. How much better he felt to dwell on these than his occasional nightmares about Robert Dudley and a lame executioner wearing a blood-stained butcher's apron!

Each time Ned came to Court in the early summer, he

took to whistling tunes as he sauntered along to see Jennie and Catherine, either in his sister's sitting-room or chamber. His buoyant frame of mind meant that he was not in the least disquieted by an even gloomier atmosphere at Court, after Elizabeth ordered William Cecil away to negotiate a peace treaty in Scotland.

Court gossip then tended to praise Mr Secretary's moderating influence over Elizabeth and his competence in arranging a treaty which expelled the French from the northern realm. But in Cecil's absence, Robert's influence over the Queen increased. Ned became vaguely aware of scraps of scandal which arose when Cecil returned to Court in July, with the air of a task well done. Elizabeth was said to be considering Robert for an earldom, but no reward was planned for her hard-working Secretary.

Ned's good mood stayed with him and he continued whistling tunefully on his way to meet Catherine. He even found a strangely genial William Cecil falling into step with him one day at Whitehall.

"My Lord Hertford, this tune is played for Her Majesty by your sister, is it not?"

"Indeed, sir. It is a favourite both of Lady Jennie's and of mine."

"Do you go to see my lady, your sister, now?"

"Yes. Yes, I do . . ."

"Lady Jennie has a most dutiful brother visiting her so happily and so often."

Cecil had no reason to be amongst those naming Ned "Little Hertford", being only of similar height. But he scrutinized him no less disconcertingly than if Ned had been looking up at a man of much taller, mightier build.

Ned tried to deflect their conversation by calling to his aid a well-practised theme of his talks with Sir John Thynne. "My sister greatly appreciated that story she heard from you - about English soldiers buying back cannonballs from the Scots at whom they'd fired them, during one of our lord father's wars there!"

"From which experience, tell her that a clear moral was learnt, my lord. Funding should be adequate for fresh supplies of munitions."

"I will tell her, sir," smiled Ned engagingly. "Yet all of England is proud of you for saving money, by disbanding our army soon after this latest -"

"*All* of England?" interrupted Cecil, sounding dubious. A few steps further on, he asked, "Does your lordship also see the Lady Catherine as often as your sister?"

Ned stalled himself from gulping, though inwardly he cursed - fluently - in case this was the death knell of their tranquil interlude. "The lady is my sister's closest friend, sir."

"But don't you also seek her out as specially, when you're at Court?"

"For my sister's sake."

"Come, come, my Lord Hertford! Is there not *goodwill* between you and Lady Catherine?"

"There is no such thing!"

Under the ongoing scrutiny of Cecil's steely-eyed expression, Ned was sure his words of denial were right to protect Catherine's safety. Her pretty face swam approvingly before him. He ached for her now to be his wife infinitely more than at that idyllic outset of his six faithful years of waiting. But he would not, could not, endanger her.

"A pity," observed Cecil. "The lady's alliance with their Good Duke's son would be more popular with *most* of England than that of - others."

Such unexpected openness from Elizabeth's Secretary of all people sounded curious. It did not invite Ned to consider a new initiative of support for his marriage. Instead, it lent substance to the general gossip that Cecil's position had lately become insecure. Ned knew firsthand the swift downfall which changing fortunes under the Tudors had caused various men and women. After he parted company with William Cecil, he faced up to an unpalatable truth: in order to distract unwanted notice away from his beloved and himself, he may have to start paying attention to other ladies of the Court . . .

"Dead?" hissed Elizabeth. "You choose a moment like this to tell me that your wife is dead!"

In the light of an early September day, a steel blade glinted in Robert Dudley's hands as he knelt before the Queen.

From the vantage point of her horse, Rhone Grey, Catherine saw Elizabeth scowl as she seized the knife from him and strode towards the dying stag.

Catherine could not bear to watch Elizabeth perform the final act of slitting the animal's throat. If I were Queen, she thought, my Court would *not* go hunting day after day like this!

She continued to look instead at Robert, who stumbled to his feet, the colour draining from his face. A burst of cheering informed Catherine when the slaughter had been accomplished. Then Elizabeth stormed into view again and was lifted back into her saddle.

Catherine exchanged a baffled glance with Jennie as they heard the Queen snap, "You are now excluded from Court, my lord, while a formal inquest is held."

She rode off, followed by her ladies. A few of them ventured to glance back at Robert Dudley. Elizabeth was usually so familiar and exuberant with him on each hunt, but now he stood, a dejected and isolated figure.

The next day, Elizabeth announced to the whole Court, "We would curb all your rumours about the death of Lady Dudley. The facts are that she sent her servants out of her house two days ago and they returned to find her body at the foot of the stairs. She had broken her neck."

"Poor Lady Dudley," whispered Jennie to Catherine. "It's easy to think she was murdered or committed suicide."

"And she was all alone," sighed Catherine.

On their way to Jennie's sitting-room, they were aware that the Court still buzzed with speculation about the demise of Robert's wife.

"I wish Her Majesty hadn't seemed so casual when she gave us the details of this matter," said Jennie, after she closed the door behind them.

"Callous as well as casual," murmured Catherine.

Jennie came to settle beside her. "Catherine, is there something else amiss?"

"Well, I wish that Helen would restrict her gossip to Lady Dudley."

"What has she been saying?"

"'Tis probably nothing, Jennie. You know how fanciful Helen can be. She reckons to have seen Ned chatting with various ladies recently. But the other day, he seemed to flirt with Sir Peter Mewtas's daughter."

"*I* haven't noticed him with anyone else."

"Neither have I."

"But if we do, let's bring word to each other. All the insults against the Queen and Lord Robert will seem as nought if I ever tax him about any proven infidelity!"

"Please, Jennie, think no more about this. I wouldn't wish for you to risk your health on my behalf."

Again, Jennie's reply was characteristically emphatic. "On the contrary, Catherine, 'twould be a pleasure for which I'm neither too ill nor tender-stomached!"

Later in September, the two friends were both in attendance on Elizabeth when William Cecil was admitted to the Privy Chamber. They had seen her become more appreciative of her Secretary during this month, and now he came to tell her the result of the inquest on Robert's wife.

"The verdict was accidental death, Your Majesty," he said.

Elizabeth appeared more pale and gaunt to Catherine, but she answered him amicably, "I wonder how many of my people will believe this verdict, my Spirit! Yet I will allow Lord Robert back to Court now. Send word to him immediately."

"Yes, Your Majesty. And do you wish the patent to be prepared for Lord Robert's earldom of Leicester, upon his return?"

"Bring it to me when it is ready."

When Cecil left, Elizabeth enthused to her ladies about virginity and single blessedness for the first time in many months. Catherine and Jennie recounted the incident to Ned on his next visit to Court.

"Who knows the workings of her mind!" he shrugged. "It's typical of her to prate on about virginity again when her Eyes, her 'Sweet Robin', is now free to marry her."

"I think, though, that even would-be brides who are amongst her favourites couldn't ask her blessing at this time," said Jennie gravely.

"Not now. Not ever!" added Catherine in despair. She brightened when Ned comforted her in his arms and Jennie reiterated some words from the summer that their love would find a way.

After Robert Dudley came back to Court, Catherine noted that Cecil's long, florid face appeared more sombre. He obeyed his orders promptly, however, to bring the patent for Robert's earldom to the Queen for signature.

Elizabeth snatched the document from him. "Daughter, fetch me my knife from my writing desk," she commanded. Catherine curtseyed and soon returned with the knife. She looked on without expression as the Queen slashed the patent cleanly in two.

"Now, Mr Secretary," declared Elizabeth fiercely, "be assured that I shall keep my throne as Virgin Queen, despite men who would undermine my sovereignty, and my very integrity and ability to rule England."

Cecil's face remained the same as it was when he produced the document. "Your Majesty is a very capable ruler. The people will be pleased that you are now adding good sense to this quality."

"May *your* good sense long continue in my service, my Spirit - although my moods will still sometimes be wild!"

Whatever mood Elizabeth is in, thought Catherine ruefully, she's liable to sting!

The third year of Elizabeth's reign began in November, with her moods veering back to favour the company of her Eyes again. Her ladies of the Privy Chamber even observed her arm in arm with Robert, when she returned by river from a private visit to Baynard's Castle. Kat Ashley's round face flushed and Blanche Parry maintained a stoic silence, while some of the ladies conjectured that Elizabeth had at last wedded him there, before only a handful of witnesses.

Catherine smiled passively as Jennie joined in with their colleagues. The mere mention of a wedding at Baynard's Castle, with its unhappy associations for her, had touched a tender nerve.

She was relieved when Kat's voice shrilled above the chatting, "Kindly stop talking such nonsense! Her Majesty has suffered enough turmoil concerning my Lord Robert. She refuses to make him an earl, so why should she suddenly take him as husband?"

Catherine often viewed the watergate from window-seats inside the palace. And since Ned would be back at Hertford House from another visit to Savernake any day, she consoled herself with picturing his next arrival at Court by this entrance. Although she did watch out for him in reality, she accepted that he might land at the watergate when she was not at a window to see him!

The grey November afternoons purpled into dusk too soon for her liking as the month neared to its end. But in the twilight of the final day, Catherine saw what she had never dreamt of witnessing.

She strained forward at first in her window-seat, stared, blinked and stared again. No, her eyes were not deceiving her. Ned was *leaving* the palace, and strolling away across the deserted gardens towards the watergate.

"Oh, Ned, how could this be?" she gasped, with her

hand discreetly covering her mouth.

Even if she tried to scurry after him for an explanation as darkness gathered, Catherine knew she would not reach him before he took boat to Hertford House. She might also betray their secrecy.

When he was about mid-way along the broad path, he turned to look back at the palace. Catherine's spirit rose in delight, but she noticed that the gardens were no longer deserted. A figure - nay, a *female,* a cloaked and hooded female, was dashing towards him. Towards Ned! Who was she? Mewtas's daughter?

In the fading light, Catherine could not tell, although the girl dropped her cloak on the path and the skirts of her pale gown billowed out.

"My lord, your explanation had better be good," Catherine whispered tearfully.

She discerned that a matronly chaperon moved in Ned's direction more sedately and stooped to pick up the heap of cloak. But beyond this woman and the mystery girl . . . Ned took up a very familiar stance. His arms reached out in front of him! But they were not destined to encircle her and Catherine was faced with the shock that they were about to hold another.

Catherine's tears permitted her sight no more. The darkness, the pale gown and Ned's outstretched arms all blurred into a mist as she turned away. She fled to her chamber, to her pets, before any more of her loved ones left her little world.

An urgent and thunderous knocking sounded on the door of Ned's bedchamber at Hertford House. He paused from his letter to Sir John Thynne about Wolf Hall and commanded, "Enter!" Christopher Barnaby, one of his valets, burst in breathlessly.

"My lord, Lady Jennie has just arrived by river."

"Well, that's no reason to break my door down, man!"

Ned glanced through his window as calmly as he was able, and noted that Jennie had indeed already climbed up his water-stairs. She was approaching uninvited across his garden with two of her servants, as if she was battling into a wind.

The lifelong habit of a sinking feeling overcame him in the first instance. But he decided that as head of the family now, and in his own house, he would no longer tolerate any sermonizing from her. And if she had come about an increase in her allowance, she must be made to understand that was secondary to his projected expenditure on Wolf Hall.

"Show my lady into the parlour," he ordered hastily, as he resumed his letter, "and ensure that she and her servants are offered goodly refreshments."

"Yes, my lord. And what shall I say to my lady about when you will see her?"

"Tell her I will be with her anon," said Ned, poring over what he had already written. He did flinch at the prospect of his adopted new demeanour with Jennie, but waited till Barnaby went off to receive her.

Within minutes, the knocking began as before. This time when he called, "Enter!", the door opened for Jennie to brush past Barnaby into the room.

"I countermanded your orders to Barnaby," she said with a cough.

"Well, sit my lady near the fireside, Barnaby," said Ned. He was exasperated at her ongoing attitude of assault towards him, without any hint of apology. "My lady shouldn't have ventured out."

"But for you, I wouldn't have taken the risk," she retorted, plonking herself in the high-backed, cushioned chair which Ned's servant brought forward for her. "What mean you by -"

"Thank you, Barnaby. And easy on my door!"

The servant bowed, and made his exit, closing the door so feebly that it stayed slightly ajar. Ned went to ascertain that the man was not eavesdropping on them, and having thus satisfied himself, slammed it shut anyway.

He grumpily wished he could achieve the same with his sister's mouth as her complaints started in earnest! Or else that he could grow deaf to her.

"What mean you by . . ." How quickly she reeled off his alleged misdeeds - amongst them, returning from Savernake and hobnobbing at Court without even the courtesy of a message to her, let alone a visit.

"And how *dare* you reduce Catherine to the state of nervous prostration she was in, when I set off for here?"

"Nervous prostration? But I haven't had the blessing of being near her yet."

"No, but Catherine saw you yesterday. In the gardens at Whitehall - about to take someone else in your arms! That much I did glean from her, oppressed as she was by her tears."

Ned stood over her aghast. "And you, *both,* accept as unquestioned fact something which isn't true at all? This will become clear to you when *my* point of view is considered."

"Don't try to evade your wrongdoing through riddles, my lord," snapped Jennie. "Are you accusing Catherine of lying?"

"I love Catherine more than life - and always will," he said passionately. "I wish that she hadn't given my conduct in the garden a meaning it doesn't possess. And as for you, sister, you never thought to credit it to higher motives, did you - oh no!"

"Higher motives?" she scoffed.

"I suppose I'll never convince you. I've felt great distaste for the deception I've been obliged to practise these past three or four months." Finding himself drowned out by a bout of coughing, Ned slouched away from her. He went back disconsolately to the table, which was strewn with his writing materials. "I might not even convince you with this."

He held out his arms towards Jennie. But his hands were clenched, inviting his sister to choose which one contained a gift. She stood up quizzically and tapped his right hand, and when this opened, a ring with a pointed diamond lay in his upturned palm.

"Take this to Catherine," he implored more gently, "and pray her to renew her love for me. But hear me out first, Jennie, for yesterday I was only doing what I've just shown you."

Jennie admired the ring, but continued regarding him reproachfully. "And your gift to that girl?"

"A mere cheap trinket to Frances Mewtas, to ensure her quietness."

"With our perfect accord, Ned, why did you endure this deception without telling us?"

He pressed the ring into her hand, a move which she did not resist. And when they were seated again, he told her of his encounter with William Cecil in the late summer.

"I took fright, I do admit it unashamedly," he added. "I believed if many eyes were on us, if Catherine and I were observed too oft together, we might be prevented from being united forever. So I pretended to woo elsewhere in order to stem general gossip about us."

"My poor Ned," Jennie sympathized at last. "And the Court was soon afterwards fully absorbed by the death of Lady Dudley and all the backwash that has involved."

"Aye," he shrugged, "but the Queen has been an even greater mass of contradictions since then. So I thought better to keep on with my new diversion strategy! When I was at Savernake, I informed our folk there that Elizabeth had inclined again to virginity. They were almost in uproar, Jennie. A story had somehow taken hold amongst them that she'd berated Robert Dudley for being married and assured him such obstacles could be removed. Hadn't Henry VIII rid himself of her mother so as to marry our Aunt Jane?"

"There's no truth, as far as I know, that she said

anything of the kind."

"And no truth in this rumour about her secret wedding at Baynard's Castle, while I was away?"

"None in that either! But every truth in your conclusion that she has become impossible . . ."

Ned half-guessed what Jennie would talk of next. The gold and diamond ring glinted and sparkled while she held it delicately between her finger and thumb for closer study. She ventured airily, "If Catherine dries her tears on receipt of this gift, would my Lord of Hertford obtain from his goldsmith a ring for another occasion?"

"And what other occasion might that be, my lady?" he feigned ignorance.

"A wedding, my lord," she replied. "A secret wedding of your own, in defiance of Elizabeth! It could be here, with your loving sister as your witness."

"If Catherine is willing, Jennie, I wouldn't hesitate to defy Elizabeth now. The sooner, indeed, the better. How else can we be joined?"

"I know not," she said briskly, and she beamed at him as he handed her a velvet pouch into which she placed the diamond ring for Catherine. "Well, I'll go back to Court now. There's work to be done! And unlike someone not too far from me, *I* will send a written message if the Lady Catherine wishes to be reconciled to you."

Ned helped Jennie most courteously down to his water-stairs and into the boat to return her to Whitehall. He was happy for her to be forceful when she wasn't with him, especially if her efforts were on his behalf!

Once he was back in his bedchamber, Ned completed his missive to Sir John. It speeded the hour or so before Jennie's maid came with his sister's promised message. Catherine had accepted his ring of assurance. She loved him so much!

"Does my Lord Earl wish me to take an answer to my lady?" the maid enquired.

"Yes! Yes, girl. Meg, isn't it?"

"Aye, my lord," she confirmed.

He scribbled feverishly to Jennie that his infinite love for Catherine so overwhelmed him, he must see her at once. After half an hour, Meg was back with yet another note to say that Catherine would see him with Jennie in the private sitting-room.

Ned smiled to himself while he unlocked a drawer in a small, wooden cabinet on the table.

"No need to visit the goldsmith at all, Jennie!" he mused, as he lifted a wedding ring out of the narrow drawer and slipped it into the purse at his belt. The wedding ring he had commissioned many months ago! He set off straightaway to show this to Catherine in proof of his true love.

## CHAPTER 11

# *Knot of Secret Might*

"Sweet Catherine, will you still marry me?"

"Oh yes, my lord. But I know not when."

"As soon as possible. Then there'll be no more misunderstanding between us."

"But what about Elizabeth?"

"We could marry the next time she takes journey from here."

Catherine smiled tentatively at the handsome young Earl kneeling before her in Jennie's presence. She saw in his deep-set grey eyes the same warmth of expression of the boy who had fallen in love with her when she was a lonely girl of fourteen. For a few moments, though, she settled back in her comfortable chair to smile her contentment at his diamond ring on her finger.

Ned addressed her again from his position of worship, "Beloved, I hope that with this you will have no more doubts."

Her face lit up in happy agreement and then she realized that he was referring to another gift. He put his clenched hands towards her and she chose the left one. This unfolded, and in his palm lay the nuptial band of gold destined for her.

Catherine took it gently from him, hoping that it was one of the 'posy' wedding rings she had so dreamed of, with two or three linked compartments and a little love motto engraved inside. Ned arose and indicated to her the secret spring which opened the gold not into two parts, or three, but *five.* Five, which she soon discovered were needed for the touching inscriptions placed in them. Her lilting voice murmured with delight in reading:

*'As circles five, by art compressed, show but one ring in sight,*
*So trust uniteth faithful minds, with knot of secret might,*
*Whose force to break (but greedy Death) no wight possesseth power,*
*As time and sequels well shall prove. My ring can say no more.'*

"So trust uniteth faithful minds with knot of secret might," she repeated. "Are these lines of your own composing, Ned?"

He nodded, and finally she said, "My lord, I am well content to marry you the next time Elizabeth journeys from here. Jennie and I will find an excuse to stay behind. Let the consequences be what they may."

Jennie looked proudly at the wedding ring. "Whatever the consequences, Catherine, I'm glad to have brought you and Ned back together," she enthused. "Queen Mary served you well, after all, in repealing those old laws, which made it treason to marry a member of the blood royal without our Sovereign's consent!"

"Aye, we have that to thank her for," Ned agreed.

He gave the 'circles five', still fully expanded, into Jennie's temporary safekeeping, and raised Catherine into his embrace. And with no ceremony beyond their kisses and joining of hands, they formally pledged themselves to each other.

Jennie carefully closed the wedding ring. "Now, let's consider how the day for this can be brought about," she mused. "Perhaps when the Queen goes hunting again . . ." With an impish smile, she planted a kiss on her brother - and then on her new sister.

One early December day, Elizabeth chose to set aside all matters of state. She would have a private sojourn of recreation at her palace in Greenwich and the excitement of some hunting at Eltham. She decided to leave Whitehall the following morning, around daybreak.

The Queen still thoroughly enjoyed issuing her absolute, non-negotiable orders to the multifarious members of her household and this time was no exception. But hark! Who was that suffering a coughing fit? It came from amongst the ladies of her Privy Chamber whom she had instructed to overhaul their riding outfits. Who else could it be but Jennie Seymour?

Alas, poor soul, thought Elizabeth. We shall enquire how she fares on the morrow before permitting her to accompany us.

By six o'clock in the morning, the Queen was further advertised of no improvement in Jennie's distressful ailment. The coughing was now interspersed with her complaints of feeling shaky and dizzy. As if this wasn't irksome enough, the general noises of sympathy for Jennie's symptoms were amplified to include also another lady's painful indisposition: *toothache.*

Elizabeth imagined a gnawing twinge of pain before demanding to know, "What's going on? Hast been eating too many sweetmeats, daughter?"

Catherine winced as she pressed slender fingers into a cheek, which was slightly swollen beneath the kerchief tied up around her face. "I . . . fear so, Your Majesty."

"Well, let that be a lesson to you," said Elizabeth sharply. She was miffed that her quelling look could make little impact on the piteous pair. The visage of Jennie had all but disappeared behind her handkerchief and that of Catherine appeared so woebegone, with downcast eyes!

"Hm, we do not care to think that either of you might *pretend* an indisposition," Elizabeth sounded a further warning note.

Although this remark attracted renewed evidence to the contrary while she continued appraising them, she could not feel sorry for Catherine Grey. Rather, she regretted that she had been unable to maintain a close check on Catherine for several months. Her spy system had been in such disarray while her Eyes and her Spirit were at variance with each other, and even with herself, during the turmoil of recent memory. Such disarray, that some work was still required to rebuild its efficiency.

"Get you gone from us back to your bedchambers, you unhealthy pair!" she concluded at last. "Yes, you are both excused from coming with us this time and we trust to find you better upon our return."

"Most humble thanks, Your Majesty," acknowledged Catherine, still with lowered eyes.

And Jennie emerged intermittently from behind her handkerchief to cough and splutter. "Most humble thanks . . . but we can only *try* to get better, without the beams of Your Majesty's smile to bless this place."

Catherine nodded. "Can only try . . ." Then she pressed her fingers to her cheek again and winced.

Such annoyingly dainty fingers, seethed Elizabeth inwardly. But she soon felt mollified by the attitude of abject disappointment from both Jennie and Catherine. "Off now to your rest," she said.

As they helped each other away, Elizabeth flattered herself about the reason why Jennie Seymour bothered to show such friendship for Catherine Grey. The latter had a *vague* Tudor resemblance to their Sovereign Lady, though she was not, of course, as beautiful.

Catherine was pleased that she had behaved with dignity before Elizabeth, in spite of her discomfort. A small piece of gauze, which was padding out her cheek, had begun to cause some chafing inside her mouth. She removed this material when she reached Jennie's chamber and her eyes registered satisfaction in the looking-glass that her cheek had returned to its usual size. As soon as Elizabeth left for Greenwich, Catherine untied the kerchief from around her face.

Jennie watched her regally and shook a reprimanding

finger at her, "Let that be a lesson . . ."

"Shh! Or else I shall laugh so much I won't be able to stop," whispered Catherine. "What with *her* teeth being so discoloured now through eating many sweetmeats."

Jennie nudged Catherine with her elbow. "I was afraid your kerchief would fall off when you nodded, 'Can only try'!"

"So was I! That's why I put my hand back up to my cheek and made sure it didn't happen."

"But now we've each staged a miraculous recovery with no effort at all," smiled Jennie. Their gowns swished while they danced in a joyous, momentary circle together. "Let's swap this kerchief for your new finery."

Catherine eagerly let go of the kerchief to Jennie. Her heart quickened as she received in return a coif made of white linen, which could only be worn by a married woman. She smoothed its triangular shape and went back at once to Jennie's mirror.

"'Tis an odd name my new finery has - a froze-paste!" murmured Catherine. The small hands of her reflection held it up to cover the front of her hair - the part normally left showing by her headdress. "I think I'll wear this all the way back here, just for today. But I promise it'll be safely in my pocket, afore Helen has any chance to see it."

"Good!"

Jennie pressed the bride's shoulder affectionately and bustled away. She returned a moment later with one of her own spare cloaks and wrapped it around Catherine's shoulders.

"'Tis eight o'clock," she added. "And no time for fond farewells to your pets."

"Apart from Poll, they've already been well-hugged. And even she gave me a peck!"

"Of all the errands and tasks we've given to our servants this morn," laughed Jennie, "I'm sure Helen will be fully occupied with the feathered and furry in her charge, when she tries to clean that raucous parrot's cage."

Before Catherine could reciprocate with helping Jennie to put on her cloak, the heavy garment was in place. Within minutes, the two friends stole out of the palace, through the orchard and down the river steps leading from there - thus avoiding the main watergate.

Their route to Westminster then lay along the pebbly mud-bank of the Thames, for the tide was out. As best they could, they sped along in the dismal light, cheerfully lifting their cloaks and skirts while their feet sloshed through the squelchy mud.

Catherine mused with a chuckle that her wedding should have been a grand occasion of ceremony and feasting. But the idea of this suddenly seemed unimportant when she took in her sense of pleasure at outwitting Elizabeth so far. She was not merely bidding for happiness against the blight of another domineering woman overshadowing her life, but belatedly hitting back at Mother Dragon for all the years of harsh treatment.

My children will have a kind mother, whether sons or daughters! she thought happily.

Jennie steered Catherine hurriedly past a group of snowy-plumaged swans, towards the green-slimed stairs to ascend to Hertford House. And on reaching them safely, without incident, Catherine's mind was entirely on her future . . .

Ned's pocket watch ticked on to half-past eight and he was in deep throes of suspense as to whether they would carry their purpose through.

He had heard from his sister yesterday evening of the Queen going early this day to Greenwich and so he had risen from his comfortable bed about three hours ago. Meanwhile, he had given orders in line with what her plotter's brain had suggested.

Now here he was, waiting frantically in his bedchamber. Food and drink were arranged on the table and cupboard.

The house was virtually empty of servants, whom he'd dispersed on various errands. Only two remained behind, and they were under strict instructions to stay below stairs until midday . . . And, yes, he had remembered to lay out the two pairs of embroidered slippers which Jennie had also sent in a package, via her servant-messenger Glynne.

But the absence of Jennie and Catherine to change into these, from muddy outer footwear, precluded all activity except pacing his room and traipsing towards the mullioned window to check for any sign of them. In the course of this, his mind had traced Catherine's direct line of descent from King Edward III two whole centuries before. As a result, Ned realized that in each generation except one - her mother's - the ancestress had been a woman of beauty. Such a beguiling discovery made him the more impatient to be wedded to the twenty year old girl, who had inherited her Tudor grandmother's good looks.

Ned sighed as he went to peer through the leaded panes yet again. His hopes seemed, as of habit, to have ebbed low like the morning tide.

Suddenly he grinned, and used Jennie's chiding tone of voice, "Oh, ye of little faith!"

He was glad that he could watch his sister and Catherine making their way along the bank, rather than them seeing him in the state of agitation he had reached. How fine he felt to be quite his relaxed, youthful self once more as he raced down to let them in!

"God give you good morning, my ladies," he greeted, breezily. He glimpsed beyond them someone replacing a doffed cap, much askew. Barnaby was running down the river stairs which they had so very recently come up.

Jennie shrugged as she bid Ned, "Good morning." But her face assumed a look of mock superiority: servants who snooped? They only belonged to people without her genius for organizing!

Catherine greeted him more diplomatically and also murmured, "Ne'er mind. We saw no-one else all the way from the palace."

"Hm, trust our luck to be spotted right outside our destination!"

Ned felt riled by that remark, riled enough to retort, "I ordered that sluggard to go to the City over an hour since, there to await me till this afternoon. He'll regret his disobedience."

He deemed further justification to be necessary, however, after Jennie led him with Catherine up to his chamber. The precision of his preparations was surely apparent: he rattled off the details of where he had sent other servants, some also to the City, some into the country. He pointed out the refreshments - sweetmeats, banqueting meats, wine . . . and, of course, here were their embroidered slippers to wear.

Catherine's eyes shone. She removed her cloak and began to change into her slippers at once, as if Hertford House had always been her London home too. Whereas Jennie . . . Ned *groaned* beneath his breath, for Jennie did not follow Catherine's example.

"I was at first impressed by your efficiency," she observed, "apart from Barnaby, of course. But alas, this good impression has not lasted."

"What fault do you find now?"

"Haven't you . . . *forgotten* something, my lord?"

"Forgotten something!"

He was aware suddenly of Catherine stifling a tinkle of laughter.

"Where's the priest?" asked Jennie.

"The priest," Ned repeated, woodenly.

"Well, even the most secretive of secret weddings must needs have one!"

"Jennie, didn't you say that *you* would arrange to have a minister standing by? Before you spoke to me so scornfully, I was about to ask you why he hasn't appeared yet."

Brother and sister eyed each other. Then laughter won through from all of them at the truly makeshift nature of their planning for this morning.

Jennie hurried off brightly in search of a priest. But she still muttered a parting tease at him, "Must I undertake everything!"

"Well, not quite *everything,* sister," he quipped, as the chamber door closed behind her.

Left alone with Catherine, Ned sensed their passionate love immediately pulsate through them. There would be nothing makeshift about the consummation of their marriage! Her exquisite young face looked up at him, lovelier in its radiance than even in the early idyll of their courtship. He regretted that he had been distracted into staring so hard at Jennie, while Catherine had removed her headdress to let her glorious, Tudor red-gold hair flow loose to her waist, in readiness for the ceremony.

He kissed her hair, her smooth and tender cheeks and neck as he caught her to him. Catherine's rosebud lips responded with a completeness such as his own in releasing some pent-up longing. In the rapture of holding her so close in his own house, Ned turned her petite form slightly so that while they continued to embrace, he lifted her in his arms and onto the bed.

Smiling at him from the coverlet, Catherine drew him swiftly down beside her. He kissed her again, caressing the soft swell of her breasts, and she stirred so their bodies could press together as near as their layers of clothing would allow. He loved her the more, because he knew she did so in total trust that his desperate manhood would not pierce her maidenhead till they were married. Never in his own heart and mind would he be guilty of the sin and crime of deflowering a lady of the blood royal.

They were content therefore to cling to each other thus - "lying in wait for the priest", as Ned murmured to amuse her.

"And 'tis much more to my taste, this sort of 'lying in wait', than the thought of Spaniards lying in wait to abduct me for Philip's son!"

"There'll be no danger of that soon, beloved."

She rubbed the tip of her nose gently against his before they next kissed. A distant cough alerted them that Jennie was back.

They tactfully left the bed, straightening clothes and coverlet speedily. The pocket watch, such a useful diversionary item when anyone was coming towards them, re-emerged for consultation.

"Nine of the clock. My, my!" noted Ned.

Jennie hastened into the room, wheezing that here was a clergyman who had known exile. Catherine went to her side, to help her at last take off her cloak, while Ned quickly welcomed him in. He was a man of average height, with a fairish complexion and auburn beard. His long, black gown had a white collar, turned down indeed in the style of ministers who had come home from Germany, at the start of Elizabeth's reign.

In after years, with the benefit of hindsight, Ned knew that they should have asked the man his name. But on the day itself, no-one thought to pose or answer questions except those relating to the wedding vows. Speed was much more vital to the occasion, if their knot of secret might was to be a *fait accompli*.

Whoever he was, wherever he haled from, his proceedings were certainly in harmony with this chief requirement. It was with obliging speed that he borrowed Jennie's proffered copy of the Book of Common Prayer and conducted the ceremony from it, with them all standing near the mullioned window. With speed also he blessed the ring of 'circles five' before its smooth placing on Catherine's finger. And lastly, he pronounced the pair to be husband and wife - from this day forward.

With positive alacrity he received his fee of ten pounds from Jennie, made a peremptory bow and courteously took his leave, guided by her out of the house.

"Ten whole pounds?" grimaced Ned, still hand in hand with Catherine when Jennie returned to them forthwith.

"That's more than most clergy earn in a year!"

"And it has all come out of my allowance," she informed him.

"I'll reimburse you. Now if you don't mind . . ."

"There's something else," she went on.

"Yes? What?"

"I gave him my prayer book in token of his help. Only, I've realized too late, that I was still pressing a four-leaf clover from last summer inside it for you, Catherine. Sorry!"

"Don't worry, Jennie. 'Twould seem that the clover has brought me the good luck I needed," said Catherine dreamily.

"Now if you . . ." Ned began again.

"Mm, all this hurrying and scurrying about has made me so hungry," said Jennie.

She started helping herself to food - lots of it. She poured a glass of wine and raised this to them. "A goodly repast, brother. Come partake, you two! Catherine?"

Catherine politely declined, for the time being. The extent of Jennie's intended eating seemed strange to Ned, when she who had done so much to bring this situation about, was now stalling him and Catherine from their hunger of a different kind.

"Ned?" asked his sister, offering him some meat.

He too declined, then motioned with his head and eyes impatiently towards the door. Jennie continued chewing, looked at him, looked at the door - and the bed, and furrowed her brow. She put a half-bitten morsel back on the plate she held and pointed to herself with her right hand, "Me?"

He beamed and nodded. And motioned head and eyes towards the door once more.

She stuffed the morsel into her mouth and picked up the glass of wine. Carrying this and her food-laden plate, Jennie flounced out through the door which Ned happily opened for her. "I'll be in the parlour," she rejoindered.

"Best not to tarry too long, else Mistress Ashley might make inconvenient enquiries if Catherine and I are not back at Court for the midday meal."

Best not to tarry? After shutting the door on Jennie, Ned did not tarry at all in starting to undress! He took off his neck ruff and threw it from him. The top buttons fronting his doublet were next undone and Catherine brought her fingertips deftly to his aid with the lower ones. Fumble, fumble, was how he, in contrast, attempted to entice her upper gown away from her shoulders. But she eluded him and with her flair for making the smallest of movements seem enthralling, she beckoned him to the greater warmth by the fireside.

There she kissed him and he was divested of his doublet, charmingly and without the fuss of struggling out of it himself. He would probably have flung this garment from him too - still containing his pocket watch! Although they had neither dressed nor undressed before without the assistance of servants in such elaborate palaver, they exhilarated in their notable achievement of helping each other with the untying of awkward laces and points, so that their clothes peeled away. Eventually, he was down to his shirt and she to her chemise.

As he kissed her deeply, Ned loosened the draw-string at Catherine's neckline and her low-cut chemise fell away from her also. And while she stepped lithely out of it, his view of her was obscured for an instant as he yanked his shirt over his head . . .

She was all he had dreamed she would be.

"Beautiful, beautiful," he whispered, as their arms encircled each other, bare flesh at last touching bare flesh.

Would his passion ever be more intense than it was now to make their twosome into one flesh? In a haze of tenderness, he lifted her to the bed as before, but next, their bodies pressed together where they were destined to be: beneath the covers. Catherine cried out softly as he first entered her, and subsequently with joy when they became truly one and gave themselves totally to each other.

"Eleven o'clock, you two," called Jennie, knocking on the bedchamber door. "Time to be a-stirring!"

"Thank you, Jennie," replied Ned. "And no need to sound like your skirts are almost tripping you."

"Tsk! I shall be back in a quarter of an hour, if not before."

Catherine, resting her head on Ned's shoulder, nestled closer to him in the curled-up, comfortable position they had now begun to adopt after *each* time they made love. "A minute or two here yet," she murmured.

His arms tightened around her. "I wish we could stay here for ever. My Lady Countess!"

He kissed her brow as she smiled at that. "Me too," she confided, pertly. "As Jennie might say, though, this has in various ways been such a *momentous* morning . . ."

"So it has! And no doubt another piece of raillery from her will be about our building a love-nest in Savernake Forest - meaning all my work on Wolf Hall."

However, when Jennie reimposed her presence on them as promised, her immediate raillery derived inspiration a-plenty from another predictable source.

"Who'd ever believe it - your getting yourselves so neatly garbed all on your own!" she exclaimed. "I expected to come in and find you still as dishevelled as the bed."

"Well, I trust that your first good impression will last this time," hinted Ned genially.

Catherine also looked enquiringly towards Jennie, but went on adding the finishing touches to her attire. The froze-paste was duly positioned in place, concealing all the front of her hair. Her headdress, with its long, flowing veil, then quickly hid the rest of the Tudor red-gold.

A further smile, meanwhile, played about Catherine's lips. Not just because she contemplated the achievements of the morning, but also that she saw Jennie using thumb and forefinger literally to 'hold her tongue'.

"Surely my favourite sister isn't speechless!" Ned cajoled.

"Hm, anyone could be forgiven for thinking that you've acted in collusion with several other accomplices, apart from me, if only to help you dress."

Catherine sped to hug her. "Jennie, when my lord and I helped each other with that task . . . it was part of all of us helping each other, in this lovely time of escape from the formality in our lives."

"Dearest Catherine, ever the one to show that your quality comes from much more than your birth and title," she teased mildly. "My first good impression of you has always lasted."

"And, Jennie - *you* have done more for us than several accomplices might have managed," said Ned. "So thank you, my sister. Thank you a thousand times!"

He too hugged Jennie. And his next words came her way soon after he released her. "Here's recompense and more for the money you paid to the priest."

Jennie pretended to reel under the weight of it while she thanked him for the bag of coins which he gave her. They laughed together, and again she seemed curiously stuck for something to say.

"I . . . I'll tidy up the bed for you," she offered.

"Nay, that'll be dealt with afore Barnaby's return," Ned assured her, "though I've a good mind to crumple it up further and set him to the work of tidying it!"

Amid more laughter, Ned poured glasses of wine for all of them. "This will warm you for your journey back to Court," he said. "As for me, I've worked up such an appetite now, I'm eating *my* midday meal in here, with what food Jennie has left me!"

They raised their glasses and drank their wine. Two pairs of muddy shoes again encased the ladies' feet and cloaks were donned. Water was rippling over the river stairs when Ned escorted Catherine and Jennie back down there. He hailed a passing boat for them and its water-man heeded his call. Yet as he prepared to help Catherine, after Jennie into the boat, his reluctance to relinquish hold of her overwhelmed her too. The intensity of their farewell kiss would have lasted longer but for the on-rush of noon.

"We'll be in time for dinner," said Jennie reassuringly as the boat set off. Catherine nodded in reply.

They had earlier agreed to slip back only to Jennie's chamber to make themselves ready for the midday meal. Catherine was already missing her new husband's company. And in the absence of Elizabeth from Court, she felt suddenly tempted to keep wearing the froze-paste during the meal. The self-abasement so long required of her in her girlhood, to conciliate Mother Dragon, was over. Catherine would never willingly repeat its depths 'from this day forward' in her adult life to appease Elizabeth.

"What's Helen prattling on about now?" said Ned, when he visited Catherine and Jennie the next morning. "She's just asked me if I think the Queen of Scots will return from France to Scotland!"

Catherine embraced him and smiled. "Well, it's all very timely for us, Ned! On the very morn of our secret knot, the news broke here that the Queen of Scots has been widowed."

"Never in my wildest dreams could I have envisaged such a distraction to aid you," added Jennie. "The speculation was so rife yesterday about the Queen of Scots that Catherine wore her froze-paste to dinner virtually unnoticed!"

"But surely someone noticed," gasped Ned. "What about Kat Ashley?"

Catherine linked her arm through his, melting him with her look of innocence. "Kat Ashley did notice, Ned, but she was busy tutting at this new outbreak of gossip. She seemed pleased when Jennie told her that I'd dared to wear the froze-paste as a jest, to cheer our spirits because we couldn't go to Greenwich with Elizabeth."

"You each deserve a halo for fooling her," he smiled. "Even more so, of course, for fooling Elizabeth yesterday morning!"

"Years of practice with Helen stood us in good stead," Jennie chuckled. "Fear not, my lord, Helen had no chance to see the froze-paste. Catherine removed it here in my chamber straight after the meal."

"I trust Helen was too busy anyway, tittle-tattling about the Queen of Scots."

"I think she had more or less planned out the entire future of my Scottish cousin!" laughed Catherine.

"Let her continue to do so," said Ned. "I'd rather talk about *our* future. I have here, beloved, a deed written in my own hand this day, signed and sealed . . ."

He sat down and beamed complacently at the avid audience which gathered on either side of his chair, to read the document he opened. *Fully* did he intend to bask in their expected expressions of approval!

"Well, this does put things on firmer ground for you, Catherine!" said Jennie, after studying its details. "A thousand pounds a year from Seymour lands if he leaves you widowed."

"Er - not that I wish to be bereft of life just yet."

Catherine flung her arms around him, kissed him and pressed her cheek against his. "Or I, ever to be bereft of you . . ."

"Of course not! God forbid, brother," sniffed Jennie, and bent to kiss his brow. "'Tis well done. A generous settlement."

That sounded better, he thought. Much more akin to what the ears liked to hear!

Ned folded the deed and gave it to Catherine. He revelled in another show of affection from her and a gracious word of thanks, before she went away briefly to store it safe in her coffer with other treasured belongings.

"You know this settlement means we must tell my brother Henry about our marriage," he said softly, upon her return, "as he is at present my heir."

"As long as 'tis only Henry we tell," smiled Jennie. "Probably best if you invite him to Hertford House. And I'll come there with Catherine and talk to him while you two - um, have company."

Ned hoped that she would let them have company in her chamber before many more minutes passed. "Your support will certainly strengthen what *I* shall say to Henry," he replied. "But will the Queen allow you to bring Catherine with you to see me?"

Jennie began to cough and Catherine went straight to her, with warmth and compassion. Ned's question was partially answered for him by her response to his sister. He realized that in their great and enduring friendship, formed soon after Catherine's loss of her own sister Jane, she and Jennie had rarely been apart for long. And this was clearly enhanced by their close kinship now because of the knot of secret might.

Jennie wiped below a watery eye with her handkerchief - her other eye seeming *maybe,* just maybe, to wink at Catherine.

"How can the Queen refuse me the comfort of a true friend, for my health's sake?" she said to him hoarsely. "If I request such, wherever I go?"

She exchanged a smile with Catherine as she handed her the chamber key. "Come and join me in the little nook when he's gone," she whispered.

Ned brimmed with good humour at Jennie's departure there. He had long accepted that her actions on their behalf stemmed more from her attachment to Catherine than to himself or Seymour family ambition. Besides, joint rapture awaited, once he was alone with Catherine . . . behind a locked door . . . And so he found! They were enthralled with each other. Enthralled, whether they lay together on Jennie's coverlet, their outer clothing removed, or naked in bed at Hertford House.

Yet his heart seemed pierced with feelings which were bitter-sweet. How could he spend a whole night with Catherine, without danger of discovery?

As Christmas approached, Elizabeth allowed Catherine to accompany Jennie to Hertford House. And brother Henry Seymour was so amenable to news of the marriage that Jennie prevailed upon him to be an extra carrier of messages between the newly-wedded pair, if required.

The festivities at Court were a whole world of improvement for them from the Christmas before, when Catherine had been at Sheen after her mother's death and any likelihood of their marriage had slowed from snail's pace to complete standstill. As usual, in the company of no matter how many other people, they communicated their love with their eyes. They did so even in the most cursory of glances, during the banquets and masques. And when they danced together, their hands touched and their feet stepped in complete harmony with each other as well as the music.

By the end of the Twelve Days of Christmas, they had been married for a month and Ned decided to mark this with a special present for Catherine. So the first time they were alone in his bedchamber at Hertford House in the New Year of 1561, he sat her on his lap and rocked her merrily like she was a child. She clung to him, laughing as she managed to maintain her balance.

"If we can be so happy, Ned," she began, "despite -"

"Happy, despite the long shadow of Elizabeth haunting us?"

"Yes."

"Aye, sweetheart. Our lives will be in seventh heaven without that! But in the meantime," he smiled, taking from his pocket a tiny book bound in red velvet. "For you."

She gasped when she first held the book, its square

shape hardly bigger than the palm of her hand. "But this is one of your most cherished possessions."

She opened the front cover to reveal the inscription written to Ned by his father 'from the Tower the day before my death'.

"Keep it safe, won't you, with the Bible your Jane sent to her 'good sister Catherine' from that place."

Catherine nodded compliantly and kissed him. Soon, they were abed and she took the lead in their love-making. While they lay in each other's arms afterwards, she confided, "I *may* be carrying another Seymour gift."

"Another gift? D'you mean . . ."

"I know not yet! But I have missed my monthly course."

"Is it not perhaps late, sweetheart?"

" Tis most unusual - for it to be late or missed . . . but let's await what happens next month, shall we?"

"Aye, we'll do that," he agreed, and kissed her.

Ned thought back to the time when Catherine had joked about the mighty tree called the Great-Bellied Oak in Savernake and he had bantered in retaliation that he would render her great-bellied. Could it be that the much-maligned "Little Hertford" had fulfilled his promise to his beloved after only a month of secret marriage, while his virile taunter Robert Dudley remained childless despite a ten-year marriage and had prospect of none by the Queen?

He thanked God that Catherine seemed so well. Months would elapse yet before she might face the rigours of childbirth. But at night, without her in bed beside him, his natural concerns for her welfare combined with other anxieties. What if this missing of her monthly course was the start of infrequent ones like her cousin Elizabeth's, or else of a phantom pregnancy such as that suffered by Queen Mary Tudor?

Although Ned knew such fears about Catherine were truly unfounded, they still persisted at times when she was not with him. He was even immersed in these thoughts when he went along his much-trodden way to Jennie's chamber at Whitehall in mid-January. His nerves were fairly under control and he paid little heed to the stiff rustle of a gown and several purposeful steps in his wake, particularly as he sensed their stride-length belonged to a female taller than himself.

It was only when a shrill voice called out to him that the situation changed.

"My Lord of Hertford, why do you scrape your feet? We were never aware that you walked in such manner before."

Ned did not flinch as he whirled round, but the gist of words once spoken to him by Sir John Thynne, outside Wolf Hall, flooded through him: *"I have seen men quail before her at more paces away from her than the length of your Long Gallery . . ."*

"Your Majesty." He bowed low and sank to his knees.

"Well?"

"I . . . suppose 'tis these ill-fitting shoes," he excused himself. "Haven't broken them in yet."

"Hm, we do perceive you to be unsettled in your mind - not your feet, my lord," she retorted.

Ned gulped inwardly, and allowed Sir John to his imaginary rescue again. "I was merely mulling over some building matters to do with my house at Wolf Hall, Your Majesty."

"Ha! And no doubt you will eventually acquire much experience of such matters, thanks to your keen neighbour at Longleat."

Ned felt unnerved by her homing in on the drift of his mind. He wondered how much longer he would have the mettle to conceal the knot of secret might from her, if she didn't send him on his way soon.

Elizabeth's grilling of him was a mild preamble, however, to the impact of her next statements.

"But if these building matters are so worrisome to you, we have an alternative which would enable you to widen your experience of them."

"An alternative?"

"Observe the architecture in France and Italy, my lord."

"Forgive me, madam, I do not understand."

"Another neighbour of yours, Mr Secretary Cecil, intends to send his unruly son Thomas abroad, to complete his education," she said. "The lad needs an older travelling companion to be a steadying influence on him. And 'tis our firm belief, as also our express desire, my Lord Hertford, that you shall be most suited to the task."

The Queen's commanding voice and whole demeanour told Ned that there was no right of appeal against her decision.

"How soon before -"

"March or April, and firstly you will go to Paris. So rise to your scraping feet now! Put all your building matters and other affairs into such order as is needful in the meantime."

She swept away as he scrambled up from the floor and bowed. Even so, he did not dare to let his feet scrape any more for the rest of his walk to Jennie's chamber.

## CHAPTER 12

# *Comings and Goings*

Snowdrops were gradually being replaced in bloom by the flowers of early spring near Comfit's grave. Ned watched from a respectful distance as Catherine bent to place a bunch of them on the small mound of earth and patted it.

Let them scoff - those who would say, " 'Tis only an animal!" he thought. Catherine had had more love from this pet dog than from all of the Grey family combined. And Ned was glad that Jennie had persuaded him to let Comfit be laid to rest in his garden at Hertford House - by the river, which had been such an element in the little spaniel's life.

He noted Helen standing tearfully beside Catherine and reflected that to her, as well the rest of the outside world, his action was a favour for his sister on her closest friend's behalf. That interpretation would have to suffice for the foreseeable future, all due to the ongoing whims of their Sovereign. But it was exasperating that his wife couldn't use Seymour property for the burial of a faithful pet if she so chose. His wife, who may be almost three months pregnant with their child!

Ned became aware of Jennie's eyes glancing from Catherine to him, while Helen sobbed, "Dear Lady Catherine, 'tis a shame all this upset over Comfit has made you unwell! Let's hope you get better now."

"Thank you, Helen. I try to feel comforted that we were both with her when she died."

"An' with her mistress caressin' her head and cradling that old left paw."

"Aye, it reached out to me in farewell!"

Seeing again Catherine's sorrow as she stepped away from the grave, but her solace too at coming back towards Jennie and then himself, Ned wondered what else but love was of any true worth.

She still trembled when they settled with Jennie to talk more freely in the parlour, so he clasped her hands to his lips. He kissed each of the slender fingers, the palms, the backs of her hands, even the pulse throbbing at her wrists.

"I can't hide my state of health from my women servants," she sighed. "Old Mistress Cousins is adamant that my courses have stopped and I've been sick in the mornings because of my distress over Comfit."

"I wish we could establish for certain that you're with child," said Ned. "Then I could stay in England with you, beloved. I'd no longer be thought an exemplary companion for Cecil's wayward son!"

"But if Catherine seeks any midwife's opinion on this," said Jennie, "she must disclose about your knot of secret might, perhaps needlessly just yet."

"You know that I shall be at Savernake soon, for the last time for maybe a year or more," he reminded them. "I trust you'll send me a message, Jennie, if there is any news."

"Of course. And you won't tarry at Savernake, will you, if you hear from us that Catherine is definitely a mother-to-be?"

"I shall leave post-haste."

"Not abroad post-haste, I hope, but to Court - to ask for the Queen's clemency."

"Jennie, give me credit just for once! I've already said I wish to remain in England."

"My apologies, Ned."

"And mine too. I should've said I'll *return* from Savernake. So content yourselves it would be as promised. Let's not part soon in anything less than our perfect accord."

"Of that, my heavy heart would be glad, you two," said Catherine.

Jennie smiled at her. "I thought I was running out of things to organize for you!"

"There'll be renewed scope for organizing, if I'm sent abroad," Ned offered, though sharing Catherine's clear sense of dejection at that prospect. "And if I learn in France or Italy of our impending parenthood, sweetheart, then likewise neither walls nor waters would separate us for long."

"Talking of walls," said Jennie, "must the work on Wolf Hall be halted completely during any absence of yours overseas?"

"Aye, for this spring and summer at least."

"I feel as disappointed as both of you."

"Well, the old house needs more than the repairs of the past two summers to reverse the years of neglect," Ned grimaced.

Jennie's preceding remark, so close to his heart, caused him to sympathize more readily when a bout of coughing beset her a few moments later.

Catherine went anxiously to her. "'Tis another bad one," she murmured, meeting Ned's gaze. As the coughing left Jennie struggling for breath, he had a worrying impression of her, wilting like the snowdrops.

He watched Catherine with tenderness in her efforts to comfort his suffering sister. She still looked to be as petite as ever. He realized reluctantly that they would perhaps only know more surely of her own state of health if her stomach started to swell. And that may not happen till the early summer - a month, or maybe even two months after Elizabeth ordered him to France . . .

*Martinsell Hill, Wiltshire*

The bulging girth of Savernake's Great-Bellied Oak was a topic of ribald repartee amongst Ned's forest officials when they rode past it with him towards Wolf Hall. Their talk and laughter still concerned Elizabeth's unmarried state, and probably even more coarsely when he was not present to restrain them. He felt sure that if any of them had ever experienced at close hand the unerring way she could home in on matters as yet unknown to her, they too would limit their derision of her to private comments in the company of trusted confidantes.

Ned did not discourage his men from channelling their jests onto the subject of pot-bellied oaks, of which Savernake had several. Neither did he seek to participate in banter as to which ones most resembled certain of his officials who had reached middle life. His whole being was too sombre, because he was here to follow Elizabeth's command and put his estates and finances "in such order as was needful" before he sailed from England next month.

"We 'ears Lord Robert Dudley be a pot-belly now'days, m'lud," ventured Richard Weeks.

"Bet 'e don't look pregnant - like missus says about I!" chuckled John Berwick.

"My friends, you have heard wrongly about my Lord Robert," Ned informed them politely. "So there's an end to this, please."

"Very good, m'lud."

He darted bland smiles around at them in general acknowledgement, being careful not to convey that their words had inadvertently touched raw nerves with him.

A mass of important decisions demanded Ned's attention during the following days, and making them seemed an uphill struggle to him. A struggle steeper than the scarp slope of Martinsell, which always drew him towards it whenever he saw the hill from the western edge of his Forest.

Yet step by step, needful order was set in place. He assessed the crumbling buildings of all his inheritance, in addition to Wolf Hall, and noted the most urgent repairs to be done upon his return. He appointed his gentleman-usher, Anthony Penne, to take charge of his financial affairs for the period of his absence - and his other gentleman-usher, Fortescue, to supervise the servants forming his retinue in France. Ned also arranged for Esturmy to be stabled with other Seymour horses at Hanworth.

When he visited Longleat, he asked Sir John Thynne to inspect the condition of Wolf Hall, once he knew the date of his homecoming. And amongst other tasks, Ned decided that some refurbishment of his ancestors' tombs at Easton Royal would begin with that of his grandfather, Sir John Seymour, when spare revenue allowed.

Until the day after the spring equinox, Ned found hardly a free moment to experience his usual sheer enjoyment of his local surroundings. On this Friday, he rode on Esturmy from Wolf Hall to Easton through sun-flecked woodland and open space. And Savernake at last intoxicated him again, with such a release of pent-up enthusiasm that he could give his attention to little else.

He was accompanied by his youngest servant, Tom Goddard, who came from a long-established family of Seymour tenants at Easton. The boy was here to bid his kinsfolk goodbye for some while, as he would be with Ned in France. Along the old village lane which was also part of the Forest boundary, they stopped outside the cottage of Tom's parents.

"Spend as much of today as you wish with them," Ned instructed cheerily, as Tom dismounted, "and I'll see you back at Ulfall tonight."

"Back at Ulfall, m'lord. And thank you."

Ned had intended to return there himself once his business at Easton was concluded. But his own words stayed with him: "Spend as much of today as you wish . . ."

He needed no further persuasion! Other things may encroach upon him before he was ready, and there'd be precious few chances of an exhilarating ride with Esturmy in this area for many a month.

And so, instead of turning eastwards to Burbage and then Wolf Hall, they veered northwards and westwards close to the Savernake boundary. Across streams, through woods and undergrowth, and at full gallop over open stretches of pasture until they reached Martinsell. The grassy slopes edging up from Pewsey Vale beckoned Ned as usual to the curious, tufted fir trees within the ramparts girding its summit, and up he encouraged Esturmy in acceptance of its invitation. The hill seemed to him to have such character unique to itself, as if a lingering aura still attracted him from the olden times when it had been part of Savernake.

The wind rushed past them once they were over its crest and on the gentler dip slope, as they picked up speed again. It then became a ride to remember along the undulating ground between Oare Hill, Huish Hill and the forest in miniature of West Woods. They slowed after a while to skirt around steep gradients back east to Martinsell. And when they regained the summit there, Ned feasted his eyes on a clear view of Savernake. He leant forward to pat his horse as they stopped.

"How I shall miss you, 'Sturmy, and my lovely Catherine, and all of this," he sighed.

This stop astride Esturmy was partly reminiscent of that time when he had seen Savernake from the Ridgeway almost three years before. But then the lump in his throat had been for the first of many homecomings. Whereas now . . .

He sighed again, though with a half-smile. For in the buffeting wind on Martinsell and overlooking Savernake, he knew he would long carry fond memories of the freedom of their ride - whatever circumstances may predominate the next time he was home in Wiltshire.

He soon broadened into a fuller smile when he reflected on a way of deterring potential poachers. He would wink at his officials fuelling rumours that his return may be imminent any day! As for the latest Court rumours about Elizabeth and Robert Dudley, though, these had no meaning here and Ned was glad to be so well away from them.

The few miles back to Wolf Hall were mainly through his Forest, the most pleasant end there could possibly have been to his outing. When Esturmy cantered into the courtyard of Wolf Hall, Ned had the horse's sugar-work reward already to hand and he himself felt much better prepared to face *anything.* He was only mildly surprised to find his brother Henry there, all travel-stained and agitated, and drinking from a stirrup cup handed to him by Barnaby.

"Greetings, brother," Ned called from the saddle. And after dismounting and rewarding Esturmy, he added, "Has Lady Jennie sent you?"

Henry Seymour nodded uncomfortably and sipped at his drink. A sense of excitement overcame Ned, while he gave a final pat to Esturmy and handed him to the care of his groom.

"Barnaby - more refreshments!"

"Yes, my lord."

Ned went to stand close beside Henry. "Is there news of Lady Catherine?" he asked in a low voice.

"Ned . . . my lord . . . I'm sorry, but I bring bad tidings."

Henry took Ned by the arm, in an attempt to lead him indoors. But Ned immediately shrugged him off. "Bad tidings? Then tell me *now* what they are. I'll read our sister's message inside."

"There is no message from her."

"None at all? What *is* all this?"

"I'm afraid that my lady, our dear sister Jennie, died suddenly on Wednesday."

"Jennie? Oh, my God!" said Ned, feeling so stunned that he leant heavily against a wall and put his head back, closing his eyes. "H-how - an accident?"

"Nay, 'twas her illness, worse than any of us knew,"

Henry commiserated. "The Queen has ordered a state funeral for her - next Tuesday, Ned, and we must leave here first thing in the morning if we're to be there in time. I've arranged for frequent changes of horses for us all the way to Westminster."

"'Twas well done," replied Ned. He had half-readied himself to return all of a sudden to Court, but never with his sister dead. "And - Lady Catherine? How has she taken this?"

"She . . . was distraught, poor lady, when I spoke with her. But she sends you her love," whispered Henry. "And all the Court is full of condolence. For 'twas Lady Catherine who found Jennie . . ."

"Catherine f-found her?" A tremor shook Ned from head to toe. This time he accepted his brother helping him indoors.

Barnaby brought their refreshments and Ned sent him away again, before sitting and slumping over his drink while he learnt more details from Henry.

"Lady Catherine told me that Wednesday morning began like many others," Henry explained. "She and Jennie decided to enjoy some time together in Jennie's chamber after their early duties attending the Queen. But her knock on our sister's door wasn't answered and she entered to the shock of seeing Jennie . . . already snatched away by death."

"I must comfort Catherine as soon as I can," Ned asserted.

"And I will do my best with regard to messages between you."

Ned thanked his brother, but the difficulties of messages and meetings between himself and Catherine, without Jennie's assistance, were only beginning to dawn. She had been so reliable and he had taken her too much for granted.

"We'll raise a monument for Jennie in Westminster Abbey," he said, partly to atone for his sense of remorse. The money for restoring tombs at Easton would therefore be subject to longer delay. "The finest monument in tribute to her."

While Henry Seymour approved wholeheartedly of this, Ned wondered to himself whether Elizabeth would have determined on a state funeral if she had known of Jennie's part in the knot of secret might.

"Wherever she is, let's hope Jennie will find great joy," Ned added, earnestly. "Free of illness and strife."

"Amen to that."

For her two closest companions left behind to mourn her, however, the path to obtaining royal mercy over their marriage would have proved so much smoother with Jennie's vital support.

Later, when Ned had retired for the night, his sorrow and the undoubted severity of Catherine's seemed to merge all into one.

"Oh, Jennie, Jennie," he wept, "there was indeed much scope for organizing yet . . ."

The Queen and all the Court allowed Catherine a public show of mourning at Jennie's funeral in Westminster Abbey. But this time, unlike at her mother's funeral, Catherine's expression of grief was genuine. Tears streamed down her face as she watched her friend's coffin being lowered into the cold vaults in St Edmund's Chapel.

The cruel truth of her sister Jane's words, penned in the Tower, came through her thoughts: *'Trust not that the tenderness of your age shall lengthen your life, for as soon as God will, goeth the young as the old.'*

At least Jane had been able to send a final farewell letter before her death, which Catherine could still read sometimes. With Jennie, however, there had been no goodbye, no fatal outcome even contemplated, despite her ill-health.

Catherine knew that Ned's grief at the loss of his sister was also very great. She had managed to speak to him briefly, amongst the openly familiar expressions of deepest sympathy between herself and various Seymours before the ceremony. And as a consequence, Ned had had the chance to arrange to visit her the next day, ostensibly to ask if she could offer employment to one or two of Jennie's servants in her household. His eyes had told Catherine how much he longed to hold her in his arms. Through her tears now, she imagined them comforting and supporting each other, while the only witness to their secret marriage was interred.

The following morning marked the first full week since Jennie's death. Catherine's eyes began to water again as Mistress Cousins helped her to dress in her chamber at Whitehall.

"Hold still, please, my lady."

"Sorry, Mistress Cousins. I was reflecting on this time last week. It seems so strange without Lady Jennie being in here, or nearby in her own chamber."

" 'Twill take time, Lady Catherine, for the grieving to go. Well now - I wish my hands were young and nimble-fingered like yours, instead o' these creaky old joints struggling to fasten your sleeves and bodice!"

"I thought my dear Mistress Cousins wasn't feeling well," replied Catherine. "You should rest for today."

"Nay! Hot possets'll help my aches and pains, Lady Catherine. I'm already doing lighter duties nowadays."

Catherine looked warmly at the former nurse who had given her many years of loyal service. "I insist that you rest today," she said. "Helen can attend me when I talk with Lord Hertford."

Inwardly, she resigned herself to this prospect, as Mistress Cousins complied. But she feared for the old woman's health.

When Helen found out about the change of plan for attending Catherine with Ned, her plump face lit up. To Catherine, the maid's forehead seemed to move as if she were wearing an invisible pair of antennae.

"If it pleases you, Lady Catherine," she enthused, "I'll leave the pets with Meg Woodford, 'cos o' Lord Nedward's comin'."

"Meg Woodford?"

"She's *ever* so good with them, Lady Catherine. Helping me with 'em makes her feel less forlorn, as she's taken Lady Jennie's loss as bitter to heart as any."

"And Lady Jennie . . . I believe, was fondest of Meg," sighed Catherine.

"Yes, she was, wasn't she? And just think of poor Lord Nedward," Helen whined, "havin' to find places for his sister's servants afore he goes o'er the sea."

"Nothing more of this now, Helen, please, until I've spoken with my lord!"

Despite her words, Catherine was thinking of Ned much more than Helen could ever guess. She was sure that she caught frequent echoes from his mind about their love and also his worries over her, and his Wiltshire home and Forest. But when she walked beside him later, along the corridor outside her chamber, she could only mention the last two of these subjects and his extra responsibility now for Jennie's household. Helen strode eagerly in their wake, yet could not see their faces conveying to each other the compelling attraction between them.

"My lady mother is demanding that she has two of Jennie's maids at Hanworth," Ned groaned, "but that still leaves one to place elsewhere."

"What is to become of Meg, my lord?"

"I understand that all three maids would happily serve the Lady Catherine, but Meg is especially keen to do so."

Catherine heard an indrawn breath as Helen anticipated her reply.

"Very well, my lord," she murmured. "I'll welcome Meg into my household for Lady Jennie's sake - providing that you approve."

Ned smiled his agreement. "I'm sure you won't regret employing Meg."

They heard Helen utter a sigh of relief. Catherine glanced at Ned, afraid that this brief time together must end soon, unless they could find other topics of conversation in Helen's presence.

"My Lady Catherine," said Ned gently, "as we are both so grief-stricken over Jennie, would you tarry with me yet a little while and let us reminisce about her?"

Catherine nodded, and they went into a small alcove nearby that contained a window-seat. They each had favourite times with Jennie to recall, once they settled there. But they were very careful which ones they remembered out aloud, because of Helen standing so close at a panelled corner of the alcove!

Eventually, Ned pretended to consult his pocket watch and said reassuringly to Catherine, "I'll call by again in a day or two, to see how Meg is getting on."

Helen turned her head to look away from them towards some chattering sounds from down the corridor.

"I think we have an idea already, my lord, how Meg is getting on!" said Catherine, half-smiling.

"Lucy, you naughty girl, not staying with t'others!" Helen remonstrated. "Come here at once."

It was Catherine, however, who coaxed her white-whiskered marmoset monkey down from the ledge above some wall-panelling. Lucy's tail clung round Catherine's back as she carried her pet to Helen. "'Tis best for you to take Lucy back to Meg now, thank you, Helen. My Lord Hertford and I have just about finished our talk."

"As you wish, Lady Catherine."

"Oh, and tell Meg that all is well."

Helen curtseyed and clumped back down the corridor, prattling at the marmoset.

Catherine at last gave her loving looks towards Ned free reign and felt comforted as always by the wonderment in his eyes. They may only have minutes alone together. They must make the most of these!

The thought of her chamber beckoned them invitingly

and when they reached it unseen, the door was closed swiftly. Ned's arms encircled her and he kissed away her tears as she clung to him. They caressed each other, whispered endearments, kissed again - and then again even more passionately.

*"Lady Catherine!"*

Catherine and Ned fell apart and saw Helen looking at them, mouth agape.

The room seemed to whirl about as Catherine motioned to her maid to shut the door and she heard Helen gabble, "I came back to take the cover off Poll's cage an' knocked, but no-one answered. So I came straight in an' . . . Oho, Lady Catherine! I ne'er thought to find you in here . . . with him . . . on yer own . . ."

"Helen, there's something we shall have to tell you," Catherine rallied herself to say. She exchanged a glance with Ned and he nodded.

"What is it, Lady Catherine?"

"Before I tell you, I'd like you to swear to secrecy. Absolute secrecy that you'll seal your lips about this."

"Absolute secrecy? I promise!" said Helen, crossing her heart. "What could it be?"

"Well . . . Lord Hertford, he . . ."

"Yes?"

"He is my husband."

Helen gasped, and Catherine sighed inwardly that an accident of fate had caused her to tell a compulsive gossip their great secret. But her next thoughts counselled her not to worry about the danger of any tale-telling at the moment. She noted that Helen was too shaken to talk!

"Would you keep watch for us for a few minutes, Helen?" asked Ned.

"K-keep watch, aye, Lord Nedward," the maid croaked breathlessly. She bobbed a hasty curtsey and shambled wordlessly back outside.

Two days later, when Ned came by as promised, Catherine observed Helen curtsey to him hastily again and shuffle, tongue-tied, from the chamber to keep watch.

"She does that to me whenever she sees me nowadays," he frowned. "Curtseys abysmally and moves off in the opposite direction like an overloaded old washerwoman!"

"She is not herself at present," Catherine excused her gently. "I've been afraid to praise Meg too amply, in case of making Helen jealous."

"Well, let's praise Meg now," he beamed. "Didn't I assure my Lady Catherine that she would be excellent if placed with my sister's dearest friend?"

"Excellent? She is indeed, my Lord Earl."

"Even so, 'tis best not to confide our secret to Meg or anyone else for the time being!"

Catherine agreed wholeheartedly. "But enough of that now," she murmured, and kissed him.

"Beloved," he whispered, as he lifted her tenderly on to the bed which awaited them.

Early in April, Helen came to see Catherine one morning, rushing into her chamber in a highly flustered state.

"Oh, Lady Catherine," she began, and then the torrent burst forth from her, "I'se had some letter sayin' as my mother's ill unto death in the country an' prayin' me to go see 'er. But I've not 'nuff money an' how can I leave you at a time like this an' all these little creatures, bless 'em, an' Meg only just started? An' yet if I don't go from Court today, she might be dead afore I get there . . ."

"You must set off to her today, of course you must!"

"But the money - I've not got -"

"Helen, I'll pay you your wages that are owing and give you more for your journey."

"Oh, Lady Catherine, thank you," she sniffed. "Always did say you're the kindest of hearts. The best mistress to me there could ever have been."

"Hush now!"

Catherine hugged Helen goodbye later the same day.

She anticipated her maid's return ere long, but during that evening she began to suspect that this situation might be otherwise.

"Lady Catherine," said Mistress Cousins, looking more than a little puzzled, "why Helen Leigh has taken all her things with her for this short visit to her mother's, I ne'er can guess!"

"Taken all her things? I can't make any sense of that either, Mistress Cousins," replied Catherine.

She decided that she would tell Ned about Helen's strange departure and seek his opinion at their next stolen meeting. They had already arranged when they were last together in her chamber that they would meet soon in the gardens at Greenwich on Easter Day.

The Court moved from Whitehall downstream to Greenwich during Holy Week. Catherine knew by then that Ned had received his passport documents. She had been in attendance on Elizabeth when the dreaded royal command was formally handed to William Cecil for his son and Ned to travel to Paris after Easter.

The soft magic of the springtime formed a happier background than either her mood or Ned's on that Sunday. They wandered together along hedge-lined paths, screened by interlaced branches and foliage.

"Where's Helen?" he asked. "I thought she'd be keeping watch for us again."

Catherine recounted to him the details of Helen going from Court several days before.

Ned drew her arm comfortingly through his. "Helen put fresh flowers on Comfit's grave after she left you," he mused. "One of my servants saw her. I did wonder why she hadn't brought a message from my sweet Catherine."

"I would have sent one if I had known. Yet I am glad that she showed her love for Comfit in this way."

"How I long for the time when *you* can place flowers on Comfit's grave whenever you wish," Ned sighed. "But even if Helen had been a lookout for us now, our present meeting is what William Cecil would call 'dissolute and refractory conduct' - the very thing he expects me to stop young Thomas Cecil from doing in France!"

Catherine saw the hope in his face that an open avowal of their marriage might yet keep him in England. As Jennie had rightly hinted, though, during the last hours Ned had seen his sister alive, they could imperil themselves unnecessarily if her condition proved to be unfounded.

"*Does* our blood mingle gently?" he asked, lightly touching her stomach.

"Would that I were sure, Ned, although my monthly courses have not resumed."

"And you still think this may be the effect of bereavement?"

"One of bereavement's many effects on me. I feel so weepy and listless much of the time, Ned. My daily life has changed too rapidly."

"You're still very slender, Catherine."

"If only I could confide in someone experienced in matters of pregnancy," she murmured, "a woman who is also reliable! But sometimes I recall how much even the doctors and midwives were deceived, when Queen Mary seemed to quicken with child . . ."

Ned reiterated his promise to return to her at once if she needed to send for him urgently. Catherine warmed to his attempt to console them both with their unity of spirit, if not of body during the coming months.

"My foreign journey seems inevitable," he added, "but no-one ever went on their travels more reluctantly!"

"Will you write to me soon?" she pleaded.

"I'll write before I reach Paris." His arms tightened round her as her head came to rest on his shoulder. "My letters both to you and Henry will be brought by Jennie's old servant, Glynne. He's still a Seymour servant and my beloved can trust him to despatch all her own letters to me."

"God keep both of us safe, Ned."

"So many preparations to finalize yet," he said ruefully. "Tedious farewells to various kinsfolk, servants to be kept busy with sundry tasks . . ." He gave her a full purse of money. "Use some of this to pay for a replacement maid if Helen doesn't come back."

Their lips met in a lingering and tearful goodbye. "I shall cherish these moments alone with you here, Catherine, for a long time," Ned whispered. He released her gently after their final kiss and away he went with his loving thoughts of her.

Ned honoured his promise to write at the earliest opportunity, by putting pen to paper at Rouen. His companion, Thomas Cecil, was already half-drunk and spending freely despite his father's numerous instructions to the contrary.

The letter was sealed and wished bon voyage back across the narrow sea to Catherine. Only at the end of April, however, did Ned hear news of her. He and Thomas were dining in Paris with the English ambassador to France, Sir Nicholas Throckmorton, and were about to be presented by him before the widowed Queen of Scots.

"As for our other heiress to the throne, the Lady Catherine," reported Sir Nicholas, "I am told that my Lord of Pembroke seeks to remarry her to his son. But whatever is the cause, pretty Catherine will have none of him and the Queen is entered into a great misliking with her!"

## CHAPTER 13

# *Summer Progress*

The Court was still at Greenwich. Catherine paused from the letter she was composing at the table in her chamber and looked through what she had written so far:

> *To my loving husband,*
>
> *It was a great joy to me, my dearest lord, to hear Mr Secretary Cecil tell Her Majesty that you are safe. I would ask how matters stand between us now that you have been gone a whole month. I have sent many letters to you through Glynne, so please, please will you write to me at last? I love and miss you very much.*

Catherine fought back her tears. Why hadn't Ned replied? She had already told him in previous letters how upsetting had been the attempt to remarry her to Pembroke's son. *And* about the taunts she had received from her former father-in-law after she rejected this scheme. Catherine felt so drained now, even though Elizabeth had not pressurized her into any change of mind, being much against marriage herself. Yet she feared that the loathing between her and Elizabeth increased each day.

Mother Dragon seems to live on ever stronger in the Queen, she thought despondently. But as she resumed the letter, Catherine decided not to dwell on further turmoil:

> *My lord, I pray as always that you are well. I would be much comforted to hear from you that this is so, and to learn more of your life in France. Let us hope for your return this summer before I come of age!*

Catherine added other words of affection before she kissed and sealed the letter. A knock at the door made her move to conceal it in her coffer-chest, but first she had to shoo two of her marmosets off the carved wooden lid.

"Who is it?" she called, as if she did not know from a recent message to her, which remained on the table.

"Sir William's here, Lady Catherine," answered Mistress Cousins. "Come to talk about sewing of your liv'ry."

"*Suing* of the lady's livery," corrected Cecil's voice tonelessly. "To do with her lands, Mistress Cousins, not stitchery!"

"Beg pardon, sir. Lady Catherine . . ."

"Oh, just a moment." By now, the letter to Ned was out of sight and the two pets allowed back to their earlier place. She returned to the table and sat down. "Yes, come in now."

Catherine was demurely perusing Cecil's note when he followed Mistress Cousins in. She acknowledged him courteously.

"Lady Catherine," he bowed, quite unruffled by the attentions of a few of her dogs snapping at his feet.

Mistress Cousins clapped her hands at them, but Catherine persuaded them quietly to settle down. She hoped that a little delay here and there would enable her to adjust to her oncoming dealings with Cecil.

He placed before her a document to sign. She stared at the words of its legal language, and stared again. "I'm afraid I cannot understand this," she murmured, but his explanations did little to help. She gathered that it was some kind of entreaty to Elizabeth for the revenues of certain Crown lands to come to her when she reached twenty-one years of age. And that rankled with the girl who on her secret wedding day, five months before, had determined never willingly to abase herself to please her royal cousin.

"Sign it here at the bottom, my Lady Catherine," said Cecil patiently, "and then I'll be gone from you the sooner!"

"Yes, Sir William." As she scrawled her name where he indicated, she asked him casually, "And how fares your son in Paris?"

She was trying to gain news of Ned indirectly, but instead saw Cecil's grey-bearded face shed all its calm.

"He is a spending sot and chases girls in place of studying!" he declared angrily.

"I-I'm sorry to hear that."

"Nay, 'twas not unappreciated that you asked, my lady," he replied. He spoke more like his usual matter-of-fact way, but his face remained somewhat careworn. "And as for the Earl of Hertford . . ."

"Yes?"

"The Queen accepted the amount of time you were in his company when he visited Lady Jennie," said Cecil kindly. "However, if such familiarity has continued since his sister's death, 'twould be well to admit this to Her Majesty."

"But . . . the Earl is with your son, isn't he?"

"Aye, and his own good conduct hasn't influenced my son yet. The very task my Lord of Hertford was sent to do!" Cecil picked up the document from Catherine, muttering his lack of hope for the future with young men such as these in the world. And then he bowed and went away.

"Boys will be boys!" chirped Mistress Cousins.

Catherine made no comment. She could not bring herself to tell anything to Elizabeth, as Cecil had quietly suggested. In her loneliness, she had troubles enough already.

"My Lord Robert gave me this for Your Majesty," whispered Blanche Parry, handing her royal mistress a note. "From Dr Dee."

"Thank you, Blanche," Elizabeth smiled, and opened it up to reveal its strange and secret symbols. She was heart-warmed as usual to read his 'EveR' at the beginning and '007' at the end.

"But he tells us nothing new!" she added.

The single circle, dash and brackets, representing Mars, warned of a danger to her throne. And his mention that Jupiter, alias Mr Secretary Cecil, would acquaint her in more detail, also made entire sense to her. For the danger surely emanated from Mary Queen of Scots, soon to leave France for her northern realm. And William Cecil, being very worried about his son's behaviour in Paris, was probably fully conversant - through ambassador Throckmorton - with this young rival Mary's movements and plans.

"There again, my Secret Eyes generally has some puzzle for me to solve . . ."

"So he does, Your Majesty. Shall I destroy the note, unless you've further need of it?"

The note was returned to Blanche at once. "Destroy it, do, Blanche! And please bring my Spirit to me. This seems a good opportunity to clear the backlog of paperwork he's been plaguing me about!"

Elizabeth's Eyes and Spirit were still much at odds with each other, but she tolerated that more easily nowadays. Their respective spy networks had recovered from the disarray of the previous year and were competing instead to root out information of considerable use to her.

Blanche arrived back shortly with Cecil. He carried in both arms all the documents for Elizabeth's attention, but made no offer of any news.

"Sir Spirit," she said, "has your face become longer, as this pile of work has grown?"

"Not at all, Your Majesty." He met her regal glance, unperturbed while he arranged the papers on her desk.

"What is the cause therefore? That son of yours, still pursuing his pleasures in Paris?"

Elizabeth suppressed one of her wry smiles, as his high forehead creased. Parental anxiety! She encouraged him to have his latest, exasperated say, so that he could revert the sooner to his mostly expressionless, efficient self.

"He *still* has not attended to his studies, Your Majesty. Nor to his prayers morning and night, as I instructed him. My son and heir is borrowing money from all quarters. He's even stolen some from his tutor's strongbox, to pay for his pleasures! And he ignores all requests to write to my lady wife."

"'Tis not unusual for the ties between stepmother and stepson or daughter to be strained," Elizabeth cut in.

"No, indeed 'tis not," Cecil agreed, steely eyes gazing at her with an equally knowing look. He delved then into the documents and fished out several items. "Besides my son's tutor and ambassador Throckmorton reporting to me regularly about him, Your Majesty, I set some of my spies in France to do the same. And in the process, these pieces of correspondence have also come to light."

He laid them carefully in front of her and she leafed through them, as she thought, for a preliminary survey.

"God's death!" her voice rang out curtly. "Already married? How *dare* that featherheaded little goose so imperil our throne and the security of our realm with . . . a *Seymour.*"

Outwardly, Cecil appeared to be self-controlled again, but a similar outrage invaded Elizabeth now. Her forewarnings from Dr John Dee usually prepared her well for the stark reality of a threat. But this one had not forearmed her enough against the anger which tensed her in a seemingly iron grip, as she read of the strongly expressed affection between Catherine and Ned.

"One of your 'troublesome, fond matters' here, Mr Secretary, of the greatest magnitude!" she snapped. "And what dubious methods did you use to obtain these?"

"Bribery, Your Majesty."

"Bribery! Of whom?"

"Of one Glynne, a servant of the Seymours, once with your admired Lady Jennie."

"Pay him well! 'Twould seem that Jennie Seymour played more than music for others. And you, William

Cecil, aren't you and your friends also partisans of Catherine?"

"I am a partisan of my country and reigning monarch, Your Majesty. Should these letters now be re-sealed and sent on to the lady and young Hertford?"

"Not yet. There may be more to intercept through Glynne. We shall bide our time. Even though Ned Seymour is a lily-livered milksop, he's still a product of that ambitious brood!"

"Carnal marriages," said Cecil ruefully, "they may start off happily, but nearly always end in trouble."

Elizabeth was in no mood to brook the criticism this remark implied about Robert's only marriage. But Cecil gave her another knowing look, watching her more thoughtfully than before. And this quelled a tongue-lashing from her.

"My son Thomas is the product I am left with of mine, Your Majesty!" he added.

Her anger subsided briefly in her commiseration with him, before resurging again. "This union of Catherine and Hertford is no love-match, though. It is grounded in bloated ambition, a far greater danger to us."

"'Tis certainly bold presumption for a subject -"

"A Seymour!"

"Quite so - for a Seymour to mate himself with a royal lady, without Your Majesty's consent. But 'tis no longer treasonous."

Elizabeth scowled, as Cecil gathered up the private correspondence of Catherine and Ned out of her immediate sight. The queenly signature was then flourished imperiously on various letters.

"What's this?" she suddenly demanded.

"Something else from ambassador Throckmorton, Your Majesty."

"My Spirit, that is *painfully* obvious! So he asks safe passage home for the Queen of Scots, does he? Through *our* peaceful England."

"Merely a -"

"Which Queen is his loyalty with - his Sovereign Lady, or *her?*"

"Merely a request, Your Majesty. In the interests of friendship between England and Scotland."

This was too much - the second danger to her throne today, even if it was the one she had half-anticipated!

"Permission refused," she shrilled, and flung the safe-conduct request from her.

Cecil retrieved it calmly. "Shall I return to complete the rest of these papers when Your Majesty's temper has cooled?"

"Yes. Get you gone from us!"

He bowed and as he departed, he observed drily, "With respect, Your Majesty, 'tis not only your Spirit who tends to overreact. There is a certain grim consolation in that."

Thunderclap after thunderclap ended a spell of good weather early in June. The midday sky over London became darkened like a night-time pall and was only lit up by flashes of lightning amid torrents of rain and hail.

"Come, we shall watch the storm!" Elizabeth commanded all her ladies after dinner.

They followed her to one of the windowed galleries looking towards the city from Greenwich Palace. Several ladies trembled in fear that a fire-ball of lightning might strike them at any minute. In the darkness, Catherine fleetingly rested a hand on her stomach, as if to soothe the little entity now kicking inside her. She dared not give any hint of the sudden discomfort such movements caused.

"Let us hope there is no weather like this on our summer progress, daughter," Elizabeth called to Catherine.

"Progress, Your Majesty?" she replied, aware of many eyes observing her instead of the storm.

"Yes, and we shall require your presence with us."

Catherine bowed her head in apparent submission,

despite realizing how arduous the progress would be. And not only that, it would make her attempts to communicate with Ned well-nigh impossible.

She looked up, however, when she heard various gasps. A column of smoke rose in the distance across the river Thames. "I think that is St Paul's ablaze, Your Majesty!" said Catherine breathlessly.

Elizabeth glared at her so sharply in the eerie light that Catherine wished at first she had said nothing. She wished also that she had never known the lie of the land around that part of London near old Pembroke's home at Baynard's Castle.

"Mistress Blanche and I believe Lady Catherine is right about St Paul's, Your Majesty," said Kat Ashley. "Might some of your courtiers take to the boats and go to help subdue the flames?"

"Each to take his own bucket, no doubt!" Elizabeth rounded on them.

They laughed nervously, but appeared relieved when the Queen decided, "Very well. Tell any men who wish to help our citizens of London fight the flames that they may do so. Any, except Lord Robert - we would have him safe to accompany us too on our progress, Kat."

Some disapproving murmurs came from Kat as she and Blanche went off to obey this latest order. Catherine assumed that these grumbles were out of Elizabeth's earshot, for they attracted no response.

Even people in her favour can't reason with Elizabeth, thought Catherine. So what chance do I have with her, unaided?

A shocked Court learnt later of the total destruction of the spire and roof of St Paul's. But Catherine's thoughts continued to centre mostly on her own personal anxieties.

On the following evening in her chamber, she sought comfort as she often did, by taking out from her coffer chest the deed of gift which Ned wrote for her soon after their wedding. She reflected sorrowfully that it was her only proof of their marriage if he had now forsaken her.

Catherine also removed another item - the latest letter she had written to Ned. 'I am with child,' her words began, and then implored him to come back to her urgently, reminding him of his promise not to tarry from her.

"Should I send this and risk him still not replying?" she whispered, sobbing. "Or should I even brave showing the deed to the Queen on my own, like her Spirit hinted? If Ned keeps his promise, we can face Elizabeth together."

Catherine paced to and fro, her pregnancy making her move less smoothly and gracefully than in former times. She feared she could not put off telling Elizabeth about the baby indefinitely . . . but it needn't be this very evening!

For the time being, both the deed and the letter were carefully returned to the coffer. Catherine then lifted out the purse of money Ned had given her before his departure. She sighed, for the amount was an expression of his generosity. And after the fervour he had shown at their loving farewell, his lack of response to all her letters was completely baffling to her.

She considered that some of this money must soon be used to pay for new maidservants unless Helen reappeared. Meg had already mentioned that Jennie's maids serving at Hanworth were unhappy there.

Amber settled at her feet and at last brought a smile to Catherine, a smile of endearment. She put the money away and bent to stroke her now oldest pet.

"I'll miss you, Amber, and all these other little scamps while I'm on the Queen's progress," she murmured wistfully. "I must leave you all with Meg . . ."

The idea then occurred to her that Beth Isham might perhaps be brought from Hanworth to help Meg with the pets. Jennie's other maid, Joan Page, could assist Mistress Cousins during the rigours of the progress.

Next time Henry Seymour is at Court, I'll ask him about them coming to me, Catherine mused. It's a chance to find out from someone else how Ned is and whether Henry has received letters from him!

She sent a verbal request through Glynne the following day for Lord Henry to see her about Beth and Joan joining her household. Soon afterwards, a vigorous knock sounded on her chamber door.

"I was newly at Court and came here at once when Glynne gave me Lady Catherine's message," Henry Seymour explained, as Mistress Cousins opened the door.

The old woman chaperoned Catherine while she spoke to him pleasantly, but also formally, in the corridor outside.

"Did Glynne acquaint you fully with my request, my lord?"

"Yes, and I foresee no difficulties. The two maids will be much happier with you, Lady Catherine, than with my lady mother."

Catherine was about to make a more hesitant enquiry, when he added in a low voice, "I shall write to Ned about this too, out of courtesy."

"Have . . . *you* heard from him?"

"Why yes." Henry's voice then sank to a whisper. "Haven't you?"

He looked stunned as Catherine shook her head. "I've even wondered," she murmured, "if through no fault of Glynne's, something has gone wrong with the system of sending letters."

"I can't understand at all why you've received nothing, Catherine. Ned mentioned a letter he was enclosing for you with mine, the last time he wrote. But there was no enclosure, so I assumed he'd sent it to you separately."

"Please, when you write to him, could you tell him that it never came. Nor have any of his other letters reached me."

Catherine forced a slight smile when he nodded and winked at her in the same way as Jennie used to do.

"Good!" said Henry, resuming a clearer tone as he looked round briefly at Mistress Cousins. "Beth Isham and Joan Page will begin their duties with my Lady Catherine within the week."

"Thank you, my lord."

A little more heartened, Catherine shortly made another request of a Seymour. She sealed her letter to Ned, the letter telling him about their baby. . .

And as usual, she entrusted her message into the hands of Glynne.

Catherine steadied Rhone Grey in the long, slow cavalcade through Epping Forest and patted her horse to a halt. She wondered if this was like Savernake. How she wished she were there instead!

The Court had already been entertained at the country mansions of Theobalds, Wanstead and Loughton, and was now travelling further away from London into Essex.

News spread backwards that another wagon had overturned far in front of the Queen and her retinue, so bringing everyone to a standstill again.

"Crammed too full!" grumbled Bess of Hardwick. "If aught of *mine* is lost or damaged, there'll be all hell let loose."

Catherine murmured politely as always to this one-time lady-in-waiting of her mother's.

If only Ned was here by now! It was early July, and there had been plenty of time for him to receive her last letter and act upon her pleading to return. Catherine knew that when he landed in England, he would soon catch up with her on the tortuous progress. She looked out for him each day - but each day from different places.

The heat made all the moving about seem worse to her. It had also added to the discomfort of unfamiliar and overcrowded sleeping quarters at each overnight stop. She supposed that there would be little improvement in the palace of Havering-atte-Bower, their present destination.

"Run-down old pile," was Bess's ominous description of it. "Shaped like a cross gone wrong. Badly wrong!"

Catherine swallowed hesitantly at the prospect of staying in such a place. Bess was probably right, for she was building-mad like Sir John Thynne and had even loaned him one of her master craftsmen to work on Longleat.

Catherine's own connection with the lady was that of godmother to Bess's favourite daughter, Elizabeth Cavendish, so she took the chance to enquire, "I trust my goddaughter is well. She must have grown taller since I last saw her!"

"She's well enough, m'Lady Catherine."

The subject was then evidently closed from Bess's point of view. Talk of cupolas and crow-stepped gables, gilded weather-vanes, red brick, rose brick and so on, flowed more excitedly from her. Echoes of Ned's architectural conversations with Sir John suddenly stood Catherine in good stead for nodding and murmuring appropriately at Bess. At least it helped to pass the time until the procession jolted into motion along the bumpy road again. Bess had always been good company with people who agreed with her!

When they eventually reached Havering, Catherine's servants fussed around her. Mistress Cousins combed the travel dust from her hair, but assigned Joan Page to shake and brush it from her riding habit.

"Too much for m'creaky old joints," laughed Mistress Cousins, "but I ne'er thought I'd see the task done by a Book Page!"

Catherine smiled too at Joan, who had insisted on keeping Jennie's nickname of 'Book' for her. "Dearest Jennie loved her books - all of them!" murmured Catherine.

Mistress Cousins helped her into another gown. "Hm, I could've sworn I let this out enough afore we left Greenwich," she clucked. "Mind, it suits you to put on some weight, Lady Catherine. Shows perhaps you're getting over your grieving for Lady Jennie, and for Comfit too."

"Oh, yes . . . perhaps."

Until Ned came to face Elizabeth with her, Catherine had not the heart to confide in another female servant about her secret love-match and her increasingly obvious condition.

Periodic attendance on Elizabeth while the Court was at Havering seemed ever more debilitating for Catherine, however. Like other royal residences, it had its Presence Chamber and Privy Chamber, but both were as dingy as the rest of the rambling old palace. She found it very dispiriting, though she dreaded uprooting again. The next stop on the itinerary was to be at Pirgo, the home of her uncle, Lord John Grey, who had encouraged the parental severity towards her sister Jane and herself. This was not the best time to evoke memories of their childhood!

Even so, she felt an almost child-like sense of intrigue when Book approached her on the last full day at Havering and cautiously beckoned her to follow.

"Not till you tell me the reason!" Catherine whispered.

"'Tis Lord Henry here, asking to see my lady straightaway," said Book. "I think he wants to check that I serve you well. Oh, Lady Catherine, if you have no good opinion of me so far, please let me make amends rather than send me back with his lordship to Hanworth!"

"Nay, I should have poached you, and Meg and Beth from Lady Jennie's service long ago. So be comforted, Book."

Book led Catherine towards a chapel at the opposite end of the palace from the royal apartments. Henry Seymour awaited them on a half-landing of some stairs adjacent to this. His expression perked up visibly, as Catherine ascended the short flight towards him and Book sat down discreetly on the lowest two steps.

Catherine greeted him in a voice which was too gentle to be overheard by Book. She affirmed to him how pleased she was with both her new maids, if that was the purpose of this meeting. But she could not stop her gaze from straying beyond him to look about her, especially up the rest of the stairs.

"Nay, something else occasioned this," he whispered.

She beamed in anticipation. Perhaps some*one* else would walk down those steps towards them. Catherine also glanced down the stairs towards Book. If Ned had decided to creep up that way behind her, now she would catch him!

Henry reached into his pocket. "These are for you," he told her, "from Ned."

He then held before her a pair of handsome, jewelled bracelets. But she began to feel so devastated as she reached out timorously for them that she could only murmur, "Is my lord not here himself to give them to me?"

"I'm afraid he isn't, Catherine. I apologize if my visit raised your hopes of that."

"I thought at least there might be a message . . ."

"Have you *still* not heard from him?" muttered Henry, with a look of sheer consternation.

"Not yet."

"I'll ask him *again* to write to you, Catherine. I've a good mind to go over to France myself to see him!"

Catherine managed to keep her composure as she thanked him. She was battling to stave off tears, which she knew would come in a flood if allowed to start.

What was she to do, with only Ned's present and not his presence to give her some protection?

Church bells pealed to welcome Elizabeth in every Essex town and village on the route of her progress. The tumultuous receptions from her subjects set her in the highest good humour with them, if not her Court.

For Catherine, the brief time at Pirgo had thankfully proved uneventful. And so had that at Ingatestone, the home of Sir William Petre, whose lands included some which had once been part of her inheritance from her traitorous father. Her coffer chest and its contents, however, were the worse for wear even before they were carted on to Moulsham, Chelmsford, Colchester, St Osyth's and Harwich.

At the end of July, the county boundary into Suffolk was crossed and the progress halted at Ipswich. Elizabeth's mood darkened there, for her strong sense of smell was offended by the stink of the town's filthy streets. She ordered that these be cleaned and paved.

Then her anger turned on the Bishop of Norwich, who condoned married priests, and she passed an edict restricting their promotion within the English Church. Elizabeth's ever-widening circle of recriminations ultimately focussed on the Queen of Scots. She ordered that ships from all the coasts of her kingdom be on the alert to intercept her Scottish cousin, who was sailing soon for Scotland. The jittery Court seemed convinced that Elizabeth would be most vindictive if she could capture this rival Queen who had once openly claimed her throne.

And still Ned neglected to return to Catherine. She was now enduring speculative glances and stifled whispers as the bulge beneath her once-slim waist went on growing.

Childbirth . . . at some unknown time in the coming weeks! The prospect began to *terrify* Catherine. She knew she could not avoid admitting her marriage and pregnancy to Elizabeth much longer.

Sometimes, she liked to reflect that the worst Elizabeth could do to her and Ned was to impose a heavy fine and banishment from Court. After all, that was how Henry VIII had reacted when Catherine's Tudor grandmother secretly wedded her grandfather.

'Twould be no hardship, Catherine felt! She would give birth to their child at Hertford House. And later, they would all go to Savernake and she would ride up Martinsell Hill on Rhone Grey, with Ned on Esturmy, and look over the Forest from there.

Several days into August, in Ned's continued absence, Catherine opened her coffer to take out the vital deed of

Seymour lands. She wiped away a tear as she touched her betrothal and wedding rings, and also those bracelets recently from him. She rummaged through other contents, stopping to put gently aside various mementoes sentimentally accumulated over the years.

The deed must be here somewhere, she frowned. Everything has become so untidy during the progress!

She checked several times for it, but eventually had to ask Mistress Cousins and Book, "Have either of you seen some papers which I had in here? Some . . . personal papers."

Book shook her head apologetically, but Mistress Cousins tutted, "Well, it wouldn't surprise me if you've mislaid them I know not where, Lady Catherine. So much shifting about, losses are happening every day. And you forgot to lock your coffer chest two or three days, didn't you?"

"I've . . . had so much else to think about," she sighed.

Catherine searched also through her clothes, hoping that she had merely mislaid the deed and it wasn't irretrievably lost. But it still proved elusive, and she began to panic. She wished she could rush for help to her step-grandmother. That good lady, however, was far away in Lincolnshire.

There seemed to be only one person who might be able to help . . . someone who had been a friendly, familiar face on this progress, and was in favour with the Queen - the Greys' ex-attendant, Bess of Hardwick.

The matronly Bess let Catherine cordially into her chamber. Catherine's reticent, but clearly confiding manner evoked a response of wide-eyed hunger for a piece of saucy gossip. Bess rubbed her hands gleefully.

"Well, my lady, don't be shy now. Spit it out!"

Catherine half-smiled at her and settled her own hands gently on her stomach.

"I am to become a mother, in a matter of weeks."

"What madness is this for a lady of your rank, who's not yet wed?"

"But I *am* a wedded wife. My husband is Lord Hertford. I pray you, for old times' sake, that you will intercede for us with the Queen. You and I share so many memories of bygone days at Bradgate."

Bess let out a shriek. "I've but lately come from trouble as makes my heart quake to think of! A poison plot against me, foiled only in June. And now *you* would endanger me with the Queen's wrath, over this?"

"'Tis a love-match," Catherine sobbed.

"Then where's your ladyship's husband? Still in France?"

Catherine nodded, trying to avoid with lowered eyes Bess's ever-hardening expression. "I wrote to my lord and told him of our child. He promised he would return to me."

"When did you write?"

"Soon before we set off on progress."

"Ha! So he's had ample time to stick to his promise, hasn't he?"

"What do you mean?"

"You know full well what I mean, my lady. Lord Hertford can be a false knave - he can go wherever he wishes outside of Her Majesty's realm."

"*No* - oh no, he's not like that!"

"What bunkum!" railed Bess, shrilling now, in tears herself. "Oh, I rue the day your lady mother gave birth to your ladyship. Her Grace must be turning in her grave."

Catherine turned to flee. Such mention of Mother Dragon seemed truly like deadly poisonous venom unleashed into her fragile body.

"And if Her Grace were alive, she would've -"

"Would've *what?*" Catherine faced Bess again, bitterly.

"She would have done like me with any daughter of mine and boxed your ears."

"I feel sorry for my little goddaughter having a mother like you," said Catherine.

After that, she left, slamming Bess's door. Once she was

back in her own quarters, she searched frantically for the deed again, but despaired of finding it. As the day wore on, though, other ladies of the Court cast nervous looks at her with an air of sympathy. Catherine assumed that Bess had passed on her secret to them. She was sure that none of them would dare to inform Elizabeth intentionally, but there was now the danger that the Queen might learn of it accidentally.

Somehow, *Elizabeth must be told! Must be told . . .* went the monotonous echo inside Catherine's head. Images of two imperious faces mocked her. The first was that of her mother, piggy eyes full of their habitual cruelty and hardness. Then Elizabeth's demanded her attention, expression pale as alabaster, but also hard - like stone - with those glinting eyes staring straight at her, powerful in their hatred and malice.

Physical nearness to that face in the flesh, complete with Elizabeth's sharp voice, was yet an extra dimension of torment for Catherine. And it lasted into the night. She patted her stomach after she retired to bed and decided that her baby wouldn't be haunted by similar, fearful images of herself in time to come!

"Don't worry, little one," she whispered to her unborn child. "I'll never be a Mother Dragon to you."

Catherine tossed and turned for a while, and shuddered at times when the child moved within her. She heard the distant chant of a watchman, "Eleven of the clock, look to your candle, your fire and your lock."

Sitting up, and trembling, Catherine reassured herself that there were no pains round her abdomen. Her child musn't make its appearance yet! She wiped her hand across her brow, breathing rapidly. Eventually, she lay down again on her back, but soon tried to rest on one side and then the other. She went on tossing to and fro in great discomfort.

Sleep must come, she told herself repeatedly. We don't deserve this suffering, little one!

"Twelve of the clock, look to your candle -" the watchman's chant interrupted her.

Catherine sat up once more. "If Bess won't help me, I must find somebody else who will," she whispered.

Before she knew, her sense of sheer terror took her out of bed and along dark passages, wearing only her nightgown. At length, she veered towards a door. The door was unlocked, and she stepped into the chamber beyond it as silently as she could. All was quiet except for some snoring and deep grunts from behind bed-curtains. She crept across the room, still shaking, and furtively drew these aside. Then for a few moments, she watched the noisy and bearded slumberer.

The person who interceded with the Queen for her needn't necessarily be a woman, she had realized . . . *Here* was another old family connection who would have married Jane, if he hadn't already been married. The wife who had saved him from Guildford Dudley's fate, had herself died in the strangest of circumstances almost a year ago. But he was back now, in the highest royal favour of anyone.

Catherine tapped and prodded the long, prone figure in the bed several times to awaken him. "My lord . . . brother . . . Robin!"

"Er-wer. W-what is it?" growled Robert Dudley, then suddenly sat bolt upright. "What in God's name are *you* doing here at this hour, madam?"

She threw herself to her knees in anguish by his bedside. "Oh, my lord, I beseech you to use your brotherly influence and ask the Queen to be merciful to me."

"What!" he exclaimed again, shooting most anxious looks into the gloom behind her. "You'd best tell me why quickly. Her Majesty might come through that adjoining door over there any minute, and we'll both be in dire straits if she catches us!"

Catherine was too afraid to glance round, and too concerned with pouring out her own sad tale to ask him why Elizabeth might choose to enter his bedchamber.

"My lord, there was so much tragedy for both our families in our younger days," she blurted out. "I appeal to you in the name of your slaughtered brother Guildford, of whom you were so fond, as I was of my sister Jane."

"Yes, yes," said Robert hastily, "get to the point."

"Please could you tell Her Majesty that I am married and soon to bear a child?"

"I'll tell Her Majesty in the morning," he agreed. "Now name to me your husband and then, *I* beseech *you*, madam, begone back to your own room."

"He is - Lord Hertford."

"Is he so, madam? My God! Well, I bid you goodnight."

Catherine snuffled her acknowledgement as she went, feeling calmer now. She heard him mutter something about "Hertford, of all people!". Curiously, in her panic, she had given Lord Robert the chance to let bygones be bygones between the Dudleys, and the Greys and Seymours. *If* he accepted that chance, it would be all to the good for her baby.

"Such a low bow from the waist to us this Sunday morning, Robin!" observed Elizabeth. "You must tell us the cause ere your back breaks."

Robert Dudley straightened up, with a rueful smile. "The cause, Your Majesty, is that a certain little goose and her milksop are not as featherheaded and lily-livered as we think."

"How do you know?"

"My . . . spies have told me, Your Majesty. Catherine Grey and Ned Seymour are married, and he has got her with child."

"God's death, Robin, I know she's pregnant by Ned Seymour. Don't look so taken aback! There must be others who've helped her to scorn my fair treatment of her with such treachery and deceit. I shall decide on the most fitting punishments."

"What are you going to do to her, Your Majesty?" asked Blanche Parry meekly. "Surely you cannot mean to execute a pregnant girl? The people will cry out in great sympathy for Lady Catherine if you do."

"Aye, Blanche, the people's opinion *has* crossed my mind," Elizabeth admitted grudgingly.

"And sorry to say," added Robert, "but if their secret marriage was before a witness, it's as binding as any church wedding ceremony."

Blanche shrank back as Elizabeth shouted, "'Twas bad enough having to deal with Lady Catherine, but Lady Catherine and her brat . . ."

"Your Majesty, I did not bring you this news as Catherine's brother-in-law," ventured Robert. "My dislike of the task is equal to my dislike of Little Hertford, ever since he exulted at my father's beheading."

"So you've said before about Hertford! And how do you like Catherine, whose child will be of the Seymour brood? They are great begetters of sons."

His reply, initially, was to study her grim expression, open-mouthed. "You do mean to kill Catherine," he noted shortly, in a hushed voice.

Elizabeth arched her brows. "Many women die in childbirth, and their brats too. More frequently than wives who break their necks falling down stairs!"

He flinched at that. "Is Your Majesty so afraid of her and the Scottish Queen?"

"Afraid, you ask your Sovereign! Do you seek to obtain a pardon for Catherine, my lord - or will one become necessary for yourself?" her voice resounded angrily. "There is but one mistress here, you know, and no master."

"My dislike of this task waxes stronger, Your Majesty."

"Then we are right good friends again, Robin. Content yourself that I shall live for ever and ne'er grow old. Therefore I won't need any successor."

He formed the symbolic 'OO' of her nickname for him,

by regarding her, as on many previous occasions, through the encircled thumb and forefinger of each hand. "May your Eyes go on serving you to the end of his days?"

Elizabeth regally acknowledged that he could. A smile hovered about her lips, though only slightly. She longed to relax with him, as in times past before his wife's death. She wanted to melt her rage clean away and laugh with him, and more. But she had her throne to safeguard. Would her people ever accept Robert? She fumed the greater to think that pretty Catherine Grey was already with child by an English husband who *would* be popular. For he was the son of the people's champion - their 'Good Duke'.

"No need to bow so low as before, Sweet Robin," she croakily dismissed him.

She enjoyed surveying again the obeisance in the movement of Robert's virile head and shoulders. Her fury could not be unleashed in its full force against such as him, whose total loyalty to her had first been pledged during their imprisonment in the Bell and Beauchamp Towers.

Yet once her Eyes had gone, she was all the more livid that on top of the threats posed to her realm by the Queen of Scots, this matter of Catherine Grey had been brought into the open.

"Light me a candle, Blanche," she instructed, so briskly that Blanche obeyed her without further question.

Elizabeth opened a drawer of her travelling desk and removed a few documents. "Now, Blanche, would you bring Catherine Grey to me."

"Yes, Your Majesty."

"But wait outside with her until I tell you . . . I would be alone for a while - to think."

Blanche curtseyed, and went away silently and warily. *And* misguidedly sorry for the girl, so Elizabeth detected. Which was why she could not do what she was about to do, even in front of someone who had been lifelong in her service.

She separated two documents from the others and

snarled at the first one of these. It was a letter to the Earl of Hertford, beginning, 'I am with child . . .'

"Who else besides Jennie Seymour has nurtured this treachery and bloated ambition concerning a claimant to my Crown?" Elizabeth raged, as she flung the letter aside. She would consider its uses with regard to her own needs later.

The second document, in Hertford's own handwriting, was as unforgivable to her. She glowered at this, satisfied that she had not relied on Cecil's spy system to net it. Her Spirit was somewhat soft on the little Grey goose. She read again that the income, from lands restored to the Seymours by their Sovereign Lady Elizabeth, would be the widow's portion for the Earl's 'most dear and beloved wife, the Lady Catherine' to the value of a thousand pounds a year.

Elizabeth held that part of the deed over the candle first and watched a burnt hole replace those words, as charred pieces fell away. She destroyed the rest of it in a similar fashion, rejoicing at her brilliance for using an offshoot of Robert's spy system without his knowledge. Robert Dudley's sister Mary had been more impartial in finding this, than either Blanche or Kat would have proved if she had ordered *them* to search Catherine's belongings in transit!

But her fury still did not dissipate. As she put out the candle, Elizabeth wished that those two who were physically distant from her anger - namely Hertford and the Scottish Queen, would be shipwrecked on their respective journeys from France.

"Blanche, bring her in to me now!" she yelled.

Blanche complied without comment. This pleased Elizabeth, but nowhere near enough to forestall her from bristling with her usual, irritated rancour at the very sight of Catherine. That simpering subservience of the girl - how could so many others find it attractive? And yet was there a tinge of defiance about her?

"Kneel there," Elizabeth snapped, pointing to the place she had decided upon.

Catherine sank to her knees, close to the ashes of the document so important to her.

"What great presumption for you and Hertford to satisfy your lust, without first gaining our consent."

"Your Majesty, I -"

"Silence!" ordered Elizabeth, banging a fist on her desk. "We are not done with our words yet, madam." She turned her glare fully on Catherine. But her young cousin's lowered eyes were frustrating proof against that weapon.

Elizabeth's fist next struck Catherine, plumb and hard so that it dented the victim's headdress. "We treated you as became your rank," she berated the bowed figure, "even called you our daughter. Yet *you,* who once accused Lord Robert of mounting more than horses at Court, repay us so irresponsibly. Allowing a Seymour to mount you enough times to beget a brat who imperils us and our realm, one day mayhap with civil war."

"We are loyal to Your Majesty, my lord and I," sobbed Catherine quietly.

"Your Majesty," put in a Welsh voice.

"Blanche! We had quite forgot you were here . . . get up, cousin, and be grateful that Mistress Blanche deflected us from striking you again."

Blanche went to help Catherine to her feet, "Oh, shush now, my dear. Don't cry, madam. I did so try to warn you and Lady Jennie of Her Majesty's displeasure if you wedded without her permission."

Still Catherine went on sobbing, as she let Blanche re-adjust her headdress. "I thank you for trying to warn me, Mistress Blanche," she murmured. "But . . . but neither of *you* know what true love is . . ."

"Do we not?" Elizabeth interrupted her coldly. And in the brief instant when Catherine looked up at her, the royal frown shot its dagger glance home magnificently. "Since you have tasted of it rather too well, you will celebrate your coming-of-age in the Tower, madam - the Bell Tower, where you will go this very day!"

# CHAPTER 14

# *A Declaration to the World*

*'From the Queen's Majesty at Ipswich to Sir Edward Warner, Lieutenant of the Tower, 10th August 1561.'*

Elizabeth's writing stood out boldly at the top of her express message. He was to prepare the Bell Tower for a prisoner of high rank who would be brought in later today.

Very high indeed, he noted. Under English law, only one life separated her from being another ruling Queen.

He read on: *'Our pleasure is that you shall examine the Lady Catherine very straitly about how many have known of the love between the Earl of Hertford and her from the beginning. Let her certainly understand that she shall have no manner of favour unless she tells the truth . . . for it now appears that several people have been involved in this matter. And when the truth becomes clearer, it shall increase our indignation against her, if she fails to disclose it.'*

"The Earl of Hertford, eh?" grinned Warner. "Lucky young devil!"

He felt sure that if the Queen had done her duty to her people and married, she would not have been so sour against her nubile young kinswoman. Lady Catherine was merely doing what the world expected of her and acquiring herself a husband.

Warner scratched his head at the unnecessary imprisonment of the lady. But before her arrival, he had to examine the stuff to be taken out of the royal wardrobe in the Tower for hastily furnishing her apartments. An inventory must be prepared, also by order of the Queen, and an estimated value given for each item.

"Well, Her Majesty should know," he concluded, out

aloud. These were probably the very same furnishings used by her in her own incarceration in the Bell Tower - and before her, by Lady Catherine's tragic sister.

And before the Lady Jane? Were they used by Anne Boleyn? He considered this possibility, while the officer of the wardrobe, William Bentley, supervised two assistants in unrolling some worn hangings. Then Warner decided that they were more likely used by royalty long before Elizabeth's mother! All four men tried to stop themselves from coughing amidst the clouds of dust which flew up.

Bentley spluttered a description for the inventory, "Six pieces of tapestry to hang in Lady Catherine's chamber."

Warner scribbled this down, before adding his estimate, *'Very old and coarse.'*

He and Bentley cast discerning eyes over a motley assortment, prior to continuing with the list.

"Item, a tester for a feather bed," dictated Bentley to the Lieutenant, who tutted as he also wrote, *'All broken and not worth tenpence.'*

The pair persevered with their task.

"Item, one silk quilt of red, striped with gold."

*'Stark naught,'* commented Warner.

"Item, two carpets of Turkey matting."

*'The wool is all worn'*, the Lieutenant recorded, and then sighed, "These must all have been beautiful things in their prime. But now . . ."

"Time-battered relics," grimaced Bentley, "totally unfit for the royal apartments nowadays!"

"Totally unfit for the dungeons!" muttered Warner, in embarrassment. He resumed his writing, cursing at the state of the things, 'Item, one chair of cloth of gold, cased with crimson velvet, with two pommels of copper gilt, and the royal arms in the back - *Nothing worth.'*

"Er, Master Lieutenant," said Bentley.

"Yes?"

"Didn't you realize that's the throne graced by the Lady Jane Grey during her short reign?"

"Was it as faded then?" retorted Warner.

The inventory grew longer with further, terse remarks from him:

'Item, one cushion of purple velvet - *An old frayed thing.*

Item, two footstools covered with green velvet - *Old stools for King Henry's gouty feet.*

One bed, one bolster, and a counterpane for her women - *A mean bed.*'

"This is shameful. Shameful!" he declared. "To palm off such tatters to a great lady who has committed no crime."

"The lady will be allowed whatever food she likes," Bentley pointed out.

"'Tis not enough to make her comfortable - and possibly obliged to us in the future."

Bentley smiled at him thoughtfully. "I can rustle up some costly curtaining of finest texture."

"And I some unmarred chairs and a table, and a much better bed to improvise along with . . . *these* things."

Warner was justifiably proud of his improvisations on Catherine's behalf by the time he had to betake himself down to the Middle Tower to receive her. On sight of her, so exhausted and travel-stained, however, he could not comprehend why Elizabeth's indignation might yet increase against Catherine. His friend, William Cecil, would be his best source of further guidance about her . . .

He readily excused the fact that she merely nodded and murmured in acknowledgement of him. He could well imagine her feelings at being enclosed in this fortress, where her sister had been beheaded! And with her servants also visibly suffering from shock, Warner took upon himself to try and shield her from much of a view of the execution site on Tower Green. He guided her through the Lieutenant's Lodgings to the upper chamber of the circular-shaped Bell Tower, where his wife awaited them by the heavy, iron-girded door.

Catherine's oldest servant wailed, "Oh, I never thought to see you come here like this, Lady Catherine. Not where

Her Majesty was once held prisoner."

Then he heard Catherine speak at last in a pretty lilt of a voice, which was nevertheless vibrant with emotion, "I never felt so wretched, Mistress Cousins. If it wasn't for my coming child, I-I'd invoke these stone walls to fall down and crush me. Or else I'd dash myself against this door. Maybe my lord will come back yet and perish with me."

"Nay, madam, there is no such fate which you need worry about," Warner tried to reassure her.

"I must needs rest now, Master Lieutenant," she answered him dejectedly. "Somehow . . ."

"Hot possets - all round!" Mistress Cousins suddenly perked up. "We're all so over-wrought."

"The miracle cure, eh?" Warner observed, smiling at his wife.

But he had other ideas to improve Catherine's lot . . . and late the next afternoon, he opened the same door in the Bell Tower to admit the rest of her household. Master Lieutenant watched and listened, entirely satisfied, at Catherine's cries of delight as a whole troupe of little dogs and monkeys rushed exuberantly through to her. In the crescendo of hugging of servants and pets, one of the maids still held a squawking, caged parrot.

Warner bowed and left them to their reunion. He believed that the lady heiress of England would be less sorrowful, with the warmth and affection of her household around her.

In the English embassy in Paris, two young men joined ambassador Throckmorton for breakfast, as they had these past few months.

"So! I come back from seeing the Queen of Scots embark at Calais and find both of you with black eyes!" he observed. "What was it this time, Master Cecil? Another drunken brawl?"

"I'm afraid so, Sir Nicholas," admitted Thomas Cecil

sheepishly. "I vaguely remember my Lord of Hertford coming to my aid, then being set upon himself."

"For which my visible reward makes me grouch," grinned Ned ruefully. "How long do these bruises take to heal, Thomas?"

Thomas clapped him laughingly on the shoulder, but any further banter was halted by the serious expression on Throckmorton's sharp face.

"I trow you'll soon sober up, Thomas Cecil," he said. "Your father has written warning you not to associate with Lord Hertford any more. Why should that be?"

Both men shrugged. "My father was ever one for correcting and scolding me," said Thomas dismissively.

"I've decided to return home anyway," added Ned.

"And not go on into Italy?"

"Nay, although 'tis tempting, Sir Nicholas! But there are Seymour family matters to deal with."

After the meal, Thomas Cecil began to stroll in Ned's wake back to their lodgings close by.

"I would not be the cause of another paternal scolding," Ned smiled at him.

"I'm truly sorry about my father. Well . . . there's a French girl of noble birth ripe for seducing, so I'd best away before any more of his injunctions!"

They parted amicably, leaving Ned to reflect on the near-certain cause of William Cecil's latest order to his son.

*'Tis the Seymour family matter I've waited to hear about all summer,* he thought. *Beloved, why did you take so long to tell me?*

Catherine's attractive face swam yet again before his mind's eye, taking full possession of him. In his love for her, Ned felt so hurt by her neglecting to write even one reply to all his letters. Until two days ago, that was, when at last he'd heard from her, confirming that she was with child and reminding him of his promise not to tarry.

Glynne had come across to France and handed the letter over to him in person.

"I was told it's a very important letter," the servant had explained, "and I wanted to make sure your lordship got it safely."

"Then why is it dated over two months ago?"

"The Lady Catherine has been much preoccupied with accompanying the Queen on progress through Essex and Suffolk."

Ned had given Glynne a reply to take back to Catherine the previous day. He could not understand why Glynne's information about Catherine differed so much from that of Henry. His brother kept urging him to write to her, insisting that she was pining for him! If it had been Jennie playing tricks on him, he knew there would have been laughter to be found somewhere.

Aye, sister, you are sorely missed, he acknowledged.

Tom Goddard waited respectfully for him at the entrance to his lodgings.

"My lord, Glynne was back 'ere a few minutes since."

"Glynne? What is he still doing in Paris?"

"He wanted a quick word with Barnaby, m'lord."

"Barnaby, eh? 'Tis odd that Glynne isn't well on his way to Calais by now." Ned began to go up to his bedchamber. "Send Barnaby to me, Tom, there's a good lad. I would know more of this."

Ned wished he had more servants like Tom. He still had misgivings over Barnaby, although the man had behaved in an ingratiating manner since his disobedience on the wedding day. Ned felt angry now at Glynne's delay in setting off with his letter for Catherine, but he saved expressing any of this until Barnaby arrived in his presence.

"If you don't wipe that smirk off your face, I'll give you a shiner to match my own! Why did Glynne come back here solely to see you?"

"Um. He, er, thought he'd taken sick last night, m'lord, and he needed some provisions and directions for his journey."

"He was well-provisioned. And he could have asked at

the embassy for directions."

"Ah. But you see -"

"See what, Barnaby?"

"Glynne's a quiet sort, that'd rather come to someone he knows. He didn't want to trouble your lordship no more."

"On the contrary, you both trouble me very much," Ned snapped. "You may go back to your duties now."

Barnaby bowed and left. Ned had the distinct impression that these two servants were involved in something untoward. He supposed that Barnaby may well have gossiped to Glynne about seeing Catherine and Jennie arrive at Hertford House on the morning of the wedding. Could it be that Glynne was to blame for some sort of breakdown in the passage of letters between himself and Catherine? That would surely account for Henry's constant requests for a letter to her!

Ned was homesick for all that he held so dear in his native country. But in no way did he underestimate the enormity of the situation facing him and Catherine there, if Elizabeth put them in her bad graces for a while. He was bracing himself, though, to endure her wrath.

Next day, the ambassador received Elizabeth's official order, recalling Ned to her realm.

"'Tis as if Dover's white cliffs have been beckoning me for some time, Sir Nicholas," he said, when this was shown to him.

One morning in early September, Ned landed at Dover and was invited to join the commander of the Castle there, Captain Crispe, for breakfast. Two more gentlemen, a Mr Sackville and another called Strange, sat down with them shortly afterwards. All four fed happily for several minutes, grunting affably about the weather.

"Are you on your way to France?" enquired Ned.

The incoherent mutters he received in response did nothing to make him think otherwise. Sackville and Strange finished their meal, each man pushing his plate away and sitting back, belching, before Sackville passed a document to the Captain.

Crispe studied this without expression. He turned to Ned and observed, "My Lord Hertford, it seems that Her Majesty would ordain you a breakfast such as you've never known before in England. I have here a warrant for your arrest."

"What reason is given, sir?"

*"Guards!"*

Two burly men appeared and were commanded to stand behind Ned. "If you don't know the reason for the fate which awaits you, my lord, then neither do I," added Crispe. "My orders are to take you as a prisoner to the Tower. Your servants are not to follow you."

The terrible reality of loss of liberty was further enforced as he was surrounded by more guards, and forbidden to speak to anyone. Not even to a tearful and bewildered Tom Goddard, whom he saw near the exit from the Castle keep.

"Take care, Tom," Ned managed to call. But Crispe intervened to thrust aside the lad, before he could reply.

And then, leaving Tom and his other servants behind in Dover, Ned was conveyed away under heavy guard. He was concerned about what might happen to them and still unaware what fate awaited him in the Tower.

Ned was spared the ignominy of being taken into the stronghold through Traitor's Gate. But when he passed through the southern ward from Tower Wharf, he stood still for an instant, thinking he had heard his name called from far-off. He had time to glance up at a circular structure surmounted by a wooden turret before he was hurried forward again. The Bell Tower!

Dear God, he thought, was that Catherine who called to me?

As Sir Edward Warner conducted him towards the

Lieutenant's Lodgings, Ned adjudged that here was a likely enough person to plague with questions about her.

"Master Lieutenant, is Lady Catherine here? In the Bell Tower, perhaps? Pray tell me how she is."

His sole answer was a bland expression, neither hostile nor friendly.

"Am I to be clapped in a cell in here?" Ned went on.

Warner brought him courteously to a halt, so as to allow another man to pass, also under armed escort.

"Henry! What *is* this?" Ned cried.

"For God's sake, Ned," his brother appealed to him, "tell them how little I know and they'll let me go from here."

"How little you know about what? And who are 'they'?"

Warner hesitantly ordered Henry's guards to take him back to his cell. Then he guided Ned onwards and at last spoke to him, "In there, my lord, is the Council Chamber. Now, there are many questions to be fired at *you!*"

Inside the Council Chamber, a formidable array of peers, lawyers and churchmen sat waiting for him. Ned picked out at the front the old Marquis of Winchester, now married to a Seymour aunt; Sir William Petre, deaf as a post; Matthew Parker, Archbishop of Canterbury; Grindal, Bishop of London; Cecil, of course, looking inscrutable . . .

He was swiftly shown to a chair - directly facing all of them.

"My Lord Hertford," began Winchester, "we are here to enquire into the infamous proceedings between yourself and the Lady Catherine Grey, she being a lady close in blood to Her Majesty."

"Infamous proceedings? The Lady Catherine is my wife."

Several voices hooted in derision, after which Winchester asked, "So you do avow a marriage between you and the lady?"

"Yes, my lord, unashamedly."

"Do you love her?" bellowed Parker above the noise.

"I love my wife very greatly."

The Archbishop looked round at the uproar in disapproval before he continued, "Do you love her - *passionately?"*

"Yes," replied Ned, trying to maintain his own dignity.

"Did you indulge in carnal copulation?"

"Wassat?" shouted Petre.

"Carnal copulation," Winchester boomed, slowly, into his ear.

"Uh!"

Ned's answer in the affirmative caused even William Cecil to shudder at the barracking. "I do fear the very roof will come in upon us!" Cecil protested, and he allowed some moments for quiet to be restored. "My Lord Hertford, where did this take place between you and Lady Catherine?"

"On the first occasion . . ."

"The *first* occasion?" a few cries interrupted. "How many times?"

"Yes, how many?"

"The first occasion was after our wedding at Hertford House," said Ned.

Cecil cleared his throat. "I fear you inform only to tantalize further, my lord. Let us concentrate, meantime, on the details of the ceremony."

"Aye, we shall so proceed - and return later to more intimate particulars!" agreed Winchester, to background mutters.

Ned found himself being harrowed for a while over the date and time of the wedding, who else was present, the priest - his name, his appearance, and how long he was with them. The ring and its words inside the 'circles five' also attracted several questions, and so did even the food and drink, and who served them after the ceremony.

Having withstood the earlier onslaughts of his interrogation, Ned did not flinch when he was unable to name the priest brought in hurriedly by Jennie. He described the clergyman as clearly as he could remember and mentioned the prayer book which Jennie gave him, still containing Catherine's pressed four-leaf clover.

"Oh, very helpful, my lord," taunted Grindal. "Great search we may make for this divine whose name you cannot tell, nor where perchance he came from. Only that he has a flower pressed in a prayer book from my lady, your sister - and she, your chief witness, is dead!"

Ned felt regret now at not discovering the priest's name on that romantic morning. But he would not encourage more jeers by admitting this, unless he was asked.

"You say naught of the document which proves our marriage," he asserted. "The deed of jointure I gave my wife before I was ordered away to France."

A strange and heavy silence descended over the Council Chamber, before Cecil addressed Ned again, "My lord, the deed to which you refer seems, alas, to have been lost by Lady Catherine during Her Majesty's summer progress."

"Lost?" Ned gripped the sides of his chair, in case he fell off it. Everything that made his life worth living seemed to be slipping from him. "And Lady Catherine - *where is she?"*

He saw Warner receive a nod from William Cecil.

"You were right, my lord. The Lady Catherine is in the Bell Tower," the Lieutenant confirmed.

"May I see her?"

"No!" rejoined Parker. "No, my lord, you may not! Her Majesty has expressly forbidden it."

"Then how is -"

"We ask the questions!"

These were resumed vigorously in their former vein: Were he and Lady Catherine naked and in bed when they copulated? Was he abed before her? Who emerged from it first? The names of everyone who helped them strip off all their clothes and put them on again?

Ned's truthful reply that no-one, except themselves, had given any such help, caused incredulity.

"This is no time to play games, Hertford," Grindal warned him sternly. "Her Majesty will be mighty displeased with such evasiveness."

"But this answer of his lordship's tallies with what Lady Catherine told us," ventured Warner.

"Master Lieutenant," spluttered Winchester, "hadn't you best take the prisoner to his quarters for the time being?"

"Aye," others called out in agreement.

"Lock him up till he talks some sense!"

Ned stood up, trying to emulate the noble bearing that he was sure his father had shown in a similar situation in the Tower. There was something about the Archbishop, the Lieutenant, and even Cecil, which gave Ned the impression that here were no enemies to be feared.

"As my lord father was, so are my brother and I - innocent of any crime!" he declared feelingly. "My brother had no part in all this, beyond carrying a few messages after our sister's death."

He then bowed amid blank silence and knew from their reaction how well he had spoken with the authority which comes from truth. After the Lieutenant led him away, he persisted with questions about Catherine.

"My lord is very tenacious in his love for her," Warner sighed. "I have my orders for no communication whatsoever between you."

"But at least you can tell me how she is?"

"As well, my lord, as any delicate young lady who is nearing her first time of childbirth in the Tower of London!"

Ned's heart sank. He was so near Catherine and yet forbidden to console her. How could Elizabeth be so vengeful? He believed that she hoped Catherine and the baby would die in this place.

Outside the Lieutenant's Lodgings, he tried to stop and look up again at the Bell Tower. But his guards ensured that he kept moving.

"Your brother has better leisure than I do to tell you

more of the Lady Catherine, my lord," explained Warner. "As you shall see!"

Soon Ned was sharing the same cell as Henry in the White Tower.

"Would that we were meeting under happier circumstances," he said apologetically. "I'll do all I can to obtain your release."

"I don't think anyone expected the Queen to react so severely," said Henry. "I've been here since the middle of August. I was brought in for questioning a few days after Catherine."

"Oh, my God! That means Catherine was already here when Glynne brought her letter to me."

"Catherine wrote many letters to you, Ned, and in increasing despair because she heard nothing from you."

"But I wrote dozens of times."

"Well, the only things she received were those bracelets that you sent through me."

Ned felt devastated. He held his head in horror. He wanted to comfort Catherine and take her in his arms and reassure her.

"Why haven't our letters been reaching each other?" he wondered aloud, then looked extremely unnerved. "And if Catherine didn't send Glynne over to France, who did?"

Henry drew a sharp breath. "It did strike me as curious," he said, "that Glynne is the only one of Jennie's old servants who hasn't been questioned in the Tower."

Ned banged his fists on the cell wall in anger that his suspicions about Glynne were proving correct. The man had been abusing his position of trust and had badly failed them.

As the days passed, Ned wept in rage every time he heard the curfew bell ring above the Bell Tower. Catherine was in the room beneath it, but he was being held close prisoner and could not go to her! His waking hours seemed to alternate between languishing in the White Tower and enduring more ribald comments from the commissioners of enquiry, dredging up the same questions over and over again.

"Lord Hertford exonerates his brother each time I see him!" the Lieutenant reported to them.

Ned's determined efforts led shortly to Henry's release. And a similar approach benefited his own servants when they were brought to the Tower for questioning. Barnaby's terror of possible imprisonment made him so abject that Ned decided to retain him in his service and let him have another chance to improve.

He never gave up asking about Catherine and tried, by means of their servants, to send her messages of his love. One day Warner had to reprimand him for smuggling posies of flowers through to her. The Lieutenant seemed uncomfortable with this task and Ned's soul was hardly blighted with guilt. He was dreaming of being with Catherine in Savernake.

She fell ill in late September and the investigations into the marriage were halted. In his fears for her life, Ned pleaded to be allowed to visit her and still was denied. He was full of apprehension when Warner came to him on the afternoon of Wednesday, the 24th and conducted him past Tower Green towards the Chapel of St Peter ad Vincula.

He followed Warner in confusion - the guards were not so close around them! There was no sign of any out-of-the-ordinary activity on the Green and only a handful of people were in the Chapel.

An old woman came up to him, crying over a small bundle in her arms.

"Oh, my lord!"

"Mistress Cousins . . ."

"I cry for joy rather than sorrow, if you'll excuse me," she clucked. "Lady Catherine has borne you this baby boy!"

"My Lady Catherine - has she . . . survived?"

"Yes, my lord, but she's sleeping like a babe herself now and she surely needs to!"

At Warner's prompting, Mistress Cousins placed the baby in Ned's arms. "My Lord Hertford," he said, "do you acknowledge this infant as your true son and heir?"

The baby stirred within his swaddling bands and at first, Ned could hardly speak. He was suddenly overwhelmed by the pride of holding *his son!*

"I acknowledge him to be so, Master Lieutenant," he gasped.

Warner immediately beamed, "My lady, his mother, wishes to call him Edward. I know not whether that's after you, my lord, or the Good Duke himself!"

"Then Edward he shall be!"

"And now he needs to be baptized," said Warner, as Ned smilingly returned the baby to Mistress Cousins. "'Tis not of course unusual for an heir to be baptized near the tombs of his illustrious ancestors. But surely 'tis unique, my lord, to be close to so many headless ones from both his father's and his mother's families . . ."

"Delivered of a healthy son!" shrieked Elizabeth. "That will *not* be allowed to upstage us. May she rot in the Tower with her brat for such a personal affront."

"The Scottish ambassador is here, requesting an audience with Your Majesty," Cecil informed her.

"God's death!" she cursed under her breath. "That's another contentious matter." How she regretted that English ships had captured the galley carrying the Queen of Scots' horse, but failed to stop Mary herself from reaching Scotland unhindered.

"He'll have to wait," she snapped, "while we overreact by throwing a right royal tantrum!"

Cecil bowed and tactfully removed himself temporarily from Elizabeth's presence till her storm spent itself. Not so lucky were those ladies with the dubious honour of being in attendance on her!

She gave full and necessary vent to her armoury of

abusiveness against them. Slapping, berating, victimizing other females in the privacy of the royal apartments - how much wiser that was than directing her aggression towards another country! She would be less prone then to provoking an international crisis or costly war with Scotland. Eventually, Elizabeth decided she was of a calmer frame of mind to meet Mary Queen of Scots' envoy, William Maitland of Lethington.

She received him courteously, though she judged that behind his friendly smiles, Maitland was something of a clever rogue - perhaps more so than herself! No doubt he was well nicknamed 'the Chameleon', because he had often changed his allegiance.

"Your Majesty, I come on behalf of *my* Sovereign Lady of Scotland to ask that you name her as heir to the throne of England."

"We had hoped for other news from our cousin of Scotland," she said. "The peace treaty, negotiated by Mr Secretary Cecil over a year ago in her realm, has yet to be ratified by her. Let your Queen get on with that - which is long overdue for her to do."

Her suspected villain went on smiling pleasantly. "If Your Majesty would but recognize my Queen as your heir, that would serve better for good friendship between England and Scotland."

"Whoever has greatest right shall succeed us. How oft do we have to repeat this answer?"

"Does not Her Majesty, Mary Queen of Scots, have the greatest right?"

"Here's another question answered with a question," snapped Elizabeth. "Am I expected to love my shroud? As examples tell, sir, the people of my England tend to fete any acknowledged heir instead of the wearer of the crown. Like they did with me in my sister's reign!"

She fixed her gaze teasingly on Cecil, recalling his active support of her during that troubled time. "The same situation shall not arise in my reign. 'Tis true, though, that one claimant, by showing she can bear a son, has made a declaration to the world that she is more worthy of my throne than either of the reigning Queens of England and Scotland!"

Well may Cecil's officious return of her gaze imply that enough had been said! She knew that she could encourage his clear dislike of her Scottish cousin's claim. But as for that of her English cousin, strengthened by the birth of a son . . . Elizabeth had too much esteem for Cecil to dissuade him from favouring it so much. She determined that he must continue serving on the commission of enquiry into the 'knot of secret might'. Somehow, means must be found to discredit Catherine thoroughly.

With that aim in mind, Elizabeth felt able to smile as broadly as Maitland.

## CHAPTER 15

# *Only Hours Away*

As Catherine drifted through sleep and semi-consciousness, she was aware of the sounds of people and pets in her room. Sometimes a baby cried. Her little son! She would hold him again when she felt stronger.

She sensed too the face of a loved one watching over her. A hand caressed and soothed her brow.

"Catherine!"

That voice - the familiar way it said her name. She thought she must be imagining it.

Her eyes flickered open. "Did you hear me call to you through yonder window?" she asked dreamily.

"Aye, I heard you, sweetheart."

"It's such a narrow window. I feared that my good Ned hadn't heard."

He bent closer and kissed her, before murmuring, "The Lieutenant took some persuading to let us meet."

"I shall dine at his table again the sooner, if he lets you stay with me . . ."

Sleep then reclaimed Catherine, but when she next awoke, there was a foot resting against hers in the bed. She turned a little to face its owner and Ned's arms closed in warmth around her. Catherine met his embrace, forgiving him for the summer of silence between them even before she learnt his side of the story. All she wanted was for them to be together with their baby!

"The Lieutenant says that he sees no point in keeping us apart!" Ned smiled.

"He was so sorry when those commissioners questioned me about the posies that you sent me, Ned. What a joy it is now to be able to say thank you!"

Ned responded with a gentle tightening of his arms to bring her even closer to him.

"Perhaps, like us, the Lieutenant wonders what the Queen is up to," he said, "when *everyone* knows that the law of marriage allows for its celebration by a clergyman at any place or hour."

"I'm sure he also thinks that the sin is far greater on her part than any wrong of ours."

"Aye - there's much we could say on that theme!"

Catherine kissed away a tear from his face. "I didn't receive any letters from you."

"And I, only the one from you about our child, and that, many weeks late! I should have been with you, beloved . . ."

"Hush!"

"I *would* have been with my sweet Catherine if I'd known! Dear God, Glynne must've handed all our letters to one of the Privy Council and then they were passed to Elizabeth."

"Maybe we'll never know. But I can still remember some of what I wrote. And now that's for my lord's ears only . . ."

They lay together for a while, recounting as much as they could of their letters. Then they commiserated with each other deeply about their separate experiences of being arrested and brought to the Tower. Their anger over Elizabeth's injustice towards them became easier to let out because of being shared, instead of borne mostly apart like their grief for Jennie.

"I can just imagine Dudley's shock when you appeared at his bedside and confessed all," said Ned. He snuggled down with Catherine and gave a chuckle. "He's probably revelling in 'Little Hertford's' discomfort. If only he could see us now!"

After some days and nights of Ned living with her in the Bell Tower, Catherine received a visit from the Lieutenant.

"I come to enquire after your ladyship's health," he said cautiously. "Mistress Cousins tells me that you seem to be more at peace, Lady Catherine."

"Oh, more so than for an age, Sir Edward."

"That is well."

Catherine nodded at a hand signal from Ned for him to speak. "While Lady Catherine is certainly more peaceful within herself, she doesn't yet thrive, alas - unlike our son!"

"Can you rise from your bed, Lady Catherine?"

"Not for long, sir. Do you wish me to do so?"

"No, no, Lady Catherine . . . I would not cause you further ill in my custody. I will endeavour for the commissioners not to burden you more when the marriage investigation resumes tomorrow. However, I fear that I must acquaint you with two related matters."

"Yes?"

"Firstly, searches have been made for the priest and your servant, Helen Leigh, but neither of them has yet been found. And secondly - although I am myself convinced that your marriage is valid - I dare not risk allowing my Lord Hertford to remain in here while daily sessions of the enquiry are held! My lord will have to be in the White Tower during these."

Ned groaned and Catherine sank back on her pillows, her first signs of recovery seeming to recede.

"Surely I may still be with Lady Catherine at night-time," ventured Ned.

Warner looked at him benevolently. "Yes, my lord, you may! Lady Catherine has clearly benefited from your company, and I wish that to continue. I hear that the people of London and elsewhere are in absolute sympathy with you. Her Majesty usually values her people's opinion. But if need be over this matter, William Cecil will likely be stiff with her, to cause a change of her mind."

Catherine attempted to smile as she thanked him for such words of reassurance. Warner meant well, but she saw the thoughtful expression on Ned's face. She knew that, like her, he was uncertain how firm William Cecil could be, on their behalf, to make Elizabeth bow to the pressure of public opinion.

In November, the draughtiness of the Tower increased Mistress Cousins' complaints about her creaky old joints.

"It seems such a long winter upon us already," she grumbled. "Those damp mists from the river can only get worse."

Catherine offered to ask if Ned could find her a position in more congenial surroundings.

"What, and leave you and the babe, Lady Catherine!" the old woman protested. "Oh, the very idea . . . no, we'll have to make sure that our fires here are kept well stacked."

Despite the dreary prospect of the winter ahead, Catherine continued her gentle progression towards improved health. She liked to hope that her memories of suffering last spring and summer would become as faded as the musty old tapestries hanging on the chamber walls!

One morning after Ned's return to the White Tower for the day, Catherine's household bustled about her and the baby and pets as usual. But there was something different from the established routine.

Catherine realized that she had heard no noise from the Council Chamber yet. She strained to listen for a while. Amber came to settle at her feet, recalling memories for her of happier times when Queen Mary gave the little spaniel to her as a boisterous pup.

"'Tis almost *three years* since Queen Mary died," Catherine observed to Mistress Cousins. "How much has befallen us in that time! If she'd survived but another year, all of us would have been living at my lord's beloved Savernake. But now, I'm wondering if the celebrations for the third anniversary of Queen Elizabeth's accession perhaps explain the silence today in the Council Chamber."

"As far as I know, the celebrations are next week, Lady

Catherine," replied Mistress Cousins. There were nods and murmurs of agreement from the other women.

"Then why can all be so quiet from there?" said Catherine. "It seems eerie to me after all those weeks of the commissioners at work. I must ask the Lieutenant what's happening."

She smilingly turned down offers of asking Warner to visit her.

"But this infernal cold and damp!" moaned Mistress Cousins, as Book helped Catherine to don her cloak. "Are you up to braving these, Lady Catherine?

"I'll soon be in the warm again," Catherine promised her.

The iron-girded door was opened for her, accompanied by its usual echoing groan. Amber shot determinedly through the exit first.

"Best let her come with me, Meg!" beamed Catherine, with a shrug.

Along the gallery outside, she still did not hear any voices from the Council Chamber. Her belief in a plan, which had come spontaneously to her, began to grow. Ned had described to her often enough the way to reach him in the White Tower. Now her sense of adventure was becoming hard to contain . . .

"A-choo! A-a-choo!"

Catherine stopped suddenly, then felt Amber slump against her for reassurance. Would they have to turn back to her chamber after all, because of some sneezing? There seemed to be nothing else but to do so in disappointment.

"A-choo! Ugh, *damned noze*."

But wait! The sneezer's voice was recognizable, in spite of his difficulties . . .

"A . . . a-a. . .a-choo!"

"Bless you, Master Lieutenant."

"Thank you, Lady Catherine," he called, as he came out of the Council Chamber to her. "And good day to you. I ought to be used to the Tower by now not to have colds!"

"You'll have to try one of Mistress Cousins' hot possets to make you better."

"I tend to think they make her feel better!" he wheezed.

Catherine laughed with him for a moment, before asking, "No commissioners here today?"

Warner shook his head and croaked, "I was just writing this to your ladyship." He beckoned her into the Council Chamber, where a note to her lay as yet unfolded on a table.

'The enquiry has been adjourned from the Tower,' she read approvingly, 'because the commissioners have investigated all they possibly can until the priest is found, and also Leigh.'

"Not yet done a note to - A-choo - tell my lord, Lady Catherine."

"I'll save you the effort, Sir Edward," she smiled gently, "for Amber can lead me to my lord."

He inclined his head in reply. A discreet wink was just discernible above his handkerchief. Soon Catherine flung her arms happily round Ned in the White Tower and told him the news about the enquiry.

Ned kissed her and joined in her laughter as they started to undress each other like before at Hertford House. "The commissioners may not have believed us over this," she said, "but I wouldn't have wished to let them see a demonstration!"

"If it wasn't for Elizabeth, Catherine, you would be beyond reproach to them as the mother of a son."

Amber curled up and slept by the fire in Ned's chamber, near their pile of clothes, while they began early anniversary celebrations of their own in his bed.

"I'm enjoying the first anniversary of our marriage already!" Catherine whispered, as they became one.

"'Tis three weeks away yet, beloved," said Ned tenderly. "I'm looking forward to lots more celebrations like this!"

"And for many more years, my sweet lord," she smiled and kissed him.

As the winter months passed, they learnt that most of

the realm wanted them to be released - and they would have been set free, but for the Queen's opposition. Their story of love and romance amid so much tragedy in their young lives had touched the hearts of the people, especially in London.

Their baby son too was very much part of the national sentiments in their favour. He had faced his first precarious months of infancy in the winter of 1562 in the Tower! Otherwise he would have had to be separated from his parents. Although misfortune had made the lawful proof of their marriage impossible so far, the new Seymour heir's legitimacy was widely accepted.

"It'll serve Helen right if she's caught through tittle-tattling about the baby, bless him," said Mistress Cousins one bright, spring day. "Think how robust he'll be in good surroundings, Lady Catherine, as he's survived so well in here!"

Ned was so proud of their offspring that in May he began to think about having a portrait painted of mother and son.

Edward was on Catherine's lap when the idea was broached to her, and she was delighted. "Would he hold still for long enough, d'you think?" she asked with some amusement. "Even for the first sketches of us?"

"I could stand near the artist and try to distract my little lord's attention."

"I am warming to this, though it still won't be easy!"

Before Catherine could say any more about the portrait, there was a knock on the door. "'Tis only me, Lady Catherine," said Warner.

She bade him come in and noted that he did so looking rather shamefaced. "My Lady Catherine, my Lord Hertford," he said, "I'm afraid that you will have to be in your separate chambers again tomorrow."

"For what reason this time?" asked Ned.

"Some of the commissioners are coming back." Warner opened out a document and offered it for Ned to read.

Ned glanced through the contents and read out aloud for Catherine's sake, "'The Archbishop of Canterbury, with others, have commission to judge of the pretended marriage between the Lady Catherine Grey and the Earl of Hertford. Our pleasure is that when the commissioners send to have either of the parties appear before them, the Lieutenant shall lead each prisoner to answer at the place of judgement. Neither prisoner shall be allowed to have conference with any person. They shall remain under the Lieutenant's custody and be returned to their quarters. Our will is to have judgement. Given under our signet at our palace of Westminster, Elizabeth R.'"

"But this sounds more like prejudgement in its wording," protested Catherine. "Small wonder that you look sorry to have to carry out your orders, Master Lieutenant."

"I have little choice but to follow them in this instance," he mumbled.

The next morning, Warner escorted Catherine to the Council Chamber. She observed that he was attempting to appear expressionless. She still felt compassion towards him, for he was as much under Elizabeth's yoke as Ned and herself.

Parker seemed to be uneasy. Catherine recalled the Queen's invectives against married clergy at Ipswich the previous summer and realized that he and his wife were also victims of the extraordinary royal antagonism towards marriage. Like Warner, he and possibly most of the other commissioners present, were acting under orders against their true beliefs about the 'knot of secret might'.

"We have searched for the priest in much earnest, madam," he informed her. "Is there anything else which upon reflection your ladyship can tell us about him?"

"I said all I could about him the last time I answered to the commissioners, Your Grace."

Parker's aged eyes lit briefly with a faint glimmer of sympathy. "I fear then that unless the priest is found within the next few days," he went on, "Her Majesty will require us to declare that there is no marriage between your ladyship and my Lord of Hertford."

*Her Majesty will require us!* Those words bore out to Catherine that her intuitive feelings were right - these men were merely obeying Elizabeth's commands.

"But what of our son?"

"Alas, he will be deemed illegitimate."

The Archbishop stared into space beyond Catherine when he said that.

"And will Her Majesty's people think that a pity also?" she asked him quietly.

His eyes met her gaze for only a moment, but he ventured a smile of acquiescence. Parker then stood in respectful silence, along with his colleagues, before he nodded to Warner to conduct her back to the Bell Tower. Catherine gently acknowledged them, seeing their respect as another indication of the strength of popular feeling in support of her.

If Elizabeth is bent on ignoring her people now, thought Catherine, how long can Her Majesty take such a risk?

News of the people's indignation swiftly accompanied that of the judgement pronounced on 12th May. The marriage of the Lady Catherine to the Earl of Hertford was declared invalid and a sentence of life imprisonment recommended for both.

Catherine and Ned were together in the Bell Tower again when Warner came to tell them of this.

"I am appalled at the pronouncement against you," he added.

"So William Cecil wasn't stiff enough with Her Majesty about us, after all," said Ned ruefully. "And what happens to us now, Master Lieutenant?"

"I will do all in my power to alleviate your imprisonment, my lord. 'Tis my guess that Her Majesty and Lord Robert were determined upon this judgement to annoy William Cecil."

"*That* may well be true," murmured Catherine.

"As also is your 'knot of secret might', Lady Catherine. Most of the realm still believe that. Apparently, all across the land your supporters are asking, 'Why should man and wife be hindered from coming together?'."

The Lieutenant winked at them. Their contented married life went on as before, thanks to his acknowledgement of the people's opinion. In the summer, the portrait of Catherine and her son was completed. And by the end of July she found that she was with child for the second time.

*Of all my granddaughters, Catherine was ever the one most dear to me. And so I urge you, good Cecil, to help her in any way you can with Her Majesty. May the Lord have you in his keeping. With my heartiest commendations this October morning and still a sluggard in my bed at six of the clock . . .*

At Hampton Court, William Cecil contemplated the latest homily from his friend and Lincolnshire neighbour, the Lady Catherine's step-grandmother. A rare smile came unbidden to him. She was certainly no sluggard, this very active Duchess! He had himself been at work on matters of state since four o'clock in the morning, but he had not yet decided on his reply to her.

The Dowager Duchess of Suffolk possessed such great enthusiasm for the extremes of Protestant faith and now for the cause of her favourite kinswoman. How could he make her understand that his serving of God included working dutifully for the reigning monarch? If Her Majesty remained immovably hostile to anything, he might give an honest opinion which was contrary to the royal viewpoint. But he could not prevail on the Queen to change her mind.

For the last five days, Cecil had not even had any chance to speak to Elizabeth. She had fallen ill with smallpox, and he could only pray that the Lord would send her a swift recovery.

Somehow he needed to explain to the Duchess that he must obey their Sovereign, however anxious he was to aid both the furtherance of faith and the Lady Catherine. He would never understand the Queen's peculiar, devouring jealousy of her attractive young cousin. More than once he had told Her Majesty that she was stirring up a hornet's nest of sympathy for Catherine by overreacting.

Yet he had worked closely with Elizabeth for long enough to know better than to take little account of her as a ruler. Most people still tended to do so, especially because she was a woman not yet thirty years old and thought to be influenced by Robert Dudley.

Cecil often employed the Queen's own great tactic of delay when faced with apparently insoluble problems. And so the Duchess's letter was regretfully consigned to the growing amount of paperwork which was pending, until he could see Elizabeth concerning all of it.

He knew that a reply may not be feasible for some while, if her lack of mercy towards Catherine and Hertford persisted partly to tease and embarrass her Spirit. William Cecil confided only to himself that he would free both captives if he had the power! And he would undoubtedly endeavour to complete a letter to the Lady Catherine's step-grandmother before he gave any further attention to the half-written letter to the Queen of Scots which lay nearby.

Elizabeth's hot fever had prevented her from finishing this. According to the regular bulletins which Cecil received from her doctors, the disfiguring spots of the pox had not yet erupted. Was this a calculated caprice on the part of her womanly vanity? She had enjoyed such a surfeit of good fortune at dangerous times of her life in the past that he would not be surprised.

Cecil wasted no more of his trained mind on speculation. There was routine administration of the realm to be done before the evening bulletin on the Queen. He made some impression on the voluminous paperwork in front of him, until he was interrupted by Kat Ashley.

"Her Majesty's doctors have asked to see you at once, Mr Secretary. I've been sent to bring you to them."

"Of course." He stood up without demur, fully used to being at Elizabeth's beck and call. He checked himself, by way of reminder that there were no papers needed to take with him to the Queen at present, and he began to follow Kat towards the royal apartments. The skirts of her black gown rustled as she walked ahead of him.

"Mistress Ashley, forgive me for asking, but why are you so attired?"

"Oh, sir, 'tis because the whole Court must prepare for mourning!" cried Kat.

"Her Majesty?"

"Death threatens to hold every joint of her."

"Is it not somewhat premature to wear mourning apparel while she still lives?"

"Dear God, there is little time . . . The doctors will tell you more."

Cecil lapsed into silence. He opted to await confirmation of this dreadful news from the doctors. Perhaps then he would have to assess how best to try and prevent a catastrophe for the state which he had served so conscientiously with Elizabeth. Others may still think that Her Majesty would no longer be obdurate about naming a successor to her throne, but he was certain that she would never be induced to settle this most crucial matter. He could not stand by and see their hard work to bring peace, solvency and stability to her realm rendered as nothing.

He was spurred on in his duty to further these aims, by his own needs and those of people like him and his pregnant wife - people like the Lady Catherine and Lord Hertford - all of them parents with young children, who deserved a good future. His wife might bear him a son far more promising than the young fool he already had in Thomas Cecil. And if so, the child must be reared in advantageous circumstances.

Characteristically, William Cecil's expression revealed

none of his inner feelings. Rather, he watched with habitual impersonality the reactions of everyone else in the royal apartments. The doctors were huddled together in deliberation, much as he expected. There was gratifying relief on the faces of most of the courtiers and Queen's ladies at sight of him, and signs of apparent sorrow were much in evidence, not least on the face of Robert Dudley.

Cecil inclined his head in courtesy to the group of doctors, particularly to the one he preferred to speak with, Dr Symonds.

"Mr Secretary, we have little hope that Her Majesty will survive if her smallpox spots do not appear soon. She may not even regain consciousness."

"This is most dire news, Dr Symonds. How long does Her Majesty still have?"

"It may be only hours, sir. We will keep you informed at shorter intervals."

Cecil nodded in reply. His next move was to approach Robert Dudley. He noted the latter straighten up in the arrogant way which showed off his lordship's height and manly appearance. This gesture tended to attract some people and intimidate others.

Undeterred, Cecil looked up at Robert, eyeing him purposefully. "My lord, we must assemble as many of the Privy Council as are near at this heavy time. The good of Her Majesty's realm requires discussion and decision before any *foreign* intervention."

"I agree wholeheartedly, Mr Secretary."

"That is well, my lord," said Cecil. He gave no hint of his astonishment that they were both at least in accord on something. "You know that Spain may try to interfere against the other Queen in this island, and that the Scots and French may try on her behalf?"

"'Tis intolerable even to think of. With another Catholic queen, we could be plunged back to the horrific days, like under 'Bloody Mary'!"

"Let us concentrate on summoning our fellow-councillors at such short notice."

They were of similar mind so far, but Cecil doubted whether that would be sustained. He sent messengers to hasten those of the Privy Councillors who were in London to Hampton Court. He felt sure that Robert Dudley had much more to fear from the passing of Queen Elizabeth than he had. The Queen's Spirit hoped he might then cease having to be unduly careful in his dealings with her Eyes.

While he waited for the coming Council meeting, Cecil occupied himself with drawing up a memorandum to guide him with his proposals for the good of the realm. A reply to the liking of the Dowager Duchess of Suffolk may be in the offing more quickly than he had originally anticipated.

Later that night, he studied the faces of noblemen and knights as they sat round the long table in a room close to Elizabeth's apartments. The Earl of Pembroke swaggered in last and sprawled in the empty chair beside Robert Dudley.

"More friends of yours than foes here, Mr Secretary," Pembroke then sneered. "What brilliant rescue plan d'you have, for me at least to find fault with?"

"Beware that the central figure of my plan does not find fault with *you,* my Lord Pembroke!" Cecil replied coolly. "You may have cause to regret casting out a royal lady from under your roof once."

Pembroke glared at him in sullen silence, jaw jutting out, but Robert Dudley instead took up the offensive.

"And *that's* your solution, Cecil? We could be only hours away from putting a featherhead on Her Majesty's throne?"

"And what's your solution, my lord? Given the irrefutable facts that the royal wills of both Her Majesty's father and brother - the latter brought about by your own father, remember - now place the Lady Catherine next in line."

Robert preened himself to answer, but not until the

support voiced by Cecil's allies died down.

"I favour the Earl of Huntingdon to succeed Her Majesty, given the irrefutable fact that he is the only male claimant to the throne."

"The Earl of Huntingdon? Let us not forget, my lord, that he is also your brother-in-law! And he too is childless. He has no Tudor blood and his claim is at best a tenuous one. It comes through females descended from Her Majesty's great-great-uncle, who was drowned in a butt of malmsey wine."

To Robert's indignation, many councillors acknowledged Cecil's words with some amusement.

"The people may not want another female ruler, Mr Secretary," Robert snapped.

"Perhaps not a female ruler on her own, my lord. But the Lady Catherine has already borne the grandson of their Good Duke, a babe who is entirely English-born. No small advantages also that the lady is Protestant and young enough to bear more sons, and that the citizens of London are much in favour of her."

"Her marriage is invalid," scoffed Pembroke.

"Huh! A mere formality," said Cecil's Northamptonshire neighbour, Sir Walter Mildmay, to a chorus of assent.

The Earl of Arundel added, "Enjoy your purlieu of my Lord Hertford's Savernake Forest while you still can, my Lord Pembroke!"

Pembroke retaliated with a thunderous look, before Robert Dudley returned to the fray. "Little Hertford, our King!" he cried.

"If the Lady Catherine wishes so to honour her husband," said Mildmay.

"May the Lord have mercy on us."

"Young Hertford may be small in physique, Lord Robert," replied Cecil, "but he has fathered a fine boy nonetheless. Nor is his intelligence determined by his size! He could heed good advice from those of greater years and experience who would serve him."

"Of which you intend to be one," retorted Robert.

"England must not be left stranded in the midst of peril," said Cecil, to more utterances of support. "I would remind you of *your* wholehearted agreement earlier on this matter!"

"Tonight's meeting is hardly representative," grumbled Pembroke. "Some of our number are well away from London. What if *important* councillors like the Duke of Norfolk and the Earl of Shrewsbury are against another of the monstrous regiment of women on the throne?"

"My son-in-law, the Duke, will not be averse to the Lady Catherine," rejoindered Arundel.

Soon all the Council members present, except Robert Dudley and Pembroke, became convinced that the will of Henry VIII should be followed. If Elizabeth died, Catherine was to be made Queen.

# CHAPTER 16

# *A Journey Upstream*

"Her Majesty's condition remains unchanged."

William Cecil thanked Dr Symonds sombrely. "We should all stay at Court for the time being," he told his fellow-councillors, "in case Her Majesty's condition deteriorates."

The Privy Council had waited for the latest bulletin on Elizabeth before their meeting ended. For the next few hours, Cecil took such rest as he could and heard from Dr Symonds again very early in the morning.

"Her Majesty still clings to life, but she has not recovered consciousness."

Cecil was soon busy at his desk. He allowed himself a brief respite from his ever-pressing workload while he wrote another memorandum for his own reference. This one concerned a scheme of such great moment that he jotted down these particular notes in a private code known only to himself.

*'In the event of Her Majesty's death, the question of her successor can be solved by a simple strategy,'* he scribbled. *'All claimants to her throne to be invited to become members of the Privy Council and the Lady Catherine released. The Queen of Scots, the Earl of Huntingdon and others will be called to London, gathered together, then arrested and put in the Tower. Catherine would be proclaimed Queen and a peaceful accession ensured!'*

The Council members were re-assembling when the next bulletin was issued: "Her Majesty has partly regained consciousness. Her fever is less. The Privy Council should report at once to the royal bedchamber."

Cecil positioned himself at Elizabeth's bedside, so that he was near enough to converse with her. The Queen's dark eyes opened and made faint acknowledgement of him. They lingered for much longer on Robert, however, when she turned weakly towards his proud figure opposite. This single movement by a woman still in mortal danger of her life kept the power struggle between her Spirit and her Eyes to the fore.

"We would have Robin appointed Lord Protector of the realm after we are gone," she said hoarsely.

Cecil observed Pembroke's thin face turn smug like Robert's, having aligned himself supposedly on the winning side.

Elizabeth talked about her constant love for Lord Robert. "Nothing improper ever happened between us, Kat," she asserted.

Kat Ashley paled tearfully at that, and some of the Queen's ladies close by exchanged surreptitious glances. Cecil's imperturbable face concealed his strong belief that the people hated Robert Dudley too much to be ruled by him.

Elizabeth's eyes closed drowsily and did not re-open. The effort expended in speaking had evidently proved too taxing for her. Even so, Cecil thought that the wailing from Robert's sister Mary, who had nursed the Queen throughout her illness, could have waited until the doctors pronounced Elizabeth dead.

They took much careful deliberation in the tense atmosphere of the crowded chamber, before Dr Symonds said, "Her Majesty still lives. The relief of all of you is undoubtedly as great as ours. However, it would be more beneficial for Her Majesty if the chamber is now cleared."

Cecil went back to his work methodically as always, a considerable advantage to him in the present, ongoing suspense. The next time the doctors sent for him, they summoned him again to the royal bedchamber. But their message said nothing of life or death for the Queen.

He entered the chamber with the intention of proceeding to the same place at Elizabeth's bedside as before. He soon saw the pointlessness of this, however. For her bed was empty.

"This way, Mr Secretary," said Dr Symonds.

And Cecil turned his unemotional gaze to a scene which he could not have predicted.

On a mattress in front of the fire, Elizabeth lay wrapped all in red. All except her face and one of her hands. As he approached her, he noticed that the latter was reddish too. She drank from a bottle which Robert's sister held for her.

"The spots - they've broken," she croaked to Cecil.

"Her Majesty is safe," confirmed the doctor.

And Mr Secretary's face registered one of his infrequent smiles, "The Lord be praised."

The umpteenth November summons to the royal apartments interrupted William Cecil in his paperwork. It was another one demanding his immediate attendance there. But most of all, it was confidently signed 'Elizabeth R', rather than by any of her doctors.

He gathered up some more letters and documents for the Queen's signature, feeling pleased to be back in the old routine. Her Majesty had risen from her sick bed at the end of October, and there were indications already that she was returning to her combatant ways. On the previous day, he had made the first of his tactful withdrawals from her anger for many weeks.

Cecil braced himself for the impending meeting with Elizabeth. He hoped he could encourage her to see sense, if at last she was prepared to listen. His thoughts turned fully onto what he had attempted to tell her before - that Her Majesty's continued recovery was God's will indeed, bringing the greatest rejoicing to her realm. But her subjects had suffered a scare when she almost died without naming her successor. And so the Privy Council had acted wisely in making contingency plans.

Cecil's belief that Catherine was Elizabeth's best successor had motivated him to persuade his fellow-councillors into further animated discussions at the Earl of Arundel's house two nights ago. They had concluded their meeting after midnight, all unanimous adherents of Catherine's claim to the throne.

On his way to see the Queen, he brought himself into step with his host from that gathering. "Lost in thought, Lord Arundel?" he asked. "Or do you seek to free yourself from all tinge of association with me?"

"Mr Secretary! Have you been - sent for too?"

"'Tis an everyday occurrence for me, my lord."

"You can count on me for assistance with whatever you say about the other night."

"Compliment Her Majesty on her appearance," whispered Cecil. "Then we may find her in a more convivial mood. The smallpox blemishes have fortunately left no pock marks on her face, as they have on Lord Robert's loyal sister."

"Whatever you advise," breathed Arundel.

Soon they knelt before Elizabeth. "Get up, you ill-assorted pair of knaves," she shrieked. "We are not strong enough yet to box you both on the ears, so we shall resort to tears of rage."

"May I say how well Your Majesty -" began Arundel.

"Silence! How *dare* you hold a meeting of our Council under your roof without our sanction? You both know how opposed we are to the decision you all reached. Do you think to persuade us to it by your joint deceit?"

Cecil furnished her as intended with his opinion. He was calm and eloquent in putting to her the words previously worked out in his thoughts. Arundel regarded him in awed amazement.

Elizabeth, however, found an inventive means of responding without in fact making answer. She turned her wrath into a tirade against Catherine, which Cecil had heard several times before. The extent of the Queen's jealousy was shrilled out on every such occasion, with blatant intensity.

Arundel, who was not so accustomed to these extraordinary displays, directed a look at Elizabeth which was totally uncomprehending. "Well, if Your Majesty intends to rule England by frenzied emotion," he blurted out, "I can tell you that the noble peers of your realm will not stomach it!"

"And who are any of you to upbraid your Sovereign?" she retorted. "Do you wish to join those prisoners already in the Tower?"

"N-no. Forgive me, Your Majesty."

"Hm. My father would have had your head for less than this! But your Queen is merciful and sets her sights on recovery rather than retribution."

"May God bless Your Majesty," said Arundel.

"'Twas still without our sanction, though," she muttered, then suddenly switched to another matter. "What were you trying to say earlier, my lord, about how well I look?"

Arundel reeled off some nauseating and deferential flattery. Elizabeth seemed to be appeased, but Cecil suspected she was probably saving up her anger to channel it elsewhere in future.

At the beginning of February, Ned began to worry about the long-term effect on his loved ones of another winter in the Tower. Catherine was in the final weeks of her pregnancy. He had hoped for somewhere happier for her to bear their child. Somewhere perhaps of her own choosing, in freedom, and with the beauties of nature near enough to exert their usual delight on her.

From the confines of the Bell Tower, he and Catherine sometimes thought back to the autumn, when such hopes had been far from illusory. Catherine almost became

Queen of England! The smallpox had taken many lives, but Elizabeth was healed of it and so here they still were, with no prospect of release.

Catherine's labour pains came on the morning of the 10th. She called Ned and Edward to her bedside and kissed both of them. "If I don't survive the birth this time, Ned, please tell the Lieutenant that my greatest request is for the Queen to comfort you with your freedom."

He kissed her tenderly and then took Edward by the hand, encouraging the little boy to exchange waves of farewell with her.

"I know, Mistress Cousins - there's women's work to be done here," he said, as the old woman opened the door insistently for them.

Catherine's other women were scurrying about, following military-style orders from Mistress Cousins. The Lieutenant's wife claimed charge of Edward. Warner himself tried to calm Ned's worries as they ate breakfast together, but Ned soon abandoned his meal and went to the Tower chapel. He prayed that the dangers of childbirth would be mercifully quick and Catherine's recovery total.

As the vigil of waiting lengthened, his fidgety consultation of his pocket watch became more frequent. He prayed again several times. Eventually, he decided to go back to his own chamber. He was nearing the chapel doorway when the Lieutenant came in a little breathlessly.

"I thought you may still be here, my lord."

"What news is there of Lady Catherine?"

"I am instructed to tell you that her ladyship is safely delivered of another boy, my lord."

"Another son! God's blessing be upon them, Master Lieutenant."

"I hope Her Majesty's heart will now be moved in compassion towards all of you," murmured Warner.

"I must hasten to them," said Ned. The Lieutenant's words had been uttered sincerely, but the mere mention of Elizabeth had dampened Ned's sense of elation.

Back at Catherine's bedside again, he bent to embrace her. He received with her the congratulations of her women and held his new-born son for as long as Mistress Cousins would let him. Long enough to give the child his paternal blessing and to agree with Catherine that they would call him Thomas.

'Tis best that we name him as we choose, no matter what Elizabeth might do, thought Ned.

He had no doubt that the name Thomas Seymour may stir echoes for the Queen of his philandering uncle, one of those headless relatives in the chapel. Ned believed that most people would use the birth of a healthy babe as an opportunity for reconciliation wherever this was needed. But Elizabeth? She had already penalized a small, defenceless child - their first son! Yet who could know if she would live long?

After Thomas's baptism in the chapel, Ned wrote a prayer in the blank leaves of his Bible. It was a prayer of thanksgiving for the safety of Catherine and the baby through the dangers of childbirth, and also one of supplication that Elizabeth would show some pity towards her two prisoners and their children.

Later in February, he trod his well-worn route back to the White Tower one morning for a visit from his servant, Anthony Penne, concerning financial matters to do with his estates. His return shortly to Catherine's chamber was made like countless times before. He walked up to the door lightheartedly and knocked.

When Catherine gave no answering call, Ned tried twice to open the door. "God's wounds! What's going on?" he asked. "Catherine?"

"No use m'creaky old joints trying to open it from inside, my lord," wailed Mistress Cousins through the door, "as 'tis soundly locked!"

Ned pushed his full force against it in rising anger. "Why is it like this?"

"I know not."

"Well, where's Lady Catherine? And our babes?"

"In here, my lord, all sleeping. They're fine. Why don't you try coming back later?" she suggested.

"I'm going in search of the Lieutenant," he said. "I must know what's happening!" He stormed off towards the Lieutenant's quarters, hoping there was nothing sinister behind this situation.

As he approached, he heard Warner exclaim, "But some of my furniture's in there, in the Bell Tower!"

Ned came upon the Lieutenant more quickly than he had anticipated - but not in the *way* he had expected.

"Master Lieutenant! What's the meaning of all this?"

"My Lord Hertford, 'tis your second boy . . . Her Majesty's response," cried Warner.

"Sir," interrupted the captain of the guards who surrounded him, "we've been ordered to put you in a dungeon."

"What! The Tower's Lieutenant in one of his own dungeons?" protested Ned. "Master Lieutenant, if there's aught I can do to help -"

"No longer 'Master Lieutenant'," said the captain, "but a prisoner, like you, m'lord."

"Ask my friend Cecil to help me," Warner called, as he was hustled away.

Armed guards also surrounded Ned. "You will be dealt with tomorrow, my lord!" the captain promised him. "In the meantime, you are close prisoner."

He was marched back promptly to the White Tower, just like in the early part of his captivity.

Golden stars adorned the ceiling of the courtroom where Ned was taken the next day. From judgements made at the Star Chamber, near Westminster Hall, he knew there was no procedure for appeal. This was hardly the answer he had sought to the prayer he wrote inside his Bible!

Warner sat near him, head bowed. Few words had

passed between them on their river journey from the Tower. The guards had seen to that. Some of these men had no doubt enjoyed giving orders to their former Lieutenant and also taunting both him and Ned that leek juice should have been applied to his lordship's manhood to cool his ardour. Now Her Majesty would accomplish such cooling by much more drastic measures . . .

Ned was sorry for Warner, that this was Elizabeth's thanks to him for showing kindness and friendship to Catherine. If the Queen had not been cured of her disease, Warner's reward would have been a whole world of difference.

Warner cut an even more abject figure when the judges told him formally of his dismissal for failure in his duty as Lieutenant of the Tower. "You were commanded to keep the Lady Catherine and Lord Hertford strictly separate," he was reminded in no uncertain terms.

"I let my lord and lady meet once, after a great deal of persuasion," he affirmed. "Then I saw how futile it was to separate them. They're very happily married."

"In Her Majesty's eyes, they are *not* married," snapped Sir John Mason, one of the judges.

Then Mason rounded on Ned, "As for you, Hertford, Her Majesty believes there was never a more conceited youth. Never one that likes himself better nor promises himself greater things."

While others joined in deriding him in coarser ways, Ned did not flinch. He found that his earlier experiences of facing Elizabeth's commissioners in the Tower helped him to face her stern judges now. According to them, he was a danger to Elizabeth's realm.

How they exaggerate, he thought. All this, because I want a happy life with Catherine and our sons!

"Your lordship is fully aware of the declaration made about your supposed marriage," Mason went on. "Therefore you are charged with presumptuous, contemptuous and outrageous behaviour in using the Lady

Catherine as you have done, both before the declaration and since. A large fine is to be set upon you, so that a good part of your income might redress some of your offence to Her Majesty."

"A good part of my income?" repeated Ned tonelessly. He was thinking of his estates, which had not yet recovered from their years of neglect during his minority.

"The lion's share, probably!" sneered Mason. "Your fine will total fifteen thousand pounds."

Warner gasped audibly with shock. The whole sentence was then reeled off rapidly to Ned, "Five thousand pounds for seducing a virgin of the blood royal, five thousand pounds for breaking prison and ravishing her again, five thousand pounds for the birth of your second bastard son, Thomas Seymour. And your lordship's imprisonment will continue. You will thus learn what it is to have offended your Sovereign so arrogantly."

"I am lawfully married to the Lady Catherine," replied Ned. "I comforted her in her sadness and paid my conjugal duty, of which I cannot repent."

While he and Warner were being led away for their journey back to the Tower, the latter managed to whisper an aside to him, "Neither do I repent, my lord. You have suffered such a setback today - and yet a short time ago, we were near to addressing you as Sire."

"I thank you for all your kindness. What my poor tenants will make of this, though, I hazard to guess. I had such good intent to improve their lot."

Ned thought of all his plans for repairs and rebuilding, regarding his inheritance. He could well imagine his chief forester John Berwick grumbling, "'Igh time Queen Lisbet let bygones be bygones. 'Ow low can 'er stoop to take things out on little babes?"

He sighed as he looked in the direction of Westminster Abbey, where Jennie's monument had been completed - and thankfully paid for. But as yet Elizabeth had forbidden him even to visit that.

Ned was sure that for as long as she lived, Elizabeth would do all in her power to break his and Catherine's 'knot of secret might'. He was still close prisoner. Would he ever see Catherine and their two boys again?

## CHAPTER 17

# *Clubfoot Hales and Crouchback Mary*

The plague claimed many thousands of victims in London in the summer of 1563. It struck down people of all ages and ranks, and foreigners as well as English folk, amongst them the Spanish ambassador.

One August morning in the Bell Tower, Catherine's maids were in tears. "What ails all of you?" she asked, in some alarm.

"'Tis Tom Goddard, Lady Catherine," said Meg. "He's dead o'the plague."

"Oh, no!"

"It's spread near the Tower, Lady Catherine," added Book.

"None of us wants to go back to Hanworth," chipped in Beth, "all wanting to stay in your ladyship's service, but -"

"But 'tis time to leave here," said Mistress Cousins.

"I shall write to Mr Secretary Cecil at once," said Catherine, "and plead for all of us to leave this place for healthier country air."

Book dried her eyes. "Barnaby told us that my Lord Hertford has already written, Lady Catherine, and also sent condolences to Tom's folk in Wiltshire."

"Poor Tom! The loss of him will be heavy to my lord. But I shall add my plea to his with William Cecil. Her Majesty will be on her summer progress now, so if there is any delay in Mr Secretary's reply, may God sustain us all in the meantime."

When Catherine had completed her letter to Cecil, she lifted Edward gently onto her lap. She hoped that he would maintain the good health that she lacked, and continue to be like his father and baby brother in that respect. Their well-being was a source of joy to her, though her only contact with Ned for the last six months had been their reams of letters to each other, smuggled back and forth by their servants.

If only we could all be together soon and for always, she thought.

A reply arrived from Cecil, dated 21st August. Catherine proceeded to read it straightaway, with her household gathered tensely near her.

"Well," she beamed at Beth and Book, "you needn't worry about going back to Hanworth, you two. We are ordered to go somewhere that Book and Mistress Cousins will remember from that progress two summers ago - to my uncle, Lord John Grey's house at Pirgo."

She paused for a few moments, while they expressed their relief at this prospect. For her own sake, however, Catherine wished that her second visit to Pirgo would be a short one. She disliked her uncle and realized that his draughty, crumbling house would do neither her any good, nor Mistress Cousins' creaky limbs in the winter months . . .

"Nay, 'tis my lord who is bound for Hanworth," she resumed, but her voice began to falter. "My lord and -"

"Lady Catherine?"

"My lord and *Edward,*" she said, horrified, "while the baby comes with me."

Catherine flung Cecil's reply down and held Edward in her arms. "But he's not even two years old till next month!" she sobbed, feeling that her swift-beating heart would break. "And Hanworth, it's in the opposite direction from Pirgo, and so many miles away!"

"Can't you appeal against this decision, Lady Catherine?" asked Meg, as the rest of Catherine's household looked on in stunned silence.

"Once we're all away from here, I will appeal for both

my lord and Edward to be with Thomas and me!" declared Catherine. "But if I do so beforehand, I'd be in fear of being kept here for much longer."

"'Tis probably wise," agreed Mistress Cousins. "Her Majesty has already released some prisoners from the Tower to go home. And with her cancelling most of his lordship's fine, she's made a start for more clemency towards you."

"I'm so glad she released Sir Edward Warner," said Catherine.

Her son stretched his infant legs and feet determinedly towards the floor. "Down," he gurgled.

Catherine complied affectionately with his demand. She felt that somehow she must try and live for each moment of her remaining time with him, despite the wrench which their enforced parting would mean for her.

They played together with the pets for a while and a little later, Edward recouped some of his energy with a nap. Catherine began another letter to Ned, reassuring him of her undying love. She received a similar one from him before she had finished. Ned told her how upset he was about the details of Elizabeth's orders for their removal from the Tower. He sent Catherine a ring, in token of his feelings at their forthcoming captivity in houses so distant from each other. It was a mourning ring, inscribed inside with the words, *'While I live, yours.'*

Oh, Ned, don't give up hope, thought Catherine as she studied this. The Queen must relent towards us one day!

She continued with her own letter, thanking him for the ring and ending with the message, 'As soon as I received all these words of yours, I read them over with my heart as well as with my eyes.'

Catherine heard again from William Cecil a few days later. She appreciated him informing her that a royal coach drawn by four Flemish horses would take her to Pirgo, as a concession for her ill-health. But she was certainly unhappy about the man appointed to take charge of conducting her there.

"Begging your pardon, Lady Catherine," said Book, "b-but my Lord Hertford's stepfather - he's one of the main reasons why we couldn't settle at Hanworth."

"He's such a busybody," groaned Beth.

"So rude and tactless. Very sorry to speak thus, Lady Catherine."

"You're forgiven. But no more of this, please!" murmured Catherine.

Secretly, how she agreed with them! Like Catherine's mother and step-grandmother, Ned's widowed mother had made a second marriage to one of her own servants. Sergeant Francis Newdigate was as overbearing as his noble spouse, and Catherine was sure that Elizabeth had chosen him for his task deliberately to undermine her spirits further on her journey.

Newdigate hailed from a family who owned property near to the Greys' forfeited Warwickshire castle at Astley, where her father and Uncle John were captured after rebelling against Queen Mary. There was much that the Sergeant could still gloat about, if he felt so inclined, or if either Elizabeth or Ned's mother had exhorted him to do so . . .

He came to the Bell Tower on a hot day in late August. Newdigate greeted Catherine respectfully at first, but when he saw Book and Beth, he suddenly exploded, "Good God! So you intrepid pair left Hanworth for this stinking hell-hole. And you prefer no doubt to replace this for draughty Pirgo."

His elbow nudged at Book Page's arm, while she shrank silently closer to Beth. Catherine's voice rose clearly at once, "I'll thank you to leave all members of my household alone, Sergeant Newdigate! Nor will I allow you to mar my last moments with my son."

"Moments only, it must be, madam," he rejoindered. "I have my orders to take him to my Lord Hertford and there can be no converse between my lord and you."

Catherine held back her tears as she reassured herself that Edward seemed well and he had his favourite toys to accompany him to his father. Then she hugged him, kissed him gently, straightened a little crease on his sleeve and murmured her farewell blessing. She would entrust only Mistress Cousins to carry him to Ned in the White Tower, though Newdigate must fulfil his orders and escort the child there.

The sight of Edward's bewildered face, peering at her from over the old woman's shoulder, was one which Catherine knew could never be shut out from her mind. He was so very young to understand that she would always love him and that she was certainly not abandoning him. She rushed for just one more touch of his hand, till she could be with him again. Edward giggled and a bright-coloured ball dropped over Mistress Cousins, to be caught by Catherine.

She managed to smile in response as she gave the toy back to him, pressing it into his hand. After her wave of goodbye, Edward was gone from her beyond the iron-girded door of her chamber, and Catherine collapsed into the nearest tattered chair. She felt too weak to move.

Soon, however, she felt obliged to rally herself when she heard a tutting Mistress Cousins return with Newdigate.

"'Tis time to begone to the coach, madam," he bellowed. "My God. These chairs - they're worse than the one now in my family that your father used when he hid at Astley as a traitor! What a sight he must have made, sitting inside a hollow oak tree when he was arrested."

"Does it give you pleasure to remind me of that?" Catherine retorted.

"Nay, I'll pass that dubious honour on to your ladyship's uncle at Pirgo. What was it - a pile of hay that *he* was caught skulking under at Astley? Lord John Grey was very lucky to be pardoned, all because his wife grovelled to Queen Mary."

"My uncle and aunt would be even luckier if you'd

allow them to forget this matter. Now would you kindly lower your voice, in case it makes my baby cry."

Catherine insisted on carrying Thomas carefully down to the coach herself, speaking softly to him as her eyes filled with tears. They emerged outside and she heard a loving sound which she had often imagined during her baby's short life.

*"Catherine!"*

She looked over to the White Tower and glimpsed Ned, with Edward on his shoulders, at a corridor window. He called her name more urgently. A sudden surge of energy animated her. She wanted to go with Thomas towards them, but her guards were so positioned to restrain her from such a move. Catherine blew two subdued farewell kisses to her husband and elder son, and even their reply in kind was disturbed by Newdigate.

"There's no time to linger here, madam," he said pompously. "I have my orders to be back from Pirgo by nightfall and take their lordships to Hanworth tomorrow."

Catherine ignored him and waved to Ned and Edward from inside the coach till they were out of sight. The bitter blow of separation from them tempered any feelings of relief at leaving the Tower. Otherwise these would have flooded over her when the coach passed through the gates of the fortress. She acknowledged some words of comfort which Mistress Cousins was crooning to Thomas. Then exhaustion overwhelmed Catherine, as the coach rumbled and lurched along ill-kept roads through the plague-ridden city into the Essex countryside.

"You appear to have acquired many cousins lately, Mr Secretary!" observed Elizabeth coolly.

"My new son, Robert, is the only extra kin that *I* wished for, Your Majesty."

She regarded him approvingly, and resumed sifting through the batch of begging letters addressed to 'Good cousin Cecil', which he had brought for her to read.

"I'm not fooled into believing that your support for Lady Catherine's cause is other than dormant," Elizabeth went on, with one of her grim smiles. "Sometimes I think these correspondents of yours will never be satisfied that I remitted ten thousand pounds of Hertford's fine."

"Your Majesty's action was most gracious," said Cecil tonelessly.

"What's this in your letter from Lord John Grey? 'Catherine is a penitent and sorrowful woman for the Queen's displeasure', is she? About time too! Hm, and *she* herself writes that she craves our pardon 'with upstretched hands and downbent knees'. More fitting words than some I've heard her say!"

"I would advise Your Majesty to read Lord John Grey's next letter," replied Cecil, placing the relevant item before her.

Elizabeth duly skimmed over its contents, which informed Cecil that Catherine was wasting away and would not live long unless she was fully pardoned soon.

"She must learn to sacrifice happiness, as I have done before her," Elizabeth retorted. "I have my throne to keep secure and no clamouring of petitions will entice me from that path!"

"Indeed not, Your Majesty."

"You can tell your 'cousin', Lord John, not to waste time also sending appeals for her through Lord Robert. All this, my Spirit, takes *both* of us away from our work of building a stronger England."

Cecil continued to stand at her side dispassionately. "Has Your Majesty's Eyes received pleas from any others of your Spirit's 'cousins'?" he enquired.

"Aye, he has - from the Seymours! I told Robin to inform them that I'm in no mood to reply."

"I doubt not that his lordship has passed this on to Lord Hertford."

Several autumn weeks of freedom from appeals

followed, but in December 1563, Elizabeth was irked when Catherine, Lord John and even Ned's mother wrote to Cecil.

"Tell Lady Catherine and her uncle to stop their whingeing!" snapped Elizabeth. "Lord John admits himself that her women take good care of her."

"On the subject of Lady Catherine and her household," ventured Cecil, "Lord John enclosed with his latest letter an itemized bill for expenses in supplying their daily requirements. I fear this needs some guidance for response from Your Majesty, however tedious such a matter is for you."

Elizabeth groaned as she looked at the bill. "Send this to Hertford - demanding immediate payment."

"Even though the marriage is invalid, Your Majesty?"

"'Tis still his duty to provide for his bastard sons and their mother! After all, his errant bedsport with her brought her to this pretty pass. Let *him* pay for the sheets and bedding and other paraphernalia that she needs. I want the demand to be signed by both you and Lord Robert!"

The next attempt at persuasion of the Queen left her Spirit alone. Instead, her Eyes came to her rather sheepishly.

"Surely you're not here again like an errand boy for the Seymours, Robin," she sighed.

Robert sighed too. "I have been asked to give Your Majesty these. A poor token, so 'tis said, from my Lord of Hertford."

"Gloves?" shrugged Elizabeth, in some amusement. She received them from Robert for the closer test of putting the pair of gloves on and peeling them off, as was her frequent habit.

"He, er, beseeches me to send him word of your liking or no of the gloves, so that he may have them improved, if need be."

"Hm," said Elizabeth. On went the gloves again, and

off, a few more times, as she relaxed full into laughter. "Well, my lord, you may say to Hertford there is no fault to be found in them, except that the next pair he sends me should be made a little more robust."

She looked at Robert teasingly. "And incidentally, Robin, you may also inform him that I am still not moved to free him and you have done *all you can* to aid him!"

"I'll do so gladly, Your Majesty," beamed Robert. "But I haven't yet told *you* all that I can."

"Not told us all that you can! Come, Robin, explain yourself."

"Rumours have reached me that a scurrilous pamphlet is circulating, amongst certain lawyers and Members of Parliament and others. It is said to support Catherine's marriage and her right to succeed Your Majesty."

"God's death! *Most* of Parliament would have us free her at once. Who is the author of this abomination?"

"I haven't seen it yet. I only hear that Your Majesty's Spirit may have helped to compile it. At least, most of the others who may be involved are friends of his!"

"Let's hear their names, Robin, and we'll wait and see if your suspicions are correct . . ."

Amongst them was Lord John Grey, who in Lent wrote one of the renewed appeals which aimed to touch the Queen's conscience. Elizabeth observed in silence that he wished he was her confessor and able to sermonize her from the pulpit about forgiveness. In April, she placed Catherine's custodian under house arrest too, in his residence at Pirgo.

"Your 'cousin' John Grey is in trouble over this," she said caustically to William Cecil, thrusting a thin, tattered manuscript under his very nose. "Look what your favouring of Lady Catherine has led to."

Elizabeth's challenge was unavailing, as so often with him. Not even the slightest flicker of emotion registered on her Secretary's face. His steely eyes moved rapidly across the title of the pamphlet, *A Declaration or Discourse on the*

*Crown Imperial of this Realm.*

"'Tis even said that you and your brother-in-law, the Lord Chancellor, wrote some of it," she launched another attack.

"I am always careful not to do anything which would cause offence, Your Majesty."

"Huh! At any rate, the Lord Chancellor's underling, John Hales, is committed to the Fleet Prison as his reward for being its author. What is it this meddler is nicknamed - 'Clubfoot' Hales?"

"Yes, Your Majesty. His foot was deformed by a dagger wound."

"Well, he's put his clubfoot into matters which are none of his business! Your brother-in-law will be severely censured for allowing Hales to write this, Mr Secretary."

"Is Your Majesty reacting so vehemently because the Queen of Scots has also written to you, asking for leniency for the Lady Catherine?"

"Leniency?" Elizabeth almost choked. "Our cousin of Scotland would never have made such a request concerning her rival, if she'd known the worst part of Hales' activities."

She saw Cecil take a small step backwards, in preparation for one of his tactful withdrawals when she lost her temper. "Our anger will run its course with you in our presence," she ordered, "since you are not yet free of our suspicions. See here in the pamphlet - Hales sought the opinions and advice of all these foreign lawyers. Every one of them upheld Catherine Grey's claim and the legality of her marriage. If tension rebuilds with other countries, do you think that the Scots and French will forget what he's done? Or Philip of Spain?"

"I will note Your Majesty's misgivings about this matter."

"You will also arrange for Hertford to be removed from Hanworth. Can you guess who financed Hales' jaunts abroad? One Sergeant Francis Newdigate!"

Cecil grimaced a little. "Lord John will be none too pleased to learn that he was on the same side as Newdigate. He finds the man insolent."

"Newdigate is already in for questioning," said Elizabeth. "He must be reprimanded, Mr Secretary, and ordered to have no further contact with Hertford, upon pain of rigorous imprisonment."

"And what of Lord Hertford, Your Majesty?"

"He is going to stricter custody - to the home of Sir John Mason at Clerkenwell. No doubt Mason will remind him daily of his fine and his past disobedience to his Queen."

Cecil bowed as Elizabeth imperiously waved him away and he took the manuscript of Clubfoot Hales' pamphlet with him as evidence. The Queen detected that her Spirit was still reluctant to accept that the appearance of this offensive document spelt the end of any chance of mercy for Catherine.

Elizabeth believed that Hales' interfering had at least put a stop to the appeals for Catherine and Ned. And these may even be ended completely by the death of one or more of the captives under the strain of her displeasure. Yet her patience had to hold out for several months before a prisoner obliged her by expiring at Pirgo. A prisoner whose friend and 'good cousin Cecil' noted that he had died of gout and great weariness of thoughts.

After the demise of Lord John Grey in November 1564, Elizabeth transferred Catherine to the custody of deaf Sir William Petre of Ingatestone Hall, who had also given them hospitality on that summer progress three years earlier. By then, Elizabeth was in the process of attracting more guesswork about her motives. She had offered an English husband to the Queen of Scots: her very own Eyes, her 'Sweet Robin' Dudley, the new Earl of Leicester!

Catherine stepped down from the royal coach in the base court of Ingatestone Hall. "I pray that in a day or two, you'll be less startled by the effects of ill-health upon my appearance, Lady Petre," she said quietly.

"Madam, you and little Lord Thomas are most welcome here."

"Your words leave this poor prisoner thankful. And I would be even more so if I had my older boy Edward with me, the babe I was expecting when I was at Ingatestone before. Now Thomas is almost the age that Edward was the last time I saw him - twenty-two months!"

Catherine sensed that her situation was already attracting much sympathy from the wife and daughters of Sir William Petre, who were present to greet her. One of them carried in her arms an infant still in swaddling bands.

"This way, madam," said Lady Petre, and conducted Catherine and her younger son like honoured guests through the porch into the Great Hall of the rose-brick mansion.

It was pleasant to be treated thus, after the frosty atmosphere of living with those Grey relatives at Pirgo and their depressing influence on her morale. Their stringent emphasis on her pretending to express remorse for offending the Queen had worsened Catherine's health.

The arrival of Sir William Petre at Pirgo to pay his last respects to her dead uncle, and then escort her here, had also been a vast improvement on Newdigate. Petre seemed such a taciturn man, in contrast! Catherine had yet to hear him speak in much more than courteous monosyllables.

"I trust that you will excuse your host for his deafness, madam," confided Lady Petre.

"Yes, of course."

"It shouldn't trouble you over-much. My husband's membership of the Privy Council keeps him often away from home, perhaps rather more because he is a friend as well as colleague of Mr Secretary Cecil."

A friend of Cecil's? Catherine felt pleased to hear that her great supporter at Court still retained a friend after the debacle of John Hales' pamphlet! She assumed that Petre had most likely stayed aloof from the whole sorry business. And if his absences from Ingatestone led to a more relaxed regime for her here, all well and good.

The Petres next showed her with pride to the first floor of their home and allocated to her the royal suite of rooms occupied by Elizabeth on the previous visit, including one which they called the Garden Chamber. Catherine soon reciprocated their deferential treatment of her by agreeing to their earnest request for her to be godmother to the baby boy amongst her welcoming party.

As she settled more into her new surroundings, she began to lengthen her daily walks along the paths of the walled orchard near the house. She delighted in the quality of the water piped into Ingatestone Hall from its own wells and her appetite improved in the atmosphere of warmth which quickly developed with her hosts.

Yet however obliging the Petre family were about her comfort and their musical entertainments for her benefit, she still pined for the company of Ned and Edward. A sad symbol of how much they had been cheated of happiness together took material form when her hosts invited Catherine to inscribe her name on the chimney-piece in the Garden Chamber. She so much wanted to put 'Catherine Hertford' or 'Catherine Seymour'. But she used her maiden name, to prevent any repercussions towards the Petres if Elizabeth ever visited Ingatestone again.

Catherine was glad for her own little household that none of them faced restrictions in slipping away to the nearby village on the Great Essex Road. Sometimes, during Sir William Petre's absences, they even went in pairs to London and Hertford House, where they exchanged her letters with Ned's veteran message-carriers. The outside news which this enabled her servants to bring Catherine was always consistent that the local inhabitants spoke so kindly of her, and her husband and sons. But such heart-warming reports were no substitute for being with her loved ones and in the spring of 1565, Catherine wrote to

Ned that she was ill again.

When she missed her first meals in the Ingatestone parlour, Lady Petre came to her, full of concern. "If you wish for a royal physician to attend you, madam, you need only say the word and I shall *insist* that one is sent," she offered. "Her Majesty would face a furore if she refused your ladyship the services of one of her own doctors, now that the news coming out of Scotland is so dire."

"Dire news from Scotland? I know of none, Lady Petre."

"Dear madam, 'tis to your advantage to know."

"My advantage?" Catherine perked up a little. "Is Her Majesty's Master of Horse accepted as husband for the Queen of Scots?"

"No, madam. The Scottish Queen would have none of my Lord Robert - my Lord Leicester, that is to say rightly now! Instead, she seems set to make an impetuous love-match with a younger Englishman - the Countess of Lennox's son, Lord Darnley. And Queen Elizabeth roundly condemns such a prospect."

"Does she?" murmured Catherine distantly. Her thoughts ran on that she would celebrate, if Mary Queen of Scots also defied Elizabeth by marrying for love. Mary could enjoy her love-match, safe in the knowledge that the vindictive English Queen was powerless to imprison her!

"Mark my words, the Countess of Lennox will be clapped back in the Tower if this goes ahead," added Lady Petre.

Catherine stopped herself from shuddering at the mention of the Tower. "But the Countess was only released from there soon before I was sent to Pirgo!"

She kept her other memories of the Countess' release to herself. At the time she had suspected that this was a signal favour to the Scottish Queen's claim to the throne, for the Countess of Lennox was a Catholic and closely related to Mary.

"I rejoice for you, madam, that Her Majesty will no longer be able to resist all the pressure to call you back to her royal favour," said Lady Petre. "But I shall miss you, indeed I shall! My husband has decided to ask Mr Secretary Cecil to plead your cause with her again, whether the Queen of Scots marries Lord Darnley or not."

Catherine could only whisper, as emotion overcame her. "I could soon be with my lord again, and both our children!"

She wept for joy and smiled when her younger son grimaced as she hugged him. Thomas was not as demonstrative as his brother had been in affection for her, though he shared their love of the pets. He was especially fond of Misty, one of Comfit's daughters and now Catherine's favourite spaniel since Amber had died. Her dread that as Thomas grew older, he too would be taken from her, seemed to dissolve. She recovered some of her health and did not require the services of a royal physician after all.

The weeks of June and July flowed by in an atmosphere almost aflame with the anticipation of impending freedom. The good wishes of the Petres enhanced the prevailing mood of real hope, and Catherine found this was mirrored too by Ned's letters.

She was in the summer house at Ingatestone with her hosts, when William Cecil sent a message one early August evening. "Mr Secretary says that the Queen of Scots wedded Lord Darnley on the last Sunday of July," Sir William Petre broke the news in his slow, monotone voice. "Her Majesty is vexed beyond measure and has committed the Countess of Lennox back to the Tower. Alas . . . that he says naught of your rehabilitation with similar alacrity, madam, but there is no doubting the great consensus of public opinion in this matter."

As August wore on, Catherine's dreams strengthened more and more of leaving the undulating countryside of Essex and beholding hills overlooking Savernake Forest.

It seemed appropriate that Cecil's next note to Petre arrived on 21st August, two years to the day since he told

Catherine that her plea to be removed from the Tower had received Elizabeth's assent. The sheer magnitude of the joy awaiting Catherine after so much tribulation meant that euphoria reached fever pitch at Ingatestone from the moments that the message was brought to her custodian, shortly before supper.

Catherine excused Petre's ill-health as reason enough why he alone of her sympathizers there did not become so caught up in this feeling. His eyebrows knit together very low over his eyes as he squinted over the contents.

"Well?" ventured his wife, brightly.

He grunted and then handed the message to her. Lady Petre read through it and swooned. Their daughters went to her assistance, while both he and Catherine looked at her with great concern. Petre recovered possession of Cecil's words and offered these to Catherine.

"Madam," he said. "So sorry."

She was still distracted more by her immediate company, as she read, '*. . . an unhappy chance and monstrous.*' Those words were certainly not the kind expected from William Cecil! She returned to the note with fuller concentration: *'The Sergeant-Porter, Keyes, being the biggest gentleman at Court, has secretly wedded the Lady Mary Grey, the least in size of the entire Court . . . each imprisoned separately . . . offence very great.'*

The rest of the message blurred before her eyes as, totally crestfallen, she pictured her younger sister with the elderly, giant Sergeant-Porter. "Crouchback Mary", imprisoned too for a secret marriage, and to someone so ill-matched! The whole thing would have been laughable, if Catherine had not been so adversely affected by family matters again.

"Another Grey, fallen into disfavour," she observed bitterly. "And my sister's secret marriage has cost my lord and me our freedom."

One of the Petres' daughters, Thomasine, tried to put on a brave face. "Nay, madam, say not so."

"I *would,* if it were not true! Dear God, I had no prior knowledge of this. My family - I long ago tried to reduce any of their influence over me. But like rank weeds, they can shoot up unsought, even if determinedly cut down -"

That sums them up, she thought. Why, why, should you and I have to suffer, Ned, because of my accursed younger sister?

"I hope that Lady Petre will soon recover," said Catherine. She left her supper, bade the family goodnight and fled in tears to her quarters.

Catherine's house arrest at Ingatestone Hall lasted until the following May. Elizabeth then ordered her removal to the red-brick gloom of nearby Gosfield. Catherine parted disconsolately from the Petre family outside the royal coach in front of their gatehouse. All the more so, because they knew how much the return of sorrow had sent her health into further decline since that fateful August day.

"What will become of us all now?" she wondered wistfully to Mistress Cousins, as the coach began its bumpy journey along the lane towards the Great Essex Road.

## CHAPTER 18

# *"The Picture of Myself"*

*"You do not know what true love is,"* murmured a girl's voice through the Queen's thoughts. Elizabeth was at Greenwich, pacing the Privy Chamber and full of rancour over Robert Dudley's recent flirting with one of her Boleyn cousins, Lettice Knollys.

"It's five years since Catherine Grey sniped at us about true love, Blanche!" she reflected angrily. "What's so special about her that inspires Hertford's love and devotion to last so long? I would strike Catherine even yet if I ever hear her speak such words again."

Blanche sighed, "Kat always blamed herself for lack of supervision of both the Grey sisters, which gave them their chances to marry without your gracious permission."

"Dear Kat!" said Elizabeth more sympathetically, as she stopped and sat down. "I do not blame her any more for the wilfulness of Catherine and Mary Grey."

"Your Majesty's visits pleased Kat more than anything in her last illness," said Blanche. "But Lord Leicester is waiting for audience now."

"Then he can wait! I believe that Kat died happily because I assured her I'd never marry him."

"Your words brought her much comfort, Your Majesty."

"The world seems a poorer place without her," observed Elizabeth. Blanche nodded sadly in agreement.

Elizabeth reminisced about her faithful old governess for several more minutes. "We are not so forgetful of majesty," she had said by Kat's deathbed, "as to tie ourself to a servant, whom we have of our own goodness advanced."

Eventually, she condescended to see Robert. She kept him kneeling while she flew into a rage, berating him for infidelity, as if she had denied herself marriage to a mighty prince solely for him.

"Tit-for-tat, was it, my lord?" she shrilled. "You thought our Spirit worked on us to offer you as spouse to the Queen of Scots, after you informed us about his links with the Clubfoot Hales business. So you flirted with a married woman! Well, Lettice Knollys may not have spurned you, but she's lost our good favour for all time and has been packed off home to her husband."

"I beg Your Majesty's forgiveness. My affection is for you only," he answered, with a wounded look. "My actions were meant to divert you."

"*Divert us?* Or test us, my lord, by diverting yourself?"

"'Twas to be of service, and seek Your Majesty to be attentive to the poor opinions of your Eyes again, as well as your Spirit."

"If that's so, then promise never to offend us with such diversions again."

Robert gave his promise, still on his knees. He attempted a winning smile. Elizabeth's demeanour softened and became more like the last time he had been in such lengthy homage to her. She had teasingly tickled his neck then in front of the whole Court, when she created him Earl of Leicester.

"Now we are reconciled," she said and magnanimously allowed him to stand.

Elizabeth's dismay about his conduct was subdued now by her belief that part of the natural order of life was for love between a man and a woman to fade. Her feelings for Robert had certainly done so, as had her father's love for his various wives. The Queen of Scots' union with Darnley appeared to be doomed after only a year and even Sergeant-Porter Keyes had offered to renounce his marriage to Mary Grey, in an attempt to be released from the Fleet Prison!

So why, Elizabeth wondered, does the 'knot of secret might' prevail against all my efforts to sunder it? The *only* reason can be that it's an act of defiance - Seymour ambition, being fuelled by those harebrains in Parliament who want to announce Catherine officially as my successor. Huh! Gosfield Hall is ideal for the little featherhead.

Elizabeth well remembered visiting Gosfield Hall on that summer progress after she sent Catherine to the Bell Tower. The cheerless mansion with no windows on the ground floor was eminently suitable for shutting someone away from the outside world. She hoped that with luck, it might reduce the need to foist Catherine onto future custodians as reluctant as its aged owners, Sir John Wentworth and his invalid wife.

She was ever mindful too of the importance of counteracting that thistly presence in Scotland who claimed her throne. Late in June, however, during an evening of Court entertainment, Elizabeth was completely unnerved by some news which William Cecil brought her as she danced with Robert.

"The Queen of Scots is lighter of a fair son, while I am but a barren stock," she cried above the revelry of her courtiers.

Cecil ventured his advice, "Your Majesty would show gladness over this better, if the Scottish envoy has audience with you tomorrow rather than now."

Robert glared at him, but Elizabeth agreed with his words. The next day, she pretended to congratulate the Scottish Queen through the envoy, Sir James Melville, and listened enigmatically as he remarked, "The safe delivery of the little prince nearly cost my Queen's life, Your Majesty. She was handled so painfully that she wished she'd never been married."

Elizabeth saw this tale-telling as a calculated tactic to intimidate her so much from marriage that she would nominate her royal Scottish kin as her heirs. She prepared herself for a tussle with Parliament over the succession now that both the main claimants had sons.

And sure enough, during the summer of 1566, she found that the Lords and Commons pressed her more than ever to be allowed to debate this matter. Or rather, in Elizabeth's view, their members wanted to go through some semblance of a debate before they resoundingly accepted Catherine!

In the autumn, the Queen reverted to her time-honoured practice of excluding those who annoyed her most, of whatever rank, from her presence.

She discovered that Robert had also tried to promote a Parliamentary debate on the succession. "God's death! It grieves us that you have again fallen foul of us," she stormed at him. "We thought that if all the world opposed us, our Eyes would be for us."

"Your Eyes would gladly lay down his life at Your Majesty's feet!"

"That has no relevance to the present situation," she snapped. "You shall swell the numbers of those banned from the royal apartments, my lord."

By the end of the year, Elizabeth learnt that although the Queen of Scots had survived a near-fatal illness at Jedburgh, events developing inside Scotland seemed to portend that she would soon fall from power. The pendulum for the English succession would then swing totally towards Catherine.

However, news was also coming to Elizabeth regularly about Catherine and Mary Grey in their separate places of captivity. And this made her hopeful of shortly being rid of all three adult female claimants to her illustrious Crown - permanently . . .

"There is a visitor for you, my lord."

"A visitor at this hour, Barnaby? Friend or foe?"

"Er . . . brother-in-law, my lord."

*"Brother-in-law?"* queried Ned. "Surely - not my Lord of Leicester himself falling back on that old link for some more

gloves for Her Majesty?" He smiled at the possible irony of the Queen's favourite coming in person through darkness and snow to him in his narrow, dreary chamber at Sir John Mason's house, merely for another pair of ladies' gloves.

"No, my lord. 'Tis Lord Ambrose Dudley. Says my Lord of Leicester has sent him, though. But I know not if it's about gloves."

"Very well. I will see him as soon as you've cleared the remains of my supper away!"

"Yes, my lord. Sorry."

Ned would usually have groaned that some aspects of the reformed Barnaby's service still left something to be desired. But in truth this time, he was glad of his servant's laxness. Its immediate result of delay helped to strengthen Ned's resolve to deal cautiously with his unexpected and distrusted visitor.

How he wished that a letter from Catherine had arrived instead! He had sent a gift of money to Gosfield Hall for the fourth birthday of his younger son recently on 10th February. But Catherine had not written back to him yet. Her letters had unfortunately become more and more rare in the last few months, as her health declined. Her manservant William Hampton tended to communicate with Ned on her behalf.

Ned felt certain, though, that Catherine still read his letters with her heart as well as her eyes. There was no doubt in his mind either that her memories remained vivid of the February day when he had fallen in love with her at Sheen, just before St Valentine's and after her sister Jane and brother-in-law, Guildford Dudley, had died on the block.

"Thirteen years ago, all that happened!" he reflected while he was still alone in his room.

Ambrose Dudley was brought in shortly. He looked flushed and in his eagerness to state the purpose of his visit, he began to speak before he sat down. He made rapid, fidgety movements with his hands.

"My Lord Hertford, I have come here at my brother's behest to offer you hope."

Hope? As a prisoner, Ned's hopes lay in not being returned to the Tower! "Would you care to explain?" he asked.

"The Earl of Leicester offers his services, through you, my lord, for the Lady Catherine and her heirs to succeed Her Majesty! And he has himself gone to your lady mother at Hanworth with this same purpose. The news has reached London tonight that the Scots' Queen's husband was murdered on the 10th."

"On the 10th? My younger boy's birthday . . ."

"Well, God preserve both your little sons, Lord Hertford. The murder was the result of an explosion. And some accuse the Scots' Queen herself of being implicated. I dread to think - it could've been my brother's fate, if she had taken him to husband!"

Ned looked at Ambrose Dudley straight in the face. "You may rest assured that your brother will have friendly company at Hanworth. My lady mother is most grateful for his kindly reception of her at Court from time to time."

Ned dissembled his true feelings with a slight beam in response to Ambrose Dudley's smile of approval at his latest words. But he felt unimpressed that his former taunter, Robert Dudley, should change direction so suddenly in support of Catherine because her claim was clearly in the ascendant. Would Elizabeth's favourite not veer away from Catherine, like a variable wind, and revert to being an adversary whenever it suited him?

Ambrose Dudley leaned forward as he said, "The chief suspect in this murder is apparently a Scottish Border Earl, by the name of Bothwell. I believe you are acquainted, my lord, and what's more, isn't he your enemy?"

"Bothwell?"

"Surely you encountered him when he was in the Tower at the same time as you?"

"I was only very briefly acquainted with him. I do not

recall this Scots Earl being there for long."

"He was there for three months of 1563 - before you left."

"Ah . . . my memory, now that I am nearer my thirtieth year than my twentieth," Ned sighed in pretence. The Dudleys could potentially entrap him on this very persuasive line of attack. Ned recalled only too clearly the ruffian Bothwell mouthing indecipherable anger at him and gleefully raising a clenched fist towards the Tower chapel.

"It would seem that Bothwell's memory stretches all the way back to his boyhood, Lord Hertford, when your lord father led armies which ravaged the Borders with fire and sword during the Scottish wars. The news of Bothwell at Court was of his infinite pleasure over seeing where your father's remains are interred."

"He's probably an enemy of all the English," observed Ned.

"But especially of yours, my lord, because of your father. There's even speculation that he is the Queen of Scots' lover nowadays, he is so much at her side. So isn't it in your interests to join forces with my brother, in case this Bothwell ever takes revenge on you?"

"What does Her Majesty think of my Lord Leicester's approach to me over this matter?" asked Ned. He was more concerned about everything said here being repeated back to Elizabeth than he was about Bothwell's emnity.

Ambrose Dudley paused, looking very uncomfortable.

"My brother doesn't know what to say to Her Majesty," he mumbled. "Her blasts are so sharp even to him she loves best. All the years of waiting to see *if*, or *when*, Her Majesty might wed him have truly told on Robert's patience. And the more so, as both he and I are well past thirty, Lord Hertford, yet neither of us has an heir of either gender!"

"My sons are both very young. I would cause them no more hurt," said Ned decisively. "Nor do I wish to incur any more of Her Majesty's wrath on Lady Catherine or myself. Therefore I cannot accept Lord Leicester's proposed help."

"My Lord Hertford, you do indeed sound nearer to middle age than I remember of you. I'll convey your answer to my brother. In the meantime I thank you for listening to me."

If only you knew how much you will *not* be conveying to your brother, thought Ned as they parted amicably.

He was pleased that he had protected his sons from a parental intrigue like those which had marred his own life and Catherine's. Another great consideration influencing him was his knowledge, through their network of loyal servants, of the advanced state of her illness. Then there was the other concealed factor of his long-suffering tenants burdened for years to come by Elizabeth's fine . . .

Ned soon believed even more that his long imprisonment had brought him early to the maturity of middle age. He asserted himself with ease as head of the Seymour family and sent Barnaby to Hanworth with a verbal message, forbidding his lady mother to interfere over his refusal of Robert Dudley's offer.

If the offer had been simply for freedom rather than the English Crown for Catherine and his sons, freedom to nurse her back to health, he would not have let it go. And some spark of his youth might then be rekindled. Ned could only dwell in hope for these.

The October day was purpling into dusk as the royal coach entered Ipswich, with its escort of horses and riders, and horse-drawn carts. Catherine was staying overnight within the old walls of this Suffolk town, where she had been arrested six years ago. She felt too broken to look out excitedly like her son, Thomas. Broken in spirit, and more tangibly, wasting away in body.

Sir John Wentworth of Gosfield Hall was the second of

her custodians to die while she was in their charge. And after her dull and wretched year and a half of captivity in his fortress-like house, she thought that she should in all compassion have been moved to friendlier surroundings such as Ingatestone again. Or into the care of her step-grandmother, as her errant sister Lady Mary had been two months before. Or best of all, into the care of her loving husband.

Catherine could hardly summon the strength to puzzle any more about why Elizabeth was still so relentless in trying to destroy her. She could not even recollect which members of her household had told her that perchance Her Majesty feared becoming a prisoner in her own realm, like the Queen of Scots was now in hers. The baby prince, called James, had succeeded to the throne of Scotland in his mother's place.

Catherine spent a wakeful night, permeated by dark thoughts. The next day she travelled east towards the house of her new custodian, Sir Owen Hopton, at the village of Yoxford. It seemed to Catherine that the journey, near the Suffolk coast, was maybe an attempt by Sir Owen to spare her feelings. For this route meant that she did not pass too near the Castle at Framlingham, where Queen Mary Tudor had gathered her army before marching victoriously on London and dethroning Jane after those nine days of power.

Framlingham - it's only a few miles, though, from where I'm being sent, reflected Catherine in her mood of deep melancholy. Elizabeth surely does intend the Tudors' revenge on the Grey family to come full circle!

Yoxford itself appeared in keeping with many other villages which Catherine had seen in this lowland part of the kingdom. Its cottages huddled along each side of its single street. The church of St Peter's stood opposite the tree-lined approach across a small stream to the Hoptons' red-brick mansion of Cockfield Hall.

Catherine took to her bed immediately when she was

shown to her new quarters. Her bout of coughing was as bad as any which used to afflict Jennie Seymour. She stayed abed for several days, but soon found herself suffering also from the ministrations of a royal physician.

"What news is there of my lord, Dr Symonds?" she asked him, rather than about herself. "I trust you are at liberty to tell me."

"Yes, I may tell you, madam. Her Majesty has moved Lord Hertford out of London to somewhere in the wilds of Northamptonshire."

"So far away? Is it to a stricter prison?"

The doctor's hesitant mumble of an answer confirmed her suspicions. Although Dr Symonds visited her subsequently, his efforts to make her well were of little avail.

Only one visitor cheered Catherine's existence with a glow of warmth. One who pattered into her chamber, slumped for hours by her bedside and could rarely be coaxed away from her. Misty was getting old, but was even more like her ever-beloved mother, Comfit, now in the depth of an attachment formed to her mistress at a time of adversity.

What were the transient delights of music, or of reading or needlework, compared with the love of a devoted pet? Catherine declined most offers by the Hoptons of these three pastimes to distract her, though neither music nor reading for her son. In her extreme state of debility after each attack of her racking cough, she kept her precarious grip on life for Thomas's sake during the entertainments of the twelve days of Christmas.

But afterwards came the days when Catherine could no longer rise from her bed unaided. She began to prepare gracefully for her freedom, as if the whole world looked on . . .

On 27th January 1568, Mistress Cousins, and Meg, Beth and Book prayed with her into the early morning hours. As soon as one prayer or psalm was said or read out, Catherine called for another.

"Lady Catherine, be of good cheer," Mistress Cousins implored her, "and with God's help, you shall live and do well many years."

"No! No life in this world," murmured Catherine, "but in the world to come I hope to live for ever. Lord, have mercy on me! For now I begin to faint . . ."

Her women chafed and rubbed her. They revived her enough for her to lift up her hands and eyes towards heaven, as she whispered, "Father of heaven, for thy son Christ's sake, have mercy on me!"

She heard a clock strike five, heard the doctor come to her and soon her menservants also.

While the bedchamber was still dark as night, she became aware of a hum of low voices. Then Lady Hopton approached her, "Madam, comfort yourself. With God's favour you shall live and escape this. Mistress Cousins says you have escaped many dangers when you were as likely to die as you are now!"

"No, no my lady," said Catherine gently. "My time is come, and it is not God's will that I should live longer. His will be done, and not mine." She looked kindly at everyone around her bed.

Some while after seven o'clock that morning, she requested urgently that Sir Owen be brought to her.

He came to her bedside, with an expression of desolate concern on his wrinkled face. "Good madam, how are you?"

"Going to God, Sir Owen, as fast as I can," she replied. "I pray you and the rest that are about me, to bear witness with me that I die a true Christian. I ask God and all the world forgiveness, and I forgive all the world . . ."

He nodded slowly, after her voice faltered. But seeing that he waited patiently for whatever else she might say, Catherine rallied herself again, "I beseech you promise me one thing."

"Yes, madam?"

"That you yourself, Sir Owen, will make this request to Her Majesty for me, which shall be the last I ever make to her . . . that she would forgive her displeasure towards me, as my hope is she has done. And that she will be good to my children, and not impute my fault to them. I ask Her Majesty also to be good to my lord, for I know my death will be grievous news to him. I pray that Her Majesty will be so good as to send freedom to gladden his sorrowful heart."

"And my Lord Hertford, madam - any message for him?"

"I further ask of you to deliver from me certain commendations and tokens to my lord and husband."

Catherine then addressed Mistress Cousins, "Please bring me the jewel-box with my wedding ring in."

Mistress Cousins let Thomas open the box and supervised him in taking out the gold ring with the pointed diamond first brought to Catherine by Jennie.

"Here, Sir Owen, deliver this to my lord."

"Was this your wedding ring, madam?"

"No, Sir Owen. It was the ring of my betrothal to Lord Hertford. Here is my wedding ring." As daylight strengthened, the 'circles five' glinted during its brief transfer from her younger son's hands to hers and then her custodian's. "Deliver this also to my lord," she added, "and pray him that he will be a loving father to our children. I give them my heartfelt blessing."

As Thomas handed her a third ring, he held out his sturdy little arms to hug her. Meg lifted him up, to ensure this was accomplished.

Sir Owen, meanwhile, took charge of the mourning-ring with a death's head enamelled on it and the inscription, *'While I live, yours'*, which Ned had sent to Catherine before they left the Tower.

"This is the last token to my lord that ever I shall send him," murmured Catherine. "The symbol of death upon it is the picture of myself."

There was only time to stroke Misty, before Catherine noticed that her fingernails had suddenly turned purple. She raised her hands and eyes again to heaven, and overheard Sir Owen Hopton ask Dr Symonds whether they should send to the church for the passing bell to be rung.

"Good Sir Owen, let it be so," she agreed happily.

Her chamber became silent until the passing bell began its solemn, wintry tolling of each of the twenty-seven years she had lived. It signalled outbreaks of sobbing near her, and more prayers for her departing soul. It also called upon all who heard it outside to pray for her.

Thomas waved his farewell, and Catherine tried to return this like she had with Ned and her elder boy when they parted from her at the Tower.

Amid her prayers, Catherine's voice lilted clearly, speaking the same last words as her sister Jane had uttered on the scaffold almost fourteen years before.

"Lord, into thy hands I commend my spirit."

The clock struck nine, and at the final stroke she closed her eyes with her own hands. Despite the tears shed by those in her bedchamber, Catherine had found her release for ever.

## CHAPTER 19

# *Light in the Dark Depths*

Ned found little consolation from picking up the betrothal ring, the wedding ring and the mourning-ring out of Catherine's jewel box. His red-rimmed eyes watered as he handled each one in turn, yet he could not bring himself to close the lid. So much of their lives was bound up in these three symbols of their love.

He listened to the sounds of Catherine's pets romping with his sons and Meg outside in the wintry parkland of his current prison at Althorp in Northamptonshire. Sudden, delighted bursts of laughter attracted him to watch his offspring from a window of his sitting-room.

Ned lingered by the window for a while. But it wasn't six year old Edward and five year old Thomas that he saw and heard at this remote place - it was Catherine with her pets at Hampton Court. He heard the soft lilt of her voice, heard her laughter when her voluminous Tudor sleeve caught on a rose-bush in full summer bloom. Then he pictured himself playing the young gallant who released her sleeve from the thorns.

The sensation of his own delight swept over him in fresh recollection, his delight in being loved by a beauty such as Catherine. He was still hers, as long as he lived, like he had proclaimed in his words engraved in the mourning-ring.

And he realized, with an acceptance which was total, that she would live on in his memory with an extraordinary power.

"I pray my lord will be a loving father to our children. I give them my wholehearted blessing," had been part of Catherine's final message to him, through Sir Owen Hopton.

Ned observed Mistress Cousins go towards Thomas and encourage the boy to wave to him at the window. There was a clear likeness to Catherine in Thomas's engaging, but shy compliance with this. Ned responded at once, smiling as he beckoned both his sons to come to him. He so much wanted to get to know his younger son better and was already setting about honouring and fulfilling Catherine's request of him as a father!

Mistress Cousins took Thomas by the hand and proceeded to bring him back inside with his brother. Ned called to mind an earlier conversation with the old woman about him.

"He's a good boy, my lord," she had said. "But like all of us, he'll take time to recover from losing his dear lady mother."

"I gather that he takes after Lady Catherine, with his love of animals," Ned had enquired.

"Oh, he does, my lord! I suppose Lord Thomas will always remember Misty's devotion to Lady Catherine. We were all so upset when the dog died beside her mistress's grave. She wouldn't leave it and pined away there, poor thing."

Ned sighed. He and Edward had not even been allowed to attend the funeral at Yoxford. Elizabeth had at least ordered a suitably grand ceremony for Catherine, but he could not help feeling bitter.

"Probably paid for out of the fine set on me," he grunted to himself.

He removed from his purse the gift of a small coin, and hid this in one of his closed hands in readiness for his sons entering the room.

"Here's a guessing game that Edward and I play sometimes, Thomas," he said, offering both hands to the little boy. "Is there something for you in my right hand? Or in my left?"

Thomas hesitantly touched Ned's right hand, and smiled with his father and brother when his choice proved to be correct.

During the spring and summer of 1568, Ned felt proud of his sons' progress in their education with their tutor, Robert Smith. By the autumn, however, he faced a dilemma over them. He was reluctant even to think of sending his children away from him, but he believed that they would be safer in the south at a Seymour house such as Hanworth.

Rumours had spread that all the north of England was preparing to rise in rebellion against Elizabeth and replace her with the Queen of Scots. Mary was now Elizabeth's captive in the north after fleeing from Scotland, but there were further rumours that Elizabeth was about to imprison her in the Midlands. Near to Ned and his sons! If rebel northerners came into the Midlands to rescue their royal heroine, Ned feared they might try to take young Edward and Thomas as hostages.

He was also worried by a number of letters which had come to him unsolicited from Scotland. A pact was being sought with him by the Scottish nobles who had rebelled against their own Queen and dethroned her in favour of her infant son. A pact which would ensure that James would continue to keep his mother off the Scottish throne, while their support of Ned's and Catherine's sons to succeed Elizabeth aimed to deny Mary the English Crown.

Ned refused to be ensnared by such letters, and forwarded them to William Cecil instead of replying. In truth, what he dearly wanted was to be at Savernake with his sons. An irresistible sense of regret overcame him that he was missing another attractive autumn in his Forest.

I expected to be away from there and Wolf Hall for only a year, he thought. Not almost a decade!

His wish was also great that Edward and Thomas could share the mutual love for the Forest which he had enjoyed from an early age with his own father.

He wrote an impassioned appeal to Elizabeth's Privy Council in an attempt to speed the return to Savernake.

There were limits on how much he was prepared to swallow his self-respect and anger to flatter the woman who had caused his Catherine's death. But he hoped that the possible dangers posed by Mary Queen of Scots would persuade the Council to insist on Elizabeth setting him free.

Autumn passed into another winter. The Queen of Scots did indeed become a prisoner in the Midlands, before Elizabeth at last granted Ned some mercy. She promised him partial freedom to go back to his own lands shortly, but not to Court. It was all he desired, though her pardon yet eluded him!

He made the request of Sir John Thynne, which he had originally anticipated eight years earlier on his return from France - for his Longleat neighbour to inspect and advise on the condition of Wolf Hall before Ned's homecoming. What need for extra repairs to the crumbling pile had accrued during his imprisonment, he could only guess! Ned also wrote to his Savernake Ranger, John Berwick, reassuring him that they would soon remedy together the great problems caused by poachers during his absence.

The Forest foliage was already heavy in the fullness of late spring when Elizabeth officially permitted Ned to return to Savernake. By this time, he was steeped in the advice of Sir John Thynne about all that awaited him to be done. But it was rather the memories of that magnificent March ride on Esturmy over Martinsell before he left for France, which pervaded his thoughts. His relief was so heartfelt to be back in Wiltshire. He had brought his and Catherine's sons to safety, well away from the northern and Midland counties if the expected rebellion rose in favour of the captive Queen of Scots.

Old Esturmy whinnied cheerily at carrying Ned into the Forest again. Edward whooped with awed delight at the height of the tallest trees that overhung their path in canopies of branches, almost shutting out the light. And as for Thomas, Ned noticed that the boy was trying to catch his eye with one of those silent looks like Catherine's, which told him so much of her joy in the world of nature. A nimbus of sunlight broke through the dark depths of foliage and brightened Thomas's wavy, red-gold hair.

And soon, Seymours were again welcomed home to Wolf Hall.

# CHAPTER 20

## *'As Time and Sequels Well Shall Prove'*

*Hertford House, Cannon Row, Westminster,*
*this Wednesday night, 5th June 1611.*

The Earl of Hertford sat up with a jolt in his high-backed chair. He looked at the letter he had tried to begin late the previous night about his grandson William's escape from captivity in the Tower for secretly marrying Lady Arabella Stuart.

He adjusted his spectacles, pushing them up once more towards the bridge of his acquiline nose. The candles were almost gutted near the letter, but the new day was dawning through the mullioned window of his bedchamber.

Handkerchief at the ready because of his cold, the Earl shuffled his aged limbs towards the window and its clear view of the river Thames. How long he had looked through it early on the morning of his wedding to Catherine! Now, he imagined that he could see her and his sister Jennie, sloshing through the pebbly mud bank at low tide, as they approached his house for the marriage and bedding in this very room . . .

"Over half a century ago!" he sighed, shaking his head almost in disbelief.

He glanced towards his bed, unoccupied all night, and he recalled the scene of bliss it had been on that day.

Other disjointed memories followed. As so often, he pictured Catherine at fourteen, in the gardens at Hampton Court; Catherine standing as godmother to Elizabeth Cavendish - who ironically was the Lady Arabella Stuart's mother; a wedding ring expand to five; then back again at Hampton Court, the pretty girl walking beside him, laughing, and never far from her pets. Next, he saw her in the Tower, her graceful, red-gold head bent lovingly over their first-born; then she sat alone on tattered furniture, a Bible in her hands containing a tear-stained message in fine handwriting from the Lady Jane. So much he could remember, as if they were things of only yesterday.

He went back to his table, but not as the venerable grandfather about to resume last night's letter immediately. Instead, he was Catherine's "good Ned" as he opened up a small book which lay close by. He glanced at Jennie's name inside and thumbed through the pages of prayers. After several moments, he came upon what he was looking for - Catherine's pressed clover. It was very browned and thoroughly stuck to one of the middle pages, but still retained its lucky four leaves.

The memory of Jennie giving this prayer book to the priest who tied the 'knot of secret might' was vivid in Ned's mind when he heard the early morning knock on his chamber door. Two of his servants came in to help him rise and dress. He chuckled at their gasps of consternation about his empty, untouched bed.

"Morning, Tom and Hugh," he teased, and peered at them over the top of his spectacles.

"My lord!" said Tom. "B-but you've not slept -"

"Not a wink - all night. Yet I seem to be more awake now than either of you!"

He observed them exchange a sheepish glance, before Hugh piped up, "Which clothes will you wear today, m'lord?"

They assisted him in selecting his apparel, including a doublet with the flat-lace collar of the Stuarts, which was his one concession to present fashions. Not for him any more the grotesque-sized Tudor ruffs causing discomfort around his scrawny, old man's neck.

While Ned submitted to their attentions, he thought of Catherine again. No-one had ever dressed him as gently as she did after their lovemaking.

Tom cut into his reverie, "My lord, that ugly old crone is back, putting flowers on the dog's grave in your river garden."

"On Comfit's grave? Well, there's a turn-up after all this time."

"She's been wandrin' there a few times a-lately," added Hugh. "We've seen her linger by that grave for an age."

"Shall we send her away, my lord?" asked Tom.

"Send her away?" Ned snapped. "Why do you ask? Is it because she's old and so ugly that you young folk take her for a witch? Eh?"

"We've been worried lest the old woman becomes a nuisance, my lord," replied Tom.

"Huh, a nuisance, is she?" Ned chided them. Rightly so to him, they appeared taken aback once more. "Nay, she's more well-meaning than she looks."

He eyed Jennie's prayer book and decided to cause even more astonishment. "Invite this old woman in," he announced nonchalantly, "and ask her to prepare a hot posset for my cold like the ones Mistress Cousins used to make. Aye, and I would that she breakfasts with me in the parlour, if she so wishes."

The old crone did so wish. Her snowy hair was whiter than at their last encounter about three years before. Her eyes appeared dim when she first hobbled into Ned's parlour, but filled with pleasure when he greeted her.

"Mistress Stretton! God give you good morning."

"And good morning to you, m'Lord Nedward. This is a great honour."

"Nay, be seated, mistress. You are most welcome."

She took the ordered hot posset from Hugh first. "Well, here we are - a posset as I do remember Mistress Cousins used to swear by for all manner of ailments."

"'Twould more than suffice if this cures my cold!" said Ned. He drank it and they both shared an amused grimace, reminiscent of the usual reactions to Mistress Cousins' hot possets in bygone times. "Pray excuse my servants if any have been impudent towards you. They are mostly too young and ignorant to appreciate how important you and Comfit were to Lady Catherine."

"Lord bless you, Lord Nedward!" Her plump cheeks reddened in further amusement. "Oh, it makes me smile in my old age, it does, to think of them tittle-tattling about me. Like playing me at my own game, as I was once . . ."

"Ah, but no-one could ever outdo Helen Leigh," he teased.

"Mistress Stretton, as I am now, became much changed."

"Aye, indeed, mistress. Are you in London for a visit, or to stay?"

"'Tis a few weeks' visit, Lord Nedward. Maybe for the last time, as it suits me best to be serving the Greys at Bradgate again. But 'tis my longest time in London since - you know - since coming back five summers ago."

While they ate, Ned ordered Tom to fetch Lady Jennie's prayer book down from his bedchamber. He bore in mind that Helen had had to keep her own counsel over his union with Catherine for a very great number of years and he was no longer surprised to find himself speaking more than she did. He needed little encouragement to talk freely of his ceaseless quest to establish the marriage as lawful. After Catherine's death, he had fought on in the face of grief and adversity.

"Even earned myself another spell in the Tower," he recalled. "Elizabeth still showed no pity, though I was nearly sixty then!"

"Lady Catherine would've been so proud of your lordship, payin' so dearly for love of her."

"Paid dearly, I certainly did! But in the end, a story of triumph -thanks to you."

"Oh, now. 'Twas the least I could do, you know that. I fled abroad on Lady Catherine's money after she confided of your secret knot to me, and I durst not come back for all of Queen Elizabeth's long reign."

The prayer book was brought in and her face lit up in

recognition of it. Ned asked Tom to open the book at Catherine's clover.

"'Tis good to see this again, Lord Nedward," smiled Helen.

"No more so than when you came back to England with it and the priest, Mistress Stretton!" wheezed Ned.

"Took much persuasion, believe me, afore your priest would even tell me how he'd come by this prayer book! I remembered it straightway when I saw him with it one day, an' Lady Catherine's flower still inside. 'Father Lamb,' I said to him many a time - as that was the only name he owned to amongst our group of English exile folk, 'I'll keep on till I find out'."

"I would like *you* to have Lady Jennie's prayer book now," declared Ned.

Helen gasped and gave a look of sheer delight. "Are you *sure,* Lord Nedward?"

"Yes, mistress. Very sure."

"Well, I thank you!" she cried. She washed and wiped her hands most carefully at the table, before Ned presented the book to her.

"I think, Mistress Stretton, my thanks are more owing to you," he acknowledged. "If you had such a hard time persuading Father Lamb even to tell you who gave him this book, I well appreciate how much more difficulty there was in persuading him to come forward."

"He feared to return for the same reasons as I did, and being a *Catholic* priest too. In Elizabeth's England! And even when King James succeeded the old Queen, we waited to see if he was secure on his throne and the Seymour family were in favour with him."

"Some excellent hunting days in Savernake Forest made certain of that," Ned grinned. "His Majesty was enjoying my wine there when he assured me of the safe descent of my earldom and inheritance to mine and Catherine's heirs."

"What a moment that must have been for you, Lord

Nedward."

"Nothing short of miraculous. The answer to my prayers, forty-six years after my wedding!"

"All that time," Helen mused. "But if it hadn't been for that 'powder treason' nearly blowing up the King and all his lords, including you, Lord Nedward, I might never have gotten your priest to own up. Not before the passing years decayed us too much . . . 'twas the shock of what could've happened to you then that spurred me on."

"I believe your action was *meant* to be," observed Ned. "I'm very glad it came about before our grandson William made his secret match! He jeopardized my family's favour with the King."

"Oh my - secret knots and Seymours, Lord Nedward!"

"Aye, Mistress Stretton," he sighed. But noting the contented old woman now with the prayer book, he chose not to burden her with the news of William's escape from the Tower.

The meal drew to a close with her gazing at the clover in her newly acquired possession, as if life's ambition for her was fulfilled. Ned felt sincerely pleased that she had found such consolation.

After their cordial parting, Ned had little time to dwell on the reality of the situation concerning William. His next visitor hurtled into the parlour - a visitor whom Ned *had* been expecting. The greetings of the day were spoken from a flushed face adorned by a curly beard, which like the accompanying head of wavy hair was fully greyed.

"What's to be done about this son of mine, father?" demanded the breathless voice. "I wish to God he'd never clapped eyes on the Lady Arabella."

"Now, now, Edward," bristled Ned, a measure of parental agitation affecting his voice too. He tried to calm them both with a wry observation, "Who are we, *either* of us, to criticize William's exploits? We hardly set him the best example with our own secret marriages at the same age as him!"

"Aye, father, but that's a private view, within the family. What are we going to say to His Majesty?"

"I have a letter started, in my bedchamber."

Ned made his way back there, with his son following closely. Once the door was closed, Edward stood at the table.

"But you've only put the address and date on this letter!" he exclaimed. "Pray forgive me, father, I thought there'd be rather more."

"And pray forgive *me,* but I was rather hoping for your advice, Edward."

"My advice? I'm too worried that William faces a future of punishments like yours for matching himself with a lady of the blood royal. How glad I am that I avoided such a life with my own marriage."

"What - to a country squire's daughter! Marrying beneath your rank was a slur on your dear lady mother's memory," rejoindered Ned. "And as for my own past punishments . . . A-choo!"

"What of them, father?"

"If I appear to be the sage grandfather thoroughly tamed down by them, that is an outward pretence."

Edward mopped his brow before words rushed from him again. "Such spirit didn't stop you from doing all you could to separate my bride and me in our youth! *Or* from fuelling William's ambitions by once seeking Arabella's hand for one or other of our sons while they were still infants."

Ned reeled, shakily catching hold of his high-backed chair to steady himself. "After all my efforts and sufferings, I am reduced to being the target of such umbrage."

"Not so, father."

Edward helped him to be seated in the chair. "I was ever mindful that after we lost my dearest lady, your mother, her succession claims came to you," Ned snuffled.

Edward shrugged, "Only for Queen Elizabeth to say of me on her death-bed that she'd have no rascal's son to succeed her!"

"*Rascal!*" scoffed Ned. "She likened your father to the runt of a herd of deer, all because your Seymour descent means you're not fully royal-blooded." He trembled at the exertion involved in crashing a clenched fist on the table. "'Tis thanks to our so-called 'Good Queen Bess' that my work for my beloved Catherine is not yet done! 'Tis not enough for me to cherish her memory to the end of my days. I need something that's more lasting."

"I have an idea," said Edward, pressing a hand on Ned's shoulder with unexpected gentleness. He prompted his father to think about the time when Ned had the remains of his own grandfather, Sir John Seymour, moved from their ruinous burial place on one side of Savernake Forest at Easton Royal to a grand new tomb on the other at Great Bedwyn Church. And more especially, about Ned's blowing of the Esturmy Horn in welcome of King James on His Majesty's first visit to the Forest.

"Do you remember that the King was so taken with your fitting re-interment of Sir John?" Edward continued. "Don't you see there's a possible solution, based on what he learnt from you?"

"I'm in no mind for solving riddles, Edward."

"His Majesty decided to move the remains of the Queen of Scots, his mother, to a more appropriate resting-place."

"Aye! The work is now well advanced on her tomb in Westminster Abbey," Ned realized. "Oh, Edward, why didn't I think of this till now? We could bring Lady Catherine's remains from Yoxford and -"

"Yes, father, and to her own magnificent royal tomb in the Abbey."

"Nay," asserted Ned.

"Why not?"

"D'you expect me to put my sweet Catherine near her own mother's tomb in there? She deserves more honour than that."

"So, what do you suggest, father?" sighed Edward in

exasperation.

Ned beamed above his descending spectacles. "Yoxford *will* merely be her first burial place, Edward."

"I'm glad to hear that. But surely there's somewhere better for a royal lady than Great Bedwyn!"

"Of course."

"Where?"

"Salisbury Cathedral," Ned enthused, "where I will at last rest in peace with my Catherine. I would have my heir escort her into Wiltshire along the Old Bath Road and through Savernake past the Great-Bellied Oak, and then Wolf Hall, where she so often longed to be."

"I defer to the wishes of the head of the family over this, more happily than many matters!" smiled Edward.

"That pleases me well," said Ned.

He saw again the letter about William's escape from the Tower, which had caused him such alarm late last night. He handed this ruefully to Edward, thankful that if his son had earlier noticed its charred state, no comment had been made. "The candle - burnt away 'Tower' from it when I sneezed! Seemed like a bad omen at first."

"I understand how you felt!" said Edward. "I hope it doesn't seem so now."

"Not any more. You helped by agreeing with me that as the head of a noble family, I can't *officially* condone Master William's quest to be with his wife rather than separately imprisoned."

While Edward read the partly damaged letter, Ned stood up from his chair and allowed himself a few hoarse chuckles as he put aside some money for forwarding to William, once they knew the young man's whereabouts.

"Yes, the tone of this reply will be devoid of our *true* feelings regarding William, eh, Edward?" he observed. "But then, 'tis the prerogative of the old to play games with the truth somewhat, when admonishing the insolence of the young!"

"Yet if we had our lives over again, I trow we would do

exactly the same as we did!" laughed Edward.

Ned was already sitting again, as Edward placed another chair for himself at the table. They knuckled down to the task of writing the rest of last night's reply to William Cecil's son, Robert, for many a year now in the same position of power as his father had served.

"How appropriate that the King made Robert Cecil the Earl of *Salisbury!*" said Edward when their letter was finished. "I'll take this to him immediately."

Left alone once more, Ned found that his cold was troubling him less. A smile glowed on his wrinkled face, for after a night-time of thinking about Catherine, he sought his favourite refuge of loving memories of her. But he was returning now with a sense of completeness, of Catherine being with him even into his native Wiltshire.

Already, a tiny girl with Tudor red-gold hair was blowing kisses to him in the way that time had never dimmed. And as another romantic memory of Catherine came forth to its full flowering in his spirit, Ned brought to mind his words engraved inside her wedding ring:

*'. . . So trust uniteth faithful minds, with knot of secret might,*
*Whose force to break but greedy Death no wight possesseth power,*
*As time and sequels well shall prove . . .'*

"Beloved," he whispered, "even death cannot break our knot of secret might!"

*The Effigies of Lady Catherine and Edward, Earl of Hertford on their tomb in Salisbury Cathedral.*

# AFTERWORD

Ned lived on for almost a decade after William's escape from the Tower. He died in April 1621, aged 82, having outlived Catherine by 53 years. He also outlived both their sons, their eldest grandson and eldest great-grandson. And so William, the second grandson, became his heir and succeeded him as Earl of Hertford - a much reformed character by then. The 'Golden Tomb' of Catherine and Ned in Salisbury Cathedral was erected to their memory by William, and as its epitaph translates: 'after having experienced alternate changes of fortune, here at length they rest together in the same concord in which they lived'.

Elizabeth granted Ned his full freedom in 1571. But although he was again received by her at Court, she did not remit all of his Star Chamber fine until about 1580. Already, the very decayed state of Wolf Hall had caused him to give up his hopes of renovating his old ancestral home and he had made his main residence at Tottenham House, which had formerly been one of his Savernake Forest lodges.

By 1591, Ned had clearly restored his Seymour inheritance to sufficient prosperity for him to stage a costly and lavish four-day entertainment of Queen and Court at his Hampshire property of Elvetham, during the late summer progress that year. Some of his servants took part in history's first mentioned game of lawn tennis on the third day of this. His subsequent return to high favour with Elizabeth proved to be short-lived, however. For when he tried actively to establish the validity of his marriage to Catherine, Elizabeth put him back in the Tower in November 1595 and fined him again before she freed him the following January. He was appointed Lord Lieutenant for Wiltshire and Somerset in 1602 and became Custos Rostulorum for Wiltshire the next year.

Ned remarried twice: both these marriages were childless, and both his second and third Countesses were called Frances Howard. Neither of them was buried with him or even mentioned on his tomb. His second wife, a favourite cousin of Elizabeth, was the sister of Lord Howard of Effingham, leader of the English victory over the Spanish Armada.

The other Frances Howard was some forty years younger than Ned. The astrologer, Simon Forman, told in his diary that he gave her a love philtre, which she utilized to attract Ned and enabled her to marry him in December 1600 - this final wedding of Ned's also being secret! Their union was blighted at the outset by one of the new Lady Hertford's suitors committing suicide in their presence, after writing her a farewell love-song in his own blood at a Wiltshire inn.

Yet amid the marital unhappiness of his old age, Ned quickly acquired favour with James I, who made his first visit to Savernake with his Queen in the year of his accession, 1603. Ned was entrusted with the leadership of an embassy to Brussels during the spring of 1605. He wrote for the King an account of Elizabeth's investigation into his marriage with Catherine, and in 1606, the minister who had performed the ceremony reappeared. In the presence of this priest, it was legally accepted as a true marriage.

Ned had the satisfaction also of seeing William pardoned by James a few months after Lady Arabella Stuart's death in captivity in 1615. William had escaped to exile in France from the Tower and after his return to England, he settled down to become M.P. for Marlborough. He made a lasting, second marriage to Frances Devereux, daughter of the Earl of Essex. Amongst the descendants of Catherine and Ned through this marriage of William's are the present royal family.

Seymour loyalty to the Stuart monarchs continued through William's friendship with Charles I, who created him Marquis of Hertford in 1640 and appointed him governor to the future Charles II in 1641. William served as an active Royalist commander during the Civil War and in his seventies, he was one of the first peers to welcome Charles II back to England at the Restoration in May 1660.

He was given his great-grandfather the Good Duke's title of Duke of Somerset and this has remained in the Seymour family ever since. A few weeks before William died in the following autumn, an Act of Parliament declared the 'knot of secret might' between Catherine and Ned officially valid, close on a century after their wedding.

In Savernake Forest, the Great-Bellied Oak can still be seen right beside the busy Marlborough to Salisbury road, the A346. Please drive carefully!

*The Great-Bellied Oak, Savernake Forest.*